JACKALS AND VIPERS DUET
BOOK ONE

SEPTEMBER DOVES

EMMERSON HOYT

ISBN: 979-8-9872887-0-2 (ebook)

ISBN: 979-8-9872887-1-9 (paperback)

Editor: The Editor and The Quill

Cover Design: ©Sarah Hansen, Okay Creations

For my husband.

Chapter One

I'm not sure what I was expecting when I agreed to meet North Carolina's top-ranked private investigator at a dive bar, but it definitely wasn't the stern-faced man with a comb-over and polyester polo sitting across from me.

Pulling his collar away from his neck, he slides a thin, manila folder across the sticky bar-top table. "I'm sorry, Ms. Adder, but I was unable to locate your sister."

Icy shock streaks up my spine. For how much this guy charges, it never occurred to me that not finding my sister was even an option. I stare at the near-empty folder, my limbs numb with disbelief. "What do you mean you couldn't find Holly?"

The P.I. adjusts his too-tight belt and wipes the sweat from his forehead. After a quick look over his shoulder, he leans forward. "Listen, kid, I've been doing this for over thirty years. When I tell you I've *never* seen anything like this before, you have to believe me. There is absolutely no digital record of your sister since her arrest seven years ago. Not even a traffic violation. Every time I thought I found something, the files disappeared before I could access them."

My legs bounce under the table. "That can't be right. I've *talked* to her. She was at our mom's funeral five years ago. We had plans to meet up last summer. She sent me a text last month, for God's sake." I grab my phone and bring up the text thread to show him.

> Unknown Number: Rylee, I need you. Jeremy is missing. -H

> Me: Where are you? How can I help?

That was over four weeks ago and still no response.

The investigator takes a peek at my screen before sliding my phone back across the table. "Like I said in my email, the text was a dead end. She used an untraceable virtual private network and likely a burner phone to send it." He purses his lips and gives me a commiserating sigh that only makes me want to smack the pitying expression right off his face. "Sometimes people don't want to be found. Maybe she already reconnected with this Jeremy guy—"

"Her husband. Jeremy is her husband," I correct, unable to hide the annoyance slipping into my tone.

He waves me off. "Right. Well, someone who's trying that hard not to be found either has a good reason to stay hidden or has powerful friends. Sometimes both. It might be best to just let her go." He pushes back his stool and signals to the bartender for another beer. "I can't offer you a refund, but this round is on me. Good luck, kid." Ripping a twenty from his worn, leather wallet, he tosses it on the table and heads out the door.

I don't bother watching him go. I can't. I can't do anything but bite my cheek and stare at the dove logo on my empty beer bottle while trying not to scream.

A few minutes later, the bartender whisks away the cash

and replaces it with a fresh beer. Without looking up, I snatch the bottle off the table. My grip tightens around the neck until my knuckles turn white and my shock and annoyance bleed into something hot and volatile.

No wonder he had me pay before he gave me the results.

Two *thousand* dollars.

For nothing.

I never should have listened to Logan. It was his stupid-ass idea to hire the investigator in the first place. I tried to explain to him that my sister has always been secretive. That she'd pop back up whenever she was ready, like she always has, but Logan disagreed. He made me feel like I was a bad sister for not looking harder for Holly and in the end, even though I knew she wouldn't be found unless she wanted to be, I'd bitten my tongue and done it. Now I'm out the two grand I'd saved for tuition and I still don't know where she is.

I slam my fist on the table, making the couple next to me jump. Why did I listen to a boyfriend who couldn't even bother to show up on time tonight? He knew how important this was to me and he still missed the entire meeting. Glancing at the door, I search for Logan's head of bleach-blond hair, but he's nowhere in sight. With a huff, I rip the wings off the dove label and set the bottle aside to shoot him a text.

> Me: Where are you? I thought you were going to be here an hour ago.

When he doesn't immediately reply, I bring up Holly's thread and type out another message.

> Me: Where are you? I want to help.

The ridiculousness of sending the same "Where are you?" text to both my sister and boyfriend doesn't escape me. While no response is typical for both of them, it hurts less from Holly. Our thirteen-year age gap has always kept a degree of distance between us. After all, she was leaving for college when I was barely turning five, and by the time I got to high school, she was ending her career in the Navy. It's not like either of us is to blame for our lack of relationship. That's just life sometimes.

I do miss her, though. Before she got out of the military, we used to keep in regular contact. After her discharge, Holly's behavior became increasingly erratic. I saw her less and less, and she started insisting on using what she called "secure" forms of communication. Sometimes, I wouldn't hear from her for months, only to have her call and say that she was married, in jail, or moving again. With the exception of her most recent text, it's been over five months since we last spoke.

I let loose a pent-up sigh as I reread her message: *I need you. Jeremy is missing.*

A prickling sensation travels up my spine into my scalp. Despite all the moving and secrecy, Holly's never sent a message like this before. And although I don't know my brother-in-law very well, I do know that he's a good guy with a big heart. Jeremy would never abandon my sister. If he's missing, it can't be good.

The prickling sensation in my skull balls itself into a rock and promptly drops into my stomach. Regardless of the fact that I didn't want to hire the investigator in the first place, I still wish he'd found *something* that could point me in the right direction. I'm not quite ready to let Holly go like he suggested, but I don't know what else to do.

Clicking out of the text thread, I thrum my fingers across the screen, getting more and more annoyed by the second that Logan still hasn't responded. All this would be so much easier to sort through if I had a sounding board. And it really shouldn't be this hard to see or communicate with someone you live with. Unfortunately for me, this is Logan's normal.

I allow myself one last look toward the door, even though I already know he's not coming, before I knock back the rest of my beer, grinding my teeth as the carbonation tickles my throat. I don't know what's worse: that he convinced me to waste so much money on an investigator or that he stood me up...*again.* It's way too early in the relationship for him to be this flippant about our time together and, at twenty-two, I'm too young to be settling. I continue fidgeting until, all at once, my body stills.

You know what? I'm done waiting. I have much bigger things to worry about than a boyfriend who won't make time for me. I'll hear him out when he gets home, but he better have a world-shattering excuse this time or else I might be done with Logan altogether.

Outside, a gust of humid air tangles through my wispy strawberry-blond hair and brings with it the sound of laughter and the hum of passing cars. The picturesque early summer night does nothing to lift my sour mood. After tying my hair up off my neck, I make my way toward the loft Logan and I share, my quick steps slapping the pavement harder than necessary, growing heavier and faster until I'm nearly running.

Logan and I have been together for six months, living together for three, and I still feel like I barely know the guy. Looking back, I never should have moved in with him. It catapulted our relationship out of the fun phase and straight into... whatever this is. Stagnation, maybe?

It's not like I had other options, though. We'd been casually dating for only a few months when out of the blue my apartment complex was condemned. I'd just fixed my car and paid my community college tuition, so I couldn't afford the down payment on a new place. When Logan suggested I move in with him, I was on week three of living out of my car.

Exhausted, tired of showering in the school gym, and sick of eating scraps at the restaurant I work at, I'd said yes.

Although he was more attentive in those early days and I *really* needed a place to live, I think even then I knew things were moving too fast. Still, it would have been idiotic to turn him down just because the relationship was new. He was handsome and educated, and I really did think our relationship had potential.

Shaking my head, I wipe off the moisture beading on my brow and stomp the rest of the way back to the loft. It's only mid-May, but by the time I make it to our building and run up the last few flights of stairs, taking two or three at a time, I'm sweating profusely. The exertion is liberating though, momentarily distracting me from the swarming thoughts inside my head. I'm not sure if it's being stood up, the new dent in my bank account, or worrying about my sister, but my legs are vibrating with nervous energy. Not to mention how the rock in the pit of my stomach only seems to be growing. I need to burn off this uneasy feeling before it consumes me. Hopefully, I can sneak in a run before the inevitable argument with Logan.

After fumbling with my keys—dropping them twice—I'm greeted by a blast of icy air-conditioning and the sterile, white interior of our living room. The counters and cabinets are all a sparkling white, just like the sheer curtains that hang from every window. Even the boxy sofa is the color of freshly fallen snow. Thanks to Logan's minimalist style, this place has always felt more like a surgeon's office than a home. Most of the time I'm afraid to touch anything for fear of leaving a mark, not that Logan particularly likes me touching his things anyway.

At first, I thought he was just a neat freak, which I can respect, but it runs deeper than that.

Once, I remember trying to use his computer to print out a school assignment. My laptop was too old to connect to our wireless printer, and the library wasn't open early enough for me to get there before class. Logan came home and found me fumbling to connect my thumb drive to the oddly shaped USB ports on his laptop. I'm pretty good with computers, but I'd never encountered a triangular port before. As soon as he walked in, I explained what I was doing and asked him for an adapter. He exploded, berating me about *respecting his work equipment and privacy* before he ripped the laptop out of my hands. Shortly after that incident, he moved his computer to a pretentious metal standing desk in the spare room, just to make sure I knew it was off-limits. That should have been the first sign that our relationship was never going to work out.

The palms of my hands heat with the memory. I hate to admit it, but if this apartment hadn't been keeping me off the streets, I think I would have left right then and there.

I look around the loft. If that incident was the first sign that our relationship was doomed, then the second would probably be that three months later, I'm still practically living out of my car. Logan had cleared out a dresser for me and some space in the closet, but most of the time I keep my belongings—like a gym bag full of winter clothes, my school-books, and laptop—in my car. It's easier for class, but now that I'm thinking about it, it sort of feels like I was waiting for an excuse to leave. Like I already knew this was just a pit stop on my journey and I needed to be ready to go at the drop of a hat.

I can't believe I didn't see this before. Logan's clearly not giving me the support I need, and I shouldn't only stay with him for a place to live. It's not fair to either of us. Maybe confronting him when he gets home tonight won't be as much of a fight as I thought. Maybe it will just be me telling him I'm done.

Shaking my head, as if that will somehow undo my newest

realizations, I beeline for the dresser to change into workout clothes before grabbing my sneakers.

I have to burn off this jittery feeling before it consumes me.

I need to run.

Need to feel the wind on my face and the sweat drip down my back.

I know it isn't for everyone, the last guy I'd dated thought running twelve miles every other day was psychotic, but it's the only way I can sort through the thoughts in my head. And while I don't run fast, I do run far—far enough that the pounding pain from the pavement fades into a cathartic numbness and I don't have to worry about anything except the road and the movements of my body.

I won't be running far enough for that tonight, though. Right now, I just need to be able to push aside the thoughts of my sister and decide what I'm going to say to Logan when he gets home. I need to figure out a plan and a place to go if this conversation goes the way I suspect it might.

A light four-miler should do the trick.

Just thinking about running is enough to get my heart racing. I'm tucking my key into the secret pocket of my shorts when my phone goes off with a text.

Shit.

Logan is probably looking for me at the bar. I thought I would have more time—

My phone goes off again, but this time with a call. I grab it and am about to send it to voicemail when the caller ID flashes across the screen.

Unknown Caller.

Holly. Of course she would call *after* I've already wasted two freaking grand trying to find her. I pick up on the third ring, handling my phone a little rougher than necessary. I'm about to lay into her when muffled sobs seep through the line. A twist of panic constricts my throat.

Something is wrong.

"Holly?" I breathe out in a rush. "Is that you?"

"Jeremy's gone," she whispers through sniffles and choppy breaths.

I've never heard her sound so dejected before, not even when Mom died. She almost sounds afraid. My chest tightens, and my annoyance is replaced with concern. I calm my breathing and attempt to hide the trepidation in my voice. "Don't worry, we'll find him. Tell me where you are. Tell me how I can help."

She swallows with an audible gulp. "You don't understand." Her voice is full of rage and soaked in despair. "They *killed* him. They fucking killed him."

Time stops.

The room spins, rendering my brain useless. "What? Who killed him? Jeremy's dead?" I wince at the sound of my own words.

Holly smothers a cry, and I can feel her agony through the phone. "I-I need you here."

"Jesus, okay." My mind acts on autopilot as I glance around the loft. "Okay, I'm coming. Just tell me where you are." I trap the phone between my ear and shoulder and make my way to the spare bedroom to search for a duffle bag. I'm moving so fast that I slam into Logan's desk. His stupid computer gleams at me tauntingly from its stand. It teeters but doesn't fall. Moving to the closet, I grab a large black duffle and reposition the phone to my other ear. My lips part but no comforting words come.

"Do you still have the burner phone I gave you? And the road atlas?" Her voice quivers slightly with the question.

"Yes." *At least I hope I do.* She sent me a prepaid phone and the book of maps a year ago for a meetup that never happened. They arrived inside of what she called a Faraday bag, which I think is supposed to block all radio signals and prevent a person from being tracked. At the time, I thought it was absurd, a whole new level of crazy from her. But now, knowing that something happened to Jeremy and hearing the fear in my sister's voice, I'm not so sure.

"Good. I'll text the coordinates to the burner." Her voice is steadier now, but I can tell she's still crying. "Make sure you turn off your cell and take out the SIM card before you leave. We need to be careful."

"Okay." I don't know what else to say. It feels like my entire world might implode at any second.

"Rylee?" Her voice is so small that it does something painful to my heart.

"Yeah?"

"I love you." She pauses. "Don't tell anyone where you're going."

Chapter Two

My sister's words still ring in my head.

They killed him.

I'm so shaky that I have to grab the dresser to keep the room from spinning. I can't believe Jeremy's gone.

What did he and Holly get themselves into?

I want to sit. I need a moment to think and to mourn, but I know I don't have the time. Logan could be home soon, and right now I need to pack and get on the road. I guess this is as good of an excuse as any to break up and move out. Our conversation wasn't going to go well anyway and there is no point in dragging it out. All that matters right now is that Holly needs me.

I allow myself a steadying breath and set off to dig through my dresser. I wish I could pick everything up neatly and place it straight into the bag, but I don't know where I put that damn burner phone.

My movements become more frantic as I empty the contents of the drawers. Bras, underwear, and running clothes fly over my shoulder like leaves riding the wind until I finally find the phone buried at the bottom of the last drawer. Clutching the small black flip phone to my chest, a *whoosh* of relief escapes my lips. Thankfully, it still lights up when I plug it in. I set it next to my personal cell to charge, briefly wondering why Holly and the P.I. call it a burner. It's just one of those cheap, prepaid phones you can buy at a gas station, but on the rare occasions we talk, Holly always insists we use one.

While the phone charges, I move through the apartment like a storm, shoving the few items that are mine into the duffle bag. I'm fully packed within a matter of minutes. Everything but a few odds and ends, like my blow dryer and an extra set of running shoes, fit perfectly. The rest I decide to toss into a black trash bag.

I look around the room. Not a pillow out of place. It's like I was never here.

Good.

Now what? Do I just wait for Logan to come home and drop the bomb? My heart gives a little jolt of excitement, which is immediately quashed by guilt. No one should be excited about leaving their boyfriend, especially on the night they found out their brother-in-law was killed.

Not one to sit still, I take another pass through the loft to see if I missed anything. As I walk back into the bedroom, both phones light up. I reach for the burner first, finding a set of coordinates from a new unknown number.

Jesus, Holly, how paranoid can you be?

I'm tempted to type them into my map app for easier direc-tions, but I can't betray my sister like that. If she knew I used GPS to find her location, she'd kill me. I can practically hear her voice now. *"Someone's always watching, don't risk it."* I nod to myself and tuck the burner into my running shorts.

My personal cell lights up again, reminding me of my unread messages. I groan when I see both texts are from Logan.

I know I have to end it, but this is all happening so quickly. My emotions are all over the place, and I really don't have the energy for a big confrontation or breakup.

> Logan: I'm at the bar. I don't see you.
>
> Logan: Are you in the bathroom or something? I know I'm late, but I got caught up on a call with my dad. You know how he is.

I laugh a little at the last text because Logan has kept most of the details of his personal life out of our relationship. Even though his father comes into town at least once a month for business, I've never met the famous Charles Eastmann or his wife—or Logan's sister for that matter. I know virtually nothing about his family except that they all work for the family business, Eastmann Incorporated. So no, Logan, I don't know how he is because you never bothered to let me in.

I tap my fingers on the dresser, contemplating my next move. I should do the right thing and end it in person, but I really don't have the time. Holly sounded desperate, and I need to get to her as soon as possible. Also, I don't exactly *want* to see the look on Logan's face when I tell him I'm leaving. I don't *want* to hurt him. Even if he is a terrible boyfriend, it's not like he's evil. He just doesn't know how to make time for me. I need someone who's going to be around. Someone who's going to place me first.

Screw it.

I slam my fist on the dresser before unlocking my phone and letting my fingers fly.

Me: Family Emergency. I'm leaving tonight and don't know when I'll be back. I hate to do this over text, but it's not working between us. I'm sorry I have to end things this way, but I promise we can talk in person when I get back. I'll leave the key on the ledge over the door. I wish you all the best.

A second after I push send, my phone lights up with a call from Logan. I ignore it, heart pounding against my rib cage. I can't believe I just did that. I finally ended it. I feel light and heavy all at once. Relieved and guilty. I know it's for the best, but the rashness of the decision combined with the knowledge of what happened to my brother-in-law is making me a little queasy. It's important to remind myself that this breakup has been months in the making and I can always talk to Logan in person when I get back to Charlotte. For now, I need to concentrate on the big picture and sort out my priorities.

Jeremy is dead.

Holly is alone.

I have to go.

I steady my resolve, square my shoulders, and grab my bags before slipping out the door. Standing on my toes, I try to stash the key onto the ledge over the door, but it won't stay put. After three failed attempts the muscles in my back twinge from straining to make myself tall enough to reach. With an angry grunt, I shove the key into my pocket and ignore two more incoming calls. I only have the bandwidth to deal with one emergency at a time. I'll just have to give him the key later. While not ideal, it's better than leaving it under the mat and risking someone breaking in.

With one final check that the door is locked, I adjust my belongings on my shoulder and dash to the carport. A text comes in just as I reach my car.

Logan: Is this because I was late? You can't
break up with me just because I've been late
a few times. Come on, Rylee, pick up the
phone! I won't stop calling until you talk
to me.

I roll my eyes. He probably thinks this is our only issue. Never mind the fact that we have nothing in common and that we barely see each other. I throw my bags into the back seat of my rusty, gray Honda and slam the door. In the time it takes me to climb into the driver's seat and fasten my seat belt, four more calls come in. A new one popping up every time I silence the previous one. I bite my lower lip. Maybe I *should* answer. I know I owe him that much, but I'm afraid he'll tell me off, or worse, convince me to stay.

Nope. I can't risk it.

My fingers move furiously across the keypad.

Me: We both know it wasn't working. My
sister needs me right now. I'm sorry, but this
is for the best.

His response is almost instantaneous.

Logan: Your sister contacted you? Did the P.I.
find her?

Seriously? That's what he asks? Speech bubbles pop up and disappear several times, as if he can't decide what to say.

Logan: I'll be home in ten minutes. If you're at
the loft, stay there. I'll get us plane tickets,
and we'll leave first thing in the morning.
What airport?

This is how he always gets me—an apology and a grand gesture. The sparkling rose gold bracelet on my wrist from his last grand gesture glints in the light of the carport, reminding me I can't do this again. He'll never change. Even if I wasn't leaving to find my sister, my relationship with Logan was never going to work out. Holly wouldn't trust a stranger, anyway, and it wouldn't be proper to bring him along.

I send one final text.

> Me: I have to leave now. I'm sorry, but it's over. I'll call you when I'm back in town.

Absently, I toss my phone into the passenger seat and whip out of our parking structure for what I hope is the last time. My phone dings with a chorus of text alerts and missed calls, but I'm too busy searching for a place to stop that's far enough away from the apartment to look up directions.

After pulling over at the first turnoff, I park under a flickering streetlight out of sight from the road. I reach for the interior light and click the button. Nothing happens.

Click. Click. Click-click-click.

Nothing.

I punch the switch for good measure. Still, no light turns on, and now my fist and jaw hurt from how hard I'm clenching my teeth. Everything in this car is falling apart. As soon as I fix one thing, the next one breaks. Thankfully, the air-conditioning works and so does the charging port. Which reminds me, I need to keep charging the burner phone. I fish it out and plug it in, then use the flashlight feature to search for the atlas in the back seat.

One paper cut and three ripped pages later, I've found the atlas and the coordinates on the map. It's a tiny blip on the page, the town so small I have to flip to the glossary just to find the name. My fingers slide across the worn paper until they land in the right spot.

Eden, West Virginia.

It's almost a straight shot there—I-77 to I-81, then east on VA-7. There are a few more turns after that, but I won't need those directions until well after my first gas stop. I repeat the route to myself and commit it to memory. I'm usually good with numbers and directions, so I'm not worried about forgetting. If my math is correct, and accounting for stops, it will take me a little over six hours to reach Eden. Which means I'll be pulling into my sister's place around three in the morning.

I shudder involuntarily, tucking the atlas between my seat and the center console. Logan's bracelet snags on the seat belt, digging painfully into my wrist. I should have left it at the loft. It's name brand—Cartier, or something like that, and probably worth more than my car. Now that we're broken up, it wouldn't be fair for me to keep it. I guess I'll have to return it to Logan with his house key when I'm back in town.

I slip the bracelet from my wrist, thankful to be freed of the rose gold shackle, and slide it into Holly's Faraday bag along with Logan's house key and my phone. At the last second, I remember to remove the SIM card and turn the phone off before placing it back inside the bag. Holly would be proud.

As I accelerate onto the highway, I glance in the rearview mirror to Logan's apartment building, lit up with red lights in an otherwise black-and-white skyline. I wonder if he's there now, looking for me, realizing all my stuff is gone and that I meant it when I said I was leaving.

Chapter Three

Four hours.

That's how long I last before the lines on the road start to blur and I have to pull over at a desolate rest stop doubling as a gas station. I need a break and a nap, but I'm not exactly sure how safe this is. When I was living out of my car, I mostly stuck to the parking lot of my community college or the surrounding neighborhoods. This gas station feels a little rough, but it has to be safer to stop here than it is to carry on and risk falling asleep at the wheel. Besides, I just need to close my eyes until the sun comes up, then I can be on my way again.

With one hand on the wheel, I rub the back of my neck and scan my parking options. There is a line of idling semitrucks in designated oversized spots on the far right. In between them and the gas station on the left, is a wide parking lot with two dim light posts. There are also about ten cars parked under the moth-swarmed lights on either end of the lot.

I make a split-second decision to avoid parking directly under the posts, instead opting for smack-dab in the middle.

There is less light here, so anyone looking in won't immediately see a woman sleeping alone in the front seat.

Three hours later, I wake with a crick in my neck and a numb left arm. I'd forgotten how uncomfortable sleeping in your car is. Blinking away the fog in my eyes, I'm greeted by a star-speckled sky.

Wait, it's still dark out. Why am I awake?

The hairs on my arms stand on end as I register deep, muffled voices coming from outside. A moment later, something—*or someone*—slams into the back of my car. I slink down into my seat, knees digging awkwardly into the steering wheel, and double-check that my doors are locked.

Twisting my upper body, I crane my neck to see if I can spot whoever is arguing, but only the night sky and cars on my left and right are visible from this vantage point. More people must have filled in the lot while I slept. They block my view, boxing me in and making me feel like I can't breathe.

Using the old, mostly silent hand crank, I crack my window for some air and to see if I can determine the direction of the voices. Hopefully, they're just being loud and not actually as close as they sound. The second I open my window, that theory dissolves as a flood of heated words fills the cabin.

"I swear, man. I don't know anything," a thin voice screeches, followed by a thud and a squawking noise that sounds suspiciously like the wind just got knocked out of him.

A low growl follows. "Then why run when you knew we'd come for you? Why flee when you knew I'd be the one to find you?"

Fear stirs low in my belly at the second man's rough, menacing tone, and I shrink further into my seat. Whatever this is, it's the last thing I need to be involved in right now.

One of the guys backs up, stepping into my line of sight. Even in the pale moonlight I can see his buzz cut and terrified expression. "I wasn't running! I was scared, alright? I was fucking scared. I had to make sure I wasn't being followed."

The second man passes by my window. He's twice as big as the first, with a slew of tattoos stamped across his fingers and hand. The hood of his dark sweatshirt is pulled up, so I can't make out any of his other features. He takes a deep breath, making his already broad back even bigger. "If I find out you're lying, that you betrayed us in any way, I'll make you regret the day you were born." He steps toward Buzz Cut Guy and in one swift movement pins him down against the hood of my car by his neck. Face meets metal with a loud smack that I'm sure will leave a dent.

"What the hell!" I cry out in surprise.

Shit. Shit. Shit.

My window is still open.

I clamp my hand over my mouth, but it's too late. The tattooed guy's eyes snap to mine, and I freeze. Although his face is partially cast in darkness, I can just make out the cut of a sharp jaw, high cheekbones, and black eyes. He's surprisingly gorgeous and not at all what I would expect from a parking-lot hooligan.

I shake free from the temporary shock of his appearance and fumble to grab the burner phone. "Back the hell up or I'm calling the cops," I announce once I have it in my grip. My voice is louder than necessary with false bravado.

"Don't!" the men say in unison.

I hesitate.

Are they serious?

I look at the man whose face is squished against my hood, his cheek nearly covering his eye now. I raise an eyebrow and my voice so he can hear it through the small gap in the window. "Are you sure?"

He nods. "It's fine, I promise. Please don't call anyone. We're just talking."

The pretty one in the sweatshirt lets him up and dusts off the hood of my car with an inked hand. "Easy, Tiger. I'm his attorney," he says, smiling at me with a mischievous and somehow sensuous half grin.

I scoff. "If you're his lawyer, then I'm a fairy princess." I shake my head. Why am I bothering to respond at all? I should just drive away. I swish my hand through the air, gesturing for them to back up. "You know what, I don't care what you guys are doing. Get out of the way so I can leave."

I turn the key in my ignition to make a point, but the engine only makes a clicking sound. I try again, and the same damn thing happens.

Perfect.

I lean forward and lightly bang my head against the steering wheel.

This can't be happening.

A light tapping noise sounds from my window. When I look up, the tall, pretty one with broad shoulders is bending over. He's taken down his hoodie and is staring at me with bright blue-green eyes and dirty blond hair that's been pushed to one side.

Wow, he's even better looking up close. If it wasn't for the pitying look on his face and the fact that he just assaulted someone on my car, I might actually be attracted to this guy.

"Pop the hood. I'll take a look," he says, like someone who's used to giving orders.

I bite my lip and watch as his gaze zeros in on my mouth. My stomach does a flip.

Nope.

Good-looking or not, I don't want his help. There is also no way I'm getting out of this car in a dark parking lot in the middle of the night. "No thanks. I just need the gas station attendant to—"

"Pop the hood," he repeats, voice so low and full of authority that my fingers fly to the latch in response. He gives me another amused half smile and disappears behind the hood. When he's out of sight, I shove my face into my hand and mentally kick myself for not having some sort of weapon in the car.

At least I'm fully awake now.

At the sound of grumbling, I pick up my head and roll the window down an inch further to hear what he's saying. "I think it's just the battery. Go grab your car. If you don't have jumper cables, you can go get mine. Be quiet about it, though. I've got someone sleeping in the front seat."

Keys sail through the air and land in Buzz Cut Guy's outstretched hand. He jogs off and instead of speculating on if he'll return, I find myself wondering who is sleeping in the front seat of the blond's car, which is absolutely crazy. I must be more tired than I thought.

Buzz Cut returns a moment later in a black SUV that he parks a few feet from my front bumper.

He came back. Interesting. I guess he wasn't in any danger after all.

What the hell is the deal with these guys?

I don't have the capacity to process this right now. I'm just going to let them do their thing and be on my way. Despite whatever that fight was earlier, they can't be all that dangerous if they're willing to help a random stranger out. Either way, I keep the burner in my hand, just in case they decide to try anything funny.

I rest my head against the steering wheel again and wait while the SUV revs its engine.

A few minutes later, someone calls out, "Try and start it." I can't see him, but I know it's the handsome one giving the command. I do as he says, and my engine roars to life on the second try.

Oh, thank God.

I have my seat belt buckled and my palm on the gearshift before Buzz Cut Guy can step forward to remove the jumper cables.

When the hood slams shut, the tall blond wipes his hands on his hoodie and pats my car twice, watching me through the windshield with undeniable interest. His overt scrutiny makes my stomach flutter, and without meaning to, I reach up to smooth down my hair.

Ugh. What's wrong with me?

A gravelly voice rips me from my musings. "Keep it running for at least thirty minutes."

I nod, turning my attention to Buzz Cut, who's standing in the door of the SUV. "You sure you're alright?"

He gives me a thumbs-up, and that's all the confirmation I need before I throw my car into reverse and back up.

I allow myself one last look at the odd duo. The tall blond is now standing in my vacated parking spot. His hood is up again, and the only thing I can see is his devastatingly beautiful smile peeking out from the darkness as I speed off.

Chapter Four

For the next two hours, there is only the black of the road ahead. The all-encompassing darkness barely cut by the two thin streams of my headlights makes it hard not to mull over what just happened at the rest stop. None of it makes sense.

I really hope I did the right thing by not calling the cops. They were nice enough while helping me with my car, and Buzz Cut Guy didn't run off when given the opportunity. Maybe it really was just a tiff between friends? I don't know what kind of friends are that rough with one another, though, especially considering how thoroughly Buzz Cut Guy was being manhandled.

I try to imagine myself in a similar situation where I might argue with someone as volatilely as those two men did and be okay with it, but my imagination rapidly spirals out of control, my breath quickening as the picture in my head morphs. In this new scenario, the tattooed blond is standing behind me instead of Buzz Cut Guy. It's me he pushes forward and pins onto the hood of my car. It's my backside the seam of his pants presses into and my breasts that heave as they're smashed against the warm metal. I can practically feel his full lips at my throat, on my spine, trailing lower...

What the actual fuck, Rylee?

I pinch my leg to chase away the rogue thoughts. My tired brain must be trying to come up with anything to distract me from post-breakup heartache and the devastating news about Jeremy. That's the only reason I keep thinking about the stranger. It has to be.

Slapping my cheeks, I redirect my thoughts. I should be concentrating on what comes next. I was in such a rush to get out of Charlotte, I haven't stopped to consider what I might be walking into with Holly. The last time we were together was when our mother died. After the funeral, she and Jeremy stayed with me for a few months until I turned eighteen. I usually try not to think about that time of my life...

The loneliness.

The fear.

The way Mom looked right before she slipped away.

After her initial stroke and her subsequent loss of mobility, I'd taken care of her all on my own. It was a lot for a seventeen-year-old, but full-time caregivers are expensive, and she made me promise not to accept any of my dad's money. So, I tried to see to her needs while finishing high school and holding down a part-time job. I was failing at all three when Mom had another massive stroke. This time, she didn't make it.

When Jeremy and Holly came, Jeremy took care of everything so I could mourn and finish my last semester. He cooked and cleaned and made one of the darkest times in my life easier to bear. Having them there was such a stark contrast to the solitude I'd been living in that I think it softened the blow of losing my mother. We were a family. Jeremy was so vibrant and alive, and for a short time, he was the glue that kept everything together in my life.

The memory of his smile makes my chest ache. I barely got the chance to know him and now I never will. This time it's my turn to be the one who's there for Holly, the way Jeremy was there for both of us.

Grief. Fear. Guilt. I can barely sort through the torrent of emotions fighting for dominance in my head.

One thing at a time, Rylee. Just get to Eden.

Light from the rising sun finally crests over the hill ahead, painting the sky orange and pink before illuminating a beautiful landscape of rolling hills as far as the eye can see. Beside me, a greenish-brown river snakes along the highway. The sight is so at odds with the events at the rest stop and the emotions of the past few hours that it hardly feels real.

I take a mental note to make the return trip during the day.

Gripping the wheel, I lean forward in my seat to relieve the ache in my back. I should have been there by now, but besides the sign for an old coal mine with a big CLOSED sticker slapped over it, I haven't seen any evidence of a town.

I keep driving until a steel bridge looms ahead in the early morning mist, making me slow down. Although rusted with age and full of creeping vines near the entrance, the bridge appears to still be in good use. I accelerate, regaining my speed, and as I cross over the river, a faded sage-green sign comes into view.

Welcome to Eden.

I breathe a sigh of relief and relax my shoulders only to tense back up as a car whips out from behind a large hedge. The older white Ford Bronco pulls up right on my ass. Craning my neck, I peek over my shoulder. Yep, those are lights on the roof, and I can just make out a sheriff's emblem on the hood. My eyes drop to my speedometer.

Twenty over the speed limit. Shit.

I can't catch a damn break. I grip the wheel and slowly let the car decelerate.

At least the cop hasn't turned on their lights yet. It is a small town, though. Maybe the people here just pull over when this sort of thing happens? My heart sinks. I really can't afford a ticket, but I know nervously eyeballing the deputy every few seconds won't help me appear innocent. So, driving at the glacial, legal speed of 25 mph, I keep my eyes glued to the road and try to appear casual, calm, and collected, which is anything but the way I feel.

By the time I allow myself another quick peek in the rearview mirror, I catch the tail end of the Bronco as it flips a U-ey and speeds back in the direction we came from. A two-tone 1990s Dodge truck leisurely pulls into the empty space behind me. My pounding pulse slows, and I fan myself, only now realizing how much I was sweating. That was a close call.

A little less wound up, I scan my surroundings. Eden's Main Street is straight out of a 1930s postcard. The buildings are mostly brick, but some of the newer ones are made of stone or plaster. Many are undergoing renovations, but all appear to be in various states of disrepair. A few of the shops are boarded up while some, like the small bakery I just passed, are preparing to open for the day.

I crack my window and let the scent of freshly baked bread wrap around me like a comforting blanket. Mom used to bake, and this place smells exactly like home used to. I need to remember to stop at the bakery when I go grocery shopping. Holly never was one for cooking, and I'm betting she could use some fresh, home-cooked meals right about now.

When the buildings start to thin out, I grab the atlas and take a left onto an unpaved road called Locksley Lane. If my map-reading skills are correct, the coordinates Holly gave me are a few miles ahead.

There's not much out this way, so I'm a little surprised when the two-tone Dodge trails me up the dirt road. I try slowing down and pulling to the side, but the truck matches my pace without passing. I can't help but eye it every few seconds, a prickling sensation blooming over the back of my neck.

We go on like this, with the truck only about a hundred feet back, until I reach a small gray bungalow with a sprig of plastic holly on the mailbox.

This must be the place.

Hopefully, this guy will pass me as soon as I pull over.

I'm barely able to step one foot out of my car when several things happen all at once. The Dodge comes to a screeching stop inches from my bumper, spraying rocks and debris in my direction. I shield my eyes right as the screen door from the house is kicked open, hitting the siding with a slap. Holly marches into view and fires a shotgun into the air. She aims the muzzle at the truck and, with a few long strides, puts herself between me and the driver.

"Relax. She's my fucking sister," she bellows at the man opening his truck door. Her unkempt reddish-gold hair whips around her face as she motions with the shotgun for the driver to turn back the way he came.

His door slams shut and although the windows are tinted, I see two heavily ringed hands raise up in surrender. The man then points to something up the road that I can't see.

Holly nods and yells, "I know the drill." There is a strained edge to her voice, like she's barely keeping it together.

The man backs up and does a three-point turn just out of range of Holly's gun. My heart thumps violently as I choke on the dust still lingering in the air.

What the hell was that?

Before I can clear my throat to ask, Holly has her arms wrapped around me in a bone-crushing hug. The warm barrel of the shotgun taps my bare leg and Holly's chest heaves against my own. She's crying, and although I have so many questions about what just happened, there will be plenty of time for answers later. Right now, my sister needs me.

I wrap my arm around her and lead her inside the house, sparing a single look back at the dust-laden road to make sure the truck is gone.

Chapter Five

Holly's home is nothing like Logan's. It's full of well-loved furniture and a thousand different colors. It's small but clean and smells pleasantly of cedar and lemon verbena with another scent lingering in the air, something faint and a little musky, like men's cologne. Holly inhales deeply, seeming to savor the scent before her soft crying becomes incoherent.

My heart breaks for her, so I do the only thing I can and hold her. When her knees buckle, I ease her down onto the threadbare sofa. I think she's trying to talk, but I can't understand the words. I lean closer and try to make sense of what she's saying through the pain blossoming in my chest.

Then I hear it.

"Jeremy," she whimpers.

The last remnants of the wall that time and distance built between Holly and me crumbles. I'm not sure that I even knew it was there, but in this moment, I have nothing but love and compassion for her. This is my sister. She is hurting. It doesn't matter that we barely talk or that I don't know how to comfort her. Right now, I am all she has, and I'd do anything to ease her pain.

I wrap a blanket from the ottoman around us and run my fingers through her greasy hair, the same way Mom used to when we were sick, until she eventually drifts off into an uneasy sleep. At some point, I must fall asleep too, because when I open my eyes again, I am alone on the couch. My two bags are on the coffee table and the sun is low in the sky, casting the house in a soft glowing light.

In the kitchen, Holly's fussing with a smoking toaster and a bottle of dark-amber liquid. I watch her unsuccessful attempts to uncork the bottle. Just when I think she might break the glass, she bites down on the cork and frees it with a *pop*.

The Holly I remember would have celebrated opening that bottle. She would have smirked and tossed out a few colorful phrases, maybe called the bottle her bitch or something, but not this Holly. This Holly's face is entirely devoid of emotion. She moves like a zombie from one task to the next. Even her eyes appear hollow and have a new distance to them that I don't recognize. We both have our stupid father's golden-hazel eyes, but today Holly's are almost mocha. It's like a light went out inside of her. I can't help but wonder if that's what happens when you lose the love of your life.

It's hard to take my eyes off her. Now that I'm more awake, I'm noticing things I missed when I arrived. She's always been skinny, but now her cheekbones are too pronounced and her ribs show through her fitted shirt. Her hair, normally the same light copper-blond shade as my own, is so dirty that it looks brown.

For her to look like this, whatever's been going on with Jeremy has to have been happening for quite some time. Weeks maybe.

If she's in danger, I need to get her out of here. A dark realization occurs to me: if it's really bad, I'll have to call and ask our father for help. The thought alone makes me shudder. I've never asked that man for anything. Although it would be a shame to start now, I'd do it for Holly.

I scan her over once more while she scrapes a butter knife across blackened bread. She takes a swig of the amber liquor and then walks over to me, placing the bottle and a plate of burnt toast on the coffee table before us. "How was the drive in?"

"It was interesting. I had a bizarre encounter at a rest stop." I pause, trying to figure out how to explain what happened. "Two guys were having some sort of argument. One second, I was threatening to call the cops, the next, they were giving my car a jump when it wouldn't start."

The tattooed stranger's blue-green eyes hover in my memory for a second before I return my attention to Holly. She's staring off into the distance, clearly not listening to a word I've said, and I can't say I blame her. While I don't know what it's like to lose a husband, I do know what it's like to be alone and hopeless. To feel like the walls are caving in. Wanting to scream but not having the energy to do it. I wish I could ease this burden for her.

"The funeral is tomorrow afternoon," she says flatly after a minute.

I lower my brows to hide my surprised reaction. A funeral tomorrow seems too soon. It took at least a week and a half to organize my mother's and she'd died of natural causes. Won't the cops need to hold on to his body for an investigation or an autopsy? And wouldn't something as major as a goddamn murder investigation have come up during the private investigator's search?

Maybe I've been reading into the whole situation wrong. Maybe it was just some sort of freak accident? Holly only said that he was *killed*. That could mean anything, not necessarily foul play like I initially assumed.

That wouldn't explain Holly's appearance, though.

My lips slip into a frown. Although I want to, I know I can't ask any of these questions right now. Not when she's finally stopped crying.

I place my hand on hers. "What can I do to help?"

She waves her free hand. "It's all been taken care of. I just need you here. I—" She makes a choking noise before she clears her throat. "I can't be alone."

I squeeze her hand. "You're not alone. I'm here for as long as you need me."

She pushes the plate in my direction, like a silent thank you. I take a bite of the toast, which on top of being burnt is stale, and try not to look disgusted. "Anything you need, I'm here," I say through strained chews. She nods, and I force myself to swallow before standing and extending my palm. "Let's get you in the shower, okay?"

One thing at a time. Tomorrow I'll worry about the funeral and figuring out what happened. Tonight I need to get her into clean clothes and see if she can sleep.

After a long drive and sleeping away most of the day, I spend the majority of the night staring at the living room ceiling. I keep my ears open in case Holly wakes up and calls for me, but she doesn't, and eventually I drift into a twitchy, dreamless sleep on the couch.

The next day, I'm the first to wake, and I spend an hour quietly looking for something to eat while acquainting myself with Holly's home. With her and Jeremy constantly on the move, I'd expected more of a crash pad, but this place is surprisingly homey. It's not very big—just a living room, eat-in kitchen, two bedrooms, and a shared bath—but it's got that lived-in feel that only comes from time, love, and sweat equity.

The last stop on my self-guided tour is the second bedroom, which is being used as Jeremy's office. Inside I find an oversized desk with an elaborate computer setup and several complicated-looking pieces of technology.

Impressive. I had no idea Jeremy was a techie.

My hands itch to get a better look at his equipment to see what he was working with, but I suppress the urge, unwilling to disturb his things.

Recently I've developed a real interest in computers. A few months ago, I was able to fix and upgrade my broken laptop by combining old parts our school computer lab was getting rid of. I did it on my own, without any formal training, and it works better than before. Building myself that laptop is the only thing that's ever given me more satisfaction or peace of mind than running. Ever since then, I've had the itch to do more with tech, maybe even dive into programming, but with lack of access, nothing's really come of it.

For a while, I'd been considering pursuing a degree in computer engineering or information technology, but when it came time to fill out my transfer applications, I let Logan talk me out of it.

"Why would you want to be in a career field dominated by men? You'll be at a disadvantage before you even graduate," he'd said. I still wonder if that was the wrong move. Judging by the excitement I feel by just looking at Jeremy's quadruple-monitor setup and extra-large computer case, it probably was.

Regret fades to sorrow as I pass a thousand little reminders of my brother-in-law scattered around the house. A bottle of cologne. A pair of shoes. A set of free weights strewn across the floor, left frozen in the positions Jeremy last threw them down.

No wonder Holly is a mess. Everywhere she turns she's slapped in the face with a reminder of what she's lost. When she's ready, we'll need to pack a lot of this away. That was the only thing that helped me move on after Mom. But we can worry about that later. Today we just need to get through the funeral.

When Holly wakes, I make us buttered noodles, and we sit down to eat at the sun-bleached oak table in the kitchen. It's not the most nutritious meal, but it's the only food I could find besides stale bread, tea, and a can of tuna. Not that it matters. After a single bite, Holly pushes away the bowl and rushes to the bathroom to throw up.

I did the same thing on the morning of Mom's funeral. Just like Holly did for me then, I hold back her hair and hand her a toothbrush when she's finished.

I curl her hair and help her with her makeup, a weird sense of déjà vu wrapping its wispy fingers around my hands as I twist the curling iron. These are the same robotic motions we went through five years ago. Only back then, our roles were reversed...and Jeremy was with us.

Together we pick out a suitable black dress for Holly. It's chiffon with long sleeves and a hem that cuts right above the knee. Very respectable. Unfortunately, the fabric does nothing to hide how rail thin she's become. She looks like a wraith.

Once she's dressed, I set her up on the couch with a cup of peppermint tea and set out to get myself ready. Holly lets me borrow a black shift dress with a white collar and I pull my hair into a neat bun at the nape of my neck, or at least I try to. I can't remember the last time I had a haircut and there's almost too much of it to put up.

I'm trying to smooth away the loose strands in the hallway mirror when Holly's head snaps toward the door. Outside, a truck squeals to a stop, followed by the sound of steps crunching gravel. Through the window, I can just make out the two-tone Dodge from yesterday.

The screen door hinges squeak open, and my brush clatters to the ground. For a moment, I think I'm staring at a ghost. The man that walks in is the spitting image of Jeremy. He has the same golden-brown skin, dark eyes, and black hair. Even his muscular build is the same. Only the gray flecks in his hair and lines on his face give him away as likely an older relative.

Holly's eyes water, and the man takes a step toward her on the couch. He only stops when I step between them. I'm not entirely sure if Holly wants this man here. Regardless of the fact that he's clearly related to Jeremy, she didn't seem very welcoming yesterday when she aimed a shotgun at his head, and I sure as hell am not going to let him give her grief today, of all days.

He looks down at me, his eyes narrowed in an assessing manner. "You must be Rylee."

It's not a question, but I respond anyway. "And you are?"

"Not a threat to you or your sister, so move aside and let me hug my daughter-in-law."

Shit.

How did I not make the connection immediately? Hot shame coats my cheeks before I move out of his way, almost tripping over my own feet as I avert my eyes to the ground. I can't believe I was about to hassle a grieving father.

From the corner of the living room, I watch through veiled lashes as this incredibly large man drops to his knees before my sister. He sets her tea aside and takes her hands in his before placing his forehead to hers. They both close their eyes.

"I'm sorry about yesterday. I'm sorry I didn't tell you Rylee was coming and that I didn't let you in. You just look so much like him... I couldn't—"

"I know, *mija*. You have nothing to apologize for," the man says, squeezing her hand.

Holly makes a noise of protest, but it's drowned out by a poorly suppressed sob. He makes a hushing sound and wraps Holly up in his massive arms, rubbing a soothing hand over her shoulder. She melts into him.

It almost feels like I'm intruding on a private family matter. A father comforting a daughter. My mouth fills with bitter jealousy at the realization that this man *is* Holly's family.

Our real father walked out on us before I was born. Holly was thirteen at the time, but at least she has memories of him being there; memories of having a father and what it was like to be part of a whole family. Those weeks with her and Jeremy were the closest thing I've ever had to that.

I didn't know until years later, but apparently my mother did such a good job of shutting our dad out of our lives that he didn't even know I existed until he dropped by unannounced in the middle of my fifth birthday party. I'll never forget the surprised hurt on his face or the sound of my mom screaming for him to leave. The yelling got so bad that my party guests left and I went to my room to cry. Later, when Mom came in to offer me some birthday cake, my dad was already gone, having never bothered to actually meet me. Since then, he's drifted back into my life a few times—once for my tenth birthday and a second time at Mom's funeral seven years later.

I shouldn't be jealous that Holly's found a second father, but I am. It's not her fault that people love her. My abandonment issues really shouldn't matter. Especially today, when she's trying to bury her husband. I should be happy that she has someone around her to love and support her, even if that someone isn't me. Why is it, then, that my throat is so tight I can barely swallow?

Holly and the man are still murmuring comforting words to

each other when I interrupt them by clearing my throat. "Should we get going?"

Holly nods and takes the man's hand when he extends it to help her stand. "You going to be okay, *mija?*"

She nods at him and heads for the door.

I move to follow, but he blocks my exit with a toned arm. "How long are you going to be in town?"

I raise my chin, meeting his stare dead on. "As long as she needs me."

He bobs his head approvingly. "Good, because she's going to need you." The lines near his eyes deepen as he gives me a sincere smile and offers me his hand. "I'm Jack Alvarez, by the way."

My eyebrows raise. It's not what I was expecting him to say. After yesterday's encounter and the abruptness of our meeting today, I thought he might ask me to leave.

Guess I was wrong.

His palm is warm and calloused when I place my hand in his. "Rylee Adder, but it sounds like you already knew that." I soften my tone. "I wish we were meeting under different circumstances. I'm very sorry for your loss."

He makes a noise in his throat. "Thank you. Make sure you stick close to your sister today. Not everyone you meet will be family."

I follow Jack outside, where one by one, we slide onto the bench seat of his single-cab truck. During the drive, Holly fidgets nonstop, fussing with her wedding ring until I'm sure the skin underneath will turn raw. I take her hand in mine and give it a gentle squeeze, but her attention doesn't stray from the window.

Instead of heading toward the bakery, we take a left on Main Street. The buildings on this end are sparsely spaced but newer. I lean my head against the glass and watch as people stop and stare at us. I don't know how long Jeremy and Holly have lived here, but I assume news of what happened travels fast in a small town. My heart pangs in discomfort. How awful to have everyone know your pain, to have to wear it like a black scarlet letter. I give Holly's hand another squeeze.

We pass by a little white-and-turquoise eatery called Maggie's Diner. Inside a young woman with tight curly black hair scurries about in an apron, waiting on tables, and there is an obnoxiously bright-orange sign posted in the window that says: Yes, We're Hiring!

My stomach growls when the smell of the diner filters in through the air-conditioning. I'm still staring at the waitress, dreaming of whatever food she's serving, when the truck slows and shudders with a right turn. We pull into a crowded dirt lot tucked between a run-down bar called The Pack and a building with a dove logo on the front sign—the same logo from the beer I had at the dive bar. Dovetail Brewery in big bold letters is scrawled across the entrance.

The parking lot is packed. Motorcycles, classic cars, junkers, and a few black luxury SUVs take up every available space, except what's been roped off for the funeral reception. I climb out of the truck, careful not to hit my head on the doorframe, and am immediately overwhelmed by the sheer amount of people present. There has to be at least three hundred of them, all mingling together.

My mouth goes dry. I hate being the odd man out.

I pull on the hem of my dress, desperate for anything to distract myself from the eyes that press on me from every angle. The pressure of their gazes is an unpleasant physical touch. As Holly's semi-estranged sister, I'd expected to feel like an outsider amongst Jeremy's friends and family. What I hadn't anticipated was the mistrust in their expressions. It feels unmistakably like I am the wolf attempting to infiltrate the flock. Like at any moment a shepherd will appear and run me off.

"You invited *him*?" Holly whispers to Jack as we approach the gathering.

"No, but I put out a notice to the network. Everyone needs to be on alert." Jack offers Holly his arm, and she takes it. "I thought you guys were good? He's just here to pay his respects."

Holly lets out a sigh. "We're fine, but I don't want him around Rylee." At the mention of my name, I perk up. Shifting to the left, I rock onto my toes for a better view of who they're talking about.

When I see him, fire coats every inch of my skin. How could I have missed him? Even if he wasn't staring straight at us from across the crowd, I'd recognize that three-piece suit and perfect bouffant anywhere.

It's our father.

Chapter Six

The sight of Rick Adder, dad of the year, has heat creeping up my neck and into my cheeks. At my sides, my fingers ball into fists.

Holly grabs my wrist and yanks me behind her before turning to face me. "I'm sorry. I swear I didn't know he was coming." She sounds panicked, like she thinks I'm going to cause a scene. If I'm being honest, her concern isn't entirely unjustified; I did cause a *little bit* of a scene the last time I unexpectedly saw my father. But I'm an adult now. For her sake, I can put aside my feelings toward him. At least for one day.

"It's fine. Today is about Jeremy," I whisper calmly, despite the molten fire coursing through my blood. Holly lifts an eyebrow in challenge. "I promise. I'm fine."

I grit my teeth as our father appears behind her. He's flanked by three men, all dressed similarly in black suits. Of course he had the audacity to bring his business associates to his son-in-law's funeral. Everything is always about work and money with him. It's disgusting.

I try to look anywhere but his face, and in doing so, my eyes fixate on the hands of the man standing slightly behind his left side. The man, not much older than me, has an open-mouthed viper tattooed on his hand that looks ready to strike. My mind instantly conjures up an image of the tattooed stranger from yesterday.

Why can't I stop thinking about him?

I look back to my father, who shakes hands with Jack first, but never lets his eyes stray from my sister. I take the opportunity to slip farther behind her.

"How are you?" he asks Holly in a soft tone—a tone he's *never* used with me.

She shrugs before allowing him to pull her into an embrace. They've always had a cordial relationship. I knew they kept in contact, but it still curdles my insides to see her standing with the man who abandoned us. What's worse is that I can't tell if the sick, bubbling sensation in my gut is anger or jealousy.

Either way, I don't have long to dwell on it because their hug now gives my father a clear view of where I'm standing. I fold my shoulders, shrinking in on myself and shuffling to the left, but his eyes zero in on me anyway.

"Rylee?" Confusion rings in his voice.

"Rick," I say back as expressionless as I can manage.

He looks at Holly. "You brought Rylee here?" His words drip with accusation.

She pushes out of the embrace and glances around uneasily. "It seemed like the safest option. Can we not fight about this right now?"

Rick gives her a strained smile, letting his eyes drift to me for only a second, his rigid posture making it clear he does not want to let this go. "Of course. I can't stay anyway. I just wanted to stop by and offer my condolences. I'm only a phone call away if you need anything."

He turns to me. "Rylee—"

"Save your breath. I'm not interested." It's the most we've said to each other since Mom's funeral when he refused to sign my emancipation paperwork. I dig my nails into my palm to keep him from seeing how my hands shake.

With a defeated breath, he turns to Jack. "Jeremy was a good man. I am very sorry for your loss."

Jack nods appreciatively and guides Holly away by the small of her back. I follow behind them like a lost puppy, not daring to look back at my father.

Can't even stay for your son-in-law's funeral? Good riddance.

We were always better off without him anyway.

Holly, Jack, and I weave through the tightly packed crowd. Jack smiles and shakes hands with everyone, doing the majority of the talking. While Holly keeps her face polite, it's hard not to notice the way she holds onto every hand a little too long, scrutinizing every face.

After what has to be their hundredth handshake, I sneak away to grab Holly a drink. Although the crowd generally ignores me as I walk by, I can't help but notice that most conversations come to an abrupt halt the moment I'm within earshot. I try not to let it bother me—being ignored *is* better than being stared at. Still, though, it's a bit odd.

With drink in hand, I scan my surroundings to try to find Holly again. She's not where I left her. The more I look, the stranger everything seems. This isn't a traditional funeral service. There is no church, no priest, no graveyard. There isn't even a place to sit, unless you count the old picnic tables hidden behind a few of the roughly erected canopies providing shade for the food and drink stations.

I can't make sense of the guests, either. At first glance, I wouldn't expect any of them to share a space together, but here they are, mingling like old friends. There are families with small children, who I assume are the locals; a group of men with tattoos and leather vest embroidered with a snarling wolf-like emblem on the back, who have to be in a motorcycle gang; and then there is the group my dad is with, who are headed to their cars, but look like they belong in a Wall Street board meeting.

Who are all these people?

If I died tomorrow, I'd have two, maybe three people come see me off. Not the hundreds that are gathered in this parking lot.

Static from a microphone interrupts my lurking and quiets the crowd. My eyes bounce around, searching for the source of the sound until they land on Holly. She's standing next to Jack on a little platform serving as a stage, her gaze locked on the table to her left where a black urn rests in a bed of white lilies.

Jack clears his throat, and all of a sudden I can hear the buzzing insects in the nearby field. No one speaks. No one even whispers. I've never seen someone command a crowd with such little effort. The air is thick with tension and something else that feels a lot like respect. A breeze rustles through the trees, making the loose strands of my hair stick to my sweat-slicked neck. A shiver creeps up my spine.

"Thank you for coming. Although I hate what brought you here, I think Jeremy would be pleased to see most of the network all in one place and getting along." A smattering of polite laughter ripples through the crowd. "Today, we remember a truly dedicated servant of our community. Jeremy was the best among us—"

The low rumble of an approaching car draws away Jack's attention. His eyes dart to the road before glancing pointedly at a man off to his right sporting bright-red suspenders and a Kpop hairstyle. They exchange some sort of unspoken communication, and the guy backs away slowly.

Jack continues his eulogy, but I'm too distracted to listen. My attention is focused on Red Suspenders as he jogs to the street. He stops just as a faded-green 1970s muscle car rumbles onto the lot. Two men hop out, and Red Suspenders greets them with solemn hugs—the man that exits from the passenger side getting an extra-long embrace. There is something about his dark hair and broad build that's vaguely familiar. As he struggles to finish up the buttons of his black dress shirt, he turns, giving me a better view of his face.

It's Jeremy's brother. We've never met, but I've seen pictures of him. His name is Daniel or Danny, or something like that. I can't believe he's late to his own brother's funeral. At least he looks put together, unlike the driver.

While Jeremy's brother's dark hair is unstyled, it's neat. His friend's hair, on the other hand, is shaved close on the sides and fades into a floppy, dirty-blond mess on top of his head. Even his clothes are unkempt. I can see the reddish-brown stains on the back of his white T-shirt from clear across the parking lot. It looks like he's covered in some sort of oil or paint splatter. When Red Suspenders points this out, the man whips off his shirt, exposing a tattooed and heavily muscled back, like it's perfectly normal to be shirtless at a funeral. I roll my eyes but don't stop watching as he throws his discarded shirt into the car and turns in my direction.

I freeze, recognition temporarily immobilizing my thoughts and body.

What the hell is he *doing here?*

While he's too far away for me to see his piercing blue-green eyes, I'd recognize that ridiculously cut jaw and those tattooed hands anywhere, even if I hadn't been thinking of him moments ago. Hands that yesterday were pinning someone to the hood of my car.

My fingers ghost across my neck as I stare at his body. Without his shirt on, I can see he also has a score of tattoos covering his toned arms and torso. The ink flows all the way from the tips of his fingers to the top of his neck and then back down again to the deep V at his waist. From the looks of it, the tattoos might even dip lower...

He pulls on his black hoodie, effectively snapping me out of my trance. I mentally scold myself. This is my brother-in-law's funeral. I should be paying attention to Jack's eulogy. I turn away from the newcomers with a blanket of shame draped over my shoulders and face the stage again.

"Jeremy's brutal murder was meant to scare us into giving up, but our fight will not end with his death. No. This is just the beginning. There will be retribution." The hairs on the back of my neck stand at attention at Jack's menacing last words, and I'm left wondering what else I missed during my shameful ogling of the stranger from the rest stop.

Each person in attendance begins to stomp their feet in unison. It's an eerie, almost ancient sound. One made by men on the precipice of war.

It's a battle cry.

Jack puts a hand up, and the stomping stops. "I'd like to open the mic up for anyone who would like to share a story about Jeremy." He looks at Holly, who only shakes her head and moves to walk off the stage.

I toss the drinks into the nearest bin and make my way over to her. When we are just feet away from one another, I'm cut off by Red Suspenders and the two guys from the muscle car. Jeremy's brother wraps his arms around Holly. When he pulls back, she wipes the tears from under his eyes. It's a gentle, motherly gesture, even though he has to be in his midtwenties.

"Your father is furious," she says, wiping at his cheeks.

"I know." Danny smirks through the tears. "Somebody had to keep Colt here from getting himself killed."

As if that was his cue, the blond stranger from the rest stop steps forward.

Holly looks up at him with a hopeful expression. "Did he say anything?"

Colt shakes his head. "No, he was clueless. I don't think he had anything to do with it."

What are they talking about?

Holly's lips press together. She looks devastated, but she tries to hide it by digging through her purse. "You have blood on your face." She hands him a napkin. "Wipe it off before Jack sees."

"I've already seen it," Jack says from behind her, voice booming with authority and disapproval. Flinching, I glance around to see who else noticed how odd this is, but they're all staring at the stage, listening to a story about Jeremy and nodding. I should be listening too, but I'm too interested in the exchange happening in front of me.

"You boys deliberately disobeyed a direct order and put all of us in jeopardy." Jack's nostrils flare as his tone sharpens. "You're both grounded." I stifle a laugh at his declaration. How can you *ground* grown men? But these two look thoroughly reprimanded by Jack's words. "You are on protective detail with Ash until I say otherwise."

Colt takes a step toward Jack. "I can't be on babysitting du—"

Jeremy's brother smacks Colt in the stomach with the back of his hand. "We understand." His statement ends the debate and eases some of the fire in Jack's eyes.

He turns to Colt. "I need to speak with you. Privately." He glances at his son. "Danny, do you have Holly?"

I take this as my opportunity to speak up and step forward. "I've got her."

All four of them turn toward me, as if only now realizing I must have been here the whole time. Colt's icy blue-green eyes lock on mine for only a brief moment, but it feels as though someone shoved me under a microscope. His gaze runs the length of my body, hovering over every curve, electrifying every nerve. When it settles on my mouth, his tongue darts out, sweeping over his full bottom lip. That small act is like a shot of adrenaline to my system. Danny nudges Colt with an elbow, and Colt promptly averts his eyes.

I shouldn't, but with Colt's attention now diverted, I allow myself to quickly take in the details of his features up close. My eyes roams over his strong nose and hollow cheeks, lingering on the pronounced cupid's bow that sits atop that deliciously full bottom lip. I should stop there, but I don't. Greedily, I devour every aspect of his appearance from his worn, brown leather boots and fitted jeans to the tattoos covering his flesh: a rose on his hand, initials on his fingers, and that same menacing wolf from the back of the motorcycle gang's jackets on the side of his neck, which is so lifelike I can practically hear the snarling.

I only stop my perusal when I notice the tiny specks of dried red and brown liquid dotting his jaw. Up close, it's clear that what I thought from a distance was oil or dirt is actually blood.

The shock of this new discovery is enough to bring me to my senses. Guilt washes over me once again. I'm here for Holly, not whatever this is.

Jack, apparently oblivious to my disgraceful gawking, dips his chin in my direction and leads Colt away with an iron grip on his shoulder. With their departure, Holly latches herself onto my arm, looking relieved to see me.

Jeremy's brother offers me his hand with a small smile that

doesn't reach his eyes. "You must be Rylee. Nice to finally meet you. I'm Danny." His palm is warm and comforting, but his smile fades quickly, replaced by an expression of profound grief.

I have a strong urge to comfort him, which catches me off guard. We don't know each other, but his anguish has me feeling devastated—not only for his loss, but also for the loss of the relationship I will never have with Jeremy. I may never really know my brother-in-law, but maybe I could know Danny?

I squeeze his hand a little tighter and his smile returns.

We're still mid introduction when Colt comes back. He runs a hand through his disheveled hair and bumps Holly with his hip. "I'm on fucking babysitting duty for your kid sister. Where is she?" He scans the crowd, looking right over me. "The sooner she leaves Eden, the better."

My shoulders drop with that same feeling I used to get every time Logan told me he wasn't going to make it to another one of our dates.

Disappointment, I tell myself. *This is disappointment.*

Why is it that attractive people always have to go and ruin the illusion by opening their mouths? And what does babysitting duty mean anyway? Is he going to come hold my hand until I go back to Charlotte? *Ridiculous.*

After a minute of pretending to scan the crowd, his gaze lands on Holly's arm linked through mine. His face sags into a deep frown, like he just found gum stuck on the bottom of his shoe. Considering how he blatantly checked me out earlier, it's pretty clear that he's pretending not to recognize me from the rest stop and pretending not to already know I'm Holly's sister.

"How long are you in town for?"

Why does everyone keep asking me that?

There has to be something I'm missing. I frown and look to Holly for an answer.

"I was hoping you would stay at least through summer?" She bites her lip and swallows hard, like she's about to be sick.

"I can do that." All my classes are online anyway.

Colt snorts humorlessly, like my being in town is the last thing he needs. Holly doesn't seem to notice his irritation, too busy looking around. She has a slightly green hue to her face as she says, "I need a minute. Are you going to be okay on your own?"

I nod and as soon as she's out of earshot, I turn on Colt. I don't understand why I'm so mad, but there is no way I'm going to stand by and let him run me off. After seeing my dad earlier, I'm raring for a fight. "Colt, is it?" I say, stepping forward. "I don't know where you get off thinking I need someone to babysit me, but I sure as shit don't need you or that attitude."

His eyes widen in surprise, and Danny starts to chuckle, which only serves to enrage me further.

"And another thing," I snap, placing my hands on my hips, "I'm not leaving Holly or Eden anytime soon, so you better get used to me."

Colt closes the distance between us in a single step. I turn to look away, but he grabs my chin, tilting it up and forcing me to look into his icy eyes. When I try to pull away, his grip tightens, keeping me in place. It doesn't hurt, but it does have my heart racing with rage or something similar.

"First off, little Tiger, the name's Colton. Only my friends call me Colt. Second"—he exhales, the scent of mint gum and iron wafting over me—"we both know you won't stick around. It'd be easier on everyone if you left now. Holly needs to be with people who actually care about her. She needs her family."

"I *am* her family, asshole."

Who does this guy think he is?

Colton drops my chin and laughs sardonically. "We'll see about that." He turns his back on me and walks away, leaving me breathless and fuming.

Danny moves to follow, stopping to give me an apologetic half smile. I wave him off. I've dealt with assholes before.

I can handle Colton.

Chapter Seven

Holly won't eat.

The day after the funeral, Jack brought us a truckload of groceries and precooked meals, but she won't touch any of it. I've tried making all her favorites: garlic bread, burgers, tacos. Nothing works. Just the mention of food makes her queasy. Her skin tone is sallow, and her eyes have a new hollowness to them that reminds me of the way Mom looked during the last three weeks of her life, when she was slipping away. Although I've heard that a lack of appetite is a natural response to grief, seeing it happen to my own sister is a new type of torture.

I am powerless, and it freaking sucks.

On the third day of her hunger strike, I take one look at Holly's hollow cheeks and decide to leave the house in search of food she might actually eat.

As I step out onto the porch, a light breeze lifts the hair from my neck, the humid morning air coating my body in a thin sheen of sweat. It's perfect running weather. I've been craving the movement of a long, steady run, but I've been too scared to leave Holly on her own. Plus, there's been a silver sedan parked outside of the house since the funeral. I keep forgetting to ask Holly why it's there. It's probably just a neighbor from up the road, but I can't shake the feeling that someone is watching us.

Hopping in my Honda, I cruise Main Street in search of a Starbucks or a Burger King. Hell, I'd settle for *any* comforting fast food, but there isn't a single familiar chain restaurant in sight. Everything is locally owned. If I wasn't so desperate to feed Holly, the mom-and-pop shops would be charming.

The only thing I recognize is the bakery—aptly named Sunrise Bakery—I passed on my first day. With no other quick options, I pull in. Inside, the faint scent of cinnamon floats in the air and my mouth waters. There has to be something in here Holly will eat.

With its rough, large-plank wooden floors and exposed brick walls, this place looks like it's been here for a century. On one of the walls, actual black-and-white photos from the founding of the town are on proud display. Miners. Women in elaborate dresses. Main Street back when it was a dirt road. So much history in one spot. There's even an old-timey mirror taking up the entire back wall with the word Bread stamped on it in big red letters. I catch myself smiling in the reflection before a flash of silver appears on the road behind me. I turn to look over my shoulder, but it's gone.

Was that the same silver sedan that just creeped by?

Shaking off the tingling feeling of being watched, I peruse the glass display filled with colorful confections. I end up buying a dozen assorted donuts, two cinnamon rolls, and a loaf of bread from the friendly owner and bring them home. To my relief, Holly eats seven of the cake donuts in one sitting. She doesn't even spew her guts out afterward.

A weight lifts from my shoulders, and I allow myself a

quick run while she showers—though guilt has me turning around before I hit the main road. The run's not nearly far enough, but it eases the nervous tension in my limbs.

Holly and I spend the rest of the day watching old movies and nibbling on the remaining donuts. For a few moments it feels natural hanging out with her in comfortable silence. It's like the childhood we would have had if we'd been closer in age.

She rests her head on my shoulder and lets loose a long breath. "Thank you for coming and for being here with me."

"Of course," I say automatically. There is so much else I want to ask her—like what really happened to Jeremy and what the deal is with that silver sedan—but I know it's too soon.

"Holls?" I pop my head into the steamy bathroom. "Can you give me the Wi-Fi password? I need to check my grades and summer coursework." I wait a few seconds. "Can I use Jeremy's computer? Or do you mind if I use my cell?" I'm still trying to be as respectful as possible of Holly's idiotic technology aversion, but I need to get online.

Her dripping head appears from behind the blue floral curtain. "No phones. I'll show you how to use our computer in a second."

I can figure out how to use a computer on my own, but maybe she has a secret porn stash she doesn't want me to see.

Fine, I guess I can wait...

Holly is still towel-drying her hair when I follow her into Jeremy's office. The moment we step inside, I'm hit with the scent I can now recognize as his cologne. Too late, I realize this might have been a mistake, but Holly doesn't break down. She's too focused on the task at hand. I mentally file that away for later.

She unlocks the top drawer of the desk and pulls out a small rectangular device attached to a knotted cluster of chords. She plugs one into the desktop USB port and the other into an old-looking extension cord. All four screens remain dark.

"Anytime you need to use the computer, just flip this switch." She demonstrates on the device. "Once the computer fires up, make sure you use the application called Ghost Rider on the desktop. That way everything you do is anonymous, and no one can track you or steal your passwords." She wiggles her eyebrows and gives me a conspiratorial grin.

No wonder the P.I. couldn't find her. She's nuts.

"Holly." I'm not sure how to say this delicately, but she seems more like herself right now, so I just say it. "Why is this even necessary? What's going on?"

She chews on her bottom lip. "You mean the secrecy?" I nod and she continues, but not before straightening her back and taking a deep breath, the same way an actress would before taking the stage. "Well, you remember after the Navy, when I started up with those activists?"

How could I forget? She'd got herself arrested four times in a twelve-month period while protesting some factory being built in another country. Thankfully, she'd reconnected with Jeremy shortly after and things quieted down.

She bites her lip. "Let's just say I pissed off a few very unsavory, very powerful people and I am safer if they don't know where I am." She gives me a tight smile, looking anywhere but my eyes.

She's lying.

I'm not exactly sure how I know, but I know beyond a shadow of a doubt that she's lying to me. "And what does that have to do with me? Why can't I use my computer or my normal cell phone?"

"You're with me now. If they knew you were here, they could find us—" She stops abruptly and her eyes go wide, like she said something she shouldn't have. "They could find me." Her expression tightens.

Another lie. I don't want to push her, but I can't let her lie to my face either. "What about the car parked outside? The silver one? I think it followed me into town yesterday. Is that somehow connected to these powerful people you're hiding from?"

"It's a small town, Ry. You're going to run into the same people frequently." Holly shrugs in obvious dismissal of the conversation.

Frustration bubbles in my gut. Is this Holly being her normal paranoid self, or is there more to it? Something about this doesn't sit right with me, and I can't just let her get away with brushing me off the way Logan used to. Never again.

"Holls, please be honest with me. Is something else going on here? At the funeral, no one would talk around me and—"

"People need time to get used to you. It will be fine." She stands, fussing with a few knickknacks on the desk before leaning forward and flipping on the computer with a tight smile. "You're all set." She looks me directly in the eye, daring me to keep prying. After a moment's hesitation, I take a seat. We've been apart for so long, I don't want to start fighting already. I can let this go...*for now.*

If I had any concern about how to find or work the Ghost Rider program, it's completely gone the second the screen loads because it's the only icon on the entire desktop. A single click on the small, black dog icon, or maybe it's a wolf, brings me to a search engine.

"So, I just type the website into the search bar and I can operate as normal?"

Holly makes a noise of confirmation, then wanders out into the hallway. Her departure is quickly followed by my groans of alarm as I pull up my bank account. I only have forty-two dollars left—and that's *with* the most recent paycheck from work.

Work. *Shit.*

I've missed two shifts, and I never called in to request a leave of absence. There is no way I'll be allowed back at that restaurant again. I run my hand down my face. The tips were so good. *Ugh.*

Fortunately, it's much better news when I sign into my school account. A few of the syllabi are up for my summer classes, including the two courses I'm most looking forward to— Coding 106 and Cyber Security 203. I've already paid for e-books, so at least I don't have to worry about shelling out any more cash for those.

Next, I check my grades. All As. But one professor still hasn't posted yet, and I *really* need to know my grades to see if I still stand a chance at getting into one of the four-year universities I applied to...

One more time won't hurt.

I stop and listen for Holly. Judging by the clanking noises coming down the hallway, it sounds like she's in the kitchen. I quickly sign out of my account and sign in as the professor. Sure enough, she has everything graded. I swear this woman holds on to our grades as some sort of power trip—

Fuck.

She gave me a B on my final paper? Even after I helped her with all her computer issues? That drops my final grade from an A- to a B+.

All of a sudden, I'm feeling way less guilty about the

keystroke recognition program I installed to get her password. I really hope that B doesn't screw me. After four years of working full-time to pay for junior college, I don't think I could handle it if I couldn't transfer because of one lousy B.

I sign out of her account and back into mine. "Holls? I'm going to need my laptop for school. Is there any way to get this Ghost Rider program installed on it?"

Holly appears in the doorway. "Yeah, of course. I'll have Minho take a look."

"What's a Minho?"

She smiles. "Minho is a computer god. He'll get you all squared away before school starts. When is that, by the way?"

"Monday, but I need to do some coursework before then." If I'm going to be here all summer, I also need a job, but I keep that to myself. Holly doesn't need to know about my money problems.

I spend the next thirty minutes searching for jobs online only to realize no one in this town knows how to post openings on the internet. It's either that or there are no jobs in Eden. I could try cold-calling some of the restaurants in town to see if they're taking applications. Maybe that nice lady at Sunrise Bakery would hire me? I have a few years of food service experience; a bakery can't be that different. The only problem is tips. Without tips, I doubt I'd make enough to get by, let alone save for school.

I slam my palm onto the keyboard and the screen flashes bright orange. The color triggers the memory of that fluorescent: Yes, We're Hiring! sign from the diner and my heart soars. Hopefully, they haven't filled the opening yet.

I call out to Holly that I'm leaving before hopping in my Honda and speeding down the dirt road. My eyes dart repeatedly to my rearview mirror, but the silver sedan doesn't follow.

Maybe I am just being paranoid.

When my tires hit the paved street, I roll down my windows and let the wind whip through my hair, the loose strands slashing against my cheeks with a sharp sting. I turn the radio up and enjoy my short ride. Far behind, there is a flash of green as a car pulls onto the road.

At the diner, I smooth my hair and do a quick makeup check in the mirror. I should have changed. Jean shorts and a black tank top aren't exactly professional, but there isn't much I can do about that now. I'll just have to dress better for the inter-view—if I get one.

Like the bakery, walking into Maggie's Diner is like taking a step back in time. A bell chimes as I open the door, and I'm greeted by cool air that smells faintly of strawberry milkshakes. Red pleather booths line the street-facing windows and orange leather stools dot the wooden countertop facing the kitchen. Even the floor is checkered black and white. It's like I stumbled into *Pleasantville* with slightly dirtier walls.

The patrons, thankfully there are only six, all turn to examine me. Two of the ladies in a booth lean closer to one another, whispering while a female voice calls out from the kitchen, "Be right with you!"

I hover near the counter as the owner of the voice, a younger woman with short, tight curly black hair bounces out from the kitchen carrying plates of sandwiches. She sets them before two elderly gentlemen sitting at the counter. "Let me know if y'all need more fries. I won't tell if you don't." She gives them a dazzling smile before turning her attention to me.

"Oh." She halts her steps, tilting her head to the side. "You must be Holly's sister. Rylee, right?"

"How'd you know?" It's a little disarming that she knows who I am.

That bright smile of hers returns. "We don't get many visitors in Eden. News tends to spread fast." Her eyes dart to the two gossiping women. "What can I get for you today?"

I wring my hands. "I saw that sign in the window. Are you guys still hiring?"

Somehow her smile grows wider. "Do you have any experience?"

"I worked at a seafood restaurant in Charlotte for about three years and a supper club before that."

"Great, you're hired!"

"Wait, really?" *It can't be that easy.* "Shouldn't I meet with the owner or a manager or something?"

She waves her hand dismissively. "Maggie is my mom. Besides, you're the only person who applied and, between you and me, we need the help. The job's yours. Pay is $8.75 an hour, cash, and you can start tomorrow." She puffs her cheeks like she's worried that won't be enough. "Actually, if you want to stick around this afternoon, I can show you the ropes. I can't pay you for today, but you can have all the tips. Sound fair?"

"Fair enough." I extend my hand to shake hers. "Should I change? And I didn't catch your name."

"I'm Lana, and it looks like you're already in uniform." She gestures to what she's wearing: jean shorts, a navy-blue tank top, and a small apron draped over her hips. Her curves are slightly less generous than mine, and her skin is a deep, golden shade of brown, but once I put on an apron, our outfits are practically twinning.

Lana spends the afternoon teaching me the ins and outs of the diner. The menu is fairly simple, and after an hour or two, I'm confident enough to take a few tables on my own.

When the rush dies down, Lana introduces me to the cook, a quiet man in his midfifties ironically named Mike Cook. Cook, as Lana calls him, doesn't speak—like ever. But he does give me a sincere smile and a hardy handshake with his cracked, scarred hand. I also get a thumbs-up, which I'm assuming means I'm doing a good job.

Hours later, I leave the diner feeling light and accomplished with thirty-eight dollars in my pocket. I've got a job, I'm with my sister...maybe a summer in Eden is exactly the reset I needed.

That feeling vanishes as soon as the green muscle car Colton drove to the funeral whips out onto the road behind me.

Chapter Eight

Colton follows me back to Holly's in that obnoxiously loud car of his with his inked arm hanging out the window. Seeing him in my review mirror for the duration of the drive is enough to effectively sour my mood.

I've barely finished locking my car when his engine cuts off and his door slams. Gravel crunches and then abruptly stops as he takes a seat on the front bumper of his car. Once again, I'm struck by his beauty and I hate myself a little for it. Even so, it would be hard not to notice how different he looks today, more put together somehow in a clean, black T-shirt that hugs his inked biceps, fitted jeans that are cuffed at the bottom, and that same pair of worn, brown boots. All he needs is a lit cigarette to really nail down that whole James Dean vibe.

"Your taillight's out," he says without any preamble. "You should get that fixed before you head out of town."

The ember of attraction stoking in my belly fizzles out entirely.

The audacity of this guy is unreal.

"Like I said at the funeral, I'm not going anywhere."

He crosses his arms over his chest and lifts an eyebrow. "First the car battery at the rest stop, now a taillight? Someone needs to learn how to take care of the things that are important to them."

My nails dig into my palm to the point of pain, and it takes every ounce of my self-control to not punch this guy in the dick. "That's literally what I'm in Eden trying to do." I know he meant my car, but Holly is the only thing that's important to me, and the insinuation that I can't take care of her rubs me the wrong way.

His brow furrows and his lips part like he's going to say something, but no words come out. Satisfied with his silence, I walk to the back of my car, ignoring the way his face scrunches into a contemplative expression and how his muscles flex in that tight black T-shirt.

Dammit. My left taillight is indeed cracked. I pick at the loose pieces and find the perpetrating rock still lodged next to a shattered lightbulb.

I wonder how much this is going to cost me.

Colton's passenger door slams shut, and I meet Danny's sad brown eyes. My demeanor instantly softens.

"Hey, Rylee." He walks around the Chevy and pulls me into a slightly awkward side hug. "How are you and your sister holding up?"

"I'm doing okay, and Holly is..." I falter, unsure how to respond. Should I tell him she's barely eating? That she's just going through the motions? I shrug and shake my head.

Danny nods, running his hand over the center of his chest like he's trying to ease an ache there. "Same."

My throat bobs with the urge to say something comforting, but before I can act on it, a heavy palm falls onto Danny's shoulder. The tattoos on Colton's hand stretch and shrink as he gives Danny a reassuring squeeze. The gesture is unexpectedly kind and speaks of a compassion I didn't know the asshole was capable of. Confusion ripples across my brow as a small crack forms in the image I've been building of Colton. Maybe it's only me he has a problem with?

Danny moves toward the bungalow, but my eyes stay locked on Colton. What is it with this guy? How can he go from jerk to compassionate friend in the span of a minute? When he notices me staring, he glares right back. I expect to see disdain written across his face, but I'm surprised to see something else. Something that looks a lot like fear, or maybe even grief. My chest pinches.

"Are you two coming in or are you too busy having a glare-off?" Danny shouts from the porch while holding the screen door open. There is a sparkle in his eye that screams of mischief. I back away and jog up the stairs to stand beside him.

Colton doesn't follow. "I've got something I need to do real quick. I'll be there in a second."

"Sounds good," Danny calls back. He looks down at me. "You good? You've got a look on your face that says you're about to fight or fuck. Which is it?"

My eyes widen at his bluntness. "Jesus, Danny. The first option. What's his deal anyway?"

Danny directs his gaze to Colton, his face growing serious. "Colt doesn't trust easily and right now you're an unknown. With everything that's going on and what happened to Jeremy, he's feeling a little overprotective." Danny turns to me and smiles. "It's not fair of me to ask, but be patient with him."

I hum, considering his request. "He doesn't need to trust me. I'm just here for Holly. You and your dad have been perfectly pleasant, and you're the ones who lost a family member. What's Colton's excuse?"

Danny slips his hand into his pocket and scuffs his boot across the deck. "Jeremy was Colt's brother, too. We all grew up together. He's family, and as far as Jack and I are concerned, so are you."

Family.

My heart gives another painful squeeze.

Danny opens the screen door further. "Just give him a chance. He'll come around. I promise."

I'm about to say that I'll think about it when the door is wrenched open. Red Suspenders Guy, now dressed in a cut-off gray shirt and black jeans sans red suspenders, stares back at me before looking at Danny. Tattoos cover every inch of his exposed arms. "Thought maybe you got locked out or something."

"Nope," Danny says, brushing past Red Suspenders and plopping himself on the couch next to Holly. "Just refereeing a standoff between Rylee and Colt."

"Who's winning?" Holly asks.

Danny places an arm over her shoulder. "To be honest, I have no idea. Could go either way."

Red Suspenders Guy laughs before extending his hand to me. "Hi, I'm Minho. Holly said you might need some help with your computer?"

I take his hand. "Rylee, and yeah, if you don't mind. You can help me get online? All my school things are on my laptop or else I would just use Jeremy's computer. I don't want to put you out or anything, though."

"It's not a problem," Minho says with a sheepish smile.

Thirty minutes later, we are set up next to each other at the kitchen table while Holly, Danny, and Colton have a quiet conversation in the living room.

"So, you rebuilt this laptop yourself?" Minho asks politely.

I flush with embarrassment, unsure if he's impressed or appalled by my work. "Yeah. I sort of had to. It stopped connecting to wireless internet, and I couldn't afford a new one."

"And you've had no training?" I nod my head in answer. "Wow. This is really impressive. Good stuff."

"Thank you." My cheeks flush again with the compliment. "Did you go to school? Or take classes to learn all this?" I gesture to the spare computer parts and wires he has spread out over the table.

His tongue pops out the side of his mouth, and he finishes screwing a back panel onto my laptop. "No, not really. Jeremy was into computers growing up, and I idolized him. I even tried to join the Marine Corps when I was old enough, like he did."

A restrained laugh sounds from the living room as Danny recounts a story about Jeremy that's too quiet for me to hear. My eyes momentarily dart to the back of Colton's head before returning to Minho. "Tried? What happened?"

"Apparently an eighteen-year-old with a criminal record is a big no-no." He raises his eyebrows, and I must look startled because he clarifies, "Nothing violent. I just hacked into the sheriff's department's database when I was sixteen. Anyway, Jeremy taught me most of what I know, and I filled in the gaps on my own."

It's my turn to be impressed. With the way he just took apart my computer and put it back together in under twenty minutes, he very clearly knows what he's doing.

Minho turns my laptop on and starts combing through code I've never seen before, his fingers flying over the keyboard as he enters commands and changes existing code lines as if it were as natural as breathing.

"That's incredible," I say, watching him work. "If you have time, would you be willing to tutor me in my programming and cyber security classes this summer?"

His deep-brown eyes flash with delight. "I'd love to. I've

always wondered what they teach in those things." He finishes what he's doing and connects a device, similar to the one Holly used on Jeremy's computer, to one of my USB ports. "As long as you're using this, you'll always have internet access." Minho's chest puffs and his eyes squint as he tries to hide his self-satisfied smirk. "I also went ahead and cleaned up your computer. I deleted anything that could be used to track you, including the connection to that nice little program you installed on one of your professor's computers."

My head disappears into my neck.

He found that in just the few minutes he was in there?

"Don't be embarrassed. It was pretty good stuff. I approve." He slides the laptop closer to me. "Anyway, if you want to just click on the Ghost Rider app and bring up your email or any other site you frequently use, we can make sure everything works."

I do as he instructs and then look away as another bout of laughter echoes from the living room. My eyes dart over to the trio, who are huddled close and sound like they're still reminiscing over some shared memory.

Holly is smiling.

The sight should be comforting—she's acting halfway normal for the first time since I arrived—but instead, a burning sensation flip-flops in my gut. The muscles in my jaw twitch, and I have to remind myself to unclench my teeth.

A low whistle sounds from my right, and I drop my eyes to my laptop where sixteen unread emails from Logan take up the screen. I don't even have to open them up to know what they say, the subject lines are illuminating enough.

Subject: Don't leave like this.
Subject: Can we talk?
Subject: Are you okay?

Subject: I miss you.

Minho shifts in his seat uncomfortably. "That's a lot of emails from Logan Eastmann," he says, feathering his gaze to the now-quiet living room.

"It's just my ex," I explain. "I sort of broke up with him and left town on the same night. He's probably just worried." I make an awkward half-laughing, half-squeaking noise.

The air grows thick and heavy as Holly, Danny, and Colton stand in the living room. The latter two step in my direction, their fists clenched and bodies rigid, but Holly stops them with a gentle hand. "I think it's time you boys leave. Thank you for stopping by. I needed those stories about Jer, but I'm tired now."

That haunted look is back on her face, and no one argues with her as they see themselves out.

Chapter Nine

"So, you'll be working at the diner?" Holly asks, looking skeptical. "Maggie hired you?"

"Yeah, today's my first day. And no, technically Lana hired me. You sure you're going to be alright without me?" I don't know why she's giving me the third degree. She didn't have anything to say about the job last night when I mentioned it. "Am I missing something here? Is there a reason Maggie wouldn't have hired me?"

Holly bites her lip. "Maggie doesn't like Jack or his boys. Which means she doesn't like me—and likely you, by association."

I laugh. "His boys? You make it sound like they're children or in a gang or something."

Holly doesn't laugh with me. "Just be careful. Don't let her give you any shit. And don't worry about me. I'll go back to work soon anyway and I'm glad you'll be busy. Hopefully, you can make a few friends, too. Just do me a favor? Try to avoid Danny and the others. I don't want you hanging out with them."

That one stumps me. "Let me get this straight, you don't want me hanging out with the people you had in your living room last night? The same people you were laughing and smiling with?"

She lets out a huff that sends her wispy curtain bangs flying. "It's complicated. Seeing them and sharing stories about Jeremy made me forget for a minute, but they are not good company for you. Trust me."

Unease needles across my shoulders. "What are you not telling me?"

She forces a smile and then glances at the clock. "You're going to be late if you don't leave now."

Even though I know she's avoiding my question, she's also not wrong. I should have left five minutes ago. "Okay, but I want to talk about this when I come back."

She gives me a vague nod, and I rush out to my Honda. When I reach for the handle, the door is unlocked and slightly ajar. I quickly check the inside, including the glove compartment, but nothing seems amiss.

Huh. I could have sworn I locked it yesterday...

I guess I was just too distracted by Colton.

A few minutes later, the bell to the diner chimes as I walk through the door. I inhale deeply and try to push all thoughts of Holly from my mind. Today, instead of milkshakes, Maggie's smells of bacon and maple syrup. The aroma is mouthwateringly delicious.

Lana rushes to greet me and help me into my apron. Her actions are hurried and she fumbles with the bow that she ties just a little too tightly around my middle. When she's done, she spins me to face her. "Come to the back. I need to introduce you to my mom."

Maggie is nothing like her daughter. While Lana's skin is a

rich shade of brown, Maggie's is so pale it's almost translucent. While Lana's hair is cropped short and kept in tight, natural curls, Maggie's is long and pulled back into a tight bun and speckled with strands of gray. The differences don't stop at their appearance either. Unlike Lana, Maggie is stiff. With posture so rigid I'd almost bet she has a metal rod shoved up her spine.

Or her ass.

She assesses me through the rims of her half-moon spectacles, which are perched precariously on the edge of her nose. "So, you're the sister."

I plaster on a fake grin. "Yes, ma'am. It's nice to meet you. Thank you for the opportunity to—"

She holds up a single finger. "I'll have none of Jack's nonsense in my diner." Then, like a spotlight, her eyes trail from my hair to my shoes and back up again. "Have you worked in the food industry before?"

"Yes, ma'am."

Am I sweating? I repress the urge to fan myself.

Maggie pushes her spectacles to the bridge of her nose and squints as she scrutinizes my face. "Okay then, as long as you're on time and you do your job, you can stay. But if Jack and his boys come in, get them in and out the door as fast as possible. If you know what's good for you, stay away from all of them. Are we clear?"

There's that phrase again. *Jack and his boys.* "Yes, ma'am. Understood. Thank you."

Lana ushers me out of the back office, and once we're out of earshot, we both let out a sigh of relief. "That went better than expected," she admits. "I'll let you take the first table—it's the least I can do." Her smile falters. "I've been meaning to ask, how is your sister doing?"

I shift right and begin filling the salt and pepper shakers. "I think she's okay. As well as can be expected."

Lana nods and messes with the ketchup bottles. "I don't want to pry, but what exactly happened?" She glances over her shoulder to her mother's office and her eyes take on a wet sheen. "I don't mean to be insensitive, but I grew up with Danny and Jeremy. His death came as such a shock. All any of us know is that he was killed."

She seems genuinely concerned, but I don't have an answer for her, so I shrug. "I don't know. I'm ashamed to admit I haven't had the heart to ask Holly yet. It just never seems like there is an appropriate time. I'm not really sure how to bring it up."

She pats me on the back. "You'll find a way. Give Holly my best, though." She scurries off to another station, wiping at her eyes as she goes.

The clock strikes seven, and a second later the bell over the door dings when Minho and Danny stroll in. They're wearing the same clothes as last night, and they take a seat at the large corner booth on the left.

Danny greets me with a tired wink when I approach their table. "How's the new job?"

"Well, considering I'm five seconds into my first shift and my first table is you two, I'd say pretty good." I smile, trying to shake off the remnants of nervousness left over from meeting the infamous Maggie.

Minho's eyes narrow. "Then why are you so sweaty?"

"Oh," I fan myself with the menu before placing it down on the table, "I just had the pleasure of meeting the owner of this fine establishment."

Danny and Minho cringe.

"Yeah, my sentiments exactly. For a second there I thought I was out of a job, but it looks like she's going to let me stay. She did warn me that I should steer clear of you two. Actually, now that I think about it, she's the second person to give me that advice today. What's that all about?"

Minho leans back, the motion revealing an abundance of computer chip tattoos at his wrist as he man-sprawls and says, "Haven't you heard? We're dangerous. We're bad news, baby."

Danny laughs and, although I get the distinct impression that I'm missing out on some sort of inside joke, I find myself laughing right along with them. I don't realize anyone has joined us until I open my eyes to a scowling Colton glaring down at me in that same black hoodie from the night we met. I wish I didn't notice how the angry expression makes his full bottom lip even more pronounced, or how despite his horrible countenance, he's still beautiful.

"What's so funny?" he asks, turning his attention to Danny and Minho, who are still chuckling to themselves.

I guess he's sticking with the asshole routine.

Why does the Lord put such horrible things in such nice-looking packages?

"Rylee just found out we're bad news. She has orders to stay far away from us." Danny smiles up at Colton, but he only gets a snarl in return from the brooding blond.

"Relax, Colt. Take a seat." Danny looks back at me with a smile so similar to Jeremy's that for one second I forget who I'm looking at. "We'll take three coffees to start, when you have a chance."

Bobbing my head, I swallow the frog in my throat and make a quick exit. Behind the counter, Lana is fussing with the coffee machine. Thankfully, she missed the whole exchange. "I know, I know. I'm taking forever. It's almost done," she says.

I want to ask her to take over the table so I don't have to deal with Colton, but that's too pathetic, even for me. Instead, I listen to the bubbling coffee maker and watch as cars drive by, mentally preparing myself for anything Colton tries to throw my way.

I don't understand how I made an enemy so fast, but just being near him makes me feel squirmy. Like my skin doesn't fit. It feels dangerously close to attraction, and while I'd love to say I've never been attracted to an asshole before, Logan wasn't exactly a charmer.

Maybe this is some sort of deep-seated daddy issue coming to the surface? Or maybe I'm only attracted to jerks because there's no real risk when you already know exactly what you're getting. Either way, my path forward is obvious.

Steer clear of Colton.

Outside, a familiar silver sedan pulls up and the most beautiful woman I've ever seen gets out. Her hair is light brown with natural-looking golden highlights that fall in long tendrils around her shoulders. She yawns and stretches, revealing a tanned, toned stomach and the bottom part of a tattoo just peeking out under her crop top. When she bends over to get something from the car, a gleam of metal shines from her waistband.

"Who *is* that?" I only ask to figure out why her car is always by my sister's house, but there is an envious quality to my voice that doesn't escape Lana's attention.

She lets out a long sigh. "I know, right? Her name is Ashlynn. I'm surprised y'all haven't met. She's one of—" The phone rings and Lana curses. "It's my mom in the back. She probably needs me. Do you mind?"

I want to ask her to finish what she was saying, but she's already gone. I watch as Ashlynn saunters into the diner. Colton rises for her, allowing her to slide into the seat between him and Danny. That annoying little voice in my head wonders if she was the one sleeping in Colton's car back at the rest stop.

My stomach churns, and I try not to read too much into the sensation.

When the coffee finishes brewing, I head to the table with four white, ceramic cups. Ashlynn grins sweetly, introducing herself and engaging me in a polite exchange: "How are you liking town? How's your sister? Is there anything you need?" Colton snorts in annoyance at her friendly demeanor, but she continues with her pleasantries.

Of course, she would be sweet, too.

Not a competition, I remind myself.

I take down their orders: French toast for Minho, pancakes for Ashlynn and Danny, and eggs and bacon with a side of salsa for Colton. As soon as I'm done, I rush away from the table like a coward. Lana still hasn't returned, and the new customers have only ordered coffee so far, so there's not much to distract myself with. Mindlessly, I wipe down the counter and pretend not to watch the four of them talking easily at the table. I feel like Bella from *Twilight*, watching the Cullens at the cool kids' table on her first day of school.

Their food is ready all too soon, and I pass out their breakfast from right to left. First to Minho, then Danny, and then to Ashlynn, who is tying back her hair in preparation for the syrupy feast I've placed before her.

With her hair tied in a low messy bun, I notice the tiny white flowers on small fern clippings encased in resin decorating her ears. The resin is cut into the shape of a leaf and catches the light when she moves.

"I love your earrings," I say, sliding the plate closer to her.

She touches her ears shyly, as if she's not used to compliments. "Aw, thank you. I can write down the Etsy account, if you're interested?"

"I'd love that. Maybe I can get Holly a pair for her birthday."

I move to give Colton his food, but he's already shaking his head. "I'm surprised you'd be into something that cheap."

Ashlynn looks offended, but I'm confident his words were only meant to wound me. "What is that supposed to mean?" I snap.

"Come on, we all know you're the rich-boyfriend, high-end-jewelry type of girl. I mean seriously, who just leaves thousands of dollars' worth of jewelry in their glove compartment?" Colton leans back and places an arm over the top of the booth.

The memory of my unlocked car door this morning flashes in my mind.

Motherfucker.

He's the reason my car was unlocked. He must have found my bracelet in the Faraday bag. I swear, if my hands weren't already full, they'd be wrapped around his neck. "Did you go through my car?"

Everyone at the table recoils, sinking in their seats.

He did. And they all knew about it.

Heat bubbles just below the surface of my skin. "Did. You. Go. Through. My. Car?" I repeat with as much malice as I can muster.

"What if I did?" He averts his eyes, as if I'm not worth communicating with directly.

That's it. Someone needs to put this man-child in his place. A leisurely smile slinks over my lips as I let the tray with his breakfast teeter and then tip.

In slow motion, the plate, salsa and all, careens into his lap. He tries to stand, but that only sends the salsa cup bouncing onto the table, the contents splashing back up into his open mouth and eyes. His face and black hoodie are now covered in bits of tomato, peppers, and egg. He looks like a hot-mess, and I can't remember the last time I felt this satisfied.

I make no attempt to hide my smile.

Serves him right.

The table erupts into a chorus of laughter as Colton storms out through the door, ripping off his hoodie and no doubt covering the parking lot in bits of egg. I bend down to pick up the tray, and as I do, I spot some of the words from the tattoo etched across his muscular shoulder blades.

NO ONE IS FREE.

Chapter Ten

It's been a week since I started summer classes and my sister went back to work. Just like that, I'm on my own again.

As ridiculous as it is to admit, I hadn't realized that Holly working night shifts would equate to her sleeping all day. Even when she is home, she's too tired to do anything with me or leave the house.

The hospital she works at is a little over an hour away. With the extra shifts she volunteered for, this means she's gone fifteen hours a day, five days a week. When she is home, I do my best not to wake her, using my headphones during school lectures and spending as much time on the porch as possible. But it's lonely. Regardless of the fact that I've been on my own most of my life, there is something about being physically near someone but unable to connect that is more isolating than actually being alone.

Today, I finished my homework early and am itching for a run. Holly will be asleep for at least another two hours, which gives me plenty of time to plot out a ten-miler and embark on a running adventure. It's a little ambitious for my first long run in over a week, but with hours before sunset, I have enough time for a nice and easy pace.

While I stretch on the patio, I notice an unfamiliar black truck idling in front of the bungalow where the silver sedan has parked in the past. I wait for them to exit, but after a few minutes, it's clear the person has no intention of coming out while I'm here. A tightness spreads through my shoulders.

I can't just leave Holly in there sleeping without knowing who this is.

Marching up to the truck, I pound on the glass. It's only when I'm lowering my fist that it occurs to me that banging on a stranger's window and asking them to leave might not be the smartest idea I've ever had.

When the window opens, Danny greets me with a poorly hidden smirk, and my shoulders relax a smidge. "Colt was right, you are feisty."

I don't know what that means, so I ignore it. "What are you doing here? You realize it's a little creepy to sit in front of someone's house without coming in, right?"

"I'm waiting for Holly to wake up. Jack needs to talk to her."

"And you're parked out here waiting until, what? The sun goes down and a light turns on? You could have just come inside."

"Well, it's not like she keeps her phone turned on, and I figured you were busy with school and what not."

He's got me there. "Okay, fine. I guess that makes sense." I hesitate. "Hey, can I ask you something?" His posture stiffens, but when he doesn't say no, I continue. "Is someone following me? I know it sounds crazy, but there's always a car out here, and Colton's been parked at the bar across the street during all four of my last shifts. It just seems like too much of a coincidence."

Danny's head tilts to the side, considering my question. It should be a simple yes or no answer, but his face is all scrunched up like he's struggling with a decision. Finally, he says, "Jack asked us to look out for the two of you. As long as Jeremy's killer is still out there, that's what we're doing."

"What are you guys, some sort of neighborhood watch?"

A small grin spreads across his face. "Yeah. Something like that."

My eyes narrow at the vague answer. "I don't need a babysitter."

Danny just raises his hands. "Not my call."

Absolutely infuriating. "Fine. Can you tell Holly I went for a run when she wakes up?"

"Sure can."

Leaving Danny and his ambiguous answers behind, I concentrate on making it down the unpaved road without rolling my ankle. Once I'm through the worst of it, I go over my running route. Two miles down, right on Main Street. One mile up, left at the gas station on Sherwood Road. Then two miles out along the river before turning back. I tried to do a street view of the run, but the route was too pixelated to make out when I zoomed in.

The first few miles are rough. My limbs are heavy and slow from disuse. The few people I pass give me a wide berth, either too afraid I'll sweat on them or afraid I'll pass out and they'll be forced to revive me. Despite their concerned glances, I push on. Mile three is where I usually get in the zone. If I can make it to the next turning point, I know I'll hit my stride.

Sure enough, the moment I turn onto Sherwood Road, my feet lighten and my breath comes easier. I leave behind the brick buildings and my troubled thoughts over Holly and soar down a shaded, tree-lined road. The golden-orange light of late afternoon filters through the leaves, creating a kaleidoscope of shadows that dance across the asphalt. On my right, I hear the sounds of the river as it ripples over rocks and downed branches, and my mind clears for the first time since I left Charlotte.

When the road curves closer to the water, a light floral scent rides the breeze, and I spot little orange and yellow flowers in the underbrush near the water's edge. They look like the ones my mom and I used to grow in little planters on our apartment patio. I didn't think they grew wild, though. I'm tempted to stop and get a better look, thinking maybe I can take some for Holly and plant them in the yard, but that would mean I have to turn around and carry them all the way home. I will just have to look up the name of the flower and come back later with my car.

All too soon I reach my five-mile turnaround point, but I'm reluctant to stop. My body is strong. I know I can keep going. As I push a little farther, the old road I've been running on transitions into a newly paved one. The asphalt is black as night, and I instantly feel the relief in my knees.

I keep going. I might regret it on the run back, but for now my body craves more.

About half a mile ahead, there is some sort of wide, wooden bridge crossing a stream. It's newer than the surrounding road and barely wide enough for a single car to pass over at a time. It has a beautiful timber-trussed roof to protect it from the elements, and as I get closer, I can just make out intricate filigree carved into some of the support beams near the rafters.

I yearn for a closer look.

Disregarding the sign that says Private Drive, I mark the bridge as my new turnaround point and push forward. The next sign isn't as easy to ignore.

Jackal Territory. Turn Back Now.

The hackles on my neck rise, and I have that odd tingling

feeling I'm being watched again. It's like pressure on my skin from an unseen source. A twig snaps in the brush, and I immediately turn around, picking up my pace to make it back to the old road. I'm feet away when I hear a chorus of rumbles approaching. Seconds later, three motorcycles ride into view.

There is no use in speeding up, because there is nowhere for me to run to and no way they haven't already seen me. But I am back on the public road now, and I have every right to be here. I need to relax and act like I belong.

A single rider breaks away from the trio and accelerates straight for me with a thunderous, sputtering boom. When he's only a few feet from careening into me, he kicks out a leg and uses it to make a sharp, peeling turn. The smell of fuel and burnt rubber permeates the air as he circles me threateningly, inching closer and closer with each consecutive sweep.

The rider is dressed in all black, including his helmet, which is matte with a dark-tinted shield obscuring his face. Even without recognizing the tattoos on his hands and arms, I'd still know who it was. Colton just has this aura about him, like he takes all the air out of a space, and right now I can hardly breathe.

He circles closer until little pebbles from the road bounce up to hit my shins. My adrenaline surges, my heart thudding against my rib cage. He might be more pissed off about me dumping his breakfast in his lap than I originally thought. And while I don't think he'd intentionally hurt me, as his path shrinks, I am starting to worry he might accidentally run me over.

When the next two riders pull up, one of them rips a cherry-red helmet off, revealing a confused-looking Minho. He mouths something, but the sound of all three bikes is deafening. Minho and the last rider cut their engines while Colton speeds off in the direction of Main Street. Without him circling, the air rushes back into my lungs and I can finally breathe.

"What are you doing out here?" Minho repeats.

I gesture to my sweat-drenched clothes and sneakers. "Isn't it obvious?"

"But why? I thought you were into computers not...*this*." His face turns sour with visible distaste for what I assume is my choice of leisure activities. I guess running is not for everyone.

The man to his left coughs. He's already removed his helmet and is watching us with interest.

"Oh, right. Alex, this is Rylee, Holly's sister. Rylee, this is Alex, my partner."

Alex gives a small wave, which I return. He has a pleasant face with curly chestnut hair that's been matted down by his helmet and soft yet mistrusting hazel eyes. Neither he nor Minho are being impolite, but I have the distinct feeling I shouldn't be here.

I shift my weight to my toes and then back onto my heels.

Minho breaks the silence. "Where is Danny?" His voice has an odd false quality to it, like he's forcing himself to sound casual.

"I'm not sure. Probably back at the house with Holly? He said Jack needed to talk with her." I cross my arms over my chest. "What are *you* guys doing here?" I ask with a bit of an edge to my voice. "Are you following me?"

Minho and Alex exchange brief eye contact before the former gestures to where I saw the signs. "We live across that bridge. We're supposed to be here."

The implication of his words is clear: I'm *not*.

I bounce from foot to foot.

Just when I think this can't get any more uncomfortable, the roar of Colton's bike returning draws all of our attention back down the road. Only now, Colton's not alone. A white sheriff's cruiser is leisurely trailing him like a stalking animal. Colton shakes his head and makes a subtle downward motion with his hand.

Sighing, Minho says, "Play it cool. Knott hasn't pulled him over yet. He might let us go this time."

"What about her?" Alex inclines his head in my direction right as Colton pulls up and cuts his engine.

He rips off his helmet and grips it tightly, staring me down. "You don't know us. You were out for a run and we started harassing you to find out why you were here, got it?"

"I mean, that's literally what happened, so yeah, got it." I crinkle my eyes and smile without teeth to emphasize my sarcasm.

Alex chortles. "Oh, I like her."

The sheriff waits a moment before flashing his lights and chirping his siren twice, as if we didn't already know he was stopping us. Instinctually, I take a step to move closer to Colton, but before my foot connects with the ground, he growls under his breath, "Keep your distance."

Well, alright then.

Thin, gray, slicked-back hair pops up from the cruiser, followed shortly by bushy eyebrows and an unflattering goatee. Beady black eyes lock onto mine, and my blood runs cold. His boots click on the pavement as he moves to the front of his cruiser. "What's a pretty thing like you doing all the way out here?" the man says with a sneer.

Even though the sun is still high in the sky, a chill runs through my entire body, like I just noticed a shadow in a dark alley. I can't pin it down, but something is off about this guy. I open my jaw to speak, but Colton's voice sounds first. "That's what we were trying to figure out, Sheriff."

The sheriff leans against the hood of his car with exaggerated casualness, his wrinkled tan shirt rustling with the movement. "Well, well, what a good thing Sheriff Knott showed up to help solve the mystery, then." His eyebrows rise as he pauses to examine me, lingering uncomfortably on my exposed legs.

I've never regretted the short shorts I run in until this very moment. His gaze feels like insects scraping across my skin.

In the corner of my eye, Colton shifts in his seat.

"Are these boys bothering you, Miss..."

"Adder," I supply. "Rylee Adder. And no, they weren't. I wasn't aware that this was private property. They were just helping me get back to the main road." I don't want to get anyone in trouble by saying they were harassing me, even if that's what Colton told me to say.

Sheriff Knott raises both his hands and gestures to the surrounding road. "You can run anywhere you like, Miss Adder. But I suggest you run as far away from these boys as you can. A pretty thing like you doesn't need any of their trouble." His eyes narrow, like he's unsure about me.

That's the third time someone has told me to stay away from *these boys*.

Sheriff Knott unbuttons the cuffs of his shirt and begins rolling his sleeves. "Why don't you go on and run home to that sister of yours? Me and the boys have got some things to discuss."

His words feel like a threat. *Leave now,* they seem to say. Even *the boys*, as he called them, look like they're throwing out warnings with their eyes, giving me silent permission to run away.

I nod my head slowly and take a few tentative steps backward. The sheriff fixes his attention back on Colton, absentmindedly palming two sets of handcuffs on his belt. Minho gives me a subtle jut of his chin, urging me to leave, but I'm torn. Moments ago, all I wanted to do was get away from these guys and off this road. Now, I feel like they need protecting from the sheriff. Which is ridiculous. He's the *law* and they're three grown men. What could I do?

Still, something with Sheriff Knott is just not right.

He closes in on the guys, and for a second, Colton's eyes flash to mine with so much poorly suppressed rage that, against my better judgment, I take off running.

As I sprint, the wind whirls through the trees, urging me to go faster, but I can't shake the sick sensation that I just left three people in need.

I have to do something.

Less than fifteen minutes later—after what might be the fastest two miles I've ever run— I reach the gas station on the corner of Main Street. My breathing is heavy, and I'm drenched in perspiration, but at least the run gave me time to form a plan.

Stopping the first person I see with out-of-state plates, I wheeze, "Hey, are you from around here?"

The stocky man in a business suit pauses. "No, why?"

Perfect.

I put on my best damsel-in-distress face and clutch my chest. "There was a major car accident down that way"—I throw a hand in the complete opposite direction that I came from—"by the diner." I pant and point in the direction of Maggie's, which is a good five miles away from Colton, Alex, and Minho. If I can draw the sheriff away, they'll have time to run. I just need to act the part of the panicked bystander.

It's a gamble, but if Eden isn't big enough for a police department, that means the sheriff's department is covering the entire county. I'm betting Sheriff Knott is the only officer within responding distance, which means he will have to respond to any accident reports in the immediate area.

I really need to write my Criminal Justice 101 professor a thank-you note and pray this idea works.

"Can you call 9-1-1 for me?" I fan myself like I might pass out. Thankfully, he nods and pulls his phone out.

I hold my breath.

Sixty seconds later, the distant wail of a police siren cuts through the air. Another sixty seconds after that, Sheriff Knott's cruiser whizzes by.

The sense of relief that washes over me is instant, but with it comes the fading of my adrenaline. I'm exhausted, both from the odd interaction with the sheriff and running so fast. I am not a sprinter. My legs are Jell-O, and there is no way I can walk back to Holly's right now. Plopping down on the curb, I rest my head on my knees.

What was I thinking? I'm pretty sure false reporting is a crime. I pound my head against my kneecap and replay the whole scene over again. Law enforcement officials are supposed to be the good guys, but Sheriff Knott felt dangerous, though I still can't pinpoint why.

The low rumble of approaching motorcycles has me picking up my head. I still don't have the energy to walk, so I let them pull up next to me. Colton lifts the visor on his helmet. His left eye is now swollen and a trail of fresh blood trickles from his newly split lip. "Was that you?" He waves in the direction Sheriff Knott took off in.

I nod, too drained to play his games or form words.

"How... Why?" he asks in a tone I haven't heard from him before. He sounds intrigued.

I put my head back on my knees. "I had some out-of-towner report a car accident. I figured the sheriff would have to respond, and I don't really know why I did it. Guess I had a bad feeling."

I broke the law because I had a bad feeling? Good one, Rylee.

Alex slaps his thigh and points at Minho. "Ha. I knew I

liked her. Told you." Minho shakes his head, but I hear muffled laughter from his red helmet.

I pick my head up enough to give Alex a thumbs-up. I like him, too. "Are you guys going to explain what all that was or what happened to Colton's face?"

Their response is immediate and unified. "No."

Of course not.

A second of silence passes, then, "But we can give you a ride home." To my surprise, the offer comes from Colton, who has taken off his helmet and is now extending it toward me.

My brows narrow. "If this is some sort of ploy to mess with me or get revenge for the breakfast in your lap, no thanks. I'm too tired."

"You look like you can barely walk, and I'm grateful for the assist with Knott. No tricks, I promise." He gives the helmet a shake and hoists me to my feet when I grab onto it.

"Fine, but I'm riding with Alex."

Alex bounces on his bike. "While you clearly have great taste, only Colt has room for two riders."

Perfect.

I shove the helmet on and fumble with the strap. Colton drops the foot pegs, leaning the bike in my direction. He extends a hand, and it feels like more than an invitation, almost like a peace offering of sorts. I hop up and realize too late that there is no backrest and nowhere to hold on. I place my hands cautiously on Colton's belt, hoping that maybe if I grip the loops of his jeans tight enough, I won't have to hold on to him.

Beneath me, the engine roars to life, then the bike surges forward before coming to an abrupt stop. My body slams into Colton's back, my arms wrapping around the front of him to brace. He grabs my hands and locks them together across his waist.

"You could have just told me to hold on," I say, gripping my hands together and adjusting myself so I'm not as firmly pressed into him.

"Where's the fun in that?" The echo of his laughter reverberates into my chest as he peels away from the curb and gasses it. His laughter is different than it was last time at Holly's—unmarred by grief. It makes my chest ache, and I wish the bike wasn't so loud so I could hear it better.

Having never been on a motorcycle before, I hadn't realized how much work the passenger has to do to actually stay on. I squeeze my thighs around Colton's hips and press my front into his back. Every inch of this man is thick, hard muscle. He's so wide I'm finding it difficult to keep my hands clasped together. There is also something tucked into the waistband of his jeans that prevents me from getting a better grip. Whatever the item is, it's hard and cold and digs into my right forearm when I try to rearrange my hands.

My palms start to sweat with the effort of holding on. When the bike settles to a steady speed, I splay my hands to dry them on his shirt.

Mistake. Huge Mistake.

Now the only thing I can think about is the taut contours of his abs under my fingers. If he was anyone else, I'd be tempted to let my hands roam and explore, but I refrain.

When we turn onto the unpaved Locksley Lane, the slight incline and marginally bumpier road has me struggling to stay seated. With each bounce over a rock or a pothole, my butt slides precariously closer to the edge of my already tiny seat. My running shorts aren't helping either. If anything, the damp fabric makes it harder for me to keep my position on the leather. Just when I'm about to slip off entirely, Colton reaches back and wraps a powerful hand under my left thigh. His rough palm cups me right below the crease of my ass, and he pulls me up until my chest is flush with him, my breasts pushed up against his back.

I expect him to release me, but he keeps his hand there, holding me in place, the bare skin of his palm on the bare skin of my thigh. My heartbeat quickens and heat pools in my core. I am suddenly very aware of the rumbling engine pulsing between my thighs. I try to squeeze my legs together and inch away, but each part of me is so firmly pressed into Colton that there is no room for movement. To make matters worse, my new position is creating friction where there wasn't friction before. That combined with the way this seat is vibrating and the occasional bounce of the road... This ride is starting to feel too good.

No. No. No.

Taking a deep breath, I close my eyes and try to ward off the traitorous thoughts forming in my head, but it only makes it worse. Now I can smell the heat of the day radiating off Colton's sweat-dampened back, along with the faint hint of gasoline mixed with something sweet and spiced. I inhale deeper through the helmet. It reminds me of sunshine and cloves with a dash of mint gum. I open my eyes, grateful for the helmet between us that prevents me from nestling my cheek against this jerk. One kind gesture—okay, two kind gestures including the car jump—and an incredible physique doesn't excuse his behavior.

I wish my body would stop reacting to our closeness, but it doesn't.

Colton gives my thigh a painful squeeze as we pull up to Holly's. It doesn't seem purposeful—almost like his hand clenched involuntarily. Regardless, I already feel bruises forming where his fingers dig into me.

Danny is still parked outside, but now Jack's truck is also here, tucked behind my Honda with Danny leaning against it.

The three bikes cut their engines and heated shouting echoes from the bungalow. Danny, Colton, Minho, and Alex trade glances with each other in some sort of silent exchange.

I wish they would stop doing that. It's infuriating.

"He never would have gone if you hadn't asked him!" Holly screams.

If Jack responds, I can't hear it.

After a brief pause, she yells, "No. I told you it was too soon. We all did. And now he's gone. Why did you think he would succeed when I failed?"

I move to dismount the bike on the right side, but Colton stops me. "Watch the exhaust, Tiger, it'll burn you." He grabs my hand and guides me off the other side.

"Thank you," I whisper while handing him my helmet. He only dips his chin in response.

"No," Holly belts, "I have nothing left to give. You already took it all. Leave. Get out." The door bangs open, and Jack is roughly shoved through it. His eyes are red rimmed and his mouth is drawn, but he doesn't fight her.

"You!" Holly points an accusing finger in my direction, and I feel it on my chest like a hot poker. "What are you doing with them?"

I open my mouth to explain, but she silences me with a slice of her hand. "Actually, no. I don't care. Get inside."

My shoulders slump as I follow her command.

"All of you, stay away from my sister. The last thing she needs is any of this mess." One of the guys starts to interrupt, but Holly screams, "No. Get out and leave us both alone." She takes a breath. "We'll be out of your hair by the end of summer. Until then, don't follow us, don't talk to us, and don't try to help us."

Jack raises his arms at his side, palms skyward. "Holly, *mija,* please. We want you with us. You are family."

Holly silences him with a humorless laugh. "Really, Jack? Because that's not how I remember the vote going." He doesn't respond. "That's what I thought. Trust me, if it wasn't for my contract at the hospital, I'd already be gone."

As soon as I squeeze by Jack, she slams the door in his face. Once we're both locked inside, she whirls on me. "What were you doing with them?"

Her question makes me feel like I've done something wrong. "Holls, it was just a ride home."

She turns her back on me. "That's how it always starts, isn't it?"

Chapter Eleven

It's Friday night and even though the bar across the street is hopping, the diner is dead.

My hand hovers over the healing bruises on my thigh as another motorcycle pulls into the parking lot. All week I've watched a stream of people come in and out of The Pack at all hours of the day and night. Some show up in casual or business attire, while others wear motorcycle vests with the wolf-like drawing on the back. There is a word scrawled across the top of the vests—cuts, I think they're called—but at this distance I can only make out the first and last letters: *J* and *S*.

Backing away from the window, I thank the stars that Maggie's isn't as busy as the bar tonight because after staying up late last night to complete a school assignment, I am freaking exhausted. The empty diner also ends up working in my favor because it gives Lana the opportunity to teach me the closing routine.

She hands me a cardboard box. "Friday nights are always this slow, that's why we close early. Everyone is either at a bar or one of the restaurants that serves alcohol. Whoever is closing, which next week will be you, usually spends the last hour of the shift going through our pantry and tossing anything with an upcoming expiration date."

"Even if it's not expired?" I ask, keenly aware of how incredibly wasteful that is.

"If the expiration date is within the next week, Mom wants it tossed. We had one bad run of food poisoning and can't afford to have another."

"And you just throw it away? Why not take it home?"

"The portions are too big. It's only the two of us. But don't go trying to take any for yourself. Mom's a little uptight about that sort of thing. She fired our last busboy for stealing after he took home a single slice of pie." Walking into the pantry, she pulls two large tubs of chocolate pudding off the shelf and checks the dates before placing one in the cardboard box I'm holding. "Anyway, we also need to toss anything premade in the fridge. Cook will remake the coleslaw, pies, and cakes over the weekend."

When all is said and done, we end up collecting three tins of green beans, one tub of pudding, four pies, and one jar of okra. Outside, I shuffle to the dumpster behind the diner with the box of food in tow. I hate this. None of the items have actually gone bad yet. There has to be a family in Eden who could use this.

My conscience gets the better of me, and I decide I just can't waste the food. Instead of in the dumpster, I place the box on one of the AC units and make a plan to grab it after we close. Tomorrow I can figure out how to get it to someone who needs it.

I slip back inside where Lana is already turning off the lights. "You up for going out and getting a drink?" Lana asks, gathering her things.

"Yeah, absolutely." I'm really not, but I give her two enthusiastic thumbs-ups and hope it hides the guilt I feel over the food I didn't throw away.

She does an excited little jump. "Great! The bar is across town. I'll pick you up around nine? I figure it'll be easier if we drive together."

"We're not going to The Pack?" I glance wistfully across the street as another group of laughing people enter through the doors. "I've been dying to check it out."

Lana's brows scrunch together as she locks the door behind us. "Not without an invite, we're not," she says, like I should already know. "Plus, I figured you wouldn't want to run into your new best friend Colton after that salsa incident, and he doesn't go to Eddie's."

I'm not sure how I feel about running into Colton. A few days ago, I would have dreaded the thought, but after the encounter with Knott and that motorcycle ride, I'm not so sure. My hand falls to my side and hovers over the bruises on the back of my thigh. It's like I can still feel his touch. "Eddie's it is then."

"Awesome. This will be fun, I promise." Lana enters her car, and I wait for her to drive away before heading to the back to retrieve the food I left. But when I get there, the box is tipped over and empty. I look around, but can't find a trace of the food or even a glass shard from the jar.

Behind me, the bushes rustle and a small voice shushes someone.

I freeze and call out in the direction of the overgrown weeds, "Hello? Did you take the food I left out here?"

High-pitched whispers fill the silence, and I hear a distinct shushing noise. The sound is quickly followed by a smack. Still, no one answers my question. "It's okay if you did. I just wanted to make sure it went to someone who needed it."

Another minute goes by before a spindly boy emerges from

what I thought was a game path. The kid is fourteen—maybe fifteen? He's skinny and his dirt-covered clothing is so ill fitting that it's a little difficult to guess his age.

He picks at the seam of his trousers while trying to make eye contact and failing. "We thought it was trash. Are you gonna call the sheriff?"

"No, of course not."

I wouldn't call Knott for anything at this point.

I smile, trying to look as friendly as possible. "I'm glad you took it." He clearly needs it. "Actually," I say, taking a step closer as an idea pops into my head, "do you live around here?"

"Yes, ma'am. Just down the road, in Willow Park with our mama."

I thought so. "If you come back next week around this same time, I might have a little bit more food for you." I'd much rather give the food to this boy than throw it out. Clearly his family has fallen on hard times if he's willing to take scraps from Maggie's.

A squeal comes from the bushes, and a little girl darts out. She's dressed in a faded-pink jumpsuit that matches the rosy tint of her cheeks. "More food! Did you hear that, Johnny?"

The little girl, full of childlike confidence, strides over to me. Her hair is in tangles and she has dirt caked on her nose. She's about five and adorable and far too young to know the hunger etched into her face. "I'm Anna Grace."

I crouch down to her level and hold out my hand. "I'm Rylee, nice to meet you."

She gives my hand a sideways high five. "If you're gon' give us some food, does that mean we won't have to take it from the bins no more?"

"Anymore, Anna. It's anymore," Johnny corrects.

I look from her hopeful expression to her brother's. His

eyes are watering, and he shoves his hands roughly into the pockets of his dirty, torn pants with obvious embarrassment.

It's worse than I thought. They probably check the dumpster every week looking for something to eat. My muscles tense, and I wonder if there are other children like this in town. "I'll tell you what, Anna. If I'm working, I'll always set the food on the AC unit where it was today. That way you won't have to climb in the bins. Just don't let Maggie find out, okay?"

She nods enthusiastically and throws her tiny arms around me for a hug. I wave to her brother. "See you next Friday?"

He gives me a curt nod, takes his sister by the hand, then disappears into the brush.

* * *

Dumping my clothes onto the couch, which has also been pulling double duty as my bed, I mull over what to wear. I have a few casual dresses, but they show *a lot* of skin and I'm not sure if that's the vibe I want to send out. I also tend to make bad choices when I dress provocatively. My mind flips through my recent not-so-great choices, namely Logan and my unexplained attraction to a certain tattoo-covered asshole.

On second thought, maybe a skimpy outfit, drinks, and a random hookup is exactly what I need tonight.

I grab one of my favorite dresses, a peach-colored Bohemian flowy number with a neckline that dips all the way down to my navel. *Meh.* This one looks like I'm trying too hard. I frown at my clothes. Actually, nearly everything I own feels out of place in Eden. Most of it was bought with the intent to try to fit in with Logan's friends or with people from work and none of it feels like me.

I end up settling for a pair of high-waisted black jean shorts and a heather-gray halter top that makes my boobs look a full cup size larger. The combination leaves about an inch of skin showing around my waist. It's perfect for a night out. I feel sexy and comfortable, but more importantly, I feel like myself.

From the coffee table, my computer chimes with yet another email. Earlier, I'd made the mistake of signing back into my personal account only to find that Logan continued sending messages—sometimes up to three a day. I only opened the most recent one, which was less than polite and a far cry from the *I miss you* emails he first sent, before deciding to leave the other thirty-two unread. This most recent ding makes thirty-three. He never paid this much attention to me when we were dating. If he had, maybe we might have actually stood a chance.

After walking over to the laptop, I move my cursor over the new email to delete it when my heart stops. It's not from Logan. It's a response from one of my transfer applications. My pulse pounds in my skull as I open the email and read.

> MS. ADDER,
>
> THANK YOU FOR YOUR INTEREST IN THE UNIVERSITY OF NORTH CAROLINA AT CHARLOTTE. WE REGRET TO INFORM YOU WE ARE UNABLE TO OFFER YOU TRANSFER ADMISSION FOR THE COMING FALL SEMESTER.

There is more, but with my heart so low in my stomach, I can't bring myself to read it. Since transfer applications are so expensive, I only applied to two schools. With an almost perfect GPA—except for that one stupid B—I really thought I was a shoo-in for UNC Charlotte. This is a major blow to both my ego and my plans for the future.

Closing my laptop, I move to the bathroom and try to run a curling iron through some of the more unruly pieces of my hair while trying not to think about how disappointed I am about the rejection. Fuck if that doesn't put a horrible damper on my night. And to top it off, my hair won't cooperate. It was up in a bun most of the day, so it's not exactly the most glorious end product, but it will have to do because I no longer have the desire to put in any more effort.

I slip my cash, ID, and a condom into my tiny clutch.

Maybe I'll find someone to screw the crushing pain of failure out of me.

A knock sounds at the door at exactly 9:01. When I open the screen, I find Lana in a light-blue T-shirt dress with backless, strappy heels. She's looking at the house with vacant eyes.

"Are you okay?" The obvious pain in her expression pushes all thoughts of the rejection from my mind. I give her a quizzical glance, and she forces a smile.

"Sorry. A song came on the radio that reminded me of my dad, and it put me in a weird headspace." Although it's seventy degrees out, she grabs her elbow and runs her hand up her bicep like she's cold. "He passed away when I was little."

Tears are forming in her eyes, and I open the door wider so she can come in. "No need to apologize. I lost my mom, I get it. Do you mind me asking what happened?"

Her voice is bottomless and sorrowful as she steps inside and closes her eyes. "Same thing that happened to all of them: the mine."

The little hairs on my arm stand at attention. The only mine I've seen was the closed one I drove by on my way into town. But the way she said it almost made the mine sound like a living, breathing thing, not something that was condemned years ago by the look of the sign.

I wonder what happened...

I give her arm a soft squeeze. "Do you need to sit down? We don't have to go out if you're not up for it. We can stay in and have a drink or chat?" I leave it up to her whether she wants to expand on what happened to her father. I know that while I love talking about my mom, I hate talking about how she died. I would never force someone else to relive the details of how they lost a loved one.

Lana waves me off and shakes her head. "No, I'm fine. It's just with the twenty-year anniversary coming up"—she blinks rapidly—"and realizing I've been without him so much longer than I had him...it got me down for a second. But I'm fine, I promise. See?" She grabs a hip flask from her purse and takes a nip before offering the steel container to me.

Grasping the flask from her outstretched hand, I slowly let loose a breath and inhale deeply only to flinch. Whatever is in this smells awful, like licorice and paint thinner. I throw it back anyway and try not to let the pungent liquid touch my tongue. A single swig of the concoction has my throat burning and my eyes watering. It's like I ingested gasoline fumes. "What *is* that?" I sputter.

"Moonshine. My cousin makes it. It'll definitely put hair on your chest."

"Or peel the skin from your throat," I counter.

By 9:30 we're in Lana's car speeding down back roads toward Eddie's bar. Fireflies dance above long blades of grass alongside the road, and the buzz of cicadas in the surrounding trees filters in through the open window. The warmth from the moonshine has seeped into my soul and pushed the last thoughts of rejection from my head.

I'm relaxed. Almost happy.

A grinding noise bellows from Lana's engine, obliterating my content glow. "Should we turn back and take my car?" I offer. The car shudders, and I instinctively reach for the handle above the door.

"Don't you worry that little head of yours, Rylee. Rhonda here is reliable," Lana says, patting the dash. "She's just very vocal." Something inside the hood sputters and sizzles. Lana smiles hesitantly and grips the steering wheel tighter while I lean back and try to ignore the noise of the engine.

"We're almost there anyway." Lana turns on a blinker to shift lanes, and the car lets out a high-pitched grating noise as the engine sputters out with a final croak. Lana coasts us onto the shoulder of the road, screaming, "No, Rhonda, no!"

With the car in park, she turns to me. "Do you know anything about engines?" I shake my head. "Yeah, me neither. But I'm assuming all these lights aren't a good sign…"

I look over. Every single light on the dash is lit up like a Christmas tree.

Great.

We're both wearing heels, and I have a feeling we have a long walk ahead of us.

We exit the car at the same time steam billows from the closed hood. Lana goes to kick the tire, only to have her shoe fly off into the deep drainage ditch beside the road. She screams out her frustration into the night sky before hobbling over to me. "I am so sorry, Rylee. This is not how I saw the night going."

"No worries. Why don't you call a tow truck, and I'll see what I can do about that shoe?"

She nods and whips out her phone while I make my way over to the edge of the ditch. The evening air is cool on my legs as the setting sun pulls the last of the warm breeze with it. Staring at the decline, my hands find their way to my hips. The way down is significantly steeper than I thought, but I can just make out Lana's shoe in a puddle at the very bottom.

Perfect.

After removing my heeled booties, I edge my way down, the wet earth squishing between my toes. By some miracle, I only slip twice, and although my legs and arms are covered in mud, my clothes remain clean. Now that I have Lana's shoe firmly in my grasp, I realize the real issue will be getting back out of the ditch.

Eden better have hot firefighters on standby to come rescue me.

After a minute of contemplating my exit route, heavy guitar drifts through the night, growing louder as it gets closer until cutting out completely. A deep, musical voice calls out with concern, "Lana? What happened?" It sounds like Danny.

"My car broke down, and no one's answering at the tow shop."

"And your shoe?" Danny asks, a clear grin clinging to his words.

"Oh. Yeah, Rylee's in the ditch trying to find it." She sounds so dismayed it's almost comical. If I wasn't stuck down here without an easy way up, I think I'd laugh.

"Rylee's here?" another familiar voice says.

Crap. I know that voice, too.

Colton.

I glance at my feet. Of course I'm covered in mud.

Two doors slam and I look up to see Danny and Colton staring at me from the top of the ridge. I must look absolutely ridiculous. My stomach hardens as I try not to show my embarrassment.

Danny lifts a brow and calls out, "Whatcha doing down there, Rylee?"

"Oh, you know, felt like a good time for a mud bath." I fling a little mud up the hill in his direction and pretend not to notice when some of it lands on Colton's boot.

"That hill is awfully steep. You aren't stuck, are you?" He crosses his arms over his chest in a poor attempt to hide his chuckle.

"No, I'm fine," I call back. With the shoe in tow, I attempt to make my way up to the road. But my trip down must have flattened the grass and made the path even slicker, because I'm only able to reach the halfway point before I start sliding back down again. Without the use of both hands, I can't seem to find my balance.

Wordlessly, Colton descends the embankment, his boots gripping the wet earth, aiding in his rapid progression. When he reaches me, he takes the shoe from my hand and tosses it up to Danny.

Why didn't I think of that?

I roll my eyes and follow Colton out of the ravine, stumbling several more times on my mud-caked feet. The third time I slip, Colton reaches back and catches my hand, pulling me up the rest of the way. My heart hammers against my rib cage as he glances back at me with an unreadable expression, like he also feels the electric current traveling between our palms. When we reach the top, he holds on to me a second longer than necessary before moving away.

Lana takes the shoe from Danny. "Thanks, Rylee. You really didn't have to do that. Especially since it looks like we're not going out tonight. I can't even get a tow," Lana says, sounding heavyhearted.

Danny snorts. "Travis is at my place, very drunk. Trust me, you don't want him or his tow truck anywhere near your car tonight."

Lana groans and stomps her feet.

"Where were you guys headed? Maybe we can give you a ride?" Danny offers.

"Eddie's, but without a way home and with miss Shoe Hero over here"—Lana waves wildly in my direction—"all covered in mud, I guess that's out of the question. Dammit. I really needed a night out."

You and me both.

Danny bends down and picks up my heeled booties from

the street. "Well, how about a house party instead? I'll give you ladies a ride home after, and we can have Travis come get your car in the morning?"

Colton clears his throat. "Are you sure that's a good idea?" His eyes slide in my direction. "Wouldn't it be better to take them home?"

He clearly means me and I'll be damned if I let another man control what I do. Stepping forward, I take my boots from Danny. "That sounds great, I'd love to."

Lana bounces on her uneven feet. "Okay, let's do it! I haven't seen the house since you guys finished the construction project, and I need to talk Travis into giving me a deal on the tow anyway."

Danny claps his hands. "Hop in. Let's go to a party."

Chapter Twelve

Danny's truck only has one row of seats.

I have no idea how we're all supposed to fit, but I think I see a bunch of lap-sitting in my near future. Lana climbs in first and attempts to make room for me. When I try to follow, Danny's voice rings out in protest, "Not you muddy-buddy. I just cleaned this thing. Hop in the back." He points to the bed and fake kicks the air near my butt. "Get goin'. You too, Colt. I don't feel like being squished, and your boots are covered in mud."

Danny makes brief eye contact with me, and I swear I see a wolfish grin.

The bed of the truck is fairly full—a box of hard alcohol and two large Tough Boxes taking up most of the area near the tailgate, along with a few other random boxes spread through-out. The limited room forces Colton and I to sit next to one another with our backs resting against the cab. Thankfully, there is just enough of an opening that we fit without having to touch, but he's so close I can feel the heat radiating off his body. He gives the window a double smack to let Danny know we're situated, then off we go, sitting side by side as the world flies by in reverse.

The wind whips through Colton's hair, and I pretend not to notice how it makes him look like the male lead in a romantic movie. I'm still a little pissed that he didn't want me to go to the party. I thought that after the motorcycle ride home we were past this. One second, he's helping me up a hill and the next he's back to being a dick. Never in my life has one person caused me so much confusion. I cross my arms over my chest and scooch my body as far from his as possible, which isn't far.

After a few minutes, my leg starts to fall asleep from the uncomfortable position I placed it in trying to avoid contact with Colton. I attempt to move one of the less bulky boxes to make more room for myself, but only succeed in popping the lid open during the struggle.

My jaw drops.

"Is this my broken taillight?" I screech.

Colton looks inside. "Sure looks like it."

My face contorts in confusion as I try to remember if I looked at my car today. "What the hell did you do?"

Colton sighs and tilts his head toward the sky while pulling his bruised lip between his teeth. "I wanted to thank you for your help with Knott the other day."

My eyebrow lifts. "So you stole my broken light?"

I mean, what the actual fuck...

"I *replaced* your broken light. With a new one," he corrects.

Oh.

My heartbeat races as I sort through the downpour of emotions bouncing around inside me. "Thank you," I manage to stammer out after a moment. Colton says nothing.

Traveling while facing the wrong direction is disorienting. Sitting next to Colton, who makes absolutely no sense, is even more befuddling. How can I go from wanting to throttle him to speechless in a matter of seconds? I can't believe he fixed my taillight. No one has ever done something like that for me before. Not even Holly.

A thousand stolen glances later, we're turning onto Sherwood Road. In the bright light of the full moon, I can just make out little orange bursts of color. "Crap, I forgot to look up the name of those flowers," I say under my breath.

Colton opens his eyes and squints into the passing underbrush. "The red and orange ones? They're marigolds," he says flatly before leaning his head back against the glass.

"They're beautiful. I saw them on my run and remembered my mom and I used to plant them on my balcony. I didn't think they grew wild, though."

Shut up, Rylee. Stop rambling.

He looks me in the eye for the first time since we sat down. "They're easy to miss if you're not looking for them." He pauses, his eyes trailing down to where our thighs are barely touching before he scoots an inch away from my muddy leg. "A landscaping truck full of them overturned upriver a few years ago. You can find marigolds all up and down the bank now. At least until it gets cold. They bloom in early summer and die with the first frost of fall."

Wow. I didn't think he was capable of stringing that many words together—and about flowers, no less. "How do you know that?"

"My mom was into plants. Like your mom, she grew marigolds in our garden." The corner of his lip quirks up. "She knew every flower and their meaning." The usual gravel in his voice is gone, replaced by something almost wistful. He's never been this pleasant to talk to before. It's almost like he's a different person. It's unnerving and feels fleeting, like each kind word could be whipped away by the wind at any moment.

"My mom loved marigolds." I have a fading image of her

placing one in my hair on a warm summer afternoon. "Did your mom ever mention what they symbolize?" For some unknown reason, I want to keep him talking.

"In Mexico, they're associated with the sun and with grief. They're used to decorate graves and guide visiting souls on the day of the dead. In India, they represent joy and prosperity, they're used in worship and in marriage celebrations." We hit a pothole and our knees land against each other. This time he doesn't scoot away. "It's crazy how a single flower can represent the sun, good energy, and new beginnings while also symbolizing death, despair, and endings." His voice is so low that I don't think he realizes he's still speaking out loud when he says that last part.

In all our interactions, this is the most he's ever said to me, and though I'm not sure what brought on this sudden bout of civility, I am mesmerized by the melodic hum of his voice. "So, what's their true meaning, then?"

"Like anything else, you have to choose their meaning for yourself." He looks at me once more, like I'm a problem he can't decide if he wants to solve or eliminate, and then turns back to face the retreating road.

The truck bounces over the wooden bridge I saw during my run, the awning blacking out the stars for the few seconds it takes to cross. We pass several houses, none of which have fences or any other type of delineation between the massive lots. Compared to what I've seen so far in Eden, the homes here are modern and new. Each one has a well-manicured yard and tidy gravel-lined driveway. The trees and hills make it difficult to tell, but I'd say there are at least twenty homes. It's like a separate town out here.

The truck comes to a stop at the end of a car-filled driveway, the sound of music and happy chatter carries out into the street from inside the lit house. "Whose place is this?" I ask.

"Mine," Danny responds, slamming his door. "There's a hose out back. Colt can show you where."

He grabs one of the Tough Boxes from the bed, and Lana takes the box full of the alcohol, bouncing her eyebrows at me. "Guess we get to have some fun after all. See you inside."

Weaving through the sea of cars, I follow Colton's broad shoulders toward the side of the house to a water spigot and a hose. There are a few people in the backyard, drinking and smoking cigarettes, but we're fairly isolated. Faint light from the window shines just bright enough for me to see Colton as he sprays off his muddy boots. When he finishes, he hands me the hose to hold while he cleans off his hands. We lock eyes, and I can almost see the question forming on the tip of his tongue.

He takes the hose back, holding it for me so I can dust off my outfit and rinse my arms. The water is cool as it runs down my skin and, despite the warm night, my nipples pebble under my shirt. Colton swallows hard and clears his throat. "Why did you *really* help us with Knott?"

He lowers the angle of the hose so I can clean off my legs, and I scrub, considering his question. "I already told you. I had a weird feeling that you needed help." Standing, I reach up and tentatively trace the bruise on his lip with my clean hand. Almost like there are little bolts of lightning under the pads of my fingers, a thousand electric nerve endings fire off where our skin makes contact. It makes my heart pound inside my chest. "What else was I going to do?"

His face is blank and unreadable, but he doesn't pull away from my touch. "Most people would've kept running, especially since he is the sheriff. It's not like I've given you a reason to risk your neck for me."

He's so close now, I can feel my own breath bouncing off his shoulder. The reverberating heat has goose bumps running up my arms and down my neck. I shudder and hate myself for not being able to control my body's response to him. "You guys are important to Holly. Holly is important to me. It doesn't matter if you've been an asshole, Minho and Alex aren't to blame for that." I tilt my chin up so I can look him in the eyes. "And no, besides jumping my car, you haven't given me a reason to help you. But someone has to be the first one to do the right thing, right?"

Colton leans forward to turn off the spigot, his breath ghosts across my forearm, sending shivers up my spine. When he stands, he brushes the hair away from my shoulder, letting his fingers graze my collarbone before settling on the back of my neck where he wipes away at what I assume is more mud. My lungs are tight with anticipation, and my upper chest swells with each attempt at a tiny breath. I think my heart might explode from how fast it's beating. His gaze lowers to the curve of my breasts and moves back to my eyes. His mouth drops open. "I'm sorry for—"

"Colt?"

He lets his hand fall as a lanky, bearded man in a leather cut rounds the corner. "Hey, man, I've been looking for you. We've got to talk about—"

This time it's Colton who interrupts him, "If this is business related, can it wait?"

The man smooths his beard, glancing at me. He shakes his head. "No, not really."

Colton closes his eyes and sighs. "I'll be right there," he says over his shoulder. To me he gives a final warning: "Keep out of trouble tonight and stay close to Danny." He leaves without so much as a backward glance.

The wind picks up and I shiver. My skin is covered in goose bumps, and my nipples are still hard from the combination of the cold water and a single touch from Colton.

Was he about to apologize for being an asshole? Does it

make a difference if he was? I mean seriously, this man is going to give me whiplash with his mood swings.

Crossing my arms over my chest, I make my way through the back door and over to Danny in the kitchen. He introduces me to his friends, but there are too many new names and faces for me to remember any of them. At least everyone is polite, if not a little standoffish. Lana and a man named Travis are part of the kitchen crowd, but she is too busy haggling over the towing fee to take part in conversation or pay much attention to me. I mostly stand there quietly and watch, but it's nice. I don't feel out of place like I did at the funeral. Everyone seems happy to be here and in no real rush to try to impress anyone else.

After a few minutes I'm handed a beer with the Dovetail logo on the label. It's the only type of beer here.

I guess town loyalty runs deep.

Across the room, Colton is wrapped up in conversation with the bearded man from outside. His frown deepens with every passing minute, and although he never makes his way over to the kitchen, anytime I step closer to Danny, I feel his attention bore into me with renewed intensity. I really wish I wasn't so aware of him, but even as the crowd thickens, I can always pinpoint his exact position in the room as if there is a rope connecting us.

When Minho and Alex stroll in hand-in-hand, I'm surprised by how excited I am to see them. Alex smiles broadly when his gaze lands on me, and he crushes me in a massive hug before bothering to greet anyone else. "Well, if it isn't Rylee Adder in the flesh." He swipes something off my cheek and wipes his fingers on his jeans. "I'm glad you're here. I've been hoping Minho would invite you over."

Minho waves him off but gives me a conspiratorial grin, like he's glad I'm out, too. I'm a little thrown back by how good that makes me feel and how strange it is to have a sense of kinship with two people I barely know.

With drinks in hand, we fall into amiable conversation about school, more specifically my computer classes and when Minho will be available for tutoring sessions. His knowledge in everything to do with tech is astounding. He's even able to explain concepts I've been struggling with in a way that actually makes sense—something my professor has failed to do in every lecture thus far. I also learn that he works for Dovetail Brewery doing marketing and a bit of IT on the side. It seems like a waste of his talents, but I guess in a small town there's limited application for his particular skill set.

Through the course of our conversation, I learn that nearly everyone at the party works for the brewery, except for Alex, who bartends at The Pack. There are a few other exceptions, like Travis who owns the auto shop in town and some other out-of-towners. When I ask if this is some sort of work party, Minho responds with a noncommittal, "Yeah, something like that."

I'm mulling over this new information when the front door bursts open and a sheriff's deputy yells, "All right, fun's over. Hands where I can see 'em!"

A collective groan ripples through the crowd, and everyone goes about their business. The deputy greets a few people, slapping them on the back, a huge grin plastered on his face that's all bright-white teeth. After getting over the shock of nearly dropping my beer when he barged in, I take a better look at the handsome newcomer, who I now realize is here as a party guest and not here in an official capacity. He's clean-shaven with dark-brown hair and a light tan that coats his muscular arms. I've never understood the man-in-uniform fetish...until this guy walked in.

He might be the exact type of distraction I need.

"Who's that?" I ask Alex.

"That's Andy, he's—" he pauses, thinking for a second. "He's new to the friend group. We're still trying to see if he's a good fit."

Minho nods his agreement.

"You guys trial run your friends?" I raise a brow.

They look at each other but only shrug in response.

Jesus.

"Well, how am I doing?"

"Mmm, tough to say." Alex pops his lips and squints, looking me up and down. "Our friends aren't usually covered in dirt."

I smack him on the chest and laugh at the fact that bits of my arms and legs are indeed still covered in dried mud.

The party gets rowdier as the night progresses. More people show up until it becomes difficult to cross a room without bumping into another body—bodies that are almost all covered in at least one visible tattoo. I've caught multiple glimpses of that same wolf-like creature and even more of doves in various stages of flight that don't look all too different from the Dovetail logo.

It's odd, to say the least. No one loves their job *that* much. There has to be more to it.

After encountering some comments that I'd swear sound like hissing, I realize I've somehow become separated from everyone I know. I scan the crowd, searching for a friendly face, only to watch Colton disappear outside. He's followed promptly by three guys in leather cuts, their expressions so severe that I decide not to risk following.

Someone slams into me, spilling most of my beer onto the wood floor. "Watch it, princess." The lumbering form rumbles, retreating so I never see his face.

Without Alex and Minho as my buffers, the air is suddenly too thin. The walls too small.

Was it always this loud in here?

After wiping up the floor with a towel from the stove, I head off in search of the bathroom and maybe a quieter place to catch my breath.

Danny's home is nice. It's got a strong midcentury modern vibe. Lots of white accents and warm oak furniture. I make my way toward what I hope is the bathroom and notice more colors come into play, like a sudden splash of black in a painting or dark green in a curtain. It feels a little like dueling styles and has me wondering if Danny shares the space with anyone. A good-looking, nice guy like him has to be seeing someone. I wonder if she was the one to decorate?

When I pass the master bedroom, I'm surprised to see Danny prepping a tattoo gun and talking with a girl lying face down in a black padded chair. "You healed up nicely," Danny says. "This will be our last session. Just a little more shading."

The woman grumbles a reply, but I only catch the fear in her voice.

That's when I notice the other person in the room—a man sitting on an ottoman at the foot of the bed. "It's alright, baby, the line work is the worst part." He pulls his collar away and strokes the wolf-like creature on his neck. His tattoo is almost the twin to the one Colton has. "It will be much easier than last time."

Danny nods his agreement and starts cleaning the delicate outline of a dove on the girl's shoulder. I'm surprised how meticulous his cleaning preparation is and how at ease he is when he starts working—serene and completely relaxed. It's almost as if the process transports him somewhere else.

It's inspiring to watch someone so entirely in their element.

When Danny's eyes finally meet mine, I ask for silent permission to enter, and he waves me in.

For the next hour, I hover over his shoulder and observe in silence. When he's done, he cleans the tattoo and puts some sort of clear wrap over it before sending the two on their way.

"That was incredible," I say in earnest. "I had no idea you were so talented. How long have you been tattooing?"

"About nine years, but I've been drawing my whole life." There is pride in his voice that was missing when I asked him about who owned the house.

"Is that what you do for the brewery? The art?" I gesture to the dove logo on the beer I'm holding, which has a similar style to the dove he just tattooed.

"Yeah, I designed the labels, but that's not what I do for the brewery." He gives me some serious side-eye. "Who told you where I work?"

"Minho and Alex," I supply. "They told me you and most of the people here work together."

His thick brows unfurrow. "Hmm, right. I do the finance and accounting." He points to a degree from West Virginia University on the wall and a Certified Public Accountant license next to it.

I want to ask him more questions, but before I can he's speaking again, "So, are you gonna get a tattoo or what?"

I can't tell if he's joking or not, but the idea is intriguing. "Can it be anything I want, or do you only do birds and wolves? Wait, is it expensive?" I fire off the questions in one breath. Before leaving Charlotte, I wouldn't say I was one to make rash decisions. But apparently, it's become my new thing. Still, though, something about this feels right. I'm in a new town, I'm free from Logan, and I'm working on my relationship with my sister. It's a new beginning of sorts, so why not?

"They're not wolves, and I can tattoo anything you want." He winks. "The first one is free of charge, just for you."

I only have to think about it for a second before the image pops into my head. I tell him what I want and run to the bathroom while he draws it up. When I return, I look over his creation.

It's perfect.

The discomfort of the needle on my skin is less painful than I thought it would be. Don't get me wrong, the first thirty minutes are torture, like someone is using a knife to scrape a splinter out of my inner wrist, but after that, my body acclimates to the assault and I'm able to close my eyes and let Danny work.

Sometime later, I hear movement in the doorway and notice that the sounds of the party have died down. People must be leaving.

"Almost done," Danny says to whoever is at the door.

"I came by to tell Rylee that Lana fell asleep on the couch." It's the second time Colton's said my name tonight, and it sounds like honey on his tongue.

I must make some sort of noise because Danny looks up to see if he's hurt me. I shake my head and tell him to keep going.

"What are you guys working on?" Colton's footsteps move in my direction and stop off to my right. His jeans brush against my arm as he looks down at what I chose. His brows wrinkle in inspection and lift. "A marigold?"

"I decided what it means to me," I say, referring to his statement in the back of the truck. "It's..." My words trail off under the intensity of his stare and the unnamed emotion etched into his face.

What I don't finish saying is that the tattoo is for my mom and for Jeremy. It's to remind me that someone can experience life and death, joy and grief, and still be beautiful and bright. That, like the truck full of marigolds that overturned, I can find a new home and thrive.

Like this little flower, I am strong.

Chapter Thirteen

"You're good to go," Danny says after giving me tattoo aftercare instructions. "I can take you and Lana home, if you're ready?"

Colton locks eyes with Danny and cold stillness washes over the room. I'm stuck sitting in the chair between them while they engage in some sort of silent standoff. For a second, I think Colton might insist on taking me home himself and my heart soars, but he leaves without argument.

My chest deflates like a balloon.

Danny and I collect Lana, who's consumed enough alcohol that walking on her own proves almost impossible. At some point during the night, she lost her shoes again, and she wobbles on her bare feet while I struggle to keep her upright. By some miracle, we make it to Danny's truck. Lana babbles nonsense, saying things like, "My poor Rhonda," and "Travis is a thief," as I belt her into the passenger seat.

"Who is Rhonda?" Danny asks, checking her belt and shutting her door. I giggle a little as I explain and Danny laughs, holding the driver side door open for me. "She called that same car Bonnie back in high school. I think she renames it every time she has to do major work or replace a big part. She's moving a bit too quickly down the alphabet, if you ask me, but I can't wait to see what she comes up with next."

I slide into the middle seat, a little giddy. Despite how tired I am, I actually had a good time. Even with the big crowd, being here felt easy and natural. Maybe it's the beer or the endorphins from the tattoo, but everything seems to be glimmering in the light of the moon tonight.

"What's got you smiling like that?" Danny asks, firing up the truck.

Was I smiling?

"I had fun tonight. I like your friends."

"That surprises you?"

"I'm not normally a fan of large gatherings."

One of his hands thrums the steering wheel, and he shakes his head. "Yeah, neither is Colt, but I figured everyone needed a night of fun after everything with my brother. It's good to remind yourself that life goes on so you don't get stuck in the past." There is a long pause and then, "You fit in here, with us."

Those six words feel bigger than they should, like there is something deeper he's not saying. Or maybe it's just how long I've been waiting for someone to say them. Either way, it feels like a compliment, and my heart swells with the warmth of belonging.

The drive is relatively short and quiet. Lana lives in an old, yellow one-story with her mother. The shutters hang at odd angles, and the grass hasn't been cut in weeks. Even the paint on the wood paneling is chipping, and there's a random screen door in the front yard. It's not what I expected, especially from Maggie, but it's a large step above the dilapidated manufactured homes across the street.

Danny pats my forearm. "I'll take her in. I know how to get

her to her bedroom without waking up Maggie. Stay here and sit tight."

Danny returns a few minutes later, and I slide across the imitation-leather bench toward the now-unoccupied passenger seat. The material is cracked and peeling in some places, causing my shorts to snag as I scoot over.

"Have you seen this part of Eden before?" he asks, turning the ignition. The smell of diesel fills the cabin.

I shake my head.

"This is what all of Eden was like when the mine was still running. Broken, run-down, falling apart. People working seventy-two hours a week and still not making enough to patch the roof over their heads. We're just now starting to dig ourselves out."

"How could one mine be responsible for this level of poverty?"

He searches my face, but when he doesn't find what he's looking for, he puts the truck in drive. "Because some men like to bleed a place dry instead of putting an ounce of life-saving resources back into the communities they steal from."

When we pull onto my sister's gravel driveway, the house is dark and the only noise comes from the cicadas in the surrounding trees. I sigh and place my hand on the door, but I can't bring myself to walk into that silent, empty house.

"How's Holly doing?"

Lifting my palm off the handle, I lean back in the seat. "I'm not sure. She stormed off for work right after you guys left the other day. Every time I try to ask her what happened, she shuts down and picks up an extra shift at the hospital. I'm starting to think she might be avoiding me."

Geez, I sound like a lonely, selfish brat.

I force a smile. "At the end of the day, I know work is a good distraction for her. I want to support her, it's just hard when I don't fully understand what she's going through, and she won't open up."

There is a weighted pause, and I realize Danny understands *exactly* what she's going through. He lost the same person she did. How could I have been so self-involved that I never thought to check up on Danny or Jack? "How about you? How have you been?"

His knuckles tighten on the steering wheel as his eyes glaze over. "Some days are better than others. It's easier when I'm with my brothers."

"Brothers? I didn't know you had more family." Again, how could I not know that? I know Jeremy and Danny's mom died in some sort of accident a long time ago, but I never realized they might have more family.

"Colt, Minho, the guys I grew up with. They're my family. We all lost a brother, but we're keeping his legacy alive." A faint smile spreads across his lips, and he bobs his head. "You know, you should come by the bar sometime." My confusion must be written on my face because he clarifies, "The Pack. It was our first family business and Jeremy's favorite spot. Why don't you come by on a Friday? Bring Holly if you can."

"Okay, I'll ask her. Maybe we'll stop by the Friday after next."

"Sounds great, I'll see you then. Remember," he says as I open the door and step out of the truck, "keep that tattoo clean and dry. No sweating for three days; no swimming for two to three weeks."

I walk inside the bungalow with a faint smile still glued to my face. While I started the day off exhausted, the party seems to have given me a second wind. If Danny hadn't told me not to sweat for a few days, I might consider going for a run. But it is the middle of the night, and I really don't want to ruin this beautiful tattoo. I run my fingers over the wrap, pushing some of the clear liquid and traces of blood around.

Grabbing my computer, I flip on the television and settle onto the couch. Holly doesn't have any subscriptions, just the local stations and a few big networks, but that's fine with me. I only want it on so the background noise will make the house seem less empty. After a few flips, I settle on some news station talking about a vigilante group in Pennsylvania protecting sex workers and terrorizing local corrupt officials.

My computer boots up, and I click on the Ghost Rider icon to access the internet. I purposely leave my email unopened and bring up the search bar. Leaning back into the couch, I watch the cursor blink.

Something has been bothering me about what Lana said happened to her father and the way Danny spoke about the mine. I tap my fingers on my laptop and decide to try searching *Eden, West Virginia mining.*

This brings up a few links, mostly on the town's mining history dating all the way back to the 1840s, which is not what I'm looking for. I scroll through page after page of irrelevant links. On the fifth page of search results, there is a single article: "West Virginia Mining Accident Claims Four Hundred."

I click on the link, but the article's been redacted. I try adding several more keywords to my search, like *accident* and *catastrophe*, but no other results pop up.

Frustrated, I slam my computer closed and curl up on the sofa.

Okay, Eden, you win this time. Keep your secrets. For now.

Chapter Fourteen

"Holy shit. You did it!" Minho gapes at my computer screen.

Ever since the party at Danny's house almost two weeks ago, Minho has been meeting me after work a few times a week to help with my school assignments. I never imagined I'd need tutoring for an online class, but without Minho's help, I'm not sure I'd be doing as well as I am. Unfortunately, Holly is still stuck on the idea that I shouldn't hang out with *the boys,* so we've been meeting at the picnic table between the brewery and the bar, under the canopy of a massive oak.

This week's assignment was about firewalls. Minho decided the best way to understand what made a good one was to find the weak spots in a bad one, and he designed a mock-up for me to hack into.

"Seriously," he says, seeming to regain his composure. "That should have taken you three times as long. It took Jeremy a week to teach me that. You're really good at this." His hand falls on my shoulder.

My chest buzzes with delight like a happy little bee. "Must

be my tutor. Honestly, it wasn't even that difficult," I say with a hum.

Minho clicks his tongue. "Don't get too cocky. You still have a lot to learn. Have you heard back from the other university yet?"

My chin dips. "Another rejection."

Minho smiles and cracks his knuckles. "Good. Neither of those schools had good tech programs. If you're set on a four-year degree, you need to transfer to one with a good computer science program. You have a natural talent, and you'd be wasting your potential if you didn't cultivate it."

A pleasant, warm feeling seeps into my bones, lessening the blow of my most recent rejection. More and more I've been realizing that Minho is right, I do have a talent for this. But more importantly, I like computers and I like code.

Minho stands and stretches his arms skyward, his back cracking with the movement. "Have you told your sister we've been meeting like this?"

I shake my head. "She's been distant since that night you all came over, but she has found the time to make it clear I should be nurturing a friendship with Lana and not you guys." My eyes drop to my keyboard, and I brush a speck of dust off the escape key. "She hasn't even told me what happened to Jeremy. I thought we were getting along fine, but now it's starting to feel like there are too many secrets between us. Maybe if I understood what happened, I could help her move on and open up." I raise my gaze to meet Minho's.

His lips disappear into a tight line as his eyes dart back and forth across my face. He swallows, and I watch his Adam's apple bob in his throat. "I don't think I'm ready to talk about that." His eyes close. "Try talking to Holly again. I think you deserve to hear it from her before anyone else."

The next day, Holly and I are both off work and she's finally decided we should hang out. As soon as she got home from her overnight shift, she asked me if I wanted to spend the afternoon with her swimming at the river. I readily agreed, having already decided today would be the day I ask her what really happened to Jeremy.

The temperature in Eden has been steadily rising, and the humidity feels like it's at an all-time high. Even indoors, I'm practically wading through the air as I wait for Holly to wake up.

She told me to get her up at noon, but I don't see how that could possibly be enough sleep. After getting home at 8:30 a.m., she spent an hour in the bathroom before finally going to bed. Although it's already almost one o'clock, I figure I'll leave her be for one more hour. Her mood swings are crazy enough lately without adding sleep deprivation to the mix. Not to mention how I still need to shower, shave, and make sure my bathing suit fits.

Taking a cool shower on a hot day has to be one of life's finer luxuries. I bathe in the lemon verbena bodywash Holly got for us and use her mint shampoo, which stings a little as it runs over my freshly shaven legs and more intimate areas. The two scents mingle and fill up the small bathroom, creating my own personal aroma therapy session. I'm reluctant to ever leave. But I think I can hear the TV on, which means Holly must be awake. Turning the shower off, I reach for a towel, but freeze when I realize the noise is not the television.

It's Holly.

And she sounds angry.

I wrap the towel loosely around me and step out of the tub.

Holly is now whisper-yelling, like she doesn't want me to hear what she's saying, which only makes me more curious.

"I'm telling you, she doesn't know. Did Jack put you up to this? Because I already told him she has no idea. She hasn't contacted him once since she's been here. I'm sure Minho can confirm that."

I hear a set of footsteps that are too heavy to be Holly's.

"Jack doesn't know I'm here." Unlike my sister, Colton does nothing to keep his volume low. Something flutters in my chest at the sound of his voice. "It just doesn't make sense. How could it be a coincidence?"

Holly snorts. "*He* might have known, but she didn't. Regardless, there was nothing for her to give up. We've barely talked over the last few years."

They're talking about me.

I wrap my towel tighter and step toward the closed door.

"That's another thing, how could you just leave her out there?" Colton says, his voice lower now, almost feral. I press my ear against the door to hear him better, the wood cool and damp on my cheek. "You had to know that eventually someone would use her to get to us. To you."

Holly snorts. "Is that concern for her or your precious club, Colt? You know *he* has always had eyes on her. Always. That's how we found out about everything in the first place, remember?" Holly sounds defensive, but instead of feeling protective of her, I feel my blood simmer.

Who the fuck has had eyes on me? What does that even mean?

"Well, you should have brought her here sooner."

"Because you're so good at protecting people? Keeping them alive?" Holly taunts.

"There it is." Colt laughs humorlessly.

"There *what* is?" Holly spits back.

"The venom I'd expect from Rick Adder's daughter." Heavy footsteps move farther away and then the front door slams shut.

I let my towel drop to the floor, then shove myself into my bathing suit and white romper, nearly ripping both with the rage in my limbs. Fully dressed, I storm out of the bathroom to confront Holly. "What the hell was that about?"

She won't meet my eyes. "It was nothing."

"No, Holly, it wasn't. It's been weeks and I've kept quiet. What is going on?"

Holly throws her hands in the air and marches off toward her bedroom. I stomp after her. "Talk to me. I came here for *you*. Tell me something. Anything. Don't I deserve to know what's going on?"

Her eyes scan my face. "Fine. Let's do this. What questions do you have?"

So, she's going to play it like that so that she can tell me as little as possible? Okay, I can play, too. "Were you and Colton talking about me?"

"Yes."

"Has someone been watching me?"

"Yes."

"Who?"

"Dad."

"Dad?" *What the hell?* "Why?"

She sighs and pinches the skin between her eyebrows. "Because you're his daughter and it's a dangerous world."

"That's bullshit, Holly. Why?" My gut clenches in frustration, and I take several deep breaths to keep from exploding.

"It's not bullshit. You've never given him a chance, Ry."

Every muscle fiber in my body quakes with anger. *He's* the one that left *me.* He left Holly, too, but she always seems to forget that. We're getting off topic, but I have to ask, "Why would I ever give that piece of shit a chance?"

"I think you need to have a conversation with Dad to answer that."

"With what phone, Holly? Not only do you barely talk to me, but you asked me to come out here and then cut me off from everything and everyone. How exactly am I supposed to have a conversation with anyone?"

Holly turns instantly red and puffs out her chest, eyes flaming. "Oh, I'm sorry, did my husband's murder inconvenience your little life in Charlotte? Were you too busy getting railed by some rich guy in exchange for a place to live to bother to come out and support your grieving sister? News flash, Rylee, not everything is about you. There is a whole big world going on outside of your safe cocoon."

"Ouch." My voice is hoarse as her words hit me like a sucker punch. All I wanted was to ask her about Jeremy and have a nice day together. How did we go so far off the rails?

Holly crosses her arms over her chest and shrugs. "You wanted the truth? That's the truth. Sometimes it hurts. We don't always get the answers we want."

My eyes sting and I fight the urge to cry. I grab my keys and the first pair of shoes I find and rush outside, letting the screen door slap closed behind me.

Too late, I realize Holly's car has boxed mine in and I won't be able to storm off without first going back inside to get her keys. *Walking it is.* I turn left and am startled to find Colton sitting in his green Chevy, the frame of the muscle car vibrating like it's yearning to take off. Colton himself is watching me with inquisitive eyes.

Without thinking, I march up to his rolled-down passenger window. "Are you playing nice today or being an asshole again?"

His eyes roam my face, and I know he must see the hurt there. "Does it matter?" He leans across the bench seat and cracks open the door.

I wipe away a single tear. "No, I guess not, as long as you can get me away from here."

Colton throws the car into drive the second I sit. The scent of leather, oil, and cloves permeates the air before the wind rushes in and robs me of it. I sniffle once and a few more tears fall before I wipe them away with the back of my hand.

Colton has the decency to pretend he doesn't see.

It takes me a few minutes before I can slip on a more composed mask. When I do, Colton says, "You overheard us, back at the house?" I nod. "Do you want to talk about it, or about whatever happened after I left?"

I do, but I'll start crying again. I shake my head. "Not right now."

He doesn't say anything. He doesn't even look at me. He just drives.

After a few minutes he turns the radio dial and an acoustic guitar floods the cabin. The melody that fills my ears is soon accompanied by a gritty voice singing about a lost love and being called home to Appalachia. Before closing my eyes, I allow myself a peek at Colton as he bobs his head along to the music. It's not what I would have pictured him listening to, but now that I've heard and seen it, I can't imagine anything else making sense.

When I open my eyes, we're crossing the steel bridge that takes us out of Eden. "Where are we going?"

"Do you trust me?"

"Not at all."

He laughs. Colton actually laughs. It's musical and echoes deep in his chest like it caught him off guard. It's the first time I've heard that sound not buried under grief or the rumble of a motorcycle engine. My attitude lightens despite that horrible fight with Holly.

"Well, I guess there's always time for that later." His eyes stray to my neckline where the strings of my bikini top peek out, and I swear his pupils dilate. "I saw you had your suit on, so I figured we'd check out the river."

Chapter Fifteen

"Be honest. Did you bring me out here to murder me?" I swat away a tree branch, only to be smacked in the mouth by the next one. Spitting out a leaf, I continue, "Seriously. What are we doing? Was the plan to get me out of town so my body would be easier to dispose of?" I'm already having a shitty day and hiking through the forest in Holly's too-big flip-flops is not helping.

Colton looks back over his shoulder and gives me a dramatic side-eye.

"What?" I retort. "One minute we're cruising down the highway, the next you're parking near an old dirt road. There was even a rusty chain with a No Trespassing sign. This is exactly like a scene out of a teen horror flick where the audience shouts, *'Don't do it! Don't go down that clearly haunted road with a strange man!'*"

Colton's shoulders bounce like he might be laughing at me. "Relax. We're still in Eden. This route is just the easiest way to get to where we're going. Otherwise, we would've had to hike a few miles, which I figured you wouldn't be down for in those sandals." He shifts the water bottle in his hand and looks point-edly at my feet.

I glance down to my legs, which are dusted in a light layer of dirt and sweat, to where I already have two hotspots from trying to keep these stupid shoes on.

I *guess* that was considerate of him.

At the end of the road, the sound of rushing water and the smell of wet earth and something vaguely familiar fills my senses. Colton, who's stayed a good fifteen feet in front of me throughout the duration of the walk, opens a decaying, moss-covered gate, revealing a beautiful river dotted with bright orange, red, and yellow flowers.

Marigolds.

I breathe in the familiar scent. "Beautiful," I whisper. It's not just the flowers either. The entire view is picture-book perfect. Great, tall oaks and maple trees line the flowing river cascading over partially exposed boulders. There is even an old wooden structure barely visible above a waterfall that looks like it belongs on a postcard.

Colton stares at me as I take in the scene, his chin tilted up, eyes lowered and thoughtful. "That's the old mill. There's a good swimming spot up there. Can you make it up those rocks?"

I nod enthusiastically. "Of course I can. Can we go inside it?"

"You'll have to swim. The bridge washed out in a storm a few years ago," he calls over his shoulder, already climbing.

I have to remove my sandals, but otherwise, the climb is easy. Colton waits for me over the last ridge and extends an arm to pull me up. After I'm safely to the top, he flexes his hands and runs his palm down his pant leg, as if he's wiping me off. I glance down at my own hand. It's not even sweaty.

My shoulders curl inward protectively.

The water at the top is even more gorgeous than below. It's calmer and deeper and has a pleasant blue-green hue, like the color of Colton's eyes. Several Adirondack chairs sit in the shade near the waterline and to our left, a crude ladder carved into the trunk of an enormous sycamore leads to a rope swing. No flowers though. The marigolds only grow near the lower level of the river where the shore is less rocky.

"Do you come up here often?" Eager to feel the water and wash the dust from my legs, I kick off my shoes and peel my romper down to my waist. I should have checked my swimsuit first, though, because I'm nearly popping out of the thin fabric. My top must have moved during the climb. I adjust the girls and retie the strings at my neck before removing the romper completely.

Colton looks away, shaking his head. "I used to ride my bike out here all the time with my brothers. Spent almost every summer here when we were kids."

His voice is nostalgic, like he's somewhere else. I move my gaze to the river where I can almost see a young Minho climbing up the mill stairs; a young Danny flipping off the rope swing. It's like the echo of their memories and laughter still ripple in the water.

Colton removes his shirt, and I instantly snap back to the present.

Wow.

Looking at him sucks all the air out of me. He's physically perfect. An Adonis. And just like I thought at the funeral, almost every inch of him is covered in tattoos. Only now, I'm close enough to make out what they are. The mill is tattooed over his rib cage and a giant open-winged eagle over his chest. There are demons and trees. A rose on his hand. Everything and anything under the sun seemed fair game when it came to decorating his body. I can clearly see

Danny's hand in most of them. The only open space is his left hand and the left side of his neck, opposite the vicious wolf like creature.

My eyes rake over the contours of his body, stopping at the deep angular ridges above his waistband and the tufts of hair peeking out. My breath catches, and I clear my throat, not dipping my eyes lower. "What's with the wolves and doves you all have tattooed?" I know Danny said they weren't wolves, but I'm not sure what else to call them.

"Jackals."

"What?"

"The tattoos, they're jackals."

My eyes narrow in annoyance. "Okay, what's with the doves and jackals, then?"

Colton's stare bores into mine so hard that it feels like he's trying to see inside my soul. I lean away from him instinctually.

"Why are you really here?" he finally asks.

Well, that's an abrupt change of conversation. But it sounds like it's leading somewhere, and I'm curious as to what comes next, so I answer, "Holly needed me. That's what you do for family. That's what you do when someone needs help."

Despite the fight we had earlier today, and the fact that Holly and I have barely spent any time together since my arrival in Eden, I'd do it all over again, too.

He tilts his head in challenge. "Even family that let you sleep on the streets for a month?"

My jaw drops a little before I catch myself, a coldness balling in the pit of my stomach. I never told *anyone* except Logan about living out of my car.

"How did you—"

He takes a step closer, invading my personal space and throwing me off-kilter. "Why didn't you come to live with Holly after your mom died? Why come here now?"

That icy feeling in my stomach churns hot as my eyes start to burn.

Why did he wait until I was half dressed to confront me about this?

Fighting the urge to cover myself, I square my shoulders. "I was a month away from turning eighteen when my mom died. Why would I move when Jeremy and Holly came to stay with me? And as for the whole living out of my car thing, it was just a few weeks. I didn't even know where Holly was or how to get a hold of her. Besides, I can take care of myself. I always have." I suck in a breath to try to control the erratic rise and fall of my chest.

Colton is too close, both physically and with his questions. It's making my head spin.

I've wondered countless times why Holly didn't ask me to live with her after Mom died. I thought maybe she didn't want to uproot my life. I'd also been under the impression that she and Jeremy were constantly moving and, at seventeen, *I* didn't particularly want to uproot my life either. So, when she didn't offer, I didn't ask. It wasn't a big deal. But now, hearing Colton allude to the fact that Holly *knew* I was displaced after my apartment was condemned and she still didn't offer to take me in or even reach out, it makes me think she didn't want the burden of taking care of me the first time either. Betrayal burns so hot inside my stomach that I want to scream.

And to think I came all this way for her.

Colton's last four words repeat inside my head as images of Holly's home float to the surface—*Why come here now?*

My vision blurs as angry tears fill my lower lids. I take a few steps away and turn my back on Colton so he doesn't see. "Holly's been in Eden this whole time, hasn't she?"

He sighs. "Not at first, but after she reconnected with Jeremy, yeah, she's been here, more or less."

"How long have you known her?" I still can't turn to face him, but I feel him moving closer.

"A little over six years."

Jesus. Six years?

That means she's been in one place since before Mom died. I really could've had a life here with her. I could have had a home and a family. There has to be a reason she didn't want me in Eden. I've never known Holly to be spiteful or vindictive. Maybe it has nothing to do with me at all. "Why doesn't she want me hanging out with you guys? Why was she so awful to you back at the house?"

"I think she thinks she's protecting you. She's probably also misplacing her grief and anger, but I'll gladly bear the brunt if it helps her heal." Even without turning I can hear the scowl on his lips. "She's looking for someone to blame for Jeremy's death, but there is only one man responsible and he's not in Eden."

"Who?" The little hairs on my arms shift in the breeze.

His voice softens. "Listen, whatever Holly said to you today, I'm sure she didn't mean it. I didn't mean to upset you either." He gently taps me on the shoulder. "We're all on edge. But I can see now that none of this is your fault."

I turn to face him, almost slamming straight into his chest. This close, he towers over me, and I have to tilt my chin to make eye contact. Something has changed in the last few minutes. His expression is smoother now, without the fine lines of anger he usually wears when he speaks to me. Even his eyes seem brighter, a vivid shade of aquamarine. Each time I take a breath, the thin fabric of my bikini top scrapes against his skin. His attention drops to my chest for a single second before the corner of his mouth quirks up.

"Do you want to start over?" he asks.

"Start over?"

"Yeah, start over. No more spilled eggs or salsa in my lap?"

"No more hot, then cold, then rude Colton?" I counter.

"You think I'm hot?" He raises his eyebrows, and I choke down a tear-stained laugh. He steps back and extends a hand between us, never letting his eyes stray from mine. "Friends?"

I take his hand. "I guess we'll just have to see about that, won't we?"

Chapter Sixteen

The summer sun beats down on the giant rocks near the shore, creating little heat spirals of fluctuating air and giving the surrounding water a dream-like quality.

After the truce, Colton and I dipped our legs in the river and then settled in under the shade of the sycamore tree, both too lost in thought to actually speak. Sitting next to him is surprisingly peaceful, a cool breeze making the temperature so comfortable I could fall asleep. I'm pretty sure that's what's going to happen if I sit here much longer.

I stand and stretch before making my way to the water's edge. Stepping out onto one of the sizzling rocks, I bend my knees to jump in when Colton sits up abruptly. "You can't swim," he says, looking panicked. I hadn't realized he was awake.

Was he watching me? Oh no, do I have chair prints on my butt?

"Of course I can swim." I bend my knees to jump again—

"No, you can't. It hasn't been three weeks since your tattoo."

Oh damn, he's right.

Danny did say something about no swimming. I place my hands on my hips and *harrumph* in frustration.

Colton laughs, and I feel lighter than I have all day. If I could bottle that sound up, I'd carry it with me everywhere.

"You can still go in, just keep your wrist above your head and don't get it wet. I'll go in with you." He turns to unbutton his pants and, although I tell myself to look away, I can't avert my eyes when I catch a gleam of metal tucked into a secret holster on the hip of his jeans.

"Is that a gun?" I cry, shock evident in my voice. I don't know why I'm surprised. It's not like we're in California. Guns are fairly common in this part of the country.

"Never know who you might run into out here," he says without the tiniest bit of sarcasm or concern.

"Don't you mean *what* you might run into?"

He lifts a brow.

I raise my hands in defeat. "Fine. I'm just trying to, once again, make sure you're not planning to murder me."

Colton, unfazed by my accusation, steps out of his pants and sprints past me toward the rope swing, latching onto it at top speed. As the rope juts out over the middle of the water, he flips and lands with a tremendous splash. When he surfaces, he whips his soaked hair to the side, revealing a goofy grin. His smile is infectious, all pearly white and punctuated with a dimple, and I feel my own cheeks rise.

After breaststroking his way toward me, he offers me his hand. "Careful, Tiger, the wet rocks are slippery. I wouldn't want my new friend to fall and ruin that ink." He retracts his hand before I can take it. "Wait, can you grab a few things first? My wallet, the gun, my shirt, and the car keys. Oh, and the water bottle."

I cast a wary look over my shoulder. "Is the gun loaded?"

"Not much use if it isn't, but you're right. I'll grab them." He pulls himself up, abs and biceps flexing as water drips down his chest to his skin-tight boxer briefs. This time, I let myself take in his form, admiring the way his muscles move and shift, bringing the art on his skin to life. My eyes dip lower and widen. Even exiting a cold river, this man is *packing*. My cheeks flush.

Bending down, he gathers the items he mentioned and wraps them in his shirt, making a little sack. I briefly check out his ass before scanning his chorded back and the tattoo that takes up its entirety.

NO ONE IS FREE

WHILE OTHERS ARE OPPRESSED.

There is another giant jackal in the middle of the two lines. It looks like one of the motorcycle club cuts has been etched into his flesh.

He slips back into the water, once again holding out his hand. I'm not sure if I need the help but, eager to touch him, I accept the offer. His calloused fingers wrap around mine, sparking a little *zing* of energy between us.

Turns out I needed the help. Unlike on the shore, the rocks beneath the water are covered in an invisible layer of slippery slime, and if it wasn't for Colton, I would have immediately face-planted. Instead, my foot shoots right off the first rock, sending my ribcage slamming into his shoulder so that I'm left half draped over him with my ass in the air.

"That's one way to get in." He chuckles, lowering me into the cool water while keeping my wrist raised. The action reminds me of the little metal wand you use when you're trying to only dye one side of an Easter egg. I laugh at the mental image until my stomach dips below the surface and shock catches my breath.

Colton continues to lower me and after a moment of acclimating, the chill is invigorating, like my whole body is suddenly more alive. Once I've found my footing, he releases my hand, and I drop my head back and float, taking extra care to keep my wrist up in the air like a snorkel. With my ears submerged and my toes drifting above silt, I close my eyes and listen to the river passing over rocks and sand below.

When I look up a few relaxing minutes later, Colton's already on the far side of the bank, placing the makeshift bundle on the stone steps leading up to the mill. I make to swim for him, but without my feet touching the bottom and only one hand to swim with, I keep getting pushed farther away. Eventually I have to swim to the shallow end and walk back up to where I started.

I wade in until the water is neck level. I want to try again, but the river is already pushing me downstream. Colton swims over, and I wave my wrist at him with a poorly hidden frown. "I don't know if I can make it with one arm."

"I'll take you, just keep that hand in the air, okay?" He grabs my waist, pulling me toward him. I rest my arms on his shoulders as he slides his palms down the outside of my thighs before wrapping my legs around his waist, sending a shiver racing up my spine.

The contrast of the water and his warm arms and chest has goose bumps erupting all over my body. I press myself into him, desperate for the warmth and pleasantly surprised by the sensation of his skin against my own.

He moves forward with broad strokes, eyes locked onto mine. His chin and lips bob in and out of the water like a buoy as we move, the ghost of his minty breath caressing my chest with each exhale. The sensation makes my lower stomach clench and heat. This is incredibly intimate, and for one brief moment it seems like the effect he has on me isn't one-sided after all.

When we reach shallow water again and he stands, my body slides down his. One of Colton's hands moves to my back, the other to my ass to stop me, his fingers finding the faded bruises he left after the motorcycle ride. The bulge in his briefs presses against the crest of my thighs, and I bite my lip. Either he's half hard or he's considerably more endowed than I thought. I fight the urge to grind myself into him to relieve the building ache.

My tongue darts out, sweeping over my bottom lip.

He has to feel this, too.

I wait for him to lean in, to kiss me. I wait for one of his hands to slide between my thighs and under my bikini.

But he doesn't.

Instead, he lowers us back into the water, and we float, tangled up in one another, eyes fastened, breaths shallow. It feels big, like we're on the precipice of something *more*, until a cracking tree branch snaps our attention to the forest.

A single branch falls into the water off to my right and with the moment broken, Colton sighs and lets me go. He hoists himself up onto the stone steps leading to the mill. "I don't know what that was."

A cold emptiness wraps around me at his abrupt departure, and I'm suddenly self-conscious and unsure if he's referring to us touching or to the branch falling.

"Oh?" I say, exiting the water. The disappointment in my voice is all too evident, and Colton glances at me from the corner of his eye.

"I mean the branch," he clarifies, like he can hear my thoughts. "It was probably just an animal, but I'm not sure." He unwraps the makeshift parcel he created, hands me the water bottle, and spreads out his shirt for me to sit on. Only, I can't sit. My skin is too tight. I need to move. I want to run. At the very least I need to put some distance between us.

Setting down the bottle, I set off to explore the mill. I move cautiously, stepping over the bits of crumbling wood that line the ground and leaving a trail of wet footprints in my wake. The first level has a stone floor, and the entry is marked with an aged-patina plaque. I trace the etching.

Archer Family Mill, est. 1903.

It's hard to believe this building is over a hundred years old and still standing.

Footsteps pad behind me and stop. "It was rebuilt in the 1930s after flooding damaged the original structure. The flooring is original and so is the sign." He places a hand on the plaque, his chest pressing against my back, making my breath hitch.

I turn in his direction but keep my attention on his face. Knowing he's still in his briefs is too much for me to handle right now. "How do you know all that?"

His eyes lift to the rafters overhead. "This mill and the surrounding acreage used to belong to my family. My parents' old house is about four miles that way." He says, pointing vaguely to the west.

"Colton Archer?"

He spreads his arms wide. "The one and only."

"You said your family *used* to own the land?"

"They sold this plot and a few others before my dad was born. Now one man owns most of the land surrounding Eden. Including this lot." I can almost taste the bitterness in his voice, like vinegar coating my tongue. "I'm going to buy it back one day. I'm going to buy it all back." The conviction in his declaration rings out like a bell.

"What's stopping you from doing it now? The guy that owns it won't sell?"

"Oh, he will. Eventually. But right now, the price is so high only a major corporation could afford it. Jack thinks he's waiting to sell off to a developer or another mining company."

I open my mouth to ask what happened with the mine, but Colton raises a hand. "I'm having a really nice afternoon, and I'd prefer if we didn't get into any of this right now. If that's okay? Why don't you explore a little more and meet me outside?"

I don't know how he always seems to know what I'm about to say, but I respect the honesty in his request and nod my agreement before he steps back outside.

My eyes trail to the rafters where there are still remnants of a second and third floor. I look for the stairs, only to discover the wood has rotted out. Around the next corner, I find descending stone steps leading to a partially flooded basement. I take two steps down before something moves in the water and I rush back up.

Hard pass.

The central room is almost perfectly preserved, the walls lacking water stains and the floor bone dry. In a corner, I find height markers for Jeremy, Danny, Minho, and Colton carved into the wall. Seeing Jeremy's name is like a needle to the heart. Even here his absence is palpable, and once again, guilt digs her steel claws into my heart for barely knowing him.

After a few more minutes of exploration, I head outside and sprawl atop the shirt Colton laid down for me. When I look around, he's nowhere to be found. Deciding that he's probably peeing on a tree or something, I savor the warmth seeping into my muscles from the heat-soaked stones. Slowly, the last bits of tension left over from my fight with Holly ease away.

Although the thought of going back to my sister's house and having another heated conversation makes my limbs heavy with dread, I still want to fix things. If Colton and I can start over, Holly and I should be able to do the same. Besides, I like

Eden, and I don't particularly want to go back to Charlotte—at least not right now. There is nothing for me there anymore anyway.

I roll onto my stomach and catch Colton staring at me as he exits the tree line. "What were you thinking about just now?" he asks when he's close enough for me to hear.

"That I like it here."

He hums as he lays next to me. "What else?"

"I don't want to go back to Charlotte. I got rejected from both schools I applied to, what reason is there for me to go back?"

He looks up to the billowing white clouds passing overhead. "When you get in somewhere, what are you going to study?"

"I don't know. Minho's been helping me with my tech classes, and I'm really enjoying it, so maybe computer science or software engineering? I think I have the grades and the skill for it."

I close my eyes so I don't have to see his response, afraid he'll laugh or tell me to pick something else, like Logan always did. But he doesn't. "Both sound like good choices. As long as you find a way to leave an impact, you know?"

This time it's my brows that crease in disbelief. "That's what my mom always said, too."

He bobs his head in approval. "Sounds like she was a smart lady."

"She was. Hey, I never asked what you do? Do you work for the brewery like Danny?"

He shakes his head, smirking like I said something funny. "Would you believe me if I said I really do practice law?"

My jaw drops. "No freaking way. I thought you were being facetious. Are you really the guy from the rest stop's lawyer?"

Colton laughs. "Sort of. Right now, I do a lot of legal work for Jack's business ventures, including the bar, the brewery, the construction company, and a few others. I also give legal advice for the various business owners in town, and things like that. In a small town you sort of end up being a jack-of-all-trades, but I'd eventually like to venture into real estate law." He lays down, stretching his arms over his head.

A piece of the Colton puzzle snaps into place. "To get back the land?"

He nods, and I reach out to run two fingers over the tattoo on his neck, trailing them down his chest. His eyes flutter closed and his abs contract.

"I'm sure these go over well in court," I say, suddenly dizzy after watching the way he reacted to my touch.

Colton's chin tilts toward me, and he opens his eyes. After a long moment he says, "We should probably get going. Looks like a storm is rolling in."

Reluctantly, I agree, forcing myself to my feet and back across the river without Colton's assistance.

Back at the car, I glance skyward. There isn't a cloud in sight.

Chapter Seventeen

The cashier stares at me wide-eyed as I struggle to load up my cart. "Are you sure you don't need someone to help you out to your car? This is almost eighty pounds of rice."

"I got it. Thanks, though," I grunt, hoisting the last sack of rice back into the cart.

I pay in cash, like I always have since I came to town, and push the creaking cart outside. Despite one of the wheels spinning wildly, threatening to tip the entire buggy, the groceries and I make it to my car in one piece.

While loading the heavy bags and other bulk items into my trunk, I am consumed by thoughts of what I need to do today. I run through my mental checklist: grocers, school, diner... There's a nagging sensation that I'm forgetting something else, but maybe that's just my body hinting for a long run.

Still attempting to remember my forgotten task, I try cramming my change back into my clutch, only to have a bunch of ones and a condom pop out. Haphazardly, I shove them all back in and curse under my breath. I need to go to the bank. Maggie's pays in cash and, while actually having money makes me feel like a badass, using a duffle bag shoved under Holly's couch as my savings account and carrying around a ridiculously full purse has me feeling all sorts of antsy. You'd think this would be an easy problem to rectify, but each time I set out to open a new bank account, the only bank in town is conveniently closed. It's like the listed hours on the front door mean nothing to them.

Now that I think about it, I might just skip the bank today. They more than likely won't be open, and I can use the extra time this afternoon to study. It's also Friday, and even though I don't work, I still have to head over to the diner to see Anna and Johnny. It's my first time giving them food on a night I'm not working and I'm a little nervous about running into Lana or Maggie. At least this time I actually have unexpired food to give the kids.

Last Friday, when Johnny and Anna showed up for the food from Maggie's, there wasn't as much to hand over, and I've felt guilty about it ever since. I went out the very next morning and special-ordered the large rice bags and jumbo cans of beans from the grocer. I even found a massive bag of chocolates, but it still doesn't seem like enough. It feels almost like I'm trying to put a Band-Aid on a cut that clearly needs stitches, or a piece of tape over a foundation crack. I don't know what else I can do to help them though. So, until I come up with a better solution, I'll just have to keep buying them food and pray they remember to bring something to carry it all back to their house with.

Is it creepy if I offer to drive them home next time? It feels creepy, especially with the candy...

I shake my head and slam my trunk.

"That's a lot of food. You throwing a party?"

I squeal, jumping a foot in the air when I notice Danny right beside me.

Clutching my chest, I say the first lie I can think of. "Nope,

I just hate making trips to the grocery store. I always buy in bulk."

"Well, alright then." His shoulders bounce. "Hey, are you still coming tonight?"

"Coming?"

"The Pack, remember? You said you'd try for this Friday, I assumed we were on?"

Oh right, the bar.

I never got around to asking Holly, and after yesterday's argument, I don't know if I still want to. "Yeah, I have a few things to do before. You know, errands…" I gesture vaguely in the air. "Is 8:30 okay?" That should give me enough time to get the groceries to the diner.

"Sure. I'll be there around seven. Any time after that is good. I can give you a ride, if you want?"

"No thanks, I can drive." My response is high-pitched and too quick. I plaster on a smile. "See you tonight!"

Danny walks toward his truck, glancing over his shoulder at me several times along the way. Once he's gone, I let loose a long breath and head back to the bungalow.

When my sister emerges from her bedroom in the late afternoon, I automatically brace myself for another confrontation. Although spending the day with Colton and a good night's sleep helped lessen some of the residual hurt and anger from Holly's verbal assault, I'm still not entirely over it.

I stand up, ready to give her space, but before I can leave the kitchen, she engulfs me in a rib-crushing hug. "I'm sorry about yesterday, Ry. I feel crazy lately. Please forgive me for what I said. I don't know what's wrong with me and I don't know what I'd do if you weren't here. Please don't leave."

There's real fear in her voice, and for the first time ever, I feel like someone is afraid of losing *me*.

As pitiful as it sounds, the sensation of being wanted is enough to soften my rigid muscles, making me pliant in her arms. Even though I'm still upset, I hug her back, pulling her tiny frame into mine. Yes, she said some harsh things to me, but like Colton so wisely pointed out, she's hurting and lashing out at anything within scratching distance. At the end of the day, she's my sister and she just lost her husband. Who knows how I would act in a similar situation.

Besides, what she said about me and Logan wasn't exactly wrong...

The least I can do is extend her a little grace. "We still have a lot to talk about, but I'm not going anywhere. I promise."

A few hours later, Holly and I sit down to an uncomfortably cordial dinner. She's already made one trip to the bathroom to spill her guts, and now she's just pushing around the food on her plate like it's a Zen garden and not lasagna I spent two hours cooking.

"So, what are your plans for the evening?" she asks, dropping the fork with a *clang*.

Shit.

We just barely made up... I can't tell her I'm going to The Pack to see Danny. I chew a few seconds longer than necessary. If she can keep secrets, why can't I?

"I'm headed over to hang out with Lana while she closes the diner."

Holly lifts a brow that's in major need of plucking. "That's how you're going to spend your Friday night?"

I take another bite and swallow before answering. "I mean, we might go to a bar after. Lana and I tried to go to Eddie's a while back, but her car broke down." The half-truth tastes salty on my tongue.

Holly smiles. "That sounds fun. You can borrow my clothes if you want."

It's a simple peace offering, but just the idea of sharing clothes makes me feel like we're reclaiming a piece of the childhood we never had. "I'd love that. Thank you."

Most of Holly's clothes don't fit me. They're either too loose or cut off circulation to my thighs. While she and I share the same hair color and eyes, that's where the similarities stop. Her skin is pale and flawless, while mine is dotted with freckles and a few old acne scars. Where her nose is long and sharp, mine is small and rounded. Where her breasts are ample and somehow manage to look bigger despite the weight she's lost, mine barely fill a B cup.

Even with our differences, I find a black and white tube top that's flattering and a short, black, flowy skirt that, after a few spins in the mirror, I decide is too dressy. I change it out for my favorite pair of black jean shorts—okay, my only pair, but still.

With hours to spare before dropping off the food and meeting up with Danny, I decide to visit Lana while she closes at the diner so what I told Holly won't be a total lie. Maybe, if I'm sneaky, I can swipe the expired items and give that to the kids, too.

The diner parking lot is nearly empty when I pull in. The large windows, luminous in the dying light of the sun, showcase the scene inside like a movie playing out on the big screen. Lana is flitting about, dancing and singing with a mop while Cook looks on adoringly. When she spots me walking up, the dancing becomes more erratic, taking on an eighties hair-metal-band theme, complete with hair flips and kicks. I can't help but smile and clap for her.

The bell over the door chimes as I walk in and continue to clap. "Bravo! Bravo! Encore!" Cook turns down the music and Lana bows.

"You look hot. Where are you headed off to and why wasn't I invited?" Her dark brows settle into an expression of mock-scolding, too exaggerated to be serious.

"I'm meeting up with Danny at The Pack later. Do you want to come?"

Her expression melts into one of real concern. "No. I don't think I should."

"Come on, it will be much more fun if you come with me," I beg. We never really got to hang out last time, and although we have fun at work, I think it would be good to let loose a little.

She shakes her head in small, quick movements. "No. You should go, but be careful."

"What do you mean? It's Danny. We were at his house two weeks ago." I want to laugh at her ridiculousness, but something about the concern in her eyes prevents me.

"It's a different crowd at the bar. Most of the people at the house party were locals, people I went to high school with." She pauses and casts her eyes to the ground. "Are you guys together?"

"Me and Danny?" This time I really do laugh. "No. No way. He's practically family."

Lana's smile returns. "If I had family like that... I mean, damn, sign me up."

Behind the counter, Cook bends to pick up a crate, reminding me of one of the things I came here to do. I hop across the checkered tile to intercept him and smile serenely. "If that's the expired stuff, I can take it out for you." Cook shakes his head, pulling the box more securely to his chest. "No really. Let me help," I say, taking the crate before he can protest again.

He clutches his heart like I've mortally wounded him. "Oh, get over it." I give him a bump with my elbow as I move past him. I feel like I'm lying again, but I just can't let them throw out perfectly good food while there are hungry kids on their way.

Bugs circle the outdoor lighting like vultures on roadkill. Across the street, an old car engine rumbles, and I set the crate on the air-conditioning unit. It's an odd assortment of food: bagged pasta salad, a small box of pink sugar cookies, and several jars of assorted pickled veggies. There's even a jar of pickled carrots and eggs. I shudder at the thought of what that tastes like and head back inside.

Lana and I chat over the next hour until it's time to close the diner. I could be projecting my own guilt onto the situation, but something is off with her. I catch her staring at The Pack one too many times and when it's finally time for us to leave, she keeps looking at the clock and back out the front window.

"Everything okay?"

"My car is still in the shop. Mom was going to pick me up and give me a ride home, but she's not here... What if something happened?"

"I'm sure she's just running late. I can give you a ride." I regret the words as soon as I say them. How can I feed the kids if I'm driving Lana home? What if I miss them?

She looks me over and frowns. "No, you have plans. Cook will give me a ride. Isn't that right, Cook?"

He moves his head up and down and makes a *thumbs-up* gesture with his scarred hands.

Lana gives me a small, guarded smile. "Just be careful tonight." She locks the last door and hesitates as she walks away. "See you tomorrow?"

"Sure will."

She hops up into Cook's busted-up minivan and waves from the window.

I wait until the taillights are no longer visible and scramble to the back of the diner only to jump out of my skin when I see a figure standing over the crate of food.

How has this happened to me twice today?

"Colton?"

He turns to me and even in the dim light his blue-green eyes are piercing. He waves a hand at the food. "What is this?"

"It's nothing." I push my body between him and the crate protectively.

"Are you stealing from Maggie?" He looks worried or angry, I can't tell which.

"It's not *stealing*...not really. This stuff is about to expire and was going into the trash anyway." I mumble to myself, bending over to pick up the food.

Colton reaches out a hand to stop me. "Are you and Holly that hard up?"

"No." Apparently, Colton is the only person I'm not lying to today.

He glances between me and the crate, weighing the sincerity of my words. "So, you're not stealing?" I shake my head. "Okay then, I'll help." His body brushes against mine as he takes the cargo from my hands. "Where to?"

Is he serious? I half expected him to rat me out. "Just like that? No questions asked?"

He sucks in his pouty lower lip and lets it go with a loud pop and a shrug. "That's what a friend would do, right? I told you, we're starting over. Now tell me where you want this."

Ignoring the goose bumps forming on my arms, I point to the small trail leading into the woods. "Over by that tree."

Colton shakes his head in obvious confusion but moves to set the crate down by the entrance to the path as asked. "Anything else?"

I tap my finger to my lip. "Actually, yeah, can you come to my car for a second?"

He squints as if he's unsure he wants to but follows me anyway. I pop the trunk and point to the three bags of rice and the cans of beans.

"You bought all this?"

"I did," I answer, not bothering to explain further.

He pinches his brows together and grabs all the rice at once like it weighs nothing, leaving the beans and chocolate for me to struggle with. As he walks back to the trailhead, he peeks over his shoulder at me, his face still contorted and confused. With each passing second, he looks more and more upset. A zing of discomfort shoots through me when I realize I hate the thought of disappointing him, which is dumb. I raise my chin.

Whatever. If feeding these kids puts me in Colton's bad graces, then he's not a friend worth having.

Johnny and Anna emerge seconds later, pulling two rickety old wagons. Anna darts out and wraps herself around my legs. "Miss Rylee! What did you bring us?"

I crouch and hug her back. "How do you feel about pink sugar cookies and a bag of chocolates?"

She squeals in delight and claps her hands, diving to examine the crate and find the sweets.

Her brother walks forward, hands in his pockets, and inclines his head to Colton and then me. "Mr. Colton. Miss Rylee."

"You guys know each other?" I ask incredulously.

Colton turns a pale shade of pink, and a muscle in his jaw tightens "It's a small town. We all know each other." He shakes Johnny's hand. "It's good to see you, kid."

Colton helps load the wagons and offers the children a ride home, which they decline. When they disappear back into the underbrush, he kicks a rock and spits on the ground.

"How long have you been giving the Grace kids food?"

"A few weeks. This is the third time." I can't tell if he's

about to yell at me or hit something. I straighten my posture. Compassion and caring for others is not a weakness, it's a strength. I won't let him make me feel bad about this.

He balls his fists at his side until his knuckles are bloodless. "I had no idea it'd gotten this bad. Did you see how fucking skinny they are?"

"Out of sight, out of mind, right?" I don't mean for it to come out so harsh, but how could you not know this was going on in your own town? Like he said, Eden is small. They all know each other.

Colton mumbles something, but I can't make out what he said. He clears his throat. "Before what happened with Jeremy, I was away a lot. I guess I sort of lost sight of what was going on at home." His voice is strained and heavy, like he's choking on whatever words he's not saying.

"Their mom, Charlotte, is raising both of them on her own." He shakes his head and grimaces. "She won't take work from us, even though she keeps getting fired everywhere else. She can't help it when she has to miss a shift if one of the kids gets sick." His jaw hardens. "I want to help you with this. Do you do this every Friday? Are there others? What can I do?"

My heart swells. He wants to help. He doesn't think I'm weird or crazy, he actually wants to help. I'm on the verge of hugging him when I stop myself and mull over his words. "What do you mean she won't take work from 'us'? Do you mean the brewery?"

Red and blue lights flash, accompanied by the sound of multiple approaching cars.

Colton leans back for a better view of the street and mutters, "It's the fucking sheriff. Come on." He grabs my wrist and tugs me into the tree line where damp earth and the smell of decaying plant life assaults my senses.

No wonder the Grace kids are always so dirty.

He pulls us into a crouch, and I do my best not to ruin my shoes in the mud as my heart thumps against my rib cage.

From the safety of the surrounding trees, I watch Sheriff Knott and Maggie park in the spaces adjacent to mine. The sheriff emerges and shines a bright light in my window before testing the door handle. Thank God I locked it.

Maggie sashays up to his side. "They've been stealing from me for months now. Going through my garbage like heathens! There's got to be something you can do, Sheriff."

Even Sheriff Knott, looking greasy as ever, rolls his eyes at her rant. "Technically, Maggie, anything thrown away is considered abandoned property. It's not illegal to dumpster dive." Maggie gives him a disappointed expression that I'm all too familiar with. He ignores it. "The best I can do is recommend you put a lock on the dumpster, if you're really that adamant about it."

Maggie sighs, placing a hand on the window of my car to give her a better view inside.

The sheriff spits on the ground. "Now, if you happened to find out that one of your employees was taking home food before it got to the dumpster, let's say a certain new employee, and you wanted to file charges... I could help you out with that."

A sour-faced Maggie stands, glancing around the parking lot. "You know she took my Lana to a party at *their* house? If she's keeping company like that, who knows what she's capable of?" She tests my door handle and then moves around to check the trunk. "She's not working tonight, but this is her car. Can we tow this piece of shit?"

She kicks the side paneling, and before I can stop myself, I'm lunging forward to give her a piece of my mind. I don't have much, but I worked hard for that *piece of shit* car.

Colton grabs me hard around the waist, careening into the

wet dirt with the momentum, taking me with him. I land in his lap with a *thunk* and a whooshing breath escapes my lips as the wind gets knocked out of me.

Maggie snaps her head in our direction, scanning the brush. Sheriff Knott follows her gaze with his flashlight.

Shit.

Colton pulls me tighter against him and leans back, placing a hand over my mouth to keep me quiet and pinned to his chest. "*Shhh.* It won't look good if Knott finds us here."

For some reason, the first time I saw him comes to mind. The way he pinned Buzz Cut Guy to the hood of my car...the resulting daydream of him doing the same thing to me. His body feels exactly the way I imagined it would.

Warm.

Muscular.

Hard.

I shiver, pinching my thighs together, and the arm he has around my waist shifts slightly with the movement, causing his pinkie to slip below the waistband of my shorts. My stomach does a flip as he presses down on it. Jesus, this is doing absolutely nothing to help my already wild imagination.

Behind me, Colton's steady breaths push my torso forward, threatening to send his fingers even lower. If I shifted just a little, his hand would be all the way inside my jeans...

Why is this so hot?

We're literally hiding from the police and my entire body is aflame. The heat from his palm is now pulsating down the length of my body, settling into a throbbing ache between my legs. I squeeze my thighs together to quell the sensation, but that has the opposite effect.

Shit. Shit. Shit.

I squirm under his touch. I have to get up. I can't breathe, and I'm about to make an absolute fool of myself.

Colton must sense my panic because slowly he slides his hand from my mouth down to my neck.

Oh fuck. A hand necklace? Jesus, that's even hotter.

Blood rushes to my cheeks and lower belly. I inhale sharply, which only makes his hand tighten around my throat.

I moan.

I fucking moan.

If I could bury my head in the dirt right now, I would.

Behind me, Colton's breath hitches, and he puts just a little more pressure on my throat. I squirm beneath his touch, both desperate for more friction between us and eager to hide what he's doing to my body.

Colton's chest rises and falls behind my back with increased frequency, his breath is hot and heady against my hair. With his thumb, he tilts my neck up, bringing his mouth to my ear. "That's not the reaction I expected with my hand wrapped around your neck, Tiger."

Goose bumps erupt on every surface of my flesh, and I shudder. I should be embarrassed, but when I shift to move away, I feel a growing hardness pressed into my backside.

At least the same thing is happening to both of us right now.

Colton uses his thumb to trace my jaw and turn my face toward his. His eyes drop to my lips.

Oh God, he's going to kiss me, and I'll be damned if that's not exactly what I want right now.

His lips are so close I can almost taste the mint on his breath.

A blinding headlight rips through our surroundings, and Colton flattens us further into the dirt. Maggie's tires squeal as she reverses out of the lot, and Colton and I are cast back into inky darkness. The sheriff curses to himself and follows shortly after, his cruiser backfiring as he starts it up.

For a moment, Colton and I lay unmoving with quivering breath, waiting until we're sure the coast is clear.

I consider flipping over to face him. I imagine the way his hands would feel on my back...on my ass. I've almost worked up the courage to turn over and make the first move when a panicked voice calls out from nearby. "Colt? Where the hell are you?"

It's Danny and the fear in his tone is almost tangible, siphoning away the remaining tension in the air between Colton and I. We stand, careful not to touch one another.

Colton is still brushing the leaves and twigs from his clothes when we emerge from the tree line. Danny races over to him, grabbing his shoulders and looking him over. "Fuck, man, when I saw Knott and I heard a gun fire... I didn't know what to think. You alright?"

"I'm fine." Colton's eyes shift to mine.

"Are you sure?" Danny, still frantic, begins patting Colton down.

Colton grabs Danny's face, realizing what's happening before I do. "It was just a car backfiring. I promise I'm fine. Okay?" He wraps an arm around Danny. "But I do have to run home and change. *Someone* pushed me in the dirt while we were avoiding Knott."

Danny nods a few times too many, as if waking himself up. He runs both his hands down his face, casting me a quick look, like he hadn't noticed I was there before.

Colton tightens his arm on Danny's shoulder and kisses his temple. "I'm okay, brother, and so are you. I'll be right back. I promise."

Chapter Eighteen

Fluttering insects continue their dance around the streetlights as the roaring engine of Colton's Chevy fades into the night.

After a quick trip back to my car to grab my clutch, Danny offers me his arm, and we make our way across the street in the direction of the bar. His forearm shakes slightly, like he's suffering from the aftereffects of an adrenaline surge.

"Are you okay?" I ask in a hushed tone.

"I'll be fine." He gives me a small smile and pats my hand on his arm. "I feel like I owe you an explanation. Has Holly told you what happened to my brother?"

"You don't owe me anything. But no, she hasn't. It never seemed like the right time to ask." I opt not to tell him about how poorly it goes any time I start asking her questions.

"I figured as much. Your sister's not really a sharer." Danny sniffles, and the chorded muscles in his forearm tense. "Andy, the sheriff's deputy that was at my party, was the one who found Jeremy's body out on the old iron bridge that leads into town. He was...unrecognizable." There is a long pause as I take in his words, and he opens and closes his mouth like he's struggling to say the next ones. "He'd been shot twice in the back of the head."

Holy shit.

We stop just shy of The Pack's doors. I am lightheaded from his revelation, and I think I might be sick. Danny's not looking much better. "I saw Colt pull up to the bar earlier, and when he didn't come inside, I went looking for him. Then I heard the car backfire and I thought—" He sucks in his lower lip and closes his eyes. "In my head, I kept seeing Jeremy and thinking that I can't lose another brother." His words tumble out, and he leans over like he's going to puke.

Oh God. I rub his lower back. "Colton's okay, it was just a car. He's fine."

"I know." Danny stands and places his arms over his head before pushing out a gush of air.

I shouldn't pry, but I can't help myself from asking, "Have they arrested anyone? For Jeremy's murder?" I need to know what happened, and Danny seems to be the only one willing to give me answers. I give his back one more comforting pat.

Hands on his head, he looks down at me from the corner of his eye. "No. Sheriff Knott closed the case. He said there wasn't enough evidence and implied that Jeremy probably did something to deserve it. We've been looking into it, but it's difficult with—"

A car door slams, and Jack appears around the corner of the brick bar, talking on his cell phone. When he sees us, he lowers his voice and abruptly ends the call, striding over to Danny.

"You good, *mijo?* You look pale." He places Danny's face between his palms, similar to the way Colton did earlier, and examines him.

"I'm fine." Danny shrugs out of his father's touch.

"Well, stiffen up before you walk in." Jack's chin juts in the direction of the bar. "I need to speak with Rylee for a second."

Danny takes a step toward the door but leans against the wall in obvious defiance of his father's command.

With the tiniest shake of his head, Jack directs his attention to me. "You seem to be getting along well with my boys."

I cross my arms over my chest, suddenly defensive at the underlying accusation. "Is that a question?"

Jack tilts his head and blinks. "*Tiene razón, ella es una tigresa,*" he says in Danny's direction before turning back to me. "No, not a question. I'm happy to see it. I'm just checking in. How is Holly doing?"

The concern written on his face is the same expression I see in the mirror every day. I soften my tone. "She's working a lot, but at least she's eating again."

"Do you guys need anything?"

I shake my head. "No, we're good. But thank you." I uncross my arms, letting them fall awkwardly to my sides. I don't know why I'm always ready for a fight. Jack has been nothing but kind to me since day one.

"Well, stick close to Danny tonight and let me know if you ever change your mind about needing anything, okay?"

I nod, and he places his phone in a box hanging on the wall next to Danny before heading inside. A burst of cigarette smoke and laughter filters through the cracked door, then disappears again when it closes.

Why did he put his phone in that box?

I squint to get a better look at the sign above the container.

NO PHONES INSIDE THE BAR.

Noticing my attention on the sign, Danny asks, "Do you have a phone, smartwatch, anything like that on you?"

"Nope. Not with Holly's weird rules." If I'm being honest, I don't miss my phone. No one called me anyway, and it's one less bill to pay.

Danny nods in approval and places his own phone inside the box, extending his other arm to hold the door open for me.

I raise a brow. "You're not going to explain the no phone thing?"

"We value privacy in this town. Nothing that happens in here needs to be recorded or overheard." He pushes the door open farther, and a blast of laughter, classic rock, and stale cigarette smoke hits me like a tidal wave. I close my eyes to adjust to the hazy new room, and when I open them, every single face is turned toward me, mouths and bodies frozen in whatever activity they were previously engaged in.

In an instant, I know I'm not welcome.

Maybe they don't allow phones so there are no witnesses when they beat up the outsider.

I brush away the ridiculous thought as Danny places a hand between my shoulder blades and guides me through the whispers to a stool at the bar. Thankfully, the music is loud enough that I can't hear any of the specific things being said. To me, it just sounds like low hissing. Slowly, conversations resume, and when most of the faces have turned away from us, I lean back and whisper, "What the hell was that? What kind of place is this?"

"You're a new face. Try not to worry about it." Motion behind the counter has Danny waving. "Hey, Ashlynn, can you get us two beers, please?"

Ashlynn, just as beautiful as the day I met her, stares at me wide-eyed. "Ash?" Danny repeats with a circular wave of his hand.

"Yeah, of course." She sets two chilled bottles on the bar.

"Thanks. Can you watch out for Rylee until Alex gets back? I need to talk to Jack before the meeting."

"You call your dad by his first name?" I shouldn't judge, I

call my dad Rick, but I feel like Jack has more than likely earned the title of Dad, while my father has not.

Danny snorts a laugh but doesn't answer my question as he waits for Ashlynn to respond.

"Sure," she says a little stiffly with just the quickest of glances in my direction, but it's enough for Danny, who promises to be back in a few minutes. He heads over to the booth on the other side of the room where Jack sits, arms stretched out like a king on his throne.

I glance around, taking in my surroundings. It's not unsimilar to other dive bars I've been in, with its rough, wide-planked floors and smoke lingering near the ceiling. Off to the left, there are three pool tables tucked into a side room along with several shuffleboard tables and a few vintage arcade games. Opposite the bar, a small stage takes up one corner of the main room, along with several booths and even more standing tables scattered evenly throughout the space. The only thing that jumps out at me as abnormal is that the building appears way bigger on the outside than it is on the inside. I thought it would be three times this size.

Although the space could hold about two hundred people in a pinch, I'd say there are maybe sixty meandering about tonight. Some throw occasional looks in my direction, but most act like eye contact with me might turn them to stone. I recognize one or two of them from the house party, but it really is a different crowd, just like Lana said it would be.

After I'm done taking in my surroundings, the silence between Ashlynn and I grows unbearable. Neither of us have anywhere to look besides each other, but each of us seems determined to avoid the other's gaze. I don't understand why this feels so weird, especially when she was so nice to me the first time we met. "Have you worked here long?" I ask in an overly friendly tone.

She busies herself cleaning the same glass she's already cleaned and dried. "I don't really work here. I just help out Alex when he's shorthanded. He's out back on a smoke break."

"Oh, okay. Well, thank you for the beer." I wiggle it in her direction, and she laughs.

"This is awkward, isn't it?"

I relax my shoulders, grateful that she's mentioning it out loud. "Yeah, why is that?"

A gust of wind flows from the opening door, and Colton strides in, followed closely by Minho and Alex. All conversations hush, but instead of scowls and angry brows, Colton receives tilted glasses and inclined heads. His eyes find mine at the bar, and my skin flushes with heat until I have to look away. I can still feel the tingling imprint of his hand on my belly and on my throat.

Ashlynn catches my blush, and the words that were about to leave her mouth never come. In my peripheral, Colton and Minho take seats next to Jack, while Alex wanders over to relieve Ashlynn. She smiles at me tentatively and leaves to take a seat next to Colton. My stomach tightens at how close she sits to him, so close their thighs are touching, and I quickly turn away.

Alex scans the mess of rags and clean glasses Ashlynn left on the counter and places his hands on his hips, shaking his head.

"Rough night?" I inquire.

"Not really, but I swear Ashlynn makes a bigger mess in fifteen minutes than I do all night. I could really use a second bartender."

I only half hear what he's saying as three more people I don't recognize join Jack at the table. Their eyes occasionally flicker in my direction, and I get the distinct impression they are talking about me. "Hey, Alex, what's that about?"

He follows my gaze. "I think a decision was proposed. They're voting on it."

"Voting?"

"You really don't know, do you?" His tone is playful and amused. I hate it.

Tapping my fingers on the table, I make a fist. "If you all could be less cryptic, I'd appreciate it. I swear, Eden is one of the most confusing places I've ever been." I tap my fingers again. "Talking to any of you is like trying to wade through quicksand. Every time I think I'm getting somewhere, I just sink further in."

Alex places his hand over mine to stop my tapping. "I don't think that's an expression but noted." He suppresses a grin and turns to stack the clean glasses next to a wall of black-and-white photos.

In the center, there is a large picture of Jeremy with the dates 1989–2026 etched into a silver plate on the frame. In the photo, he's smiling at something just outside of view, the sun lighting his hair like a halo.

God, he was handsome.

I hope Holly didn't have to see him after he died. I hope she gets to remember him like this—young and perfect.

I glance over at the table to compare the image of Jeremy to Danny but find Minho staring daggers in my direction. The fierceness in his expression makes me jump and immediately return to my inspection of the picture wall.

There are several other photographs, some with date plates under them and some without. I assume the ones with date plates, like Danny's, are other patrons of the bar who have passed on. Most are surprisingly young, except for a single picture of several hundred miners of varying ages, June 2006 is written in black sharpie on the bottom right corner.

Above that picture is another photo, this time of a handsome man surrounded by four boys. The metal plate on this one says Jackal Originals. I lean closer, recognizing the handsome man as Jack in his early thirties and the boys around him as Jeremy, Danny, Minho, and Colton, in that order.

Jackals, just like the tattoos, and the sign. I look around the bar again, noticing all the jackals inked on arms and hands. There are a few doves mixed in, but mostly it's the vicious-looking canine. Over by the pool tables, a large black flag is draped across the wall with a snarling jackal in the center of it. It's an exact replica of the image on Colton's back.

Slowly the pieces start to click into place. "Is this some sort of clubhouse?"

Alex shrugs.

"Are you going to answer any of my questions?" I'm starting to feel like this is a repeat of my conversation with Holly.

"Depends on the question." He grabs a dirty glass and starts washing it.

I pause to consider for a moment. "Do you have any tattoos?"

Alex leans forward, pulling down the collar of his short-sleeve button-down to reveal a beautiful dove across his chest.

Interesting.

I expected a jackal. I wonder if Danny has any tattoos. He wears long sleeves most of the time, so I haven't thought to ask. I turn on my stool but am stopped dead in my quest for answers when I make eye contact with Minho again, who is still scowling and staring holes into me.

"Why does Minho keep looking over here like he wants to unalive me?"

Alex laughs, pausing his cleaning to look up at the ceiling. "Have you ever seen *Schitt's Creek?*" I shake my head. "Well, to bastardize and butcher one of their quotes: Minho only drinks whiskey. I, however, like whiskey, red wine, beer, and have tried just about every type of alcohol there is."

I shake my head because I don't get it.

"He's afraid I want to try the new drink on the menu." Alex raises his eyes at me suggestively.

"Oh, me?" I ask, crossing my arms. I didn't think I was flirting. "I'm not trying to—not that you're not... I'm just...and I know you guys are together—"

Alex graciously cuts me off with a dismissive gesture. "You're beautiful, but after all that sampling, I now know there is only one person for me." He casts his eyes to Minho lovingly, and I see his partner's shoulders relax from across the bar. I love how even unspoken communication can put them at ease.

"Forgive me for asking, but why partner instead of boyfriend?" I ask, remembering how Minho introduced Alex the first time.

Alex grabs a new glass and starts wiping. "Jeremy's death hit us all a little differently. For me, I realized I didn't want to spend my life waiting to live. I was with the man I wanted to be with forever, why not make it official? It was probably the wrong time, but I proposed to Minho the day after the funeral."

"He didn't say yes?"

"He said *not yet.*"

My face scrunches up. "What does that mean?"

"For Minho, Jeremy's death showed him how fragile life is. He's afraid of doing to me what Jeremy did to Holly."

My muscles go rigid.

What the hell did Jeremy do to Holly?

Alex must sense that I'm about to have an outburst because he shakes his head. "I mean dying. He's afraid he'll die and I'll be left alone without him, or vice versa."

Oh, that's dark.

"Is the risk of dying high for bartenders or people in

marketing and IT?" I laugh, trying to bring some brevity to the situation. Alex only frowns.

"You'd be surprised," he says, humorlessly. "Anyway, even though he said no to marriage, he said he still wanted to move forward in our relationship. He suggested calling ourselves partners to show our commitment, and he gave me this promise ring." Alex holds up his hand where a simple gold band with a black stone in the center sits on his left ring finger.

It's a romantic gesture, but I wonder how I would feel in the same situation. "Is that enough for you, being partners?"

Alex gets a dreamy look in his eyes that contrasts dramatically with the serious set of his jaw. "I want to spend every minute with that man in any way that he'll have me. Especially if a minute is all we get."

"That's beautiful." It really is. It makes my heart hurt a little because I want that. That's what Jeremy and Holly had.

Ugh. How did this conversation take such a serious turn?

I peek over my shoulder for a distraction and to see if Danny is headed back yet. He's not. Jack is still in the center of the booth, holding court. He finishes what he's saying and extends his palms to the table. Danny immediately raises his hand, followed by Minho. The three men I don't know are slower to raise their hands. Colton raises a single finger and then they all turn toward Ashlynn expectantly. She casts a tentative glance in my direction and then fixates on Colton before dropping her eyes and raising her hand as well.

Jack sets his palms on the table and nods with an air of satisfaction, his eyes flashing to me briefly with a subtle grin that deepens the lines in his face. My heart thumps once against my ribs. Jack has this whole *dad vibe* about him. A simple smile from him makes me feel like I just earned a proud father's approval, something I really know nothing about. I wish Holly would patch things up with him. It would be nice to be around a family, to have a dad figure in our lives.

When the odd little meeting adjourns, Colton is the first to stand. When he rises from the booth, the crowd unconsciously shifts out of his way, leaving an unobstructed route to the bar—and to me. A small sigh escapes my lips as I watch his body move, all power and muscle. When he's close enough for me to reach out and touch, I take a deep breath, savoring the scent of spice and soap and a faint hint of sunshine. Now that we are *friendly,* I really would have loved to push that physical boundary with him, but I still plan on leaving Eden at the end of summer for school. There's no need to overcomplicate things here.

Alex pours a whiskey neat and sets it in front of the stool to my right. Colton downs half the drink in one go and twists the glass in his hand, watching the light shine through the crystal and the single rainbow it casts on the shellacked wood of the counter.

"Need me to top you off?" Alex asks with a wink, ready to pour more.

"I'm just having the one tonight," Colton says, missing the joke. His eyes turn to me, sparkling with mischief.

"You look clean," I say, desperate to hear more of his voice.

"I took a very cold shower." His tone is hard and firm, just like his body was against mine.

A little wave of satisfaction slides up my spine at his response, and my skin crawls with renewed need.

He pulls out the stool next to me and takes a seat. "So, you've lied to the sheriff, you partied with the townies, and now you're at my bar? You trying to make a life here, Tiger? Or just trying to weasel your way into mine?" He grabs my stool and pulls it closer to his, making the legs squeal as they drag across the floor.

My pulse is so rapid I can feel it in my throat. "Neither," I manage to squeak out. Heat radiates off his chest as he leans in, overwhelming me with even more of his scent. Where did this flirty Colton come from? It's like our encounter in the trees flipped a switch.

Or maybe I infected him with my horniness?

He tosses back the rest of his whiskey and points to my beer. "How many of those have you had?"

"Just the one." I lift an eyebrow. "Why?"

"I want to make sure you have a clear head when I ask you to leave with me later."

"Wh-what?" I can't breathe, and now my heart is threatening to beat through my chest.

"You heard me." He leans in closer, his lips brushing against my ear. "I haven't stopped thinking about you since that night at the rest stop. All that strength. All that fire. Your brazen, idiotic disregard for your own safety when you risked pissing off a dangerous stranger because you thought someone was in trouble and needed your help. I thought I could ignore this feeling. I thought I could ignore you. But I can't."

My jaw drops.

Warmth spreads through my body and a floating feeling fills my chest. That's the best compliment I've ever received.

He shakes his head, ghosting his hand across my jaw and down my neck. A small gasp escapes my lips, and he smirks. "I know you feel this, too. I can barely fucking think straight anymore, but I'm only going to ask if you're sober enough to make a sound decision." He places a hand on my upper thigh and squeezes, using my body to push back his stool. Without another word, he leaves to rejoin Jack and the others, who've all moved across the room toward the pool tables near an emergency exit.

What the fuck just happened?

Chapter Nineteen

"You might want to close your mouth," Alex says with a smug chortle.

I attempt to seal my lips, but I can't. I'm stuck gaping. "Did he just..."

Did Colton just proposition me?

Chuckling to himself, Alex raises his hands. "I heard nothing. I saw nothing. I know nothing."

Ironically enough, that's exactly how I feel right now.

I take a deep breath, composing myself before grabbing my beer and heading over to where Danny's motioning me over. My brain spins as he introduces me to a few people, including the three unfamiliar men that were sitting at his booth. One is a skinny guy with a motorcycle cut on, another has black eyes and scar across his lip, while the third has red hair and a suit on, which is somehow not out of place in this back-hills bar. Again, it's too many new faces and names for me to remember, especially when all I can think about is Colton, but I appreciate being included, and the men are friendly enough, inquiring about my time in Eden and even inviting me to play pool with them.

I play a few rounds, but mostly I watch and try to steal glances at Colton. Despite my obvious lack of skill, Jack tries to teach me the rules and proper technique. It's of no use. I can't think of anything except Colton's body pressed against mine and how hot it suddenly is in this bar.

I mean seriously, is the air-conditioning even on?

"You're as hopeless as your sister," Jack says with a deep belly laugh when I miss my sixth shot of the night. He pushes out a large breath of air, like the sudden thought of Holly has led him to painful memories. "I think I'm done for the night. Colt, you take my spot?"

Colton dips his head and takes Jack's pool cue. The entire bar falls silent as Jack approaches the door. People who are sitting stand, and people who are mid-sip lower their drinks.

Jack looks over his shoulder. "Have a good night, Jackals."

In unison, every person present, except for me of course, stomps their foot and makes a *haroom* sound—almost like a bark or a battle cry from ancient Sparta. It sends a chill up my spine, making the hairs on my neck stand straight up, just like at the funeral.

When the door closes, the noise picks back up and everyone resumes their activities as if what just happened was nothing out of the ordinary.

I turn to Colton, who's taken Jack's place beside me. "So, you're in a cult?" I gesture to the door and the jackal flag on the wall. "You know this is all pretty weird, right?"

He laughs, and I feel it resonate deep down in my stomach. He leans down over the pool table for the first shot. The balls scatter as he breaks. "The Jackals are not a cult, we're a club."

I raise my eyebrows, a silent request for him to continue.

"We're like a family, a group of people with a similar outlook on life."

"And that is?"

He takes a few more shots, each ball landing its mark, then inclines his head toward the flag. I read the familiar words out loud. "No one is free while others are oppressed. Like your tattoo."

Colton nods in answer and steps out of the way for Danny to shoot. With the rest of the group momentarily distracted, he backs me into a corner and moves some of my loose strands of hair behind my shoulder. I revel in the way his fingers trail across the hollow of my collarbone. "Are you having fun tonight?"

My head tilts automatically to give him better access, and I try to form words, but *mm-hmm* is all that comes out.

He leans in. "Have you thought more about what I said?" He slides a finger from my collarbone down my side to the hem of my shirt, grazing the exposed skin of my belly. My back arches into him, and I nod. A sound of approval rumbles deep in his throat. "Do you want to leave with me, Tiger?" His nose skims the ridge of my ear.

My brain is fuzzy and lust clouded, but I still have the presence of mind to ask, "Just this once, though, right?" I need to get this attraction out of my system, but I won't be in Eden forever and I can't afford to get attached. One and done. Then we can both move on.

His finger freezes but only for a second. "That's usually my line, but sure. Just this once."

"Then yes, let's get out of here." My voice is husky, almost unrecognizable.

He leans away from me. "I'll wait outside for you for ten minutes. If you change your mind, that's fine. No hard feelings." He locks eyes with me. "The choice is yours. I promise

I'll respect your decision either way." He lifts a brow, as if making sure I heard him. I bob my head, and he pushes off the wall, heading straight for the front door.

"Well, byeee," Minho calls out after him, his voice bringing the room back into sharp focus. "It's not like it was your turn or anything."

Colton's sudden departure sends a rush of cool air into the space he left behind. I take a step toward the door only to stop. It feels like there is a force pulling me after him, a rope wrapped around my rib cage, dragging me in his wake.

But is this what I want?

I can't deny that I'm attracted to Colton. I can't stop thinking about him, but it's not like I have a track record for making smart decisions about men.

Fuck it. It's just one night.

I turn to Danny to excuse myself, but he's already propping open the back door. He gives a quick jut of his head and rolls his eyes when I hesitate. "Just go."

I mouth a quick "thank you" and slip outside.

Colton is there, leaning against the brick wall with his hands in his pockets, the dim parking lot casting most of his face and body in shadows. He reminds me of a painting I once saw of a fallen angel. Beautiful and perfect.

He only looks up once the door bangs closed, relief washing over his face when he sees me.

I smile to myself. *I guess I surprised both of us.*

We move toward each other without a word, closing the distance in seconds. The moment I'm within arm's reach, he wraps a hand in my hair at the base of my neck, his lips slamming into mine, soft for only a moment before his tongue dips into my mouth like he's desperate to taste me.

Caressing.

Exploring.

Hungry.

I've never been kissed like this. Sparks erupt behind my eyes, and my lungs feel like they might burst. Beneath my hands, Colton's body stiffens, and he squirms like he might push himself away, but I crush my mouth to his and suck his tongue until he melts under my touch. When I bite his lower lip, he grunts in pleasure, wrapping an arm around my waist and pulling my body into his. His hands move to my ass, kneading until I'm so slick my shorts could slide right off.

Fuck. I want him so bad.

Pushing a hand between us, I rub the seam of his pants and find that he's already rock-hard. Desire pulses through my core in heated waves. Almost frantically, I work myself inside his jeans and wrap my palm around his cock. My eyebrows shoot into my hairline when my fingers don't meet.

Holy fuck, he's too big for me to wrap my hand all the way around.

Colton thrusts against my grip and groans. Then he's moving, one hand dips to the back waistband of my shorts and slips inside while the other undoes the front button, creating more room for him to work. Painstakingly slow, he kisses me, sliding his fingers farther down until he's cupping my ass with one hand and diving deeper with the other, where he finds just how ready I am for him.

"Fuck, that's hot." He adjusts me, ripping my hand from his cock and picking me up so I'm higher on his torso. My breasts swell in his face, threatening to suffocate him with each breath until he pulls my head down for another kiss. I slide my hands through his hair, eliciting soft moans from his mouth as he kisses me, and spiking my need for him until I'm guiding his hands back down into my shorts. It only takes a moment before he begins to explore. Sliding my lace thong to the side, he slips two fingers inside of me, moving them in time with each stroke of his tongue.

I moan as Colton's lips trail down my neck to my chest where he draws one of my nipples into his mouth, fabric and all. His fingers pulse in and out, teasing the outside of my pussy before diving back in. I whimper, trying to ride his hand, but the angles are all wrong. I can't get him as deep as I want him. As deep as I *need* him.

"Fuck, you're so wet." A guttural noise erupts in his throat that reminds me of a wild animal, and I grind myself into his stomach, desperate for more attention on my clit. He lets me ride him like that until my moans bleed into a panting cry for more.

I'm already so close, just a little bit—

He slides his fingers out of me and plunges them into my mouth, glancing around the parking lot. I seem to have forgotten we're in public, but as long as he keeps doing what he's doing, I really don't care who hears us. Especially now that I can taste myself on his skin. It's so dirty and so fucking hot I want to scream. I've never tasted myself before and having his fingers thrust into my mouth the same way they plundered my pussy just heightens the experience.

Colton's lips move back to my neck, and he exhales warm air onto the sensitive skin near my ear. I close my eyes and breathe him in while he slides me down the length of his body until the seams of our jeans line up perfectly. Then he slams me into the wall, his lips reclaiming mine as he thrusts against me, dry fucking me into the brick with new vigor.

Rocking against him, I deepen the kiss and devour him like his tongue might hold the answer to every question I've ever asked. This crazed feeling taking over my body is like nothing I've ever experienced before. It might be the culmination of every interaction Colton and I have ever had, or maybe it's just how long it's been for me, but whatever it is, it's not enough.

I need more.

Reaching up, I lock my hands behind his neck and arch my back to give him better access to my core. "Please," I beg, grinding my pelvis against him. "Please."

"I don't have a condom here," he whispers, slowing his movements.

"There is one in my purse." I move to capture his mouth with mine, but he pulls back and sets me back on the ground. With a calloused hand on my cheek he looks at me, his hooded eyes roaming my face before he leans in and steals another kiss.

Slowly, so that I can see every movement, he removes a sleek black gun from the back of his waistband, clicks the safety on, and sets it on the ground before grabbing the condom out of my purse, which has been lying discarded on the concrete this entire time.

He leans down, places a hand in my hair, and kisses me, unhurried, sliding his tongue across my lower lip and pulling away again. "Say it." He slips the condom into my hand, and I fumble with the zipper of his jeans. "Say it, Rylee."

His cock springs from his pants and twitches. It's so incredibly hot that he wants me as bad as I want him. I slide my thumb back and forth over a bead of precum before covering it with the condom.

Colton shudders, picking up one of my legs to wrap it around his waist and leaning into me. "I need to hear you say it," he growls again.

"I want you to fuck me, Colton Archer."

His next movements are so fast, I hardly register what's happening. He whips something out of his pocket and there's a ripping noise a second before cool air hits my pussy through my panties. I catch a glint of metal as his hand slides into his back pocket, and I realize he just cut through the crotch of my shorts with a pocketknife.

Pushing my underwear back to the side, he runs the pad of his thumb over my clit and I moan, closing my eyes and rocking into his movements. Just a few quick strokes and I'm already on the edge. Right when I think it can't get any better, he drives the head of his cock between my pussy lips without penetrating, paying special attention to my swollen clit. It feels incredible, better than it should. Leaning back against the rough brick, I thrust against him until the ridge of his head is right where I want it.

The added friction is too much to bear and my legs turn to jelly. I can't wait any longer and Colton must feel the same because he grunts before grabbing the backs of my knees and lifting me. He lets me change the angle, giving me much-needed time to adjust as I lower myself onto him. Colton's cock is by far the biggest I've ever had, and I catch a small quirk of his lips when he realizes I'm struggling to fit him.

Once he's fully seated inside me, I ride him through the burn and pleasure of adjustment until I'm wetter than I've ever been. I kiss him again, and he kisses me back with renewed force. Then he begins to fuck me in earnest, his movements feverish and vicious, like he still can't get enough of me.

In this moment, I want to give him anything, everything, and Colton seems to have the same idea.

He releases one of my legs and moves a calloused hand to my throat, placing the slightest bit of pressure against my pulse, pinning me in place.

Heat courses through me.

"Oh God." My breathing becomes wild, and Colton's eyes struggle to stay open as he pounds into me with a steady rhythm. "I'm close," I moan.

He pushes me harder into the wall, fucking me faster and

faster, that steady pressure cuffing my throat heightening every sensation until I almost feel high.

It's too good.

Too much.

My pleasure builds, and the muscles in Colton's arms quake. He looks panicked, his brows furrowed and almost confused. "You feel so fucking good, Tiger," he pants against me.

He slows his thrusts, locking eyes with mine. Hand still on my neck, he tilts up my chin with his thumb so that we're eye to eye.

I'm about to come. I want to look away, but I can't. It's like that rope in my rib cage has wrapped itself around him and now binds us together. I don't know what I'm feeling, but it's so much more than I expected.

Each stroke of his cock has pleasure rippling through my entire body in scorching waves, but there's something else, too, something sweet I can almost taste. The pleasure builds until my pussy clamps onto him as my orgasm blasts through my body, robbing me of all rational thought.

"Fuck," Colton grunts between thrusts. "You feel too fucking good. I'm not going to last." He rests his forehead against mine and continues to pump, our eyes still locked, our breath one, until his lips connect with mine and he shudders, spilling himself into the condom right as a second orgasm ravages my body.

Colton's chest rises and falls as he lowers my feet to the ground. He's still inside of me when he wipes my sweat-drenched hair from my forehead. I can barely stay on my feet, and he seems to be struggling just as much, if not more. Sweat dots his brow, his shoulders rising and falling with each sharp breath. He looks beautiful. Younger somehow. Vulnerable. I'd almost say he looks dazed, maybe even like he's in pain?

"Did I hurt you?" I ask, reaching for his face.

He shrugs off my touch and shakes his head. "No, you were perfect." His head keeps shaking as he laughs. "We didn't even make it to the car."

"You cut off my shorts." I'm still breathing hard, but now I'm laughing, too.

Colton rubs his hand over his face. "Fuck."

I couldn't agree more.

Chapter Twenty

Beep. Beep. Beep.

I slam the snooze button on my borrowed alarm clock and blink open my weary eyes. An instant smile spreads across my cheeks the moment the room comes into focus. Despite Holly's lumpy sofa, I haven't slept that hard in years. Turning onto my side, I nestle my face into the collar of the sweatshirt I'm wearing and inhale the distinctive smell of sunshine and cloves.

Colton offered to drive me home last night, and when I declined, he insisted I borrow his sweatshirt to cover up my ripped shorts before he walked me to my car. I was going to decline those offers, too, but when I heard the sound of approaching people from the parking lot, I gave in.

That might have been the best sex of my entire life.

I can't believe it was in public.

Flipping onto my back, I squeal and kick my legs under the blanket on my makeshift couch-bed, only stopping when a slight tenderness between my thighs and a light soreness in my shoulders stills my movements. The memory of being pushed up against the brick as Colton thrust into me has my lower stomach clenching all over again. Need sparks in my veins, warm and unrelenting.

I slide my fingers into my sleep shorts and rub my clit with slow, methodical circles while my free hand wraps around my throat. With memories of last night and the smell of Colton's sweatshirt surrounding me, it only takes a few minutes before I'm coming.

I can't remember the last time I felt this good. Sex was exactly what I needed.

As the morning progresses and I prepare for Holly's return, guilt coats me like a wet blanket. I woke up happy and smiling, even though I know how miserable Holly has been. By the time her car door slams outside, I'm showered, cooking breakfast, and questioning whether or not to tell her about the bar. Should I at least bring up that I now know how Jeremy died? I still have a million questions.

Like, if the sheriff already closed the investigation, then shouldn't we get an attorney or something to reopen it? Logan's dad has connections. Although not ideal, I could call my ex and ask for help. Hell, our dad has money, he could hire an attorney and an investigator. Rick would help Holly in a heartbeat if he knew she needed it, though the thought of calling him and asking for anything still makes me shudder.

I bound to the door and take Holly's bag. Without a word, she bristles past me, heading straight to the bathroom and spilling her guts into the toilet before collapsing on the floor. I grab the paper towels from under the sink and hand her one to clean her mouth with. "I'm taking you to the doctor," I say forcefully. "This has been going on for too long."

"No, I'm fine. One of the other nurses brought shrimp lumpia to work last night, it sat out for eight hours before I got around to eating some. I don't think it's sitting right. It's just food poisoning."

"Are you sure?"

"Positive, but don't touch me. I had some sick patients last night, and I really need to shower."

Hands raised, I back out of the bathroom. I learned the hard way that when Holly says don't touch her, she means it. A few weeks ago, she had to explain to me what C. diff was while she bleached her shoes out on the deck. She recounted a story involving copious amounts of yellow, gelatinous feces that I would rather not relive ever again. Even Holly wrinkled her nose as she told me, like the smell still haunted her. Now, when she says not to touch her until after she's bathed, I listen.

The sound of the shower echoes through the house for twenty minutes, but Holly doesn't emerge. When I open the door to tell her that breakfast is ready, I find her still wrapped around the toilet with one towel draped around her waist and another resting over her shoulders. Judging by her wet hair and the evidence in the bowl, it looks like she got out midshower to throw up again. I crouch down to place a hand on her back, just above a tattoo peeking out from under the towel. I start to move the fabric to get a better look, but only reveal a single wing before she bats me away.

Holly shifts on the floor. When she vomits again, the towel around her waist rides up, revealing the very edge of another tattoo, this one coiling around her upper thigh. I didn't know she had one tattoo, let alone two. But I suppose asking her about them while she pukes her brains out isn't a good idea. After her next round of being sick, she pushes me out of the bathroom, requesting that I "let her die in peace." I leave, but even when I'm back in the kitchen, I can't stop thinking about the tattoos.

Those feathers peeking out from her shoulder looked an awful lot like one of Danny's doves. I don't have long to dwell on it though, because I need to get ready for work.

Begrudgingly, I force myself into a pair of high-waisted, ankle-length jeans. Since my favorite, and only, pair of shorts now have the crotch cut out of them, I'll have to suffer through the heat of wearing pants. I briefly thought about trying to sew the hole, but my sewing skills are limited and I would hate to have a wardrobe malfunction at work.

Holly is still in the shower when I knock to say I'm leaving. Part of me wants to call in sick in case she needs me, but I think Maggie would fire me if I did. Over the past week, she's become less and less tolerant of my little mistakes, and after last night's overheard conversation with Sheriff Knott, I don't want to give her any excuse to get rid of me.

"I'm fine," Holly says between heaves. "I'm glad you're going to work so I can sleep this off. Trust me, I need the quiet."

The diner's parking lot is overflowing, forcing me to park in the adjacent overgrown field. The tall grass nearly reaches my knees, and as I exit my car, something slithers through the bushes to my left. I quicken my steps and rush to the asphalt. My gait feels awkward, and I realize I might be sorer than I originally thought. I try to hide my satisfied smile.

The bell over the door dings and I only make it ten steps inside before Lana is dragging me to the back with a demanding expression plastered on her face. My chest constricts.

Did Maggie see me in the tree line last night?

I wipe my sweaty hands on my jeans as Lana corrals me

next to the fridge and whispers with wide eyes, "Why are you walking funny?"

"What?" Her question is not what I was expecting.

"You had sex last night, didn't you?" When I don't respond, she keeps going. "Judging by that walk, it was good." Her shoulders slump. "Who was it?"

Images of Colton run through my mind like a movie. "No one," I mutter, looking over to Cook, who is pretending we're not in his kitchen.

"Then why are you walking all bowlegged like you had the night of your life?" The corner of her mouth perks up, but there is something else there, too. Jealousy?

"I think I over did it on yesterday's run. Then I spent the morning crouched in the bathroom with Holly after she came home sick from work." I didn't run yesterday, but Lana doesn't know that and something about last night makes me not want to share. That was the best sex I've ever had, and if it was a onetime deal, I don't want to taint the memory by overanalyzing it with a friend.

She grabs an apron off the wall and chucks it in my face. "Fine. Lame, but fine."

The Saturday morning rush is hectic. If I drank more than one beer last night, I'd say a hangover was slowing me down, but really, I just keep looking across the street and blushing every time I see the brick exterior of the bar.

Did anyone see us? More importantly, do I care if they did? I'll be leaving in a few weeks, so it shouldn't matter.

The bell over the door chimes, and Danny's voice briefly echoes through the diner as he greets Lana and a few others. Several older ladies turn to dole out rude stares, but he doesn't let them dampen his spirit. He and Alex give me brief side hugs and take the big corner booth, which has oddly been the only unoccupied table throughout every single one of my shifts, even though it's the best seat in the house. Lana watches our interaction with laser focus, but with the way my heart is thudding in my chest, I hardly notice.

I glance out the window, searching for a green Chevy.

If Danny is here, that means—

No.

I brush away the thought. Colton and I agreed it was just the once. I got it out of my system, and now I need to focus on my future and move on. I need to keep reminding myself that I'm leaving at the end of summer. I shouldn't get excited or nervous about the idea of seeing Colton. He's just a pretty face attached to a perfect body and a huge...

I look out the window one more time and then clear the table, taking the dirty plates to the kitchen and cleaning up my thoughts.

Unfortunately, Maggie is also in the back, training a new dishwasher. She doesn't look pleased to see me. After the way she kicked my car and threatened to collude with Sheriff Knott against me, I can't say I'm too pleased to see her either—which is crazy because until yesterday, I thought she was just uppity. I'd mistakenly assumed she was your run-of-the-mill, cranky middle-aged woman. I had no idea how hateful she could be or that any of those feelings were directed toward me.

Over my shoulder, I ask Lana to pick up Danny's table, and she eagerly agrees. Although part of me is dying to see Colton again, I've never had to talk to a one-night stand the next day, and I'm not sure how I'm supposed to act. This way, on the off chance that Colton does show up, Lana will be their server and I won't need to interact with him.

There, problem solved.

On my next run out of the kitchen, my arms ladened with breakfast trays, I notice Jack, Ashlynn, and the redhead from the bar have now joined Danny at the table. Minho and Colton are conspicuously absent.

Jack waves at me before carrying on his conversation with the redhead. I'm mouthing a silent "hi" when the bell over the door chimes again. I sense Colton before I see him. I can't say exactly how, but I know it's him.

His muscles tense when he sees me, and although I turn away before he has the chance to say anything, I feel his gaze like hot pokers on my back. My eyes flutter closed as I remember his hand on my stomach, his hot breath on my neck. The mere memory of the sensation has me almost dumping a plate of waffles onto one of my patrons. The white-haired woman purses her lips at me. "Just what I need, a third-degree burn from breakfast so close to the anniversary of my Jim's death." She begins brushing off her dress, and the woman she's with clicks her tongue. Several of the ladies seated around them shake their heads in agreement. I've never noticed before, but there sure are a lot of women in this town.

"I'm so sorry, ma'am, did something spill on you?" I scan her up and down for any sign of syrup or food, but she's pristine. Not a crumb to be found.

"No, but you very well could have! Haven't I suffered enough?"

I open my mouth to apologize, but Jack is already looming over the table. "Is there a problem, Ethel?"

The woman, Ethel, darts her gaze back and forth between me and Jack. Her eyes soften when they settle on Jack's handsome, tanned face. "No, no, Jackie. I'm fine. You know how it is around this time of year. Everything seems bigger than it is." She smiles at him and pats the ringed hand he placed on her shoulder. "Will we be seeing you at the memorial?"

Jack lets go of a heavy sigh. "I wouldn't miss it."

Ethel turns to me. "Well, can I have those waffles, or would you prefer I wear them?"

Setting the plates down, I give Jack a grateful smile before hurrying back to the kitchen. Once inside, I lean against the wall. Colton didn't even acknowledge me. I don't know what I expected, maybe a side hug like the one I got from Danny? I think I would have even settled for a small wave, like the one Jack gave me. But really, what sort of greeting *is* proper after you fuck someone's brains out in a parking lot behind a bar?

A small laugh escapes my lips, and Cook gives me a concerned glance from the griddle. I'm definitely overreacting. What was Colton going to do, come talk to me while my arms were full of plates? Interrupt my lovely conversation with Ethel? I snicker again. I shouldn't even be thinking about this right now anyway. Tapping my fingers on the counter, I look over to where Lana is trying to load up six plates onto a tray.

"Hey, Lana," I say, putting myself in her line of sight as she grunts with the effort of lifting the tray onto her shoulder. She's distracted, but that seems to be the only way I get any answers in this town, so I keep going. "What memorial is coming up?"

"What?" she asks, swaying a little. She lowers her voice with a quick glance to Cook. "Do you mean the anniversary of the mine collapse on the fourth?" She frowns and motions to the kitchen exit in a silent plea for me to help. I open the double doors for her, barely missing a tray to the head as she bustles through.

The mine. Of course.

How did I not put it together before? A mining accident. Jesus. In my internet search, the article mentioned that over four hundred people died. I can't even imagine a loss of that magnitude or the effect it would have on the community. Maybe that's why everyone is so weird here? I feel like this is something I should have been aware of before now. All the subtle hints, the picture of the miners from the bar, what Lana said when I asked what happened to her dad...

A crash of shattering ceramic plates and glass ricochets off the walls, followed closely by Lana's voice. "Crap on a stick."

A few of the surrounding diners gasp in horror at her use of language, but this only makes Lana laugh. Danny is the first one off his feet, strolling across the room and dropping to his knees to help pick up the broken plates. I grab a few of the bins we use for busing tables and meet them on the floor, purposefully ignoring the booth where I know Colton must be watching.

Keep it casual, Rylee.

Lana looks up at me with grateful eyes. "At least I got all the food to the table. These were the dirty dishes from table nine."

"Small victories," I assure her while picking up a cracked glass.

I'm still concentrating on not looking in Colton's direction when a sharp stabbing sensation rips through my palm. Something warm trickles down my fingers, but instead of stopping, I reach for the next piece of broken glass.

"Um, Rylee? You're bleeding..." Lana grabs my wrist to stop me.

Danny stops what he's doing, too, and takes my hand from her. "There's a piece of glass in the cut," he says, prodding the flesh of my palm. "Let me get Colt, he has the steady hands—"

"No," I blurt, cutting him off. "I'm fine. I'll go rinse it in the bathroom." I stand abruptly, ignoring the sudden wave of dizziness, and rush to the bathroom, doing my best to catch the dripping blood with my clean hand, but a small trail of red dots the floor in my wake.

The rushing water from the faucet stings as it hits my wound. Luckily, there's enough water pressure that a shard of glass slips out without much effort, but the resulting flap of skin is nauseating. Sighing, I wrap the cut in a paper towel, but when I flex my fingers, a sharp, radiating pain rips through my palm all the way up my arm.

Perfect, either there is still glass in there, or I have permanent nerve damage.

Frustrated, I smack the faucet with my good hand to turn it off. I'm more embarrassed than anything, but still, I shouldn't have let myself get so distracted. And to think, today started off so well.

There is a knock and Lana cracks open the door. Her mouth smooshes to one side. "Mom wants you to go home. Says you can't work with an injury."

"I'm fine, it's not that bad." I lift my hand to show her, but the paper towel is already soaked through with bright-red blood.

"She said it needs to be healed before you can come back in. We can't risk you dropping something hot on a customer."

This can't be happening. "How long does she want me to wait before I can work again?"

"Let's plan for next Saturday." Lana shrugs apologetically and ducks out. We both know there's no use arguing with Maggie, but that doesn't stop the angry heat coursing through my veins or make me want to punch the mirror any less. That's *five* shifts.

Grabbing another wad of paper towels, I slam it onto my palm and apply pressure. Pain pulses through my hand, up to my wrist and down into my fingertips, but I ignore it and rip open the door to the bathroom. With my head down and palm clutched to my chest, I hurry out of the diner.

Once I'm back in the safety of my car, I let out an irritated groan. I lost out on half a day's wages and triple as much in tips today. And now I have to be out until Saturday? How am I ever going to afford to transfer schools without taking on a loan I'll never be able to pay back?

Not that I can actually get in anywhere...

I close my eyes and mash my head against the headrest, the entire car rocking with the violence of my movement. Someone taps on my window, and my lashes flutter open, only to be met with a pair of icy blue-green eyes.

Colton.

Chapter Twenty-One

Colton taps a single tattooed knuckle against my window again, and something in my chest pinches. This is eerily similar to the first time I laid eyes on him at the rest stop all those weeks ago.

He makes a circular motion with his finger for me to roll down the window. I raise my bloody palm. Not going to happen.

Colton's brows draw together and in the blink of an eye, he's ripped open my door and has my hand in his. He peels off the saturated paper towel, and I flinch as portions of it tug at the wound.

With his free hand, he swings my legs out of the car and crouches between them for a better look, one of his hands staying on the back of my knee, gripping me tighter than necessary. "Danny told me you cut yourself," he offers with a quick glance, as if that explains why he's here.

"Do you have some sort of medical background I don't know about? Or are all lawyers trained in first aid?" I ask, trying to sound composed while my pulse pounds in my temples.

"No, but I used to fight a lot." He looks up at me through

his thick lashes and points to a faint white scar over his eyebrow. "Had to learn to patch myself up."

"Oh." I find myself wanting to reach out and touch the scar, to brush the hair away from his forehead and search for others.

I don't. Obviously.

"There is a first aid kit at the office. I can clean this out and close it up, if you'll let me?"

I nod and climb out of my car. He holds my uninjured hand for a few feet before he lets it fall, fisting and flexing his fingers at his side.

It's like a kick to the stomach. Maybe last night wasn't as good for him as it was for me—

No, stop.

It was a one-night stand, the only thing that's important is that I had a good time, and I did. Judging by the satisfied ache in my body, Colton also had a good time. I need to stop ruining it by overanalyzing. I wipe my good hand on my jeans and mentally erect a flimsy wall between us.

We cross the street and head toward the brewery. My pulse kicks up a beat. I must have stared at the Dovetail sign a thousand times from the window at Maggie's, but I've never once considered heading over to check it out. Come to think of it, I've never actually seen anyone go in, but since it shares a parking lot with The Pack, maybe I just didn't notice?

My eyes drift to Colton's shoulders. I know he said that he works for Jack, but it seems odd for an attorney to work out of a place that makes beer.

Throughout the short walk, Colton stays a pace or two ahead. I'm concentrating so hard on being nonchalant about our post-hookup interaction that I only realize we're headed toward The Pack, and not Dovetail, when we're walking through the front door.

"Your office isn't at the brewery?"

"Nope, that building across the lot is just for production. Only the foreman, the brewmaster, and our head of distribution have offices over there. The rest are across town."

Colton leads us through a small door behind the bar and down a wood-planked hallway. Furious typing ticks away from the office to the right, and I peek in to see Minho sitting behind a massive computer monitor. There are several other large screens on his half-circle desk and he seems to be bouncing back and forth between them.

"Alright, Minho?" Colton asks, taking note of his frantic movements.

"No," he replies with an exasperated breath. "I told you I need at least one more body to do this shit properly. Without Jeremy there are too many things to watch all at once." I hear the telltale *pop* of knuckles, then, "But they just made a large cash withdrawal and so far, no one's noticed the siphon."

Minho looks up for the first time and notices me. His eyebrows lift, and he starts to bounce in his seat. "Rylee, my fellow computer goddess, do you—"

"No," Colton cuts him off. "She's hurt. We're just here to patch her up."

Minho blows a raspberry and disappears behind his screens once more. "If you can't help, then get out of my hair."

Colton moves to leave, but I step into the office. "I can help."

Minho's head pops back up with a toothy grin right before Colton grabs my good hand. My head snaps and my hair flies like I'm some sort of cartoon character as he drags me down the hallway.

I am going to get literal whiplash from this guy.

When we're almost to the end of the hall, Minho cries out, "It's inevitable, bro. You're fighting a losing battle!" Colton snorts disdainfully as an emotionless mask takes over his face. I want to tell him I can help, that if it has to do with computers, it's no trouble and I don't mind. I want to ask him what the hell Minho meant by *it's inevitable*, but I also don't feel like poking the bear.

Without warning, Colton grabs my waist and hoists me onto the counter of the small hallway kitchenette. His shirt lifts as he fishes out a large first aid bag from an overhead cabinet, drawing my eyes to his exposed flesh and the gun holstered at his hip. After washing his hands at the small sink, he flushes out my cut with iodine and saline before setting in with a pair of tweezers. If I flinch, he stops and flashes me a pained expression, like I'm the one hurting him, so I do my best to school my face and hide away my emotions. But I've never been a good poker player.

"You don't need to do that. I know this hurts."

"It doesn't. I'm fine," I say, covering my grimace with an awkward smile.

He pulls out a shard of glass, and this time I kick my feet as the nerves in my hand scream in protest. When I stop, he looks at me with a face that shouts *I knew it.*

I roll my eyes. "Fine. It would help if you'd try distracting me."

"My hands are a little busy right now."

"I meant with your mouth." The words are off my lips before I realize their implication. Colton's eyes dart up in surprise, and I blush at my unconscious insinuation.

"Not like that!"

Although that would be a nice distraction...

I bite my lip and watch his gaze follow the movement. He leans forward, and the heat from his body has my head spinning. Right when I think he might kiss me, he blinks—almost as if startled—and drops his head before bringing the tweezers back to my palm.

Disappointment weighs heavily on my shoulders. "I meant you could talk to me. You said you used to fight?"

He looks up at me briefly before answering. "Boxing in high school, mixed martial arts in college and law school. I still get in a fight or two when I can. When the rings are running."

"Ouch." I wince, and Colton takes that as his cue to keep talking.

"I thought about coaching the high school boxing team. I used to help out at their practices for a while."

"Used to? Why'd you stop?"

"Work. Jack had me on assignment *out of town*," he says, like it's a dirty phrase. He also sounds a little ashamed. "Until last night, I hadn't seen the Grace kids in a year. I looked into it this morning. Their mom was injured at her last job and has been out of work for a few months."

"At least they're getting food now," I offer, feeling the need to soothe him.

"Thanks to you. What would have happened if you hadn't taken the job at Maggie's and realized what was happening? I should have been here. I should have known. There are probably others just like them."

Maybe I shouldn't have been so harsh with him at the diner. He seems to have really taken my *out of sight, out of mind* accusation to heart. "You're not responsible for that. How could you have known?" I pause. "You're right though, there are likely others just like them. I wish there was some sort of place they could go after school or on the weekends where they would be safe and we could feed them. Maybe even teach them to cook or help them with homework?"

Colton gives me a look that I can't begin to describe. "What else?"

"I don't know, maybe a couple computers they could use?

I'm sure a lot of kids don't have access to the internet up here. I didn't when I was their age."

"Where would you get the money for something like that?" Colton looks down and won't meet my eyes, suddenly laser focused on placing tiny adhesive strips on my palm.

"I don't know," I admit.

"Well, think. The Grace family, along with most of the families in Eden, don't have enough to pay for after-school care. You can't charge them because they can't afford it. How are you going to pay the employees, rent the space, or keep the lights on?"

"Donations? I'd give my time to a place like that."

Colton shakes his head. "Do you think anyone cares what's happening here in Eden? Or any of the hundreds of other towns like ours? Do you think anyone's willing to do anything about it?"

His eyes meet mine, and it's like he's staring into my soul.

"I care." My voice is small, almost childlike.

He's done with the bandages, but he's still holding on to my hand, his grip borderline painful. "I can see that, but sometimes caring isn't enough. What would you *do*? How far would you be willing to go to make that idea a reality? To help them?"

I don't know what kind of answer he's looking for. Actually, I don't even know what my options are. Up until a second ago, I thought this was all hypothetical. What I do know is that when I close my eyes at night, I see little Anna's dirty face and torn pink tracksuit. I hear the growl of her hungry belly and see her brothers' hollow cheeks. I sit up straighter. "I'd do whatever it takes."

Colton is still gripping my injured hand, eyes roaming my face, when Jack enters the hallway. Colton lets go of me so quickly I almost fall from the counter. Jack does a double take, clearly not expecting to find us here.

"Rylee, I saw what happened," he calls out, taking longer steps to close the distance. "Can I see it?" I give him my hand, and he assesses Colton's work with a critical eye. "Looks good, *mijo*. You did well. But don't think I didn't notice how you left your food uneaten at the diner." Jack pats Colton on the back of his neck with his free hand, and Colton's chest swells at the compliment before he looks away.

Jack releases my hand and clamps down on my shoulder. "He's always looking out for everyone except himself." He gives me a wink. "Looks like your afternoon just opened up. We're headed to the brewery to do a tasting of the new batches. Would you like to join us?"

I rack my brain for an excuse, but I'm caught up on homework and I really don't feel like going for a run with a cut-up hand. Holly is most likely already sleeping, so if I did go home, I'd just be stuck alone and forced to be quiet.

What the hell. Beer might be just what the doctor ordered. "Lead the way."

Chapter Twenty-Two

Hopping off the counter, I follow Jack outside. Colton falls in behind us, and I can't help feeling like his distance is purposeful.

After crossing the parking lot and passing through dual sets of security doors at Dovetail, I'm led to a small outdoor space covered by a wooden pergola canopied in creeping vines. There are several dark-wood tables placed neatly under the rafters and delicate string lights draped throughout the space that I'm sure look whimsical at night.

It's like a private little oasis, secluded enough that you can't hear the noise from the road. I could see myself wasting many an afternoon or evening here, sipping beer and enjoying the breeze.

"Come sit next to me," Jack says, motioning for me to take the bench seat beside him.

As I sit, the set of wood-and-iron double doors we just came through open back up, and an older man sporting a handlebar mustache and overalls walks out carrying seven pitchers of beer. Ashlynn trails behind him with a tray of small glasses, followed by Danny and the redhead in a suit.

Ashlynn's eyes catch mine for a moment, and I give her a soft smile that she doesn't return. A little surprised by the brush-off, I follow her gaze as she glances around the table, noting the way her attention hovers over Colton, who's chosen the seat directly across from Jack and the farthest away from me.

Under the table, my leg starts to bounce.

After Danny takes the seat next to Colton and the redhead finds a spot at the end of the table, Ashlynn asks, "Is it just the five of you?"

"We'll have one more joining us shortly. Everyone else is tied up this afternoon," Jack replies. Ashlynn sets out place settings, which consist of a long sheet of paper with seven shot glasses, and then excuses herself. "Are you not joining us, Ash?" Jack asks with a hint of concern.

She shakes her head. "I'm waiting on an order. Next time, though." She's through the double doors and out of view before I can even process her departure. Jack and Danny exchange a glance.

The doors open again, and I expect to see Ashlynn, but when I look up, it's the sheriff's deputy from Danny's party.

The one who found Jeremy's body.

He nods to Danny and Colton, clasps the redhead with the suit on the back, and comes to shake Jack's hand. "Thanks for inviting me, sir."

"Have a seat, Andy, we're just about to start." Jack gestures to the open space to my right.

Andy looks at me and smiles. "Looks like y'all saved the best seat in the house for me. Is this my initiation present?" He confidently takes the spot next to mine and extends a hand. "Andy," he says, his eyes twinkling in the afternoon sun. I place my uninjured hand in his, and he pulls it closer to his chest. "It's a pleasure to finally meet you, Rylee."

I smile and blush a little. He really is pretty to look at and damn if that uniform doesn't do wonders for his physique. I don't know why he's still wearing it when he's clearly not working, but I'd be lying if I said I hadn't checked out his ass when he walked in. Still, though, I'm not one to jump from one bed to another...or one bar wall to another, I should say.

Across from me, Colton bristles, but before I can figure out why, Handlebar Mustache Man claps his hands together, drawing my attention. "Let's get started." He passes the first pitcher of bubbly, light-yellow beer to Jack, who pours for me before pouring his own and passing along the beer to the redhead.

"Twice a month we taste the product for quality and sample any new flavors. Tommy here is quite the brewer. We stole him from a brewery out in Colorado about ten years ago. He single-handedly made the beer what it is today." Tommy gives me a small smile with a silver shine to his eye.

Jack turns his attention to me. "Do you drink beer?"

"Doesn't everybody?"

The corners of his mouth twitch up. "Your sister doesn't. She and Colton usually sip whiskey during these things just to wash away the flavor." Jack smiles, but Colton only sucks his teeth. "My Jeremy had the real palate. He could have worked with Tommy if he hadn't been so gifted with computers."

The air around the table grows heavy. I lift my glass. "I wish I had known him better. To Jeremy." The table echoes my statement, and we drink in unison.

"Oh, what is that?" I say, as a wash of fruity sweetness covers my tongue.

Tommy smiles widely, and his mustache ticks as he answers, "Strawberry Summer Shandy. My favorite."

We move through the pitchers, tasting twice per batch. Tommy explains the beers to Jack, and the redhead—who's name I've finally remembered is Lee—pops in with questions about which markets certain beers will do better in. After the fifth pitcher, I have a slight buzz, and I stop paying as much attention to the technical aspects of the conversation.

Andy takes this as his opportunity to lean in. "How are you liking Eden?"

"It's beautiful." My eyes long to dart to Colton, but I keep them trained on my glass. "Are you from here?"

Andy takes a sip of the latest beer. It's dark and foamy and sticks to his upper lip. "No, I'm from a town over, but same county." He taps the Marion County patch on his uniform for emphasis.

"I didn't think you were allowed to drink in uniform?" My eyes scan his sculpted body, hovering too long on his bulging biceps.

Crap. I think the beer might be hitting me harder than I thought.

"I'm off duty. I can do whatever I want when I'm not on the clock." He licks the foam from his lip and scoots an inch closer. "Do you have any suggestions how I might spend the rest of my time off duty?" A roguish smile spreads over his lips.

I don't want to give him the wrong impression, so I roll my eyes and change the subject to safer territory. "So, how do you know everyone if you're not from here?"

He puffs out his cheeks and exhales. "I saw a few things on the job that didn't sit right with me." He leans back with two hands on the table. "I approached Jack with the information, which I suppose is why my vetting process has been so long. Hard to trust the nephew of the *evil* sheriff."

"Vetting process? Wait, you're related to Sheriff Knott?"

"Unfortunately. But you of all people know that we can't

always be held responsible for the sins of our family or our fathers." He looks sad, but I don't know what his family relations have to do with me.

"What's that supposed to mean?" I move farther away from him, uneasy with the fact that he's speaking to me like he knows something about my dad and I, and bump into Jack's side.

Andy opens his mouth with a slightly confused set to his jaw, but a deep, gravelly voice stops him from answering.

"You're in my seat," Colton says without an ounce of civility.

Andy raises his hands and slowly stands. "Hey, man, we're just talking."

"I don't give a single fuck what you're doing. I'm telling you the seat next to her is mine. Move."

My stomach flips, unable to decide if I'm angry or turned on by Colton's sudden appearance and overbearing attitude. Is it possible to be both?

Andy leaves, finding space on the other side of Jack while Colton claims the spot next to me, straddling the bench instead of sitting like a normal person. He grabs one of my belt loops and slides me away from Jack until I'm nearly between his thighs. "Are you done?" he asks with a slight shake of his head.

My heartbeat quickens, and I raise a brow at him. "Done with what?"

"Flirting with Andy. It worked, I'm here. Are you done now?"

What an ass.

"Me talking to Andy has nothing to do with you. And I wasn't flirting," I say indignantly.

He sighs and drags a hand across his face with a slap. "You're driving me crazy, Tiger. Last night was a onetime thing, remember?"

I cross my arms over my chest. "Yeah, I remember. I'm just sitting here talking to people who talk to me. How is that an issue?" Bolstered by the beer, I lean closer to him and stare into his eyes. "Speaking of remembering, I thought we agreed not to do this hot-and-cold thing? You can't just tend to my hand one second, ignore me the next, and then accuse me of flirting like I'm not allowed to flirt with whoever I want to. I thought we were friends? If that's not the case, then what do you want from me, Colton?"

Without looking away from my eyes, he says, "I don't know what I want. That's the problem."

After the sampling, we sit around draining the rest of the pitchers. And by we, I mean everyone except Colton. He's silently taken a sip of each sample but not a drop more. I, however, have continued to drink and mull over what exactly he meant when he said he doesn't know what he wants. Does that mean he regrets what we did last night?

While Jack has engaged me in polite conversation, he seems to be the only one who still knows I'm here. Andy won't look in my direction, and Danny only looks over to laugh any time I pout. The whole thing is off-putting and confusing. Actually, I'm a little pissed off at most of the men at the table—even Tommy and his silly mustache for getting me drunk.

When I move to stand, Colton pulls me back down by the same belt loop he hasn't let go of. "Where are you going?"

"I need to pee. Is that okay with you, warden?"

The table erupts in laughter, and a satisfied smirk settles over my lips. If he's going to act like an ass because he regrets fucking me, then I can act like one, too.

"Danny, can you show her inside and give her a ride home?" Jack asks.

"Danny's been drinking," Colton says, as if that's the end of the conversation. I want to interject that I'm fine, but I know I shouldn't drive like this.

"I'm okay to drive," Danny pipes in.

Colton crosses his arms over his chest. "Good, then you can follow behind in her car."

After a quick trip to the bathroom, I head out through the front door. I've barely stepped a foot outside before Colton rips my keys out of my pocket and tosses them to Danny twenty feet away.

"Where are you parked?" Danny calls out with two hands near his mouth. I point to the dirt field, which has mostly emptied, and he proceeds to bound over to my Honda.

When we get to Colton's Chevy, I run my fingers over the faded hood. "Have you ever thought about adding two black racing stripes or giving her a fresh paint job?"

"Absolutely not." He looks offended that I even asked. "This is a 1970 Chevelle with the original paint. Why would I fuck with what's already perfect?" He steps over and opens my door, slamming it behind me once I'm seated.

Jesus, testy much?

We drive in silence, and I bounce my legs while the old engine takes on the ancient roads with a purr. The ride is uncomfortable, tense even. It's like we took two steps forward in our friendship only to fall back down an entire flight of stairs. Maybe it's because we've barely acknowledged that we slept together yesterday? Ignoring casual sex makes it a little less casual.

I clear my throat, the sound cutting through the silent cabin like a knife. "I had fun last night."

The gearshift grinds as Colton sneaks a glance at me and

momentarily loses his footing. After a long pause and a coy smile, he says, "Yeah, me too."

I smirk to myself and when I peek over at Colton, he's running a finger lightly over his lips, exactly where I bit him. He laughs and the wall I erected starts to crack.

"I'm not interested in Andy," I confess.

Colton swallows, his Adam's apple bobbing with the motion. "Good."

Good? Glad we cleared that up.

"Are you coming Wednesday?" he asks with a slight hesitation in his tone.

"To?"

"Jack wanted you to come to the mine. Danny was supposed to invite you last night. The whole town gets together on the anniversary of the collapse. Jack thought it would be a good idea for you to experience more of Eden."

"Danny never said anything."

"Maybe you were a little preoccupied?"

I huff out a breath and the soreness between my thighs pulses. "Little is not a word I would use to describe anything that happened yesterday. I could hardly walk this morning."

I slap my hand to my forehead.

Damn all that beer, where is my filter?

Colton giggles. This grown-ass, tattoo-covered man giggles, and the musical sound has the last bits of the wall I built crumbling down.

Tires crunch over gravel when we pull up to the bungalow. There's a light on inside, which means Holly's awake.

Still, I find myself reluctant to leave. "Colton..." I press on my thighs to keep them from bouncing. "Did it have to be just a onetime thing?"

I regret the words as soon as they're out. What am I even

asking him for? To be fuck buddies? To ravish me right here in this car?

My shoulders curve forward protectively as I fold my hands in my lap.

Colton keeps his eyes forward, jaw tight. "I—" His bottom lip falls slightly agape before he frowns.

He's going to turn me down.

I have to stop him before this gets any more awkward. Even as my heart shrivels from the crushing pressure in my chest, I straighten in my seat and force a fake smile. "I get it. It's probably for the best anyway. Still friends, though?"

He looks away, tilting his chin down with an even more pronounced frown. He almost looks...disappointed? That can't be right. Colton's made many faces in the short time I've known him, but disappointed isn't one of them. I must be reading him wrong.

"Yeah," he says. "Friends. Sounds good."

We sit in silence a long moment, the air thick and weighty, neither of us daring to move a muscle.

When Colton rotates his body, placing a hand on my thigh, my heart speeds up dangerously.

Fuck friendship.

That tiny touch is enough to change my mind all over again. I tilt my head in anticipation of an earth-shattering, soul-crushing kiss, but he keeps rotating and reaches into the back seat to grab something. My lips sour and my stomach plummets. That's the second time I've made an absolute fool of myself in the past five minutes.

He places a small, brown paper bag—similar to what you'd pack a lunch in—onto my lap and leans across me to open my car door. I shrug out from under him before I embarrass myself again and shut the door right as Danny parks behind us in my car.

Danny opens an arm for a hug, and I pull him against my side, grateful for his steady presence. "Thanks for bringing my car."

"Anytime. Hey, did Jack talk to you about Wednesday?"

I lean away. "Colton did. I'll be there."

Danny looks surprised and then confused, like his brows can't decide whether to rest near his hairline or obscure his vision. Finally, he glances toward the Chevy and then back to my face. "Did he now? Interesting. Parking will be tight, so I'll pick you up around noon."

I bob my head, and he hands me my keys before lowering himself gracefully into the green muscle car. Colton revs the engine, gravel spraying across the drive as he cuts an unnecessarily sharp turn.

I make my way up the porch with heavy steps, my injured hand throbbing with the ascent. *I might as well get this over with.* The lunch bag crinkles when I remove the staple and pull out the contents: A pair of black jean shorts in exactly my size.

I shake out the denim to examine them under the porch light, like that will help me decipher what this gift means. It doesn't. If anything, it confuses me further. Not only are they my exact size, but they're the same brand as the ones we ruined.

I'm marveling over how he could have possibly had the time to find and buy these when a single marigold falls from the pocket and floats onto the deck. My heart beats in an off-kilter rhythm as I turn my head toward the road, catching the last glint of Colton's taillights before he disappears down the dusty drive.

Chapter Twenty-Three

Today is the Fourth of July. Independence Day. Not that you'd know it by looking around.

Eden appears exactly as it did the day I arrived. There are no little flags in flowerpots. No cartoon depictions of Uncle Sam in any of the shop windows. There isn't even a hint of red, white, or blue anywhere in sight, and I have yet to see a firework stand.

The only thing that's different from any other day is that every shop is closed and when I went for a long walk in place of my normal run, I didn't see a single living soul. It was eerie. If I'd had a phone on me, I would have checked to see if I missed the rapture or the start of the zombie apocalypse.

After my run, I'd nervously asked Holly if she wanted to come to the memorial with me, and she adamantly declined before heading to bed. She didn't ask who I was going with, and I didn't offer up the information.

I wish we spent more time together. I came here to support and reconnect with her, but all I do is watch her pick at food and sleep. At least she's starting to put back on a little weight, which means she must be doing better, right?

I've been dying to talk to her, though. To tell her that, with Minho's help, I applied to four more universities. They all have great computer engineering programs. One is about two hours away, one's back in Charlotte, and the other two are in Boston, where I know she spent some time after she got out of the Navy. Hopefully, if I'm accepted into one of those schools, she might consider moving with me. I just have to find the right time to ask. It will be good for her to get out of Eden. To not have a daily reminder of what she lost.

Maybe we could actually reconnect if we got away from here.

Although I might be jumping the gun by extending Holly an invitation before knowing where I'm accepted, I don't care. Sometimes you have to let the people in your life know you want them with you.

Musing over what I'm going to say to Holly gets me through folding both our piles of laundry. I set the neat stacks of her clothes on the kitchen table so she can't possibly miss them once she wakes.

By midmorning, the house is dusted and spotless. I even put a roast in the slow cooker, which will be ready in time for Holly to take some to work. Now, the only thing left to do is pick out what to wear for the memorial. It's hot out, but I put on a loose, black sweater and pair it with Holly's black skirt from the other night. I don't know what the protocol is for an event like this, but my outfit is modest and respectful. It should be good enough.

Car tires crunch on the driveway, and I scramble to intercept Danny before he can knock and wake up Holly. In my hurry, I end up stumbling through the door, making more noise than knocking would have. Instead of falling, I slam into a hard chest that smells of cloves and a little like whiskey. Colton braces me by my waist and sets me straight.

I glance up, ready to thank him and expecting to see a small mocking smile, but I'm met with a gaunt face that I barely recognize.

"Colton?" My hand drifts up to cup his face. Instead of pulling away, he leans into it and closes his eyes, and I trail my thumb across the stubble on his cheek and watch as his blue-green eyes flutter open.

He slowly takes my hand, threading his fingers through mine and leading me to a sleek, black SUV parked on the road.

From the driver and passenger seats, Minho and Alex tilt their chins in my direction. In the back, Danny scurries into the third row to make room for me next to Ashlynn. She gives me a polite smile before zeroing in on my hand clasped in Colton's. Her smile doesn't falter, but the tightness in her lips suggests it's taking considerable effort to keep it in place.

The drive to the mine is quiet. Colton keeps his forehead pressed against the glass of the window and doesn't let go of my hand. Actually, when my palm starts to sweat and I try to loosen my fingers, he slides my hand into his lap and gives it a soft squeeze. I squeeze him back and let my free hand rest in the crook of his elbow.

I thought I might be able to ask questions on the drive over, but clearly everyone in the car prefers silence today. At least I'm not overdressed. Ashlynn's wearing a black dress, and the guys are in button-downs and jeans. Minho's the best dressed of us all in his red suspenders and dress pants.

About twenty minutes later, we pass the old sign I saw on my way into town and turn into the mine. After seeing parked cars lining the main road during our drive, I should have expected it, but the sheer number of vehicles here is outrageous. Even inside the gate, each side of the tiny one-lane road is packed. There is no way we'll be able to find parking. I'm about to suggest we back up when Minho pulls into a single open spot near the front next to Jack's two-tone truck.

Colton continues to hold my hand as we walk along a barbed-wire topped chain link fence surrounding several crumbling buildings. My palms sweat with both excitement at being so close to him and nervous anticipation of what this means.

We make our way toward the old entrance, where a crowd has gathered. Just visible above the sea of heads is a beautiful bronze statue of a dove in flight. The sculpture is much newer than the neighboring fence, and appears to be serving as some sort of monument. Its base is surrounded by hundreds of bouquets of flowers and a long plaque etched with names. To the left, a small tent has been erected with a few boxy speakers and a microphone.

Colton leads me to the left, where Jack gives me a quick hello through the curtain of people stationed around him, reminiscent of secret service agents in a protective formation around the president.

As I take in the people near the memorial, I notice the crowd is separated into two groups. The group I stand in is mostly wearing black, their faces painted with somber expressions. The other half is much smaller, dressed in colorful prints with angry eyes all pointed in one direction.

At Jack.

Lana and her mother are in that group, and for some reason Lana won't meet my eye. After a moment or so of trying to catch her attention, she slinks behind a greasy, narrow-shouldered Sheriff Knott.

There is a much smaller third group poised right in the middle, but their only distinguishing characteristic is that they keep their heads pointed straight ahead, occasionally throwing tentative glances to their left and right. Among them is a petite, disheveled woman with a purple, full-length cast on her arm. Anna waves at me with a tiny hand, and I give her a small wave back and stick my tongue out at her, which makes her smile and earns her an arm yank from her mother.

High-pitched feedback screeches, and a small woman with short black hair and dark eyes steps up to the microphone. Colton leans down. "That's Minho's Aunt Jin. She took him and his mom in after his dad died. She works for the mayor now."

"Minho's dad died?"

I don't know anything about these people, do I?

Colton gives me a look that says *not right now*, and I turn my attention back to Minho's aunt.

"Thank you for coming. We're gathered here today to remember the four hundred and eighty-one lives lost on this day twenty years ago. I will ask, on behalf of the mayor and Eastmann Incorporated, that you do not step foot on East Mining Company property. Please stay on this side of the fence. Eastmann Incorporated is not responsible for any injuries that occur on their private property. I will now ask Reverend Tuck to step forward with a prayer."

A kind-looking, mostly bald man in a brown suit approaches the microphone. He lifts his arms, and the crowd bows their heads when he begins to pray.

A buzzing noise takes over my brain as I try to rationalize what I just heard. Eastmann Incorporated? It can't be. There is no way that Logan's family is somehow involved in the mining accident that killed so many people in this tiny town. It has to be some sort of freak coincidence, right?

And yet, Logan did always keep his family and the business side of his life separate from our relationship... Maybe there was a reason for that.

No.

There is no way.

The reverend finishes his prayer, and as he does, several of the people surrounding Jack, including Ashlynn, glance my way with less than welcoming expressions. Colton repositions himself so I'm mostly out of view from the mean-mugging offenders, but I can't shake the feeling that somehow everyone knew about my connection to Logan's family—not that I'm admitting they are connected to what happened here.

I shift on the balls of my feet and tap my fingers against my thigh as a ceremonial wreath is placed on the head of the dove. After a short speech from the mayor, parts of the crowd disperse while others head toward the fence with coolers and lawn chairs in tow.

Within a matter of minutes, the iron lock on the gate is cut open and tent canopies are being hoisted into place. Colton lets go of my hand to help carry a cooler, and I busy myself, trying not to get lost in the throng of movement.

A moment's distraction has me swept along with the horde marching onto East Mining Company ground. I soon find myself pressed against a second chain-link fence, staring into a giant sinkhole. Chunks of concrete and partially submerged brick line the bottom, and a single crumbling wall stands guard at the leftmost edge.

It's horrifying. If anyone was in that building when it collapsed, they would have been swallowed whole. My throat constricts and I audibly gulp. I want to step back, to move away from the terrible sight, but all around me others press toward the fence to get a better view. I'm pinned. Forced to watch their grief and overwhelmed by the sheer magnitude of the gaping pit in front of me. Tears prick my eyes as the fence grates painfully against my rib cage and into my injured hand.

Then the crowd stills. While some form the sign of the cross, others murmur words of silent prayer. I use their reverence to make my escape. I back away, not caring who I bump into, until I run into Ashlynn. She takes one look at my face and grabs my elbow, leading me away.

We stop at a blue-topped canopy, and she sits me in a folding chair, smoothing back my hair. "Hey, you're okay," she coos.

"No. I'm not," I croak. "What the hell happened here? Four hundred and eighty-one people?" I sound hysterical.

"Shit," she whispers, taking the seat beside me. "You really don't know, do you?"

"Why do people keep saying that to me?" I'm trying to keep my voice low but there is a panic-stricken pitch to it that makes a few heads turn in our direction.

"Okay, *shhh*." She sighs. "If you can keep your voice down, I can explain." She looks a little annoyed as she glances over to where Jack's gathered a small crowd. He's currently touching shoulders and hugging crying women. Danny and Colton stand at his side, writing things down in a notebook like scribes following a general. Once Ashlynn's sure they're not listening, she continues.

"Twenty years ago, East Mining Company was the only job in Eden. Nearly everyone worked for the mine. They were underpaid with no benefits, no insurance, and barely any days off. But there wasn't another option. The company started off offering fair wages, but once they ran every other business out of town, they started paying less and less every year. At the time, Jack was one of the people advocating for a worker's union. He was trying to get everyone safer working conditions or health benefits at the very least. The owner of the mine hated this and threatened to fire everyone if they unionized.

"A few of the men, including Jack, were so insulted by his threats that they began reporting the unsafe conditions to one of the national reporting agencies." Her eyes dart briefly back to Jack. "On the day of the collapse, Jack was in a small car accident on the way to work. He was supposed to be meeting a team of government officials to walk them through the mine to point out the safety issues. Instead, he had to call one of his buddies who was off that day and ask him to take his place.

"Around three o'clock that same day, there were a few loud pops reported. People in town brushed it off as fireworks until they saw the massive plume of brown dust. Everyone rushed over to the mine. Not only had there been a collapse, but the aftershocks caused that sinkhole over there to swallow up the administrative offices on this end of the property."

She looks over to where Alex has his arms wrapped around Minho, the sides of their foreheads pressed together as they stare at the gaping hole in the earth.

"That's awful. How many people made it out?" I ask.

"One."

"How is that possible?" Chills cover my body. "Who was it?"

"Mike Cook, the fry cook over at Maggie's Diner. But technically he wasn't in the mine, he was in the elevator shaft when it happened."

Cook? My sweet, silent coworker? That poor man. The survivor's guilt he must feel...

My mind races. "What were the loud pops?"

Ashlynn shakes her head and looks down. "No one knows for sure. Cook hasn't said a word since he crawled out of that shaft. Jack says there were safety issues, but only a planned demolition could have caused a collapse of that magnitude."

My blood runs cold. "Are you saying that it wasn't an accident?"

"Yes." She pauses. "There wasn't even a payout to the families. The owner had to fork over a small fine, and that was that. They put this fence up around the property and called off the rescue effort after two weeks." She spits on the ground, the perfect ringlets of her loose curls bobbing with the action.

I can't breathe.

So many people gone in an instant. So much corruption. Poor Cook. Poor Eden. If this happened twenty years ago, why hasn't anyone done anything? It's disgusting that the owner of the mine was allowed to walk away scot-free after so much devastation.

The owner.

The hairs on my arms lift in slow motion as the puzzle pieces fall into place.

"Who owns the mine?" I blurt.

She looks at me, silently asking if I'm really going to make her say it.

"Who owns the mine, Ashlynn?"

"I think you already know the answer."

"Say it anyway."

"East Mining Company is a subsidiary of Eastmann Incorporated. Charles Eastmann owns the mine."

Chapter Twenty-Four

"Charles Eastmann? My ex's father? You've got to be shitting me." I stand and begin pacing. "And you're saying the collapse was purposeful, that he had something to do with it? Is that why I get all the weird looks? People think I knew?" I run my hands through my hair. "Fucking hell, Ashlynn."

I'm glad I never met Logan's dad, the fucking murderer.

Did Logan know? He couldn't have. He'd be devastated if he knew and there is no way he'd continue working for the family business.

Slamming my ass back into a chair, I dig my fingers into my scalp. I feel so dirty. I unknowingly lived in a loft paid for by Logan's job with Eastmann Incorporated. I shake my hands out in front of me. I need to shower. I need to run, but I settle for standing back up and pacing again.

Danny walks over after noticing my distress and nudges Ashlynn. "What happened?"

Ashlynn crosses her arms over her chest and waves a hand in the air. "She's connecting some dots about her ex's family."

"Oh." Danny brings a hand to his chin. "See, told you she didn't know."

"Clearly, I believe you now," Ashlynn grumbles.

Danny places an arm around my shoulder. "It's okay, Rylee. It's not your fault. It's not like you're the one that killed my mom. Just your ex-boyfriend's prick father."

He's trying to make light of the situation, but a bout of nausea racks my stomach so hard my lip quivers. "Your mom?" I ask quietly. Oh God. Her accident wasn't an accident. She must have worked in the administrative building.

My eyes dart to the sinkhole, and a silent sob escapes my lips. Danny wraps me in a hug, and Ashlynn hands me a beer. She's clearly uncomfortable, but at least she's not looking at me with mistrust anymore. How could she think I knew about Logan or about his father's company? More importantly, how did she even know about Logan and me in the first place?

Poor Jack.

Handing off my beer, I stride toward him, my skirt billowing behind me. I'm fairly certain I'm flashing anyone bothering to look, but I don't stop moving until I barrel into Jack, crushing him with the most supportive hug I can muster. The few remaining people around him disperse, and he tilts my face up to get a look at me.

"I'm so sorry," I mutter. "He needs to pay for this. I promise I didn't know, but now that I do, I want to kill him for what he did to this town." I sound like a child threatening retribution I'm not capable of, but I don't know what else to say.

How do you live with this sort of knowledge?

How do you move forward?

Jack hugs me, patting my upper back. "It's not your fault, *cariño*. But thank you for caring."

I wipe my eyes and adjust my posture, suddenly ashamed

of my outburst. Today is not about me. "What can I do? How can I help?"

Jack's eyes twinkle, and he glances over his shoulder to Colton, who remains standing right behind him like a silent sentinel.

"Today? Nothing. Today is a day of remembrance. We spend the day here, with the people who never came out of the ground, to show them they are not forgotten. We show them that we have not stopped fighting." He places a hand on each of my shoulders. "Today we remember, tomorrow we return to the fight."

Turns out, remembering means getting shit-faced.

The crackle of bonfires and the somber clink of toasting glass bottles sound from all around the condemned mine. What started off with the quiet exchanges of hugs and tentative sips of alcohol has slowly morphed into beer guzzling and people half slumped in their chairs.

Everyone is drunk.

They drink to celebrate the lives of those lost.

They drink to forget their pain.

It's as if the lack of justice and retribution against the man responsible has kept their wounds open and festering.

Across the fire from me, Danny takes a swig straight out of a whiskey bottle and passes it around our small circle. The bottle skips over Jack, who hasn't been drinking but has been silent since he folded in on himself hours ago. Alex and Minho each take a sip and then continue watching the fire, as if in a trance. Minho lost his father in the collapse, and Alex lost a cousin and an uncle.

There are other faces, both familiar and not, scattered

around the nearby fires, but Colton's been conspicuously absent since sunset. The last time I saw him, he was so wasted he could barely walk, which seems to be the common theme around here. Actually, the only one besides Jack that's keeping it together is Ashlynn.

"Did you lose someone in the collapse?" I ask as she passes me the whiskey bottle.

"I'm not from Eden," she says with a small shake of her head. "I'm from a small mining town in Pennsylvania. My dad runs another branch of the club up there."

"Of the Jackals?" I clarify, not expecting an answer.

"Mm-hmm," she hums, taking back the whiskey bottle when she notices I'm not drinking.

Around us, fires start to sputter out. Danny stands and shuffles over to take the bottle from Ashlynn. He takes a large swig of the light-brown liquid and plops down between us on the ground, wiggling his hips and shoving us aside until there's enough room for him to fit.

He puts an arm around each of our shoulders, the bottle clinking against my collarbone. "Ladies, it's almost midnight. We should start packing up and head back to my place."

"What about Colton?" I ask.

"We can find him before we leave. He likes to stay with them as long as possible. This is the only day of the year he really lets himself feel it."

"With them?"

"Colt lost both of his parents that day."

"Fuck," I say, my throat going dry.

"I sometimes forget that you don't know." He squints and pushes out a heavy sigh. "After the collapse, Colton was alone in his house for nearly three weeks waiting for his parents to come home. He was six."

Danny takes two more big mouthfuls of whiskey and passes

the bottle across the fire to Minho. "Both his parents were at work that day. It was chaos. No one thought to check on him. No one knew what to do. I mean, a fourth of the town was dead. The rescue effort itself opened up two new sinkholes and killed ten rescue workers. We only realized he'd been alone after Jack found him in the forest near our house. He was starving and terrified."

Danny glances up to the hillside and hiccups, slurring, "My house was five miles from his. Can you imagine a six-year-old walking five miles? When Dad asked Colt why he didn't leave sooner, Colt said he only left his own house because he ran out of stuff to eat and that he didn't need help. I guess he's always been a stubborn motherfucker."

Ashlynn excuses herself to start packing up with Minho and Jack. Danny wraps his arm tighter around my shoulder. "Jack took him in, and Colt became my brother that day." He laughs. "He refused to call Jack dad. So Jeremy and I started calling him Jack, too, that way we were all on equal footing in the house. No brother above the other."

My chest cracks with the tenderness of his words.

"It did something to him, though, all those weeks on his own. He still hates being in the house alone. I hear him scream in his sleep sometimes." Danny sits up straighter and pulls back his arm. "Fuck, I'm drunk. Don't tell him I said that, okay? He'd beat the shit out of me if he knew."

I bob my chin and force back the tears threatening to spill. I can't imagine a child having to go through all that. They all lost someone, but Colton lost everyone. I'm sure there are others like him, too.

"Where is he?" I stand, brushing the dust from my skirt.

Danny casts his eyes back to the ridge overlooking the sink-hole. "Somewhere up there."

Sticks and blades of grass reach for my lower legs like small greedy hands as I follow a thin, overgrown trail up the ridge-line. When I reach the crest, I find Colton perched atop a large, flat rock with his legs dangling dangerously over the edge and a half-empty bottle of amber liquid clutched in his hand.

I take a seat next to him, and my head instantly spins at the sight of the drop.

Scooching back from the edge, I tuck my knees under my chin and look out at the view. All around the sunken ground below, glowing ochre bonfires blink out of existence.

Colton swirls the bottle. "How's your hand?"

I run a finger over the bandage on my palm. "Tender, but fine."

He makes a humming noise. "Is it close to midnight?"

"I think so. Everyone's packing up." I wrap my arms tighter around my legs and rest my chin on my knees.

"And you thought it was a good idea to hike up here with a fucked-up hand and in a skirt? I thought you were smarter than that, Tiger."

It sounds like he's trying to pick a fight, but I'm not going to rise to the occasion. "I didn't want you to be alone, but I can leave." Although I make the offer, I don't move a muscle. If he wants me to go, he'll have to say so.

After a stretch of silence, the crickets start to chirp and a breeze rustles through the trees and grass, drowning out the noise from the people below.

It feels like the world itself forgot we exist.

After another long stretch of quiet, Colton leans forward, clasping his hands together over the bottle neck and resting his elbows on his knees. His hair falls into his eyes, and the tattoo on his hand flexes as he stares straight down into the pit. "Did someone tell you they're all still down there?" His lips twitch into a scowl that is eerily similar to the Jackal's on his neck. "Not one of them made it back up. I watched in 2010 when those miners in Chile were rescued after sixty-nine days underground. I watched again in 2015 when the Tanzanian miners were brought up after forty-one days. Do you know what the difference is between what happened there and what happened here?"

I shake my head, unsure if he expects a response.

"The difference is those were accidents. Here, there was no one to rescue because they were executed. Dead after the first detonation collapsed the entire mine. There was no one left to save. Fucking Eastmann got a payout for it, too. Not only did he have insurance on the mine, which was no longer making any real money for him, but he also had insurance on all his workers. He actually *made* money from their death. It's fucking disgusting."

"I didn't know." I reach out and take one of his hands in mine. "I'm so sorry. I swear I didn't know."

He looks at our hands, and his expression softens a fraction. "I believe you."

"He's going to pay for this, right? We're going to make him pay? I could tell Logan, maybe he could do something?" I refuse to believe Logan knew.

Colton shakes his head. "I'm going to take everything from him. Destroy his whole fucking empire."

"Good," I say back, surprised at my own bloodlust. "Someone needs to."

Chapter Twenty-Five

As the only sober party present, I draw the short straw and have to drive everyone back to Danny's.

Apparently, the tradition is that they all get together to play board games and chase away the melancholy of the day with more alcohol. Everyone's in a better mood now that we're leaving—everyone except Jack, who looks crestfallen, like he's reliving the loss of his wife and friends all over again. Still, he helps us load the SUV, makes sure I'm sober, and ensures that we all have our seat belts on before he lets us leave. I invite him back to Danny's, but he respectfully declines and checks my seat belt one more time before shutting my door with a wink.

I feel like a little old lady as I push the button to slide the driver's seat forward and adjust the mirrors to my height. Even with the adjustments, I have to sit on the edge of the seat with my best posture just to see over the dash. By the time I pull into Danny's driveway, my back is exhausted from the effort.

Danny's house looks different when it's not full of partygoers. Last time I was here, the boisterous crowd gave it a bit of a frat vibe. Without all the commotion, it really is a beautiful home, complete with a manicured lawn and neatly trimmed shrubs. I only have a second to admire it before a laughing Danny falls out of the back seat and lands facedown on the driveway. Colton takes a step to help him up, but trips over his own feet and ends up splayed out right next to him. They take one look at each other and burst into uncontrollable, high-pitched laughter.

Minho wobbles up to them and places his hands on his hips. "How drunk are you dipshits?"

"Sober enough for this," Danny shouts, and with movements quicker than my eyes can catch, Minho's feet are swept out from under him and he's locked into a wrestling match with Danny and Colton.

Alex walks up and stops beside me. "Are they always like this?" I ask, staring disbelievingly at the tangle of arms and legs tussling before us.

"Unfortunately."

"Kinda makes a girl feel left out."

"I know what you mean." His shoulders bounce as he leads me in through the open garage. Inside, Ashlynn is busy in the kitchen making what looks like Bloody Marys.

"Is more alcohol a good idea, Ash? I think they've had enough for today," Alex says, taking a seat at the island.

"I went light on the vodka." She shrugs. "Plus, look at the clock. It's officially a new day. The vitamins in here will help with their hangovers later." She grabs a packet labeled Hangover Cure from the pantry and dumps the contents into the Bloody Mary mix before pouring out five glasses. She hovers over the sixth glass and looks at me. "Are you staying for a while?"

I hadn't thought about it, but without my car and no one sober enough to drive me home, I think I'm sort of stuck. "I'm not sure—"

"She's staying," Danny says, entering through the garage. He has a swollen lip and is trailed by a bickering Colton and Minho. Colton's eyebrow is busted open, a delicate trickle of blood running down the length of his face. Minho's clothes are ruffled, but he's the only one not visibly injured.

"Did you win, dear?" Alex calls out.

Minho straightens his shirt and hooks his thumbs through his ruby suspenders. "Of course I did."

"That's my man," Alex replies, standing to offer Minho his seat and placing a soft kiss on his head.

Ashlynn fills the sixth cup and passes out the glasses. She raises her drink. "To a new day."

Her words are repeated, and Danny raises his glass, clasping me on the shoulder. "To family."

"To family," we repeat, drinking our fill of the most disgusting Bloody Mary I've ever tasted.

There are coughs and sputters, followed immediately by the sound of Alex ripping open the refrigerator door. He begins pulling out ingredients and setting up an assembly line of pickles, bacon, cheese, and hot sauce before adding them to everyone's drink. The result is something much better, but still not anything I would classify as appetizing. When he sees my pursed lips, he adds a splash of lime and another hit of hot sauce to mine and suddenly the concoction becomes tolerable.

The next few hours are spent laughing and playing dominoes. There's a moment where, midlaugh, I glance around the table and realize how easy it is to be here with these people. I smile wider and laugh easier with them than I ever have with anyone else, including Holly. My insides feel like they're full of glowing embers.

Warm.

Safe.

As I scan their faces, which are in various stages of cracking up, my own smile starts to strain my cheeks. Despite what I learned today, being a part of this group of friends makes me feel like I can handle anything. Makes me feel like I belong. Since our conversation at the mine, even Ashlynn seems to be warming up to me.

The table juts forward as Minho stands and immediately tips over. From his position on the floor he says to Alex, "I don't think I can walk home."

"The bed in the spare room is yours, unless Colt wants to let you guys use his." Danny looks at Colton, who I hadn't realized also lives here, but Colton just shakes his head, rubbing his eyes as if fighting off sleep. All that alcohol must finally be catching up to him.

Ashlynn laughs in a musical tone. "Um, I don't think so. I have permanent dibs on Colt's bed." She gets up and saunters away, my body turning to stone in her wake. Colton's eyes snap open like he's suddenly awake and eager to follow her.

A cold knot settles in my stomach.

Permanent dibs?

Is that why she's been so reserved around me? Colton made it abundantly clear that what we did was a onetime deal. Was that because of her?

With the hand holding and everything else, I thought that...

A strained grunt interrupts my spiraling thoughts as Alex and Colton hoist Minho off the ground. They heft his half-conscious form between their shoulders and carry him down the hallway toward the spare bedroom. Two separate doors open and close, and after a minute or two of silence, it becomes clear that Colton isn't coming back.

My head falls forward until my forehead slams onto the live-edge table with a loud *whack*.

How could I be so stupid?

Danny chuckles and begins collecting glasses. "Help me

clean up? The box for the dominoes is on the chair next to you."

I lift my heavy head and start placing the dominoes in the hand-crafted wooden box with sloth-like speed. Somewhere in the house the hot water heater gurgles angrily and a shower turns on. The cold, hard feeling in my stomach leaches into my extremities. I wonder if that's Minho and Alex, or are Ashlynn and Colton showering together? I imagine both of the latter two's perfect, tattooed bodies dripping wet and tangled together.

My cheeks and neck flush and I have to blink away the tears pooling on my lower lids.

"So," Danny says, seeming much more sober than earlier this evening and entirely oblivious to my internal meltdown, "Jack told me what you said today at the mine. About wanting to help the club. Did you mean that?"

I blink a few more times and place another domino in the box. "I still don't really understand what *the club* is. But I meant what I said. I don't know what I have to offer, but Eastmann Incorporated has to be held responsible for what happened."

"It's not just Eastmann Incorporated. There are thousands of other companies like them and countless men like Charles Eastmann. Eden isn't the only place where something like this has happened." He places a rinsed glass into the dishwasher. "Haven't you ever wondered what Holly saw that made her leave the military?"

I shake my head, too embarrassed to voice my confession. I always assumed it just wasn't for her.

"Did you know the Army sends their engineers into developing nations to practice building hospitals and schools? Or that some companies outsource jobs so they can use cheaper, younger labor with less safety regulations? Or that rumors have been circulating that government and pharmaceutical companies are illegally trial running new medications on unwitting and impoverished populations under the guise of free health care?" He laughs bitterly. "Holly and Jeremy were both running from the truth until they saw it firsthand. That's why they both got out. They were tired of being on the wrong side."

I shake my head. I haven't had time to process what I learned about the mine, now this? My face contorts into a pronounced frown as I try to comprehend.

Danny shakes his head, and his tongue darts out to the small cut on his lip as he thinks. "Minho needs help."

My head tilts to the side. "I think he's just drunk. I'm sure Alex has it covered."

"That's not what I meant. If you really want to help us, you'd do it by helping Minho."

"By *us*, do you mean your club, the Jackals?" I feel silly using the word *club*, like we're kids again, but Danny doesn't bat an eye.

He nods and starts loading the bottom rack of the dishwasher. "I can't really give you more details yet. You should know, though, that what we do is illegal and dangerous. But we also do a lot of good."

This is the sort of thing you read about in fiction or see at the movies. "I feel like you're asking me if I want to take the red pill or the blue pill... How can I say yes without knowing what I'm signing up for?"

"That's a choice only you can make."

"I'm assuming you can't tell me what illegal activities you're involved in?"

"Minho said you may have overheard something outside his office. I'm sure you can put a few things together."

I rack my brain for what I heard outside his office the day I sliced open my hand. Something about bank withdrawals? A siphon? Do they monitor bank accounts? Play the stock market? I shrug and move my head slowly from side to side. "Can you at least tell me what good things you do?"

"We help the community. We create jobs. We give out interest-free loans. We started a construction company that built this entire neighborhood and created even more jobs. Now that same company is renovating Main Street, bringing in tourists and more cash to the town. We provide people stuck under the thumb of men like Charles Eastmann a way to get out and make a life for themselves."

One of my eyebrows perks up. "Sounds too good to be true."

"Everything has a price, especially being a Jackal. Normal people with normal lives don't get executed in the street for trying to do the right thing, like Jeremy did."

His last words hang heavily in the air. I gulp. If this is real, then the Jackals are accomplishing more than I could have dreamed of doing. But it could be dangerous.

Shit. Am I seriously considering joining what sounds like a do-gooder gang?

The thought is so comical I have to stifle a giggle. Maybe I'm drunk.

"Where do you get the money to do all that?"

Danny pulls his lips into an exaggerated frown and raises an eyebrow, the expression very Robert De Niro and screams *do you really think I'm going to tell you that right now?*

He closes the dishwasher and leans across the counter, taking my hands in his. His stare is intense as his dark eyes bore into me. "You need to think about this. It's more than a huge commitment, it's a blood oath. It won't be easy. This is our entire life. People get hurt. Jeremy died." He squeezes my hands, and his mouth twists open as if he's stuck on what to say next. His jaw settles, like he's resigned himself to say what's on his mind. "Rylee—"

A door smashes open followed by loud thundering footsteps. Colton takes one look at my hands in Danny's, kicks a chair, and tosses his hands in the air before storming outside. He slams the sliding door closed with such force that it bounces back open. How the glass doesn't shatter upon impact is beyond me.

With a sigh, Danny releases my hands. Only then do I realize how intimate we must have looked, hand in hand, leaning in toward one another over the counter.

Good.

I hope Colton thinks something is going on. He deserves to feel a fraction of what I've been going through since Ashlynn announced her *dibs,* especially if they've been together this whole time.

Serves him right.

Danny inhales, overinflating his lungs as he watches Colton's shadowed form make its way through the yard. "We unloaded a lot of information on you today. Get some sleep, and I'll take you back in the morning. We can talk about this tomorrow."

He's right. This isn't a decision I should make tonight, and definitely not one I should make without asking for more details. Honestly, this all feels like a fever dream at this point. My whole world view has been turned upside down. "Do you have blankets for the couch?"

"Fuck no, you can take my room. I washed the sheets this morning, and you can borrow some clothes. It's bad enough that I drank so much that I can't drive you home. Colt is usually the designated driver and I guess I got used to not having to worry about that. He doesn't normally drink as much as he did tonight." Danny gives me a half grin and touches his stomach like he's already feeling the effects of his impending hangover. "The least I can do is let you sleep on a real mattress. I'll take the couch. I'm out here every other night anyway. The noise from the TV helps me fall asleep."

I take a quick peek into the living room where a navy-blue pillow and blanket sit crumpled on the sofa. It makes me think he's telling the truth. Still, the thought of stealing someone's bed doesn't sit right with me. I open my mouth to decline, to insist I be the one to sleep on the couch, but a yawn smothers my argument before it begins. Danny takes this as his opportunity to playfully push me toward the hall in the direction of his bedroom. Holly used to push me around playfully like this when I was younger. It's kind of nice having someone look out for you in a brotherly fashion.

Five steps away from the kitchen, Danny belches, blowing his rancid breath in my direction. His burp smells like spicy bacon and old beer, and for some reason it makes me want to double over with laughter. I must be more tired than I thought. Bodily functions are not usually part of my sense of humor. I turn to push him away from me or smack him, but as I do my laugh lodges in my throat. Colton is staring at us from the patio, his mouth set in an almost snarl.

Oblivious to our possibly homicidal spectator, Danny points me in the direction of his bedroom with a forceful nudge. Inside, he shows me to the bathroom and hands me a clean towel, one of his T-shirts, and a brand-new pair of boxers. He makes a big show of tearing the plastic wrapping open in front of me before dangling the black briefs between us. "These are too small for me, but I figure they're good enough to sleep in?"

He glances at me hesitantly, and I shrug, taking the boxer briefs with a quick "thank you." Minus the crotch flap, they're similar to my running shorts. I couldn't care less if they're technically men's underwear. He leaves me to bathe, and I hear the soft click of the bedroom door closing a second later.

In the shower, I scrub myself clean, tinging the water with bits of gray and brown earth from the mine. The scent of Danny's shampoo fills the steamy air as I dig my sudsy fingers into my scalp and scrutinize everything I learned today, trying not to think about Colton.

What a roller coaster of emotion.

Logan's father is a murderer. I don't technically have proof, but something in my gut tells me I can trust Jack. That I can believe what Danny and Ashlynn told me, even if I do currently want to throttle Ashlynn in her sleep.

Hot water pelts my flesh, turning my skin an angry red as my mind flashes to the faces of the crowd gathered at the memorial service. To the sinkhole. To the bits of mangled elevator shaft still half buried in the clay after twenty years.

I close my eyes and see Cook with his scarred hands and sad eyes. I see Jack and the weight he must be carrying with those strong shoulders of his. I see Colton's face when I opened the screen door this morning, his expression as he sat perched atop the boulder overlooking the grounds that still entomb his parents and 479 others. I imagine him as an orphaned six-year-old, starving because his mom and dad never came home. I see Danny's face in the kitchen just minutes ago, asking me if I really want to help them.

The soap-streaked, murky water swirls the drain before finally running clear, and I exit the shower.

Although clean, I smell distinctly of Danny. I never realized before, but he smells exactly like his cedar and citrus bodywash. It's a comforting, homey scent that somehow settles my nerves. Fresh and calm, I climb into his oversized bed.

As promised, his navy-blue sheets are crisp and clean, crinkling when I shift around to get comfortable. Once I'm settled, there's a soft knock at the door, and I smile to myself when I realize Danny has come to check on me. I feel like I missed out on having a brother by not coming here sooner—having two brothers, really, if I include Jeremy in that depressing train of thought.

I'm not wearing a bra though, so I pull the comforter up to my chin and make sure I'm decent before responding with a quiet "come in," keeping my voice low so as to not wake Alex or Minho in the next room.

To my surprise, it's not Danny who enters.

It's Colton.

I sit up straighter as he takes a quick scan of the room. He fidgets with a bundle of clothes in his hands and hangs his head. "Can I use Danny's shower? Ashlynn's in mine."

I nod, my heart racing. His eyes bounce across the bed and around the room again, almost as if he's checking to make sure I'm alone, before he disappears into the bathroom. I don't breathe until I hear the water from the shower hitting the tile. Then, without warning, my imagination once again conjures up an image of Colton's chiseled, tattoo-covered body in the shower—only this time, it's me in there with him.

I shove my face into a pillow and scream.

How I can go from being furious at him to wanting to jump his bones in a matter of seconds is beyond me.

If he's with Ashlynn, why did he come in here to shower? Was it just to torture me? To show me that our single night together really meant nothing to him?

I turn over and shriek into the pillow again. This feeling, whatever it is, is suffocating.

The hot water heater gurgles down the hall while I search for shapes in the ceiling texture to distract myself. Unfortunately, every shape turns into something that reminds me of Colton.

A rose.

An eagle.

A dick.

I tap my fingers over my stomach. With every second he's in there, my anger rises closer to the surface. I need to get my emotions under control. Colton made it clear that what we were doing behind that bar was just sex. Rational me knows he does not need my wrath after the horrible day he had. Irrational me is a different story. Irrational me hates the idea that he might leave this room and search for comfort in Ashlynn's arms —or worse, between her legs.

What feels like decades later, Colton walks out of the bathroom in a pair of black sweats and a dark-gray T-shirt with a skull on it and Fiend Club in big white letters along the bottom.

It's almost comical how perfectly that describes this demon who's clearly come to steal my sanity.

He stares at the door leading out of Danny's bedroom, hesitating. A single drop of water drips from his head onto the floor.

"Can I stay in here, with you?" he asks, not turning to face me.

I cross my arms over my chest. "Won't Ashlynn be waiting for you?" I cringe at the ring of jealousy in my words and readjust myself in the bed, hopeful that the noise might muffle the bitterness.

"No." He shakes his head and more water droplets fall to the ground.

"Is there something going on between you two?"

"No."

"Does she know that?"

"I thought she did."

I sit up entirely. "Colton, I understand that you don't owe me any explanation. But if you want to sleep in here, I'm going to need a little more information. I'm not going to step on anyone's toes. If you and Ashlynn have something messy going on, I really don't need any more complications in my life right now."

Colton throws a towel over his head and drags it down his face.

"We slept together a few times. I thought it was casual. She never seemed interested before. I assumed we were on the same page, but I guess I was wrong. Tonight, I made it clear that it's never going to happen again."

The news that they've been together prickles, but the sensation is almost immediately soothed by the fact that he officially ended it and then came here.

Why would he do that unless—

"Listen, I promise I won't try anything, but I can't go back to my room, and my head hurts. Today has been absolute shit."

I feel the ice around my heart melting. "One more question?"

He nods.

"When was the last time?" I hate that I'm asking, but for my sanity, I need to know.

Colton pauses. "A year ago."

The breath that whooshes out of me is pure relief. The burning acid in my stomach stops churning and the tense muscles in my shoulders release their grip. I didn't know him a year ago. He didn't know me. At least I can rest assured that I didn't sleep with a man that already belonged to someone else. I'm not the other woman.

I scoot over and lift up the comforter to make room for him. I expect a smirk or a witty comment. I expect some sort of reaction, but I only get the same loathsome expression of grief he wore this morning. He looks defeated, like the day's events, and maybe even the conversation with Ashlynn, have finally exhausted him and he's ready to tap out.

He crawls into bed and lays flat on his back, keeping a respectful distance.

"I think I might have just lost one of my best friends," he says, staring up at the ceiling. "I fucking hate July fourth."

My chest caves and the last of the ice melts.

I turn over on my side, letting my hair cascade over my arm as I prop myself up delicately with my injured hand. "I'm sure you guys will work it out."

"Even if we could, I'm not sure I want to. It's not fair to her. I can't give her what she wants."

If he doesn't want to be with Ashlynn, one of his self-proclaimed best friends who's physically perfect and who's dedicated herself to the same cause, then what chance do I have?

My thought startles me because I realize that's what I want —a chance with Colton. Despite my best efforts to convince myself otherwise, I'm not just attracted to him physically. I want to know what's underneath that icy exterior. I want to figure out what makes him smile. I want to prevent him from experiencing anything that makes him frown. I want to hold him right now and make him feel better.

My eyes rake over his face, noticing the deep lines in his forehead and the goose egg on his eyebrow. "You said your head hurt? Can I get you something?"

"No, it's my own damn fault, just like everything else that went to shit today." He lifts his fingers gingerly to the bump. The cut looks much smaller now that it stopped bleeding. Hopefully all the swelling will be gone by morning.

"How did you do that, anyway? The three of you were fine when we left you." I need him to keep talking, to distract me from examining just how much my feelings have changed.

"My head connected with Danny's lip when we were wrestling. I think one of his teeth is still embedded in my skull."

My hand raises to meet his, sweeping his blond locks off his forehead. His eyes flutter closed as my fingers comb through his hair. When I repeat the motion, the rest of his features relax too. His expression is so peaceful and content that I scooch down in the bed and do it again.

After a few minutes of rubbing my hand through his hair, he scoots closer, flipping over and draping one arm across my stomach while resting his head on my ribs, just below my left breast. He inhales deeply, and his face contorts, nose wrinkling.

"You smell like Danny." He opens his eyes and peels back the comforter. "You're wearing his shirt and you smell like him. I hate that." Groaning, he tosses his head back onto his own pillow.

I bounce my legs under the covers and revel in the idea that he hates me smelling like another man. It gives me just a sliver of hope.

"I'm not interested in Danny as anything more than a brother," I say in a single breath. My declaration makes me feel vulnerable and somehow seems more significant than when I told him I wasn't interested in Andy.

Colton moves an inch closer. "Good," he says, turning back in my direction. He wraps an arm over my hip and pulls me against him, molding our bodies together and lighting my skin on fire. Oblivious to my reaction, he takes his time rearranging the pillows and comforter before resuming his position on me. I run my fingers over his scalp and through his hair again.

His eyes close, and I swear his chest rumbles like a purring lion.

"Tiger?" he says after a moment.

"Yeah?"

"Thank you for coming today."

The weight of his head leaves my torso, and I look down to see those icy eyes staring up at me, a question hidden in their blue-green depths.

My breath bottoms out as he moves a single muscled arm over my head and lifts himself until our faces are even. He hovers inches above me, his free hand gliding up to cup my cheek. My pulse hammering so violently I know he must feel it. When he trails his thumb across my bottom lip, my mouth parts of its own volition. Colton waits a breath, as if giving me the opportunity to pull away, and then he moves his lips to meet mine.

The kiss is deceptively soft and painstakingly slow. The heat of his body pressed into mine makes my head spin and light dances behind my eyelids as I lift my head to deepen the kiss. He tastes like sweet mint and I want more.

As if satisfied with my response, Colton's tongue dips in, speeding up little by little before slowing back down. I suck his lower lip, encouraging him to keep going, and moan when his hand moves to the back of my neck. After a few seconds, he repositions himself, sliding a knee between my thighs to part them before reclaiming my mouth with deep, possessive pressure.

The new angle and new intensity of his mouth's caress has blood pulsing low in my belly. I buck my hips, grinding into his thigh with each rock of his body against mine. As he moves his mouth to my neck, I gasp for air, desperate to be closer, desperate for more friction, desperate for more of him.

Colton's breath quickens, his hard cock pressing into my inner thigh.

Then he pulls back.

His chest heaves against my breasts, and he looks into my eyes with an emotion I can't name. I take his face between my hands and lightly kiss his swollen lips. I wait for him to bring another leg between my thighs. I wait for him to lower his sweatpants and climb on top of me.

But he doesn't.

Instead, he kisses me reverently on the mouth, trailing his lips over my cheek and stopping at my jaw where he nuzzles his nose into the soft skin behind my ear. My heart skips a beat, and a shiver runs up my spine at the sensation.

Pulling up the blankets to cover us with a heavy sigh, he wriggles his shoulders as he settles in for the night. He leaves a leg half draped over mine and places one arm securely around my waist, enveloping me in a comforting warmth that I nestle into.

After a few minutes, Colton's breaths even and slow into the peaceful cadence of sleep. I, however, am left breathless with my heart pounding and an unsatiated ache between my legs. I run my hands through the strands of his blond hair and drift to sleep surrounded by the scent of cloves and mint and sunshine.

Chapter Twenty-Six

Early morning sunlight filters through the thick branches of the maple tree outside, casting shadows over Danny's bedroom, making it look like leaves are dancing across my hands and forearms and Colton's sleeping face.

He doesn't seem to notice them at all. His breath is slow and even, and his arm is still wrapped around my waist. Now and then his hand contracts and his muscles tremor like he's deep in the throes of a dream.

I run the pad of my pointer finger delicately over his upper lip, noticing how much more pronounced his cupid's bow is while he slumbers. His face is so different when he's relaxed, like in sleep he is somehow able to escape the burdens of his waking hours.

If only we could stay like this forever.

I close my eyes, hopeful that I might fall back asleep, when a quiet knock sounds at the door. Pulling the comforter over my chest, I sit up. Colton's head slips into my lap as I offer a soft "come in," and Danny enters carrying three mugs of coffee.

Although the porcelain glasses clink with each step, Colton doesn't stir or open his eyes.

"Scooch over," Danny says with a flick of his head.

Where does he expect me to go?

Before I can voice my confusion, a powerful arm hauls me across the bed, creating enough room for Danny to slide in next to me. I hadn't realized Colton was awake.

With his face still buried in my lap, he blindly makes a grabbing motion in Danny's direction, like a toddler begging for snacks. His eyes are still shut tight when Danny places the steaming mug into his waiting palm. Colton barely lifts his head to take a slurping sip, but he makes a satisfied grunt of approval after he swallows.

Only after the second taste does he bother opening his eyes. A small smile curves the corner of his lips when we make eye contact. My cheeks burn and I have to look away.

I take the second mug from Danny, careful not to spill a drop as he slides into the open space next to me. Although I'm not a huge coffee drinker, at least the cup gives me something to look at other than the two men flanking me. Is it weird that Colton and I are in Danny's bed? Or that all three of us are having morning coffee in here, like we do this all the time?

"Are you guys going to sleep in here all day?" Danny asks.

A quick look at the bedside clock tells me it's only 7:12 a.m., so I know he's just giving us a hard time. He doesn't seem to be the least bit bothered that he found Colton in here with me. Actually, he can't seem to wipe the grin off his face, and he did come in with three coffees.

"I am way too hungover for you to be busting my balls this early," Colton says with a sleep-drenched voice. He balances his mug on my thigh and lets his head drop back onto the pillow beside me. Each time he exhales, his breath tickles my hip through the thin fabric of my briefs.

"Well," Danny says, sounding like a chiding father instead of a friend, "if you want to get started on that *project,* then we have to be at the site by nine to meet the crew. You also need to take Rylee home so she can get to work on time, not to mention everything else you have to do today."

Colton lifts his head. "You didn't hear? Yesterday Rylee told Jack she was going to kill Charles Eastmann for us. So, basically, the situation is taken care of and I can go back to sleep."

"Did you really say that?" Danny asks, somehow managing to sound both shocked and impressed.

My neck disappears into my shoulders and warmth creeps into my cheeks. "I was a little overwhelmed with everything. I might have said that." Obviously, I'd never hurt anyone, but what Charles Eastmann did in Eden is despicable. He should be locked up for the rest of his life, but I know that's not what happens to men like him. Men with money and power.

Maybe someone should *take him out...*

"Told you she was a tiger, didn't I?" Colton says with his eyes closed. He lifts his head again to rest his chin on my thigh and take another sip of coffee.

"Why do you always call me that?" I nudge him with my leg, and he nearly spills the scalding liquid.

Danny chuckles. "I can answer that one. The first time he saw you, at the rest stop, Colt said you looked like a caged tiger ready to strike. He said he was afraid of what would happen if you got out of your car."

My jaw pops open. "I thought you letting me stay in my car was a chivalrous thing!"

Colton only grunts his disapproval at being ratted out.

While I like being compared to a tiger, I hate the caged part. Although... I guess it's a fair assessment. My life in Charlotte did make me feel like I was trapped, pacing in front of bars of my own creation.

It's time I start making decisions for myself instead of letting circumstance and other people make them for me.

Colton's raspy morning voice draws me back. "What time do you work?"

I lift my still-bandaged palm. "Maggie won't let me go back until Saturday."

"Great, then we can all sleep for at least another hour." He downs his coffee, hands his empty mug to Danny, and proceeds to nuzzle into my side and close his eyes.

Danny shakes his head, and I shrug. Can't argue with Colton's logic. We were up late last night, and I am exhausted, too.

A few seconds later, a snore erupts from Colton that has Danny and I struggling to control our amusement.

"Are you hungover?" Danny asks politely after our laughter dies down.

"No, I didn't really drink a lot."

"So, you were sober when we talked in the kitchen last night?"

"Mostly, yeah," I answer noncommittally, unsure where he's headed with this.

"Good. I thought so, I just wanted to make sure." He leans forward to peek at Colton and then grabs a large laptop from his bedside table.

"Do you mind if I hang out in here and work a little?"

"It's your house. Should I leave?"

Is this his subtle way of asking me to go?

"No, please don't. Especially not right now." His eyes dart to his closed door. "Ashlynn's out there, and I think it's best if we all give her some space."

I tap my fingers against the coffee cup. "Is she okay?"

Danny connects a boxy external hard drive with the Ghost Rider logo on it to his laptop and starts entering passwords. Spreadsheets spring to life across the screen. "It's hard to say. I think she was okay with the way things were between her and Colt because he treated her slightly better than he treated the other women he slept with. They were friends before anything happened, and I think that gave her false hope that he might be interested in having *more* with her. Now, after last night... Well, I think she finally realizes nothing is ever going to happen between them. So, no, she's probably not okay, but she will be."

I can't help but wince at his words. I don't know how I was so blind to her feelings. "Is she in love with him?"

"I'd imagine she thinks she is. Once you know Colt, he's hard not to love."

I glance down at the sleeping subject of our conversation and run my fingers through his coarse blond hair. He lets out a deep snore that makes me grin. I can't change what happened with Ashlynn, but I can change the topic of this conversation. "What are you working on?"

"The accounting books. Budget season is in October, and I like to do my prep work the quarter prior."

I shake my head. "I have no idea what that entails."

Danny's eyes crinkle. "Basically, I look at how much money we bring in through the brewery and other businesses. Then I look at how much each of those businesses cost to run. I account for inflation and new projects and forecast how much money we need to keep running in the next year and come up with a budget. That's a drastic oversimplification, but that's part of what I do in a nutshell."

"Sounds like a lot of work."

"It is, especially when I have to piss. Can you hold my laptop for a sec?"

I nod, and he places the computer on my lap before scurrying off.

Sipping my cooling coffee, I glance down at the screen. He left all the windows open to whatever he needs to work on. It's a lot of numbers in small fields, and I do not envy him for it.

The two documents taking up most of the screen space are lists of dollar amounts. Upon closer inspection, I notice it's the same document with different titles: *Dovetail Books IRS 2026* and *Dovetail Books Jackal Accountings 2026*.

It's not very difficult to assume that these two documents should match up. It is difficult, however, to not notice that the total income reported for the IRS document is significantly lower than the reported amount for the internal Jackal accountings—four times lower to be precise.

My eyes flick to the bathroom door. I shouldn't snoop, but I can't help myself. I set my coffee on the table and click on a large sum of outgoing money that's hyperlinked in the Jackal document. The link brings up a new page with a list of coded destinations where the dispersals are going. I click on the next link, which is a key for what the codes mean.

If this is correct, then the money is going to local businesses, individual struggling families, homeless shelters in the city, rehab centers a few towns over... The list is extensive.

You name it, they give money to it.

A flush of adrenaline spikes through my body. This is incredible. The organization and the laws they must be breaking to do it is unheard of. The only thing not listed here is where they get the surplus cash from in the first place, but I bet I can find it. Clicking out of the window, I bring up the task manager—

A quiet cough sounds from the bathroom doorway. "Enjoying some light reading?"

Shit.

I didn't even hear the toilet flush. My eyes widen, and I nearly drop the laptop.

Fuck. If I could vanish into thin air, I would. I can't believe I just betrayed his trust like that. "I'm sorry, I don't know what I was thinking."

Danny climbs back onto his bed and takes the computer from my lap before settling in next to me. He's quiet but doesn't seem overly concerned. If anything, he seems almost amused.

"You're not sorry and neither am I. I could have easily closed the screen."

Colton's arm reaches over me, brushing against my breast as he slams the laptop closed. "You should have kept it closed, Danny."

"Maybe next time she sleeps over in my bed, I'll remember." His insinuation is clear.

Colton growls.

"What, dude, she's family. She can sleep wherever she likes," Danny says with a smug expression.

"She's not sleeping in here next time. She might be your family, but she's my—" He sits up.

I don't know if I'm more excited to be called Danny's family or that Colton might be about to elaborate on what he feels for me.

"She's your what?" Danny presses.

"Shut the fuck up and give me a second." Turning toward me, Colton bites his lip. "Can I take you out Friday?"

"Like murder me?" It's kind of funny watching him squirm.

His face scrunches in confusion. "Why do you always think I'm trying to kill you? I want to take you out, like on a date."

"A date." My lips slip into a flirtatious smile. "I thought it was a onetime thing?"

Jesus, someone shut me up, please. Why do I keep talking?

"Yeah, me too. Turns out we were both wrong." He groans and runs a hand over his face as Danny chuckles beside me.

"Then yes, I'd love that." My smile is so big I can feel it tugging on my ears.

"Good." Colton lays back down, eyes closed, grinning like a kid in a candy store. "Now, can we all go back to sleep?" He pulls me down into the bed and throws the covers up to our necks. Yawning, he snakes his arm around my waist and burrows his head in the crook of my neck. The faint whisper of his lips grazes my shoulder.

Beside me, Danny clicks away at his keyboard, and I fall asleep to the sound of his typing and occasional soft laugh.

Chapter Twenty-Seven

We sleep too long.

After scrambling out of bed, I barely have time to throw on my skirt before we're running out the door. When Colton drops me off at the bungalow, I still have Danny's shirt and boxers on, my underwear, bra, and sweater unceremoniously balled up inside my purse. I was hoping Holly would be in the shower, but she's sitting at the kitchen table with wet hair, eating leftovers.

"Is that Danny's shirt?" she asks around a mouthful of yesterday's pot roast.

Shit.

The door creaks closed behind me, and I tuck a strand of hair behind my ear, staring at the floor. "Yeah, I went over to his house after the memorial. No one was sober enough to drive me home."

Holly sucks in her lips. "They still got together after?"

I nod.

"Did Jack go?"

I shake my head. Sometimes I forget that this has been her

life for the past five years. If I was here for the last memorial, she and Jeremy would have been at the table playing dominoes with us. I think I understand now why she didn't want to come. She's finally starting to gain back some sense of normalcy and that might have sent her back over the edge.

I take a seat across from her at the table and steal a piece of meat from her plate. "What are your days off this week? Can we hang out?" I ask while chewing.

She pushes her plate toward me to finish. She only ate half, but I'm too starved to force her to eat right now.

"I'm off Friday and Saturday. Friday would be best, though, since I work Sunday." She pauses. "Why are you making that face?"

I hadn't realized I *was* making a face. Colton and I decided on the car ride over that he'd pick me up at two on Friday. I know I should cancel on him to spend time with Holly, but I really don't want to.

Dropping my eyes to the plate, I tuck my hands under the table. "I have plans on Friday and have to work Saturday, but I can try to rearrange."

"No, don't do that. Who are your plans with? Lana?" Holly sounds happy, like she's glad I'm making friends.

"No. Colton," I reply sheepishly.

She lifts one of her blond brows, her mouth setting into a flat, hard line. "I see."

My eyes roll. "It's just a date, I'm still leaving at the end of summer."

She snorts humorlessly. "Colton doesn't date. Trust me. You should stay away from him, from all of them, but especially him. He's not who you think he is. He's...dangerous."

I don't know why the idea of me going on a date with Colton is so offensive to her, but as she crosses her arms over her chest, it's clear that she can't stand the thought.

I bottle up the anger brewing inside of me. "Whatever. I don't want to have this conversation right now. Besides, there's something I've been meaning to ask you."

"Then ask."

This is not how I saw the *let's leave Eden together* conversation going, but I guess there's no time like the present. "I applied to four more universities, and I was hoping you'd consider coming with me to whatever school I get into. I thought we could live together?"

Danny's question about helping Minho and the Jackals pops into my head.

How will I make both work—

Holly lunges across the table and wraps her arms around my shoulders. "Yes, absolutely! Let's do it!"

I hadn't expected her to be so enthusiastic, but her response transforms the entire atmosphere in the room. We're both laughing as she pulls away. "Don't you want to know where I applied and what city we could be living in before you agree?" I ask through laughter.

She waves her hand. "I don't care. I can't be in this house or Eden anymore. Jeremy's absence is everywhere."

It's the first time she's mentioned Jeremy on her own, and I don't know if I should ask more or let it go. I decide on telling her the location of the schools, revealing that one of them is MIT in Boston, and that Minho, after helping with my résumé and supplemental questions, seems to think I have a pretty good shot at getting in.

"*It's all about the admissions algorithm,*" he'd said while reworking my essay answers.

The smile slides right off Holly's face as soon as I mention Boston. "Why Boston?"

"They have great tech schools. I thought you loved Boston?"

"Dad has an office in Boston..."

While that news does bring my excitement down a notch, it doesn't change anything. Not anything important, at least. "We don't have to see him. I'd never have known if you hadn't said anything."

"I won't be able to avoid him." She scratches absently at her thigh where I saw the hint of the tattoo. "Did Colt ask you to apply to schools in Boston?"

"No, why would he?" Again, I choose to omit that Minho suggested both Boston universities and helped me apply. It's almost like she's implying there might have been some sort of ulterior motive, which is absurd.

All of a sudden, Holly starts making too much eye contact. "What do you know about the Jackals?"

"Not a lot." I shrug. "I don't even understand what I do know."

Especially after what I saw on Danny's computer this morning.

"Have you heard of the Vipers?" Her face is so taut and expressionless that it's almost frightening.

"Who the hell are the Vipers?"

"Well, let's just say that the Jackals and the Vipers used to be rival clubs. They've reached a tentative peace over the past few years. But Boston is Viper territory."

"Holly, how does that affect us?" First she brought up dad, now this Viper nonsense. "If you don't want to go to Boston with me, why don't you just say so?"

Holly reaches her arms over her head and lets out an exaggerated yawn. "Can we talk about this some other time?"

I hesitate. She does look tired. She has bags under her eyes, and she looks kind of puffy. I know she just got off an all-nighter, but I can't keep doing this. I can't keep letting her avoid telling me what's going on, especially not after what I found out about the mine.

"No, Holly. It can't wait this time. I moved here for you. I want to support you, but you won't let me in. Tell me more about the Jackals and whatever the Vipers are."

Across from me, she sets her hands in her lap and stops blinking. Her lack of response only makes my frustration burn hotter. "I was blindsided yesterday about Logan's dad and what he did to this poor fucking town, but you knew, didn't you? You knew and you didn't bother telling me."

I take a deep, fortifying breath. "You also still haven't told me what happened to Jeremy. I had to find out from Danny when he nearly had a panic attack after hearing a car backfire. At first, I accepted you not telling me because I can't begin to imagine what you're going through. I wanted to give you time to heal. I didn't want to push you. But you can't keep me in the dark like this. I'm not a child. I feel like I'm stuck in the middle of some game and I'm the only one who doesn't know the rules. Tell me what's going on."

"Why do you need to know so badly? If we're leaving at the end of summer, then why does it matter? You're not with Logan anymore. Jeremy isn't suddenly going to be alive because I told you the gruesome details of his murder. What difference does it make?"

I hate how she always twists my words and makes me feel like I'm the one in the wrong, but I'm not backing down. Not this time. "It makes a difference to me. Why did you ask me to stay in Eden if you can't trust me? You said you needed me."

"I do need you. You're my sister." Her head tilts to the side and her eyes soften. "I love you."

I sniffle as I struggle to control my emotions. "Then why didn't you take me in after Mom died? Why didn't you help me when I couldn't afford an apartment? Colton said you knew I was sleeping in my car. Why didn't you do anything? The second you needed help, I came running, but when I needed someone, where were you?" Hot, angry tears stream down my cheeks, and I'm practically yelling now.

"Rylee, I'm sorry. I wanted to protect you. I thought I was keeping you safe."

"Safe from *what*? And what about what I want?"

"What *do* you want?" The edge is back in her voice.

I throw my hands in the air. "To be included. For you to be honest with me. Even Danny, who I only met a few weeks ago, has told me more about you, about Jeremy, about their damn secret club than you have. I want the same level of trust from my own sister. You say you love me, but you've been cold and closed off since I got here."

Holly visibly recoils. "He's the one who told you about the Jackals?"

"*That's* what you got out of all this?" Now I really am screaming. I leave the kitchen in a huff and throw on my running clothes, not caring that I'm undressing right in front of her.

When I head for the front door, Holly is already standing in the frame, blocking my exit. "I need to know if they've asked you to join."

She can't be serious. "Get out of my way, Holly. Let me know when you're ready to give me some answers." I push past her and take off down the road at a sprint.

My legs pound the pavement until I can no longer hear my sister's voice ringing in my head.

I run until the pain in my heart and legs goes numb.

I run until I lose all sense of time and direction.

I run until my right shoe falls apart. Literally.

Limping my way over to the side of the road. I bend down to take a look at the damage and curse as blood droplets fall onto the pavement, only now noticing that the cut on my hand is bleeding again. Not only that, but it turns out the sole of my shoe has completely detached. My socked foot now looks like a giant tongue.

I wiggle my toes and laugh because, really, what else can I do?

Glancing around, I try to determine where I ran to, but the first thing I notice is the storm system moving in. To my right is a blue sky with bright sun in a cloudless canopy. To my left, the sky is a deep gray with low, angry-looking rain clouds. It's moving fast.

Could this day get any worse?

My knees creak as I force myself up and begin the long trek back to the bungalow. I have no idea what time it is, only that the sun's almost directly overhead now. I know I've been running for at least two hours, which means it's going to take me twice as long to walk back, maybe longer with my messed-up shoe.

Fantastic.

About twenty minutes later, the first drops of rain pelt the road. Ten minutes after that, a torrential downpour soaks me to the bone. It's so bad that I have to wipe my eyes every few seconds in order to see. I tilt my chin up to curse my luck and a growl of thunder rolls through the sky in answer.

But the grumble doesn't stop. The rain is so loud, it takes me a few seconds to realize that what I thought was thunder is actually the low rumble of a car engine.

As it draws closer, I recognize the green paint and familiar tugging sensation in my chest. Colton pulls off the road next to me, letting the car idle while he leans over to manually lower the window.

"Need a lift, Tiger?" he says with what's fast becoming a familiar smirk.

I nod my head eagerly. "You don't care if I get your seats wet?"

He looks offended that I would ask. "Not at all. Get in."

While the summer rain wasn't exactly cold, the air-conditioning inside the Chevy combined with my wet clothes and hair has goose bumps erupting all over my skin. My nipples chafe uncomfortably against my tight sports bra as I drip water all over the leather bench seat.

"What are you doing out here?" I ask with a slight chatter of my teeth.

"Looking for you."

He must see the confusion written on my face because he adds, "We passed you on the road about an hour ago. I saw the rain and figured you were still out here and might want a ride. You didn't see Danny and I drive by earlier?"

"No. I was in the zone," I reply, not wanting to get into it.

"Yeah." He hesitates and casts his eyes to his lap. "You looked deep in thought, like maybe you were rethinking our plans for Friday..."

It takes me a second to realize he's referring to our date. I turn to face him and reach for his arm. "No, it's not that. Holly and I got into it after you dropped me off, and I had to get out of the house."

The tension in his face lifts. "Do you want to talk about it?" He leans back in his seat, placing a muscled arm over the backrest like he has all the time in the world to listen to what I have to say. To be here for me. My heart flutters at the simple gesture. "I wouldn't know where to start."

"Try at the end?" he suggests.

I mentally run through everything Holly and I talked about: the secrets she's keeping, the warning against Colton. The blood drains from my cheeks. "I don't really want to relive all of it right now. But you should know, she told me to stay away from you. Again."

His mouth twitches up on one side, revealing the dimple I've only seen a few times before.

"Just me? Or all of us?"

"All of you, with special emphasis on the *you* part. She said you were dangerous." I don't know why I'm saying this, except it's almost like I want him to prove her wrong. Or maybe I'm daring him to prove her right? Maybe I like a bit of danger.

A chill runs up my arms and my teeth give a quick chatter. Colton notices and leans across me to turn off the air-conditioning and redirect the vents. In the process, his arm brushes mine, spreading heat through my skin like ripples in a pond. He's so warm that I instinctively lean into him, tucking my shoulder behind his muscular arm. Now, each time I inhale, my breasts push into the tattoo on his tricep.

When I place my cheek on Colton's shoulder, he turns his head toward me, his minty breath caressing my hairline. I'd only have to tilt up a few inches and our lips would touch.

My eyes move to his mouth.

My stomach flips as I lean in to close the distance.

Our mouths barely touch before he places a hand on the back of my neck and pulls away to rest his forehead against mine. "She's right. It is best if you stay away. Safer."

"I don't want to stay away," I say breathlessly. "I can't."

Colton takes one hard swallow and then wets his lips. "I know what you mean."

I lean in again and capture his mouth with mine. This time he slides his hand down my back and tugs me toward him until I'm straddling his lap. As the kiss deepens, one of Colton's hands roams under my shirt, teasing my stomach and the undersides of my breasts with soft touches while his other hand slips into my hair, drawing me into him. I dip my tongue into his mouth, feeling him grow hard under me, and reveling in the satisfaction that I can elicit such a reaction with just a kiss. I wrap my arms around his shoulders, and he thrusts up against my ass. I answer his yearning by rotating my hips. He moans into my mouth, and the sound is so freaking hot it has liquid heat pooling in my core.

His lips slow, dwindling to a few quick pecks. Just when I think he's done, he comes back in and claims another. When he's finally able to wrench himself away, he whispers in a husky voice, "That was a good first kiss."

I smile against his jaw. "That wasn't our first kiss."

"Hmm, well it should have been." He nips at my bottom lip "Should we practice for the next one?"

I bob my head ever so slightly, and then he's back, capturing my mouth with his and devouring my every breath. While we kiss, the rain pelts down around us, creating our own personal tin symphony.

Chapter Twenty-Eight

Colton drives me back to Holly's with an arm draped over my shoulder and my body tucked perfectly into his side, like we are two pieces of the same puzzle. Never in my life did I think I would be so grateful for a bench seat or the steady warmth of my very own life-sized heater.

When we pull into the gravel drive and it's time for me to exit the car, Colton seems as reluctant to let me go as I am to leave. Instead of letting me out from under his arm, he intertwines our fingers and glances at the house. Bashfully, he invites me to run errands with him and to eat dinner at Jack's. I readily agree. With Holly in a mood, we both decide it's best if he waits in the car while I dash inside to shower and change.

Thankfully, Holly doesn't wake up and I'm able to get in and get out without a confrontation. From the porch, I watch Colton sitting in his car with his eyes closed, listening to soft music and the sound of the rain dripping through the surrounding trees.

A surge of unfamiliar emotions swell inside my chest,

accompanied by a prattling thrill of excitement when his eyes crack open. When he sees me, a brilliant grin spreads over his cheeks, and I find myself skipping to the car before sliding back in next to him.

His pupils dilate as he runs his gaze down the length of my bare legs. "A dress? In the rain?"

"I hate the way wet pants feel against my legs." I shrug. It's a simple black sundress, and although I really do hate the feel of wet pants, this was just the easiest thing to put on. Judging by the look Colton's giving me right now, it was the right choice.

He revs the engine and peels out of the driveway without taking his eyes from my legs.

"Where are we off to?"

"I have two clients to meet with and then I need to pick up some groceries for dinner at Jack's." He frowns like he's suddenly self-conscious. "I guess that might be a little boring for you. Should we go back and get your computer so you can work on school stuff?"

I shake my head. "Nope, I'm all caught up. I'm just happy to be out of the house." The words *with you* hang in the air unsaid.

Colton places a hand on the inside of my left knee, his fingers molten against my skin. I scoot closer to him.

When we reach Main Street, he takes a right instead of a left. "We're not headed to your office at The Pack?"

"No, ma'am, we're going to a coffee shop off Main. People tend to feel more at ease when they're in a less formal setting."

That's considerate of him. Not many people would place their client's comfort over their own.

We park amid a bustling Main Street and, to my surprise, Colton darts out of the car before I have time to unbuckle my seat belt. My heart skips a beat when I realize he's coming around to open my door. Apparently, I'm a sucker for the little gestures. When I exit the car, Colton takes my hand, and we make our way to the coffee shop. The action feels meaningful, but I can't place a finger on why, so I enjoy the feeling of my hand in his and try to appreciate the brief pause in the rain.

The coffee shop is several blocks away. From what I can tell, there are at least five open parking spots in front of it. My lips part to ask if we should move the car, but when I glance up at his face, he seems preoccupied with scanning the crowds of people emerging from shops and businesses.

Everyone is trying to take advantage of the temporary respite from the rain, scurrying to their cars or bouncing from one shop to the next. When they notice us, they either wave enthusiastically at Colton or cross the street without making eye contact. Each time, he grips my hand more firmly before either waving back, greeting them by name, or scowling at their retreating forms. It's hard for me to imagine being from a town where everyone knows you, like an extended family of sorts. I wonder if they would accept me over time? If, after college, I could make a home here, like Holly did.

The coffee shop is small and cozy with soft country music playing through a single speaker on the counter. The walls are painted a deep purple with black trim. Decadent pastries line the shelves of an old-fashioned bakery display case. I love it.

How have I never been here before?

As if reading my mind, Colton leans down and whispers, "Eden's full of all sorts of gems like this. You just have to go out and find them."

I don't think his comment is meant as a dig, but he's right. It really is a treasure, and I haven't explored Eden at all. A place like this would have a line out the door in Charlotte, but here, there is only one patron.

Ethel, the woman I almost spilled waffles on, greets Colton with an animated wave that doesn't match the worried look splashed across her weathered face. She takes one look at our clasped hands and her frown lines deepen. "I saw you both at the memorial, but I hadn't realized you two were together?"

Colton just nods and squeezes my palm reassuringly. My heart does a somersault.

"Ethel, this is Rylee. She's helping me out with a few things today. Are you comfortable if she joins us?"

Ethel reaches out to take my free hand. "I don't mind at all. If she's okay with you and Jack, and she's willing to help with Jimmy, then she's more than welcome. Come sit, dear."

She ushers us to her table where Colton pulls out a chair for me. Ethel smiles approvingly and offers to buy us coffees. She's an entirely different person than the woman I met at Maggie's Diner. Or maybe she really was distressed about the mine collapse anniversary and took it out on me and the waffles?

"No," I protest. "You guys have things to discuss, let me get the drinks."

Gratefully, she agrees, requesting a "fancy mocha."

When I approach the counter, I'm overwhelmed with a deliciously spiced scent. "Mmm, what is that smell?" I ask the barista, who I recognize as the woman that Danny tattooed during his house party, the one with the dove on her shoulder.

"I just made some chai. Do you want a sample?"

She pours a little of the milky brown liquid into a large ceramic cup that looks more like a bowl than a teacup. When I lift the drink to my nose, I'm hit with a sudden feeling of desire and familiarity, but it's not until I taste the tea that I realize why. The flavor is rich, smooth, and bold. It reminds me of Colton.

"Are there cloves in here?"

"Cloves, cinnamon, cardamom, fennel, black pepper, and milk. It's good, right?"

"It might be my new favorite," I say honestly. I order the biggest chai they have, a mocha for Ethel, and a black coffee for Colton. When I get back to the table, Ethel is dragging out binder after binder full of legal documents from a blue rolling backpack she's brought with her.

Colton pulls out my chair again so I can sit while he explains, "Ethel's son, Jimmy, is serving twelve years for drug possession charges. It was his first offense. Ethel had just bought a house from Jack's construction company. The arresting officer was Sheriff Knott." He makes pointed eye contact with me when he says that last part.

"My Jimmy doesn't do drugs. I told the sheriff they were my pills, for my back surgery, you see. Jimmy was just picking them up from the pharmacy."

I can hear the guilt in her voice, but from what I inferred, this is Knott's doing, not hers. Ethel and Colton spend the next hour going over documents and forming a plan of attack to get Jimmy's verdict thrown out, or at least reduce the sentence. It's incredible to watch him work. His knowledge of the law and inner workings of the court system is astonishing. He's professional and patient with Ethel whenever she asks questions about something she doesn't understand. It's a side of him I've never seen, and I'd be lying if I said his passion for justice didn't have me swooning.

How corny is that?

When the meeting is over, Colton agrees to take on her case and keep her updated. Overjoyed, Ethel pinches his cheeks and shakes my hand with fervor, thanking us both profusely, even though all I did was listen and hand her a napkin when she cried.

In between appointments, Colton reviews the documents

and draws circles on my inner thigh with his middle finger. I don't think he's aware he's doing it, but the stolen touches have me struggling to keep my composure.

The next appointment is with a man named Little John. He's well over six feet tall and walks with a slight limp. He has tight curly black hair that's graying on the sides and a handsome face.

When I offer to buy him a coffee, he politely declines. "I can't drink the stuff without sugar, and I can't afford to lose any more toes."

"Diabetes," he explains when I look at him quizzically. "The medicine is too expensive."

Over the course of the next forty-five minutes, Little John explains his predicament. He and his wife have a special-needs daughter with extensive past-due medical bills. She's now requiring around-the-clock care, and his wife is no longer able to work—it was actually her vacancy that I filled at Maggie's. Turns out, Little John is Lana's uncle on her father's side.

Colton takes diligent notes on his yellow-papered notepad, getting rough estimates of monthly expenses and a list of Little John's job qualifications. When all is said and done, Little John leaves the coffeehouse with a promise of a onetime, interest-free loan, an appointment with Danny next week to go over finances, and a job offer to work at Dovetail Brewery as a production manager with a higher salary than he's currently making at a factory two towns over.

It seems too good to be true. Little John must share my sentiments because he bursts into tears the moment Colton is done summarizing the outcome of their meeting.

When he leaves and it's just us again, I let Colton finish his notes before I ask my first burning question. "How can you possibly offer him all that? Where is the money coming from?"

Colton's lips all but disappear. "I don't ever want to lie to you."

"Jackal business?"

He nods. Meaning he's not going to tell me.

While it's frustrating to have my question left unanswered, I'm not mad the way I was with Holly. It might be a double standard, but I respect Colton for being upfront with me about not wanting to lie. If it means people like Ethel and Little John get the help they need, then I can manage not knowing the details of exactly how it happens.

"Wait, why does Little John need an attorney?"

"He doesn't," Colton says simply before shoving the folded notepad into his back pocket. "He needs an advocate and a sounding board. Jack normally does these kinds of meetings, but I went to high school with Little John's oldest son. He trusts me."

"How do they pay for your services?"

Colton looks like I just asked him why the sky is made of slime. "I don't charge them. Jack takes care of me and, in turn, I take care of the town."

"Is that what you do for the Jackals?" I don't realize until after the words leave my mouth that this might be an inappropriate question.

"It's what we all do. It's the core of who we are," he replies without elaborating.

There is a pregnant pause where I search for the words to change the topic, but before I can, Colton starts speaking again. "This is weird for me. I don't think I've ever talked about the club with anyone before."

I want to encourage him to keep talking, but at this point I think silence might be the best way to accomplish that.

"My job is to keep the club safe. I keep the charters and the members in line. If there is a threat to the businesses or the club, I eliminate it. I also handle all of the legal affairs. But most importantly, I help protect the people of Eden, the September Doves."

My chest swells with awe and longing. He has so much drive and conviction. I only hope that I can live the same way.

He lets out a long, slow breath and offers me his arm before I can figure out the right way to ask what he means about September Doves. "That's enough about work for now. Ready to go shopping?"

The rain holds off while we stop at the butcher's, the baker's, and the farmers' collective for fresh veggies. Apparently, Colton is passionate about his shopping. Each shop owner's face lights up as soon as we walk through the door. The nice woman at the bakery even goes as far as to say, "It's about time I saw you with a woman. Happiness looks good on you, Mr. Archer."

Colton's answering smile is enough to make my knees weak.

By the time we've gathered all the groceries, it's nearly five o'clock. "One more stop," Colton promises with his hand resting on my knee. There is just enough heat radiating from his palm to turn my thoughts dirty and my body needy. The engine purrs and the sensitive flesh between my thighs pulses as we fly down Main Street and whip into the parking lot of The Pack. Colton gives me a knowing smirk and parks in front of the brick wall around the back—the same wall he fucked me against. His rough palm slides higher, and my pulse quickens, my knees falling to the sides as his fingers approach the apex of my thighs.

I don't even bother looking around. I don't care who sees us, as long as he's touching me.

Lazily, without even a glance in my direction, he pushes my dress up and runs his middle finger down the thin fabric of my underwear. "Please," I beg, urging him on while struggling to control my uneven breathing. Up and down his fingers glide before pushing aside the fabric to circle the little bundle of nerves that's yearning for his attention. After a few painstakingly slow, methodical circles, his fingers start to pulse on my throbbing clit. I arch into his touch, gasping. It's too much. Too good. "I'm going to— I'm gonna—"

I explode in a rush of heat and white light, unable to breathe or see.

"Fuck," Colton finally says, his voice bringing me back to reality. He returns my dress to its proper position and places his middle finger in his mouth to taste me. "Fuck," he says once more, his voice so low and gravelly he could stoke a brush fire.

Two hands slam onto the hood with a loud *slap* as Alex's grinning face comes into view. "You guys here to give me a ride or are you busy?"

Colton exits the car and musses Alex's hair playfully. Alex, a little more disheveled than he was a moment ago, climbs into the back seat and leans forward to give me a quick peck on the cheek before buckling himself in.

"Thanks for the ride. I'm glad you're coming to dinner, Ry. I missed you this morning and wanted to ask you, when is your birthday? You're twenty-one, right?"

That's an odd question. "Why?"

"I need help at the bar. Ashlynn used to fill in occasionally, but with her heading back to Pennsylvania for a bit, I need a bartender to help with my shifts at The Pack for the next few weeks."

Colton's shoulders tense, and I try not to read into it.

"I'll be twenty-three later this month, thank you very much," I say to Alex.

"Excuuuuse me. Listen, I know you're still leaving at the

end of summer, but I can pay you $15.25 an hour. Are you interested?"

I turn my head so fast I think I strain my neck. "That's almost twice what I make now. Hell yeah I'm interested."

A muscle in Colton's jaw feathers. "Did you already clear that with Jack?"

Alex shrugs and leans back. "He was the one who suggested it after his meeting with Ashlynn. I'll let him know you're in, if that's okay, Ry?"

I nod my agreement, and Colton grips the steering wheel tighter, accelerating. A hollow pit opens in my stomach. Last night, sleeping wrapped up in each other felt so right. And today has been so natural and easy, it almost made me feel like I belonged in Colton's life. Like we belonged together. My pussy is still throbbing with the orgasm he just gave me, for God's sake. But seeing Colton's reaction to Alex's job offer plants a seed of doubt in my mind.

With every second that passes, the roots of that seed start to spread. I can't decide whether his problem is the idea of me working at The Pack or the idea of me being so close to the Jackals. Either way, it feels like he's trying to put distance between us, and never again will I date someone who keeps me at arm's length the way Logan did.

I push my knees closer together and angle them toward the window. Slowly, the bricks of my internal defenses stack one by one until my arms are crossed over my chest and I am completely closed off, wishing I had just stayed at the bungalow.

When we pull up to Jack's house, I stay in the car and hear Colton ask Alex to give us a minute before he opens my door and crouches down so that our faces are level. I'm hit with his spicy sunshine scent and I try not to breathe. The feelings that scent elicits are exactly the type of feelings I'm trying to ward off.

"What is this?" He gestures to my rigid, closed-off posture.

I shrug in response, not meeting his eyes.

"Tiger, talk to me." His voice is demanding and rises up at the end, like he's confused.

When I refuse to concede to his request, he grabs my chin and gently forces my face in his direction. When I still won't look at him, he forces my jaw up, the index finger still under my chin. "What happened?"

"It's nothing." I feel childish and stupid for being upset and I try to shift away from him again, but he stops me.

"Rylee."

"Fine. You didn't seem to like that Alex wanted me to bartend with him." I pout, sucking my lip back in when Colton laughs in my face. Tears form in my eyes, and I try blinking them away. I hate that I'm being this emotional. I've never let anyone, besides Holly, affect me this way before. The worst part is that even I feel like I'm overreacting. "It's not funny. I can't do this again. I don't want to be kept separate from certain aspects of your life."

"That's what this is about?" A slow smile spreads across his cheeks, and his eyes seem to gleam with unsaid promises.

I blink away new tears. "I saw you work today. I saw you help people; saw the way you treated Ethel and Little John. I've seen the accounting records of all the other people you helped on Danny's computer. If that's what the Jackals do, I want that. I want this life."

I have to bite my cheek to keep from saying that I want *him*.

Colton places a single soft kiss between my eyebrows and runs his thumb over my bottom lip, pulling it down a little. "I'm not trying to keep you out of any part of my life," he says. "But you working at the bar is going to expedite everything. Minho and Jack are going to work you to the bone. You haven't even had time to finish college yet. There's no rush, Tiger. We're not going anywhere."

"But I *want* to help and not just at the bar. Isn't that my decision to make?"

Colton takes my hand, turning it to kiss the marigold tattoo on my wrist. "Fine." He nestles his nose against my skin. "If that's what you want, let's give it a try."

Chapter Twenty-Nine

Dinner at Jack's never happened.

I was standing at the front door, admiring the lilies, when Jack and Danny came rushing out into the yard. They spoke in hushed, frantic tones with Colton before sprinting over to Minho's waiting SUV.

Alex took me home in Colton's Chevy with no more than a few words except to assure me dinner would be rescheduled.

As if eating was my main concern and not the troubled look etched into each of their faces...

Their expressions are all I can think about as I work on school assignments. That and Holly's snoring, which seems to reverberate through the walls. Even with headphones on, I can still hear the god-awful sound over my professor's recorded lecture.

I was already having trouble concentrating before Holly came home and decided she needed to rearrange the furniture but wouldn't accept any help doing it. Now that she's sleeping, I thought I might be able to get some work done, but the combination of her trying to blow the house down, confusion over the dinner that never happened, and the knowledge that Colton will be here in a few hours to pick me up for our first official date, makes it impossible to concentrate.

I slam my computer closed.

I give up.

And since when does Holly snore? Thankfully, she's gained a little weight since she started eating again, but not enough to make her snore like an elderly man with sleep apnea.

Maybe I'm just annoyed because we're still fighting. Or maybe I'm annoyed because I woke up at the butt crack of dawn to drop off some food for the Grace kids in the woods behind the diner. Either way, I need to get out of this house and run before I blow a gasket. My hand is healing nicely and as long as I don't hit it on anything, I should be fine.

I throw on my exercise gear and my shitty backup pair of running shoes and am out the door within a matter of minutes.

The July air is hotter than I expect it to be this early in the day, the heat so oppressive that I cut my run short after just four miles. Even then, I walk the last mile back and when I reach the porch, I'm sweat-drenched and dizzy.

I collapse onto the sun-bleached deck, limbs sprawled and chest heaving, and watch the clouds drift overhead. I've never been one to stare at the sky for long. It normally makes me feel antsy. Too much introspection always makes me feel like I'm not doing enough with my life. Now, for the first time, when I stare at the clouds my future seems bright.

Except for my relationship with Holly, everything is going well for me. I have friends, good grades, a decent job—two if you count The Pack—and in a few weeks, I'll be done with finals and two years away from a bachelor's degree. I'm also going on a date with someone I'm actually interested in, which only goes to show how wrong everything was with my ex.

Logan's incessant daily emails also helped illuminate that

issue. There are so many now that I'd almost missed an acceptance letter from Northeastern University in Boston and an email from the private investigator back in Charlotte. I'd been so excited about my transfer acceptance that I forgot about the email from the P.I. until now.

How important could it be if I've already found Holly?

I still can't believe I wasted two grand on him, but I make a mental note to read his email later anyway.

As I lie on the deck, my breathing steadies and my muscles slowly uncoil. Things feel...good. Eden is starting to feel like home, which is only going to make it harder to leave at the end of summer.

I must doze off because when I open my eyes, the sun has shifted to the left in an increasingly cloudy sky. Scrambling to my feet, I dart inside to get ready for my date. When I emerge from the bathroom, my skin is glowing and my hair is silky straight for the first time in months. I decide to wear a tight jean dress that zips all the way down the front and hugs my curves in all the right places. Hopefully, the idea of how easily the dress can be opened drives Colton crazy enough to rip it off me before the date is over.

A quick glance at the microwave clock tells me I have five minutes until he gets here, which means I'll have to make time to read the email from the P.I. later. I'm curious as to what he has to say, but unless he's offering me a refund, my time is better spent preparing for this date. I reach for my bag under the couch and retrieve three condoms, biting my lip. It's wishful thinking, but a girl can never be too prepared.

Nervous anticipation vibrates through my limbs as I bounce from toe to toe. I'm jittery and I have no idea why I'm so nervous all of a sudden.

Then it dawns on me: This is excitement.

I'm *excited.*

When I walk out on the porch to wait, Colton is already there, worrying his lip with a beautiful bouquet of bright-red tulips clutched in his palm. His back is partially turned toward me, and he's so lost in thought, he doesn't realize I'm behind him until the screen door slaps shut. His head snaps in my direction, and an instant smile spreads over his face. "You look incredible, Tiger."

He's dressed casually, black jeans and a black Henley that hugs every contour of his muscular arms and torso. He has on his standard pair of brown boots and looks so good I have to remind myself to breathe. The effect he has on me is alarming, but more concerning than my unbridled attraction is the ashen pallor of his face and the way he can't seem to stop fidgeting with the string tied around the stem of the bouquet.

"Are you okay?"

He laughs nervously and cuffs a hand on the back of his neck. "I'm going to be honest with you, I haven't been on a date since high school. I have no idea what I'm doing."

Several birds in the neighboring trees take flight at the thunderous laugh that erupts from my mouth. My heart dances against my rib cage.

He is adorable.

"You're laughing at me? It's already that bad?" His eyebrows pinch together.

"No, not at all."

How is this the same man I met all those weeks ago?

I point to the flowers. "Are those for me?"

"Oh, yeah." He steps forward and takes my hand, running his thumb over my tattoo. "I remembered the meaning behind some of the flowers my mom grew, and had the florist help me pick these out." He points in the direction of the street. "He grows everything in a greenhouse just up the road from here, but his shop is on Main— You're laughing. I'm rambling, aren't I?"

He places the beautiful, red flowers into my outstretched hand, and I lean up on my tiptoes to kiss his cheek. "They're perfect. Let me go inside to put them in water. Thank you."

When I walk back out onto the porch, Colton is pacing. He's so visibly anxious that I find my nervous energy being replaced with the need to soothe him.

"Where are we headed?" I ask to hopefully get him out of his own head.

Colton does a quick scan of my dress, like he's seeing me for the first time, and whistles. "Jesus, Tiger. That dress." He moves his head like someone shaking off a dream. "I want to show you something in town, and after that, I figured we could head up to a scenic overlook for a late lunch? I packed a picnic for us."

"Sounds perfect. Lead the way."

The streets through town feel windier today, my stomach flipping every time we take a slight turn. Colton takes my hand in his and plays with my fingers, slightly pressing on my nail beds and rolling my knuckles between his thumb and pointer finger. He's cute when he's nervous.

Who am I trying to kid? He's cute all the time.

He catches me staring at him and lifts my hand to his mouth for a kiss. "We're almost there."

A few minutes later, we pull into the empty parking lot of a vacant brick building, if you can call it a building. It's really just a shell. Although the school across the street is clearly up and running, there is no telling how long this building's been abandoned. It's an interesting spot for a first date, I'll give him that. There aren't even windows or doors, but the roof looks new.

Colton parks the car halfway inside of what might be an old delivery bay. When I turn to question why we are driving in, he points skyward. "Looks like another summer storm is headed our way." Sure enough, dark-gray clouds are rolling in behind us.

He leads me inside. I'm surprised at how tidy the space is, like someone recently came through and removed all the rubble. The cement floors look freshly poured, too.

Interesting.

Colton leans down, his lips brushing my ear as his fingers trail across my arm. "Aren't you going to ask me if I brought you here to murder you?"

His breath sends a chill up my spine, and I clench my thighs together. "I hadn't even thought of that. But now it all makes sense." I take a playful step away from him, like I'm going to run, and he lunges, throwing me over his shoulder. My body floods with a heat that has nothing to do with the temperature and everything to do with Colton's massive, calloused hand on the curve of my ass. If he moved his fingers just a little to the left, he'd feel exactly how much I was enjoying this. After a few moments, he sets me down in the center of the building.

Once I'm stable, he extends his arms and spins around. "Well, what do you think?"

Confused, I scan the ceiling and the brick walls for something that will help me understand. When I don't find it, I shrug.

"It's the after-school center," he says excitedly.

His eyes sparkle as he latches on to my arm and drags me across the room with him. When he stops, he gestures wildly to the back wall. "This will be the kitchen area. We're going to have four of those huge industrial fridges and six stoves so we can teach the kids to cook. We'll keep the fridges fully stocked with food for them, too."

He takes my hand and pulls me into the next room. "This

will be the media lab. I ordered twenty computers so the kids can have internet access and a way to print their school assignments. Minho said he'd help teach them how. Or you can, either way."

Colton guides me from room to room, explaining what plans he has for each space. I've never seen anyone so excited, and watching him does something all twisty to my insides.

"The elementary and middle school are right across the street, so there will be a school crossing guard to help the kids get here safely. And you'll never believe who I got to accept a job. Charlotte Grace, Anna and Johnny's mom!"

His chin lifts and there is a gleam in his eye. "Minho's Aunt Jin is working on getting proper permits for us to use tax dollars to help run this place. Dovetail is going to cover the rest as a tax write-off."

He looks down at me expectantly, and I pinch my inner arm to keep my emotions at bay. "You did all this? Based off my idea?" I hadn't realized he was listening so intently to what I said while he bandaged my hand. But here it is, all my crazy notions in one place, but better because it's actually real.

The emotion that swirls inside me is overwhelming and indescribable.

"It was a great idea. After I dropped you off, I went back and told Jack. He was on board immediately. We can help so many more families this way. You can work here, too, when you come back from Northeastern for the summer, if you want."

"When I come back? Wait, how did you know about that already?"

"Minho."

Of course Minho would already know.

Colton cups the back of his neck and drops his eyes to the ground. "I know you'll be busy with school, but I figured you'd come home whenever you could. I can work remotely some of the time, too, but I'll need to be in Eden for meetings and to help run the club. So, we'll have to come back quite a bit."

Every inch of my body is overcome with warmth as I take a breath that seems to last an eternity.

He called Eden my home.

He said we.

Colton shoves his hands into his pockets. "Oh fuck. I scared you, didn't I? Listen, I know it's early, but I want to make this work. I want you to go after your goals, and I want to be there when you reach them. For the first time in my life, I want something for myself. Not for Jack or the club, but for me. I'm not going to let a little distance come between us, Tiger."

My throat constricts, and my tears fall freely as I throw myself into him. No one has put my goals above their own. Never in my life has someone shown me with actions just how important I am to them. He doesn't even have to say it. I feel it.

Wanted.

Valued.

He wraps his arms around me and strokes my back. "This is the worst first date ever, isn't it?"

"It's the best."

"Then why are you crying?" His disbelieving tone is laced with light laughter.

"It's too perfect. You're too good to be true."

His chest rumbles against mine. "Far from it, but I'm glad you think so." He kisses my forehead and then my cheek, the tendrils of his hair dusting across my face before he takes a step back to look me in the eye. "So, the after-school center is good?"

I nod and sniffle. "It's better than I could've imagined. Thank you."

"Don't thank me. This was your brainchild. It's your compassion and thoughtfulness that's going to help make sure no other kids in this town go hungry ever again. We're really setting them up for a bright future." He takes a step to close the distance between us. "We can start other places like this, too, in neighboring towns. I already put out the word through the Jackal network. We should have been doing something like this sooner. We were so concerned with the big picture that cracks started to form in our own communities." He grabs my chin with his tattooed fingers and tilts my face up. "Thank you for helping me see that."

As I look at this beautiful man before me, I see him with new clarity. Together we could accomplish anything we set our minds to. With the Jackals, we could reach so many people.

Colton leans down, still gripping my chin, and gently places a kiss on each eyelid. Then he kisses me.

Like, *really* kisses me.

His lips move gently against mine. Slowly and steadily, he stokes a fire in me. Then, just when I think he'll pull away, his tongue sweeps across the seam of my mouth, and he places a hand on the front of my neck. His thumb strokes the delicate skin over my pulse, sending molten heat straight to my core. I moan against his mouth, pressing my body into his.

The second the moan leaves my mouth, the kiss changes, taking on a wild, almost savage tempo. His tongue dives in, and in a second I'm being devoured. His mouth is everywhere, and in this moment, I want nothing more than to be completely consumed.

Running my hands up the back of his shirt, I dig my nails in for leverage, the feel of his flesh in my hands awakening the animal within. I kiss his lips, his neck. I suck on his pulse and nibble on his jaw, desperate to taste every part of him.

He lifts me, making my dress ride up to my waist, but I don't care. With his mouth still on mine, he fumbles with the hem, trying to cover my ass while he walks, but all that does is press my clit more firmly into his waist.

God, that feels good.

I adjust myself so I can reach between us. I want to make him feel as good as he makes me feel, but his pants are too tight. Not willing to give up, I rub my palm along the outside of his jeans where his rigid length strains against the denim as I struggle with the button. Just like the night at the bar, he's already so fucking hard.

After a moment's battle, I get the button undone and am able to slide my hand in and wrap my palm around the base of his shaft. I squeeze, and Colton's chest vibrates with a growl. Beneath me, I feel him stumble as he walks, but I'm too caught up in the taste of his salty skin and the feel of his hard cock in my hand to care. After a moment, warm metal kisses my bare bottom when he places me on the hood of his car.

Colton steps back, panting with a wild look in his eyes. I utilize the brief pause in his attention to spread my legs and leisurely unzip my dress. My braless breasts spring out once released from the confines of the tight denim and Colton's eyes go even more feral. I stop the zipper at my navel and spread my legs even farther apart. He lets loose a string of colorful curses, then he's on me, unzipping the dress the rest of the way and pushing against my stomach, forcing me to lie back.

The hood makes a popping sound as he climbs up and across me to reclaim my mouth. His kisses trail down my neck, between my breasts, and stop just below my belly. The hood makes more noises when he lowers himself onto the ground and plants delicate kisses on the inside of my thigh. His tongue darts out, licking its way north, and strong hands push my thighs open. Then his mouth is on my pussy, tonguing my clit over the soaked black lace that still covers me.

I buck my hips against him until he takes the hint and pushes the fabric to the side. When his tongue finally returns without a barrier between us, I see stars. He laps me up, groaning with delight. "You taste even better than I imagined."

The vibration of his voice combined with the delicious way he's sucking on my clit is too much. I come apart, exploding in a burst of liquid light and fire.

When I'm done convulsing, Colton removes his tongue.

"You're so beautiful when you come." He removes his shirt and drops his pants in one fluid motion. His beautifully tattooed torso is covered in a thin sheen of sweat, and his muscles flex as he fishes out a condom from his pocket and slides it on.

His dick pulses with the movement, and I'm instantly hungry for more.

He leans over and begins to tug at the thin strings of my thong until the fabric is sliding down my thighs and over my feet. "I'm going to need you to come again, this time while I'm buried inside you. Can you do that for me, Tiger? Can you come on my cock?"

I can't form words.

I nod my head quickly, and Colton climbs back on top of me, spreading my thighs with his knee. Blond hair falls over one side of his face as he lifts his hand to cup my cheek and run a thumb over my bottom lip. His blue-green eyes bore into mine with so much intensity my heart throbs painfully, like a piece of me is being pulled into him and vice versa.

I need him so badly I can hardly function.

Will it always be like this with him and me? All consuming?

I close my eyes to help regain some composure, but his calloused hand slides to the back of my neck, gripping me roughly, and my eyes snap back open. Colton's cock nudges at my entrance. "Don't close your eyes. I want to see them as I—"

He slams inside of me, and his words are cut off by a guttural cry of pure ecstasy. I don't know if the sound came from him or me, maybe both, but that rope around my chest tightens with each slow thrust. My legs wrap around his waist as I struggle to acclimate to the size of him while simultaneously trying to pull him deeper.

So full. So stretched. So fucking good.

I cry out with each stroke, already cresting that next pleasureful crescendo.

Overhead, black clouds roll in, and the smell of summer rain fills the brick chamber of the loading dock. The car isn't far enough inside to keep us dry, and we'll need to hurry if we don't want to be caught in a downpour.

Our pace quickens, and my pleasure rises. It's like a race against Mother Nature. Who can get there first, us or the rain? Colton pistons in and out of me as the first droplets fall from the sky. Seamlessly, he picks me up and maneuvers us from the hood to the back seat of his car before the rain has a chance to soak us.

The space is tighter here, but with one of my legs over his shoulder and the other resting in the crook of his arm, Colton slowly reenters me. I expect him to resume the same jackhammer momentum he was giving me outside, but he doesn't. Instead, he moves my leg from his shoulder to his waist and slides his newly freed arm around my back, bringing our faces closer together. He kisses me and rests his forehead against mine before burying himself to the hilt. Then, slowly, he begins to rotate his hips like he's searching for something. When he finds it, I let out a frenzied gasp. My mouth drops open into a silent scream as he pounds into that delicious spot—a spot I didn't even know I had until just now.

I can't breathe.

I can't see.

My core coils and tightens with each magnificent stroke of his cock.

"That's it, come for me, Tiger," Colton says against my mouth. His pace quickens and his breathing becomes erratic. When he swells inside me, it sends me over the edge of my second orgasm. Only this time, instead of breaking into a million pieces, it feels like I am being reformed; a star in the sky, bright, alive, glowing. And I'm not alone—when I open my eyes, Colton is right there with me, driving into me as he chases his own release. It's not until I lean up to kiss him, running my hands through his hair, that he shudders and collapses against me, our slick bodies finally one.

When we've both stopped shaking, he raises up onto an elbow and tucks a sweat-dampened strand of hair behind my ear. "How did I ever think once would be enough?"

Chapter Thirty

Family dinner, as Jack called it, happens at least once every other week when the original Jackals are in Eden. If it gets canceled, it always gets rescheduled, just like Alex said. Which is how I ended up back at Jack's two nights after my first date with Colton.

Jack's kitchen is tiny, but not once does he, Danny, Minho, or Colton bump into each other while they make dinner. The way they move and work is like a well-oiled machine. Jack explains that they've been cooking together since they were old enough to hold a knife, and I can't decide if that's terrifying or adorable. I also can't imagine the patience it must have taken to teach a bunch of rowdy preteen boys to cook. Jack is a saint.

The meal, a shredded beef dish that Jack called *ropa vieja,* is served with black beans, white rice, and large sweet plantains. It's my first time eating Cuban food and to say it was incredible would be an understatement. Jack seems to take special gratification in my enjoyment of the meal. "Next time we'll make *yuca con mojo* and maybe some *flan,*" he says once

I've finished my second helping. Even though I'm too full to move, I drool a little.

After struggling to remain upright while helping to clean up, I roll myself into the living room with Alex. Colton brings me another beer before heading back to the kitchen to finish up the dishes. Unlike the rest of us, he hasn't had a drop of alcohol all night. He was quiet throughout dinner, only smiling and laughing when appropriate. He also kept an arm over the back of my chair or under the table on my thigh, almost as if he was reassuring himself that I was there without having to look in my direction every two seconds. Every time he did happen to look at me, there was a gleam in his eye that had heat creeping up my spine and into my cheeks.

We've technically only been on one date, but this thing between us already feels weighty and solid. Being around Colton is grounding, like I'm not functioning at my best unless he's close. It should scare me, but instead it bolsters me and makes me feel like I could take on the world.

After finishing the dishes and refilling drinks, Jack makes his way toward the living room where I am lounging on one of four gray-and-white striped couches surrounding a hand-carved coffee table. On his way over, he stops to press play on a wooden record player in the corner near a wall full of old vinyls. The soft strum of a guitar drifts through the air, lulling me into cozy comfort.

Everything in this place is practical and well taken care of, and while the house reeks of bachelor living, it's comfortable and tidy. Every once in a while, though, I'll catch a glimpse of a delicate picture frame or small teapot that I assume belonged to Danny's mom. There's even a dust-covered bundle of dried lilies and roses on one of the bookcases. It's the only dusty thing in the whole house, almost as if the blooms are too precious to risk damaging by cleaning them.

Jack catches me staring at the flowers and gives me a small, pained smile before taking the seat on the couch across from me. "Lilies were my wife's favorite. Now they're mine." My mind floats back to the fragrant lilies in the front yard while my eyes dart to the fresh bouquet on the kitchen table that I caught Jack fussing with earlier. My heart aches for him, but his aggrieved smile quickly transforms into a real one as the others file in from the kitchen.

Following the direction of Jack's gaze, I turn in time to see Colton push Danny into Minho, who stumbles, but magically manages to keep all of his whiskey in the glass. I relax further into the couch. I love the way they interact with each other. Like playful puppies.

Like brothers.

Like family.

My smile sags. Holly and I have never had that, and I don't know how we're ever going to get past our most recent argument. I need honesty, and she doesn't seem to be able to give that to me.

I force my attention back to Jack, noticing how the fine lines near his eyes are less pronounced here, surrounded by his loved ones. His attention drifts from one face to another as they sit until it lands on the only empty couch in the room. The corners of his lips turn down at the sight of the two empty seats. Jeremy's seat, I realize. Holly's, too.

It's a stark reminder that life is precious. We never know when it all could end.

I tuck my legs under my side and lean into Colton, who is in the process of shifting closer to me. Without looking, he wraps his arm around me, his thumb gently caressing my waist. That small touch is enough to send a flight of butterflies through my belly. Most of his touches during dinner were secretive and just for us, but not this one. This feels deliberate and possessive.

His brothers exchange meaningful looks, and a blush blooms over my cheeks. Alex slaps Minho's knee and gives it a shake. "Who won? I know for a fact it wasn't me."

Colton looks around, confused, and Danny brings out a sheet of paper from his wallet. "Minho had June, Alex had August, and I had July. Pay up, bitches." He stretches a hand out, making a *gimme* gesture. Minho and Alex each place a twenty-dollar bill in his open palm.

"What the fuck is this?" Colton demands.

"Oh, this?" Danny responds, pocketing his wallet. "We took bets on when the two of you would get together. I won."

"What the actual fuck? Seriously?" Colton barks.

They all nod, and my blush deepens. I'm nervous Colton will remove his arm or freak out now that we've been called out so publicly, but instead, he laughs and pulls me in tighter, leaning us back into the couch. "So fucking stupid," he says with a snort.

"I forgot to ask, how did the meetings go with Ethel and Little John?" Jack asks, changing the subject with a wink in my direction.

"Good. Ethel's pleased we're taking on Jimmy's case, and Little John is coming to see you and Danny next week." He turns to Danny sitting on his other side. "I already typed up the job offer, if you can draw up the loan paperwork? I'll send you all the details in the morning."

"Works for me," Danny replies.

"What changed to finally get Little John to come work for us?" Jack asks.

"His daughter. She's not doing well," Colton replies somberly.

"Shame. I assume he wouldn't just take the money? He was the one who insisted it be a loan?"

Colton nods.

"*Ahck*," Jack says dismissively. "Stubborn *pendejo*. You let him know we're here if he needs anything, okay?"

"Will do."

Jack bends forward to grab a stack of small boxes from under the table. He sets aside several worn board games and a photo album before retrieving a dominoes box.

"May I?" I ask, reaching for the photo album.

Colton swats at my hand but backs off when Jack responds with an open palm. "Of course. There are some real good ones of the boys when they were young in there." He winks at Colton.

The plastic covering the pages sticks together when I open the album. The first picture is a wedding photo of Jack and his wife, a familiar bouquet clutched between her delicate fingers. In the photo, they stare into each other's eyes, looking happy and so in love. I glance down the couch. Danny is the spitting image of his father at that age, just without the love-sick expression.

Next are baby pictures of Jeremy, chubby-cheeked and smiling between a twenty-something-year-old Jack and a massive German shepherd. There are a few pictures of Jeremy as a toddler and then a large photo of him holding up infant Danny. Jeremy looks like he's maybe nine in the picture.

I keep flipping until I see a blond boy next to Danny. Or at least I think it's Danny. The boys have their backs to the camera, and each of them is wearing a bright-orange vest, struggling to hold up shotguns that are twice their size.

"Is that you?" I ask Colton. "What are you guys doing?"

"Jack took us dove hunting," he says with an eye roll.

"He cried." Danny laughs, holding up his beer in a mock salute.

Colton runs his free hand over his face. "It was fucking awful. I haven't been hunting since. Those poor fucking birds had no idea what was coming." He shakes his head. "September first hits and the entire county is out there trying to kill them. They were defenseless. The second they tried to take flight—*BOOM*—someone shot them down. They were trapped. Lambs to the slaughter. Just awful." He shakes his head again, like it will free him of the memory.

Danny pipes up, "Right after that picture, Colton took off his vest and started screaming and waving it around to get the birds to fly off. He was determined to save every last one of those damn doves."

"Go figure he's still trying to do the same damn thing today, the dumb fuck. Only now you're all in on it, too," Alex says with a surprisingly bitter edge to his tone.

I run my fingers over the image, trying to imagine Colton's stoic determination at that age. Then Alex's words hit me and it feels like I just unlocked a vital piece of who Colton is, of who the Jackals are. They are protecting the people of Eden—the people society has declared open season on. Just like Colton couldn't stand to watch the doves be slaughtered, he and the Jackals can't stand by and watch less-fortunate people be used and discarded for sport by rich bastards like Charles Eastmann.

"September Doves," I whisper.

Colt looks down and leans in like he might kiss me. "We have to protect them, right?"

There is a loud cough and choking noise from my right before Minho loudly dumps dominoes out on the table.

For a second, I forgot we were surrounded by people. My cheeks burn again, and I lean away from Colton to examine the wooden dominoes. Minho begins flipping all the pieces over, revealing the Jackal emblem burned into the back.

"Wow, these are really cool," I say, lifting one of them up to the light and pretending like I wasn't about to jump Colton's bones in front of everyone. "How did you guys come up with the name Jackals?"

"Oh, I got this one," Minho cracks his knuckles, looks around the group, and when he doesn't receive any protests, he continues, "My mom and I moved in with my aunt about a year or two after the mine collapsed. Her house is about a mile from here. Anyway, one day, I looked out my window to see this dirty-blond idiot kicking a rock down the road. I ran out to see what he was doing, and he told me he was waiting for 'Jack Al.' I thought this motherfucker was looking for a wild animal."

"I was seven. I couldn't say Alvarez. Sue me," Colton says as he tosses a throw pillow at Minho.

Alex deflects the projectile away from his partner's face with ease, then ruffles Minho's hair and plants a soft kiss on his temple before urging him to continue his story.

"*Anyway*, when Jack finally came ambling down the road in that two-tone Dodge of his, we climbed into the bed, and I told him about the jackals in the area. I don't think I've ever seen a man laugh so hard. It sort of took on a life of its own after that. The three of us started calling ourselves Jackals in middle school and the rest is history."

Jack smiles proudly, and from the corner of my eye, I notice Alex fussing with Minho's hair that he messed up.

"What about you, Alex? When did you join the Jackals?" It feels weird to be asking these questions so openly, especially after all the secrecy with Holly, but no one flinches at my query.

Alex takes a sip of wine and pulls down the collar of his

shirt, flashing the dove tattoo he showed me at the bar. "I'm not a Jackal. I'm just under their protection." He winks at Minho, who puts an arm around his shoulder. "Jack hadn't even started the brewery yet when I moved here for high school. All I knew was there was a group of guys causing trouble for anyone who tried to move against the town. These idiots were into some pretty rough shit when all the Jackal stuff really started to kick off. Someone tried to build a paper mill upriver and the whole thing caught fire days before completion. Everyone knew who did it." He makes aggressive eye contact with Danny and Colton and starts laughing in a way that lets me know he might be a little drunk. "There was even a rumor that Colt killed the mayor as punishment for his involvement with Eastmann Incorporated and the cover up of the mine collapse. No one ever found his body, though. No body, no proof. Right, Colt?"

The muscles in Colton's abdomen and arm go taut, and Alex shrinks behind Minho as if realizing his mistake.

My mind spins to catch up. While the words might have implied it was just a rumor, Colton's response and the guilty look on Alex's face tells me there's a chance it's not.

Colton might have actually killed someone.

Shit.

Colton removes his arm from my waist, and a sense of cold washes over me at the loss of his touch. Every face, besides Colton's, is now turned toward me, waiting for my reaction. I knew they were involved with illegal activities, but this? *Murder?* This is some serious shit.

My natural inclination should be to run away screaming, but instead my pulse thrums against my temple as images of the mine and all the names carved into the memorial flash in my memory. If the former mayor had something to do with all those deaths, then he shouldn't be the mayor. If he was corrupt, then he was just as responsible as Charles Eastmann. He deserves a life sentence, if not a death sentence...doesn't he?

I don't know if I could ever kill someone, but I have to trust that if Colton did something like that, it was either to protect the people he loves or because he had no other option. If my short time in Eden has taught me anything, it's that you can't always depend on the law to protect you. Sheriff Knott's greasy image floats in my mind. Maybe Eden would be better off without him, too.

Jesus, that's dark.

I struggle to swallow and keep my face neutral, still unsure how I feel about all this.

Colton must notice the change in my demeanor because he moves away from me, clasping his hands between his knees and leaning onto his elbows. Although he only moved a few inches, the space feels vast, like he just closed me out. I try to catch his eye, but he seems unable to see anything but the scratches on the old wooden floors.

After a painfully awkward stretch of silence, Danny is the first to speak. "The mayor *did* collude with Eastmann Incorporated. Jeremy and Minho hacked into his bank account and found a deposit for $300,000 dated the week before the collapse. The mayor admitted that he—"

Colton lifts his hand. "You don't have to defend my actions. I might not have killed the mayor, but the shit I've done is just as bad." He takes a fortifying breath. "Rylee, you don't have to get involved with this. I know you said you wanted to help, but you don't have to be a Jackal." His right knee starts to bounce, shaking his shoulders. "Alex has been with us for ten years now and he's not in the club, but he's protected and helps us when he can. He's family. No one looks down on him for his choice."

I place my hand on his bouncing knee and squeeze. "Stop."

His entire body goes rigid under my touch, bracing against whatever I'm going to say next.

Hearing that Colton might have killed someone was alarming, and I'll admit that learning he didn't sent shock-waves of relief cascading through my tense shoulders. But what's most shocking is that none of this information changes how I feel, which is the exact same way I did walking in.

I turn my face back to Jack, who's been watching me with laser focus but hasn't once opened his mouth to interrupt, and set my bottle on the table, squaring my shoulders. "I want in," I say to no one in particular.

Jack doesn't miss a beat. "It's forever. There's no turning back once you're one of us."

"I understand."

A collective breath loosens around the room. Jack looks at me like a proud father, his eyes glistening as he tries to suppress a smile and fails. My answering grin and resolute feeling of confidence are cut short by Colton's abrupt departure from the couch. He stands up so fast I fall into his vacated seat. Danny looks at me apologetically and tries to excuse himself to go after Colton.

"No, I'll go." I grab Danny's arm, stopping him.

I follow the sound of Colton's pacing footsteps until I find him in a bedroom with two sets of bunk beds. Each bed is made with matching plaid comforters, and a poster of a bikini-clad model squatting, ass out, in front of a classic muscle car hangs on the only available wall space.

I shut the door gently behind me, and Colton's head snaps in my direction.

"I'm not mad," he says. "This will be good for the club. Minho can really use your help once you're trained." He stops pacing.

"Then what is it?" I don't understand his reaction. If he's not mad, then why is he so volatile?

His eyes fall to the floor. "I really didn't kill the mayor. He skipped town after we threatened to expose what he'd done, and last I heard, he hung himself a few years later. But, once you know the things I *have* done, the things I've had to do, you won't see me the same. While I don't regret anything I've done for this club, or for my brothers, I can't fucking stand the idea of you looking at me differently."

I step toward him, closing the gap between us. His expression is so pained it actually hurts. I wish I could put into words how he makes me feel. But even I can realize it's too soon for that. I search for other words. "I won't ever see you any differently than I see you now. Protective, caring—"

"You say that now, but—"

"No buts." I place my hand on his cheek, and he leans into it. "I don't care what you've done as long as it's for the right reasons. I told you, I'm all in."

He opens his mouth to argue, but I silence him with a kiss. His strained muscles soften under my fingers before he pulls away just enough to ask, "You're sure?"

I nod, and his lips come crashing into mine. His hands slide down to my ass and clamp down, hard. After taking a doe-eyed moment to appreciate the fact that I'm wearing the black shorts he bought me, he hoists me up and wraps my legs around his waist, never letting his lips leave mine.

When we finally come up for air, I breathe against his mouth, "Which bed is yours?"

The corners of his lips tug up as he gently lowers me onto the bottom bunk on the left. When I crack open my eyes, a giant Jackal carved into the wood overhead stares back at me.

Of course.

Colton kisses me on my neck and runs his thumb across my

breasts, drawing me back into the moment and eliciting a soft moan from my throat. My nipples pebble under his touch, and a fire erupts in my belly.

"How quiet can you be?" His voice is heady and low as he slides down the strap of my bra and tank top. Bending down, he licks the curve of my exposed breast, and I arch my back into him, my breaths quick and shallow. It only takes a second for him to take advantage of the new angle by sliding his palm up the back of my thigh and up my shorts. The pulse between my legs is needy and throbbing. From this position, his thumb can almost reach my—

Knock-knock.

Colton curses under his breath.

Minho's muffled voice sounds through the wood. "Jack says you can't fuck in there while the rest of us are only fifteen feet away."

Colton shakes his head, the long blond strands dusting my chest and surrounding me with his clove-and-sunshine scent. "Give me a second! *Fucking Minho,*" he mumbles the second part under his breath with no real malice.

Slowly, he replaces the strap of my tank to my shoulder, leaving an icy trail of tingles where his fingers touch my skin. He presses his soft lips to mine. "You're incredible, you know that? Never in my life did I think I'd find someone like you. Someone passionate, strong, and generous. Someone so beautiful and fierce."

He leans down and kisses the space behind my ear, inhaling deeply before he pulls away. "Fuck, if we don't get out of this room right now, I'm not going to be able to keep from burying myself inside you."

Colton scrambles off the bed, repositioning his rather noticeable erection into the waistband of his briefs. "Come on, Tiger, let's go sit with the family."

Standing, I smooth out the wrinkles in my outfit and try to tame my hair before I take his hand and follow him into a room full of grinning men. Jack has us all pick out six dominoes, as if minutes ago I didn't make the biggest decision of my life or nearly mount Colton feet away from this room.

We laugh and exchange stories, and by the end of the night, my heart feels lighter and fuller than I can ever remember it feeling before.

Chapter Thirty-One

The next few weeks are the best of my entire life.

Colton and I have continued to feed the Grace kids, only now we bring the food straight to their house and do it with the Jackals' support. We've even added a few other families onto our grocery drop-off route, and spread the word about the after-school center being built. The hope this news elicited in the families we told could sustain me for a lifetime.

Every second of my free time is spent with Colton. When I'm not working, I'm either with him or at The Pack picking up an extra shift. Even then, Colton and I usually find an excuse to sneak off to his car.

We sneak off *a lot.*

So much so, that when Danny climbed into the back of the Chevy the other day, he instantly climbed back out and said he'd find a ride that *"smelled less like sex."* I was embarrassed for a second, but when Colton pulled over halfway through our drive so he could drag us into the back seat, all feelings of embarrassment floated away.

Most nights I sleep over at his and Danny's place. Holly

and I still haven't talked, but I've been so wrapped up in everything else that I haven't had much time to dwell on it.

I'm coming to learn that sometimes a found family is even better than the ones we're assigned at birth.

Half the time I'm so happy I feel like I'm drunk. My attraction to Colton is at a level I didn't know I was capable of feeling. It's almost indescribable. Every piece of him is incredible. He's attentive, values my ideas and opinions, and he goes out of his way to help others. Sometimes I think I've found the only good man left on the planet. Then I remember Danny and Minho and all the other Jackals I've met so far. They're all good. They all take after Jack.

I've also been learning more about how the Jackals operate. While Minho came up with the name, it was Colton who came up with the idea for the club and Jack who got the wheels turning. Jack used to run with a motorcycle club in his younger days, the same one Ashlynn's father still runs, and once he got them on board with the idea of stealing from the rich and giving to the poor, the Jackals spread like wildfire. Turns out, Eden wasn't the only town being bled dry by Charles Eastmann and his associates.

With each passing day, I realize Jack is more than just in charge. He's a true leader. He knows each member and their families by name and takes on more than his fair share of the work. Even though I haven't been initiated, he still treats me like a part of the pack, like I belong. Yesterday he even called me *mija*, which I learned means "daughter" in Spanish. I almost cried.

How is a man who's lost so much able to give and love so freely?

Even though I'm not a Jackal, they no longer whisper things under their breath when I walk into a room, and they occasionally engage me in casual conversation outside of the bar. Not that my escapades with Colton leave much time for casual anything, but still, it's nice. When I asked Danny about the change in the Jackals' attitude, he shrugged and said, "They've seen you with Colt. They trust him with their lives, so by default, they trust you."

I was hoping it was something I'd done, but I guess I have time to earn their trust on my own. For the time being, it's enough just to be accepted.

Today is my last shift at the diner. Tomorrow, I turn twenty-three and then I'll be full-time bartending at The Pack until I leave for Boston at the end of the summer. Lana didn't take the news of my quitting very well, and she's been avoiding eye contact with me ever since.

The bell over the door chimes for what has to be the fiftieth time this morning. My shoulders slump with exhaustion until I'm hit with the warm scent of sunshine and cloves and feel a familiar tug in my chest. As soon as I set my tray down, Colton wraps an arm around my waist from behind and brings his lips to my temple, his minty breath dancing across my cheek. "I missed you."

I push away from him with my ass and turn. "It's been three hours since you saw me."

He pulls me back, burying his face in my hair and tightening his grip around my waist. I didn't notice it at first, but his shoulders are hard and tense against me and there's a firm set to his jaw that wasn't there when he dropped me off this morning. My stomach sinks. "Is everything okay?"

"Jack's coming by to see you." His words are simple, inflectionless, but I can read into them just the same. Jack's coming by on Jackal business. Colton only locks up like this anytime me joining the Jackals is brought up. Part of me wonders if he has something to do with the delay in my initiation.

I lean back and cup his cheek. "I'm ready for him. It's going to be okay."

He nods into my hand before turning and kissing my open palm. "I know."

An hour later, I've just given my last table their check when the bell over the door chimes and Jack strides in, his eyes crinkling with his smile when he spots me. "I know you're busy, *mija*, but do you have a minute to talk?"

My patrons get up to leave and I wave at them, using the opportunity to take a deep breath, before turning toward Jack. "I'm about to take my break. I can meet you outside in a minute?"

Jack nods and walks back out the door. My stomach knots as he leaves. While I haven't been told exactly how Jackals are initiated, I know that each new member has to be tested. I was starting to think I might leave for Boston before ever finding out.

I clean my section and retie my apron before meeting Jack out by the picnic tables.

"Having a good last shift?"

"I'm eager to get it over with. Maggie's been insufferable since I gave my notice."

"I bet." He hesitates. "I hate to ruin your last day, but the Jackals need a favor."

My stomach clenches, and I fidget with the ties of my apron. "Anything. I can do it," I squeak out.

Jack smiles and snorts. "It's nothing too difficult. You remember Andy? The sheriff's deputy?" I nod and he continues, "Well, Sheriff Knott has caught on that Andy might have switched allegiances. We have to throw him off the trail. We need to make Knott think that the Jackals want nothing to do with Andy."

Sounds easy enough, but I don't see where this is going or how it involves me. Really, the only thing I can fixate on is that he keeps saying *we*, like I'm already part of the club. It makes my heart pitter-patter in my chest.

"This afternoon, Andy and Knott will be at Maggie's. I want you to be their server."

"Okay?" I answer, confused. "Is there more?"

Jack's mouth twists like he tastes something sour. "Andy is going to hit on you, and I'd like you to let it happen."

"Am I expected to flirt back with him?" Even the thought feels like a betrayal to Colton.

"No, not at all. I just want you to let it happen. The entire town has seen you and Colt out and about, everyone knows you're together. Andy hitting on you in public is something a Jackal would never do to another brother. While all this is happening Colt and Danny will come into Maggie's, at which point Andy will double down. It's simple, but it should send a clear message to Knott."

I think I understand what he's saying. It's like some sort of weird pissing contest. Part of me is flattered that Colton's feelings for me are well-known enough that our relationship can be used in this way. But another part of me wants to scream that I'm no one's property.

I run over the scenario in my head. It's *too* easy—not even I could fuck this up. Then I remember the way Colton reacted to Andy's light flirtation at the beer tasting a few weeks ago. I remember the look on his face as he made Andy move from the seat next to mine. "Colton knows?" I ask.

"He knows. He's not happy that we're using you, but club business and member safety are more important than his feelings. Andy is an integral part of this organization. We need him on the inside." Jack pauses for a moment. "Every few weeks or so he reports made-up interactions with the Jackals. He gives us real tickets for speeding and other small citations, too. Knott will expect that Colt would have warned you to stay away from Andy. He will expect you to be wary of him."

"Got it." I thought I would be doing something more exciting, but if it's for the good of the club, then I guess no task is too small. Though, I have to admit I'm a little disappointed it's not some big mission to save someone.

Jack gives me an approving pat on the shoulder, and I scurry back inside the diner.

An hour later, the diner is already packed with the lunch crowd when Sheriff Knott and Andy stroll in and sit in my section. Out of the corner of my eye, I see Maggie directing Lana to take their orders, but I'm at the table before she has the chance to leave the kitchen.

As I approach, I remember I'm supposed to be wary of Andy, so I step back from the table before greeting them.

"Sheriff. Deputy," I say, not making eye contact. "What can I get for you this afternoon?"

Sheriff Knott leans over the edge of the table and rakes his gaze over my exposed legs. After a quick glance at my chest, he orders two coffees and two waters and then goes back to openly perusing my body. He looks greasy as ever as his eyes roam everywhere and anywhere except for my face.

With the sheriff distracted by the shorts Colt bought me, I dart my eyes to Andy. He's in his pressed uniform with some sort of pomade taming his dark-brown locks. He looks good, handsome even, nothing like his uncle. I wait for him to hit on me, but he doesn't.

Then his mouth drops open, like he's going to speak, before he snaps it shut again.

I open my eyes wide in his direction, silently signaling for him to go ahead, but he remains mute.

Next to him, Knott shifts his head to take in the rest of my body. I know his blatant ogling is a power move meant to throw me off, but I refuse to react. When his eyes finally reach my face, they narrow, and he has the audacity to pretend he's surprised to see me. "Ah, Miss Adder. I hadn't realized it was you. I should have recognized those runner's thighs...and other assets." His eyes drop back down to my backside, and I fight the roiling in my gut.

Although the sheriff's comments disgust me, they present the perfect opportunity for Andy to chime in. As if realizing this is his cue, Andy clears his throat and quickly looks me up and down. "I don't see what all the fuss is about. Neither of them look like all that much to me."

Seriously, Andy? What does that even mean?

Knott looks just as confused as I feel. "You mean her sister?"

Andy nods. "I'd take this one over the older one, but only because she's younger."

Sheriff Knott gives a deep belly laugh and claps Andy on the back. "You'd be surprised. Sometimes the older they get, the more they know what they're doing in bed. The older sister could probably handle both of us at the same time. Actually, I'd be surprised if she hadn't already done that with a few of the boys in town."

I fight the sudden urge to punch the sheriff in the mouth. The only thing keeping me from lashing out is the fact that Andy somehow looks even angrier than I feel. His hand grips his thigh so hard that his knuckles are white, and if he was clenching his jaw any tighter, I think his teeth might crack.

Great. His poker face is even worse than mine. No wonder his uncle suspects something. If Knott sees that expression, he'll know for sure that Andy is with the Jackals. I give his boot a subtle nudge with my shoe, and he smooths over his angry expression.

I hurry away from the table as the still-laughing Knott excuses himself to the bathroom. After I grab some coffee and water, I head back.

"You're not selling this, Andy," I whisper, placing the drinks on the table.

"What am I supposed to do? Every time I go to say something to you, I feel like I'm disrespecting a friend and future sister. I just can't do it. Help me," he pleads.

Well, fuck if that doesn't melt my tiny heart. Andy really is a good guy. No wonder Jack trusts him. "Just pretend it's not me, I'll bend over and give you a clear cleavage shot, then you can smack my ass or something as I turn away. I promise I won't hold it against you."

Just then, the door chimes and in strides Colton and Danny. As always, they take the corner booth.

Andy gulps audibly. "You won't hold it against me, but he will." He tilts his chin to the corner of the diner where Colton looks ready to commit homicide.

"He'll get over it. Club business and your safety are more important than his or my feelings right now." I can't believe I just spit Jack's words back at Andy. But I did, and more importantly, they seem to be working. Andy squares his shoulders and looks me in the eye. "Thank you for doing this. Colt's a lucky man."

I bob my chin and head toward Colton's table. He stands to greet me, brushing a kiss on my temple right as the sheriff returns from the bathroom.

"How's he doing?" Danny asks, careful not to look in Andy's direction where Knott is retaking his seat at the table.

"I think he's got it now," I assure him.

Colton huffs as he takes a seat, making his displeasure at the situation known without ever having to speak. His pouting is adorable. I place my hand on his shoulder. "It's really not a big deal. This is important and I don't mind." He crosses his arms over his chest and rolls his eyes in acceptance.

I have to swallow my laugh. "Do you guys want anything?"

"We'll take some coffees and a few sandwiches when you get a chance. We're really just here for bait, so no rush," Danny murmurs.

I write down their order for Cook and head toward the kitchen, but before I get there, a hand reaches out and grabs my hip, stopping me in my tracks.

Andy loops two fingers through my apron and yanks me closer. "Is that what it takes to get some food around here?" he says, jutting his chin toward the back booth. He drops the volume of his voice an octave, but it's still loud enough that anyone can hear. "Because I'm more than willing to take you out back and fuck you within an inch of your life. You won't even remember his name when I'm through with you."

I peel his hand off me and throw it in his lap. I know he doesn't mean what he said, but it still has me rattled. For a second, his voice sounded like Sheriff Knott's and his threat felt real. My hand trembles as I try to pull my pen from my apron while the sheriff smiles at his nephew like he's never seen him before.

I steady my nerves. "Does that mean you two are ready to order?"

"Depends," Andy says. "Is that ass on the menu, or do you only bend over for dogs?"

This time when the sheriff starts laughing, Andy flashes me an apologetic smile. It's enough to remind me that, despite the crassness of his words, this isn't him. We're just playing parts.

By now, a few heads have turned our way, and I crouch

down to keep the conversation as private as possible. Unfortunately, this new stance really does end up giving Andy a clear shot of my cleavage. His eyes dart to my breasts, and his pupils dilate. I was about to say something smart, something in defense of myself and the Jackals, but watching Andy actually look like he's aroused by my actions confuses me. I lose my balance and tip forward onto one knee, barely stopping my chin from slamming into the table.

"Look," Andy mocks, glancing across the table to Knott, "she's already on her knees for me." Andy leans over and pats my ass. "Get up. You don't have to beg for it. You're embarrassing yourself."

There is a slight commotion somewhere behind me, and I sense Colton before I see him. He helps me stand and wraps a protective arm around me. "Keep your fucking hands off of her."

Andy rises, walking forward until he's chin to chin with Colton. I never noticed how tall he was before, but they're almost identical in their imposing heights. "Or what?"

In his chair, Knott leans back and places his hands behind his head like he's watching a show. He has a sick, satisfied smile draped across his face, and I realize this little argument has done exactly what was intended. It's time to put an end to this before it escalates any further.

"I said, or what?" Andy repeats, taking a step closer. Colton's muscles tense like a predator preparing to strike.

I shove myself between them and dig my fingers into Andy's shoulder to remind him this isn't real. "It's not enough that you pigs harass them every chance you get? You have to pick a fight where you know he can't hit back? It might make you feel good, Deputy, but trust me, it won't make up for the tiny prick you're hiding under that oversized gun belt."

Andy's eyes clear as he attempts to abruptly shift away. In

doing so, he bumps me with his chest, sending me flailing to the ground. I hit the floor with a loud *slap* and bite my lip in the process. A trickle of something warm and wet drips down my chin. I tentatively dab at it, and my finger comes away coated in crimson. When I glance up to Andy, I can tell he's fighting the urge to help me, regret clearly written on his face.

Thankfully, Knott can't see his expression from his angle or the jig would be up.

I spin back toward Colton. His eyes transform into saucers when he sees the blood on my lips. Before I can stop him, he lunges at Andy.

Out of thin air, Danny materializes just in time to catch Colton's fist before it collides with Andy's face.

Danny backs Colton up, rapidly whispering something into his ear before I even have time to stand. Whatever he says, it calms Colton enough that his shoulders stop heaving so heavily and he loses some of the murderous glint in his eye. I struggle to my feet, still wedged between them. People are watching now, and Knott takes this opportunity to taunt Colton further.

"Is pussy really worth all this trouble? Just let my nephew have her for a few hours and we'll return her to you. I'm sure a day with Andy could do her some good, maybe tame some of that wild spirit."

As Colton struggles against Danny's hold, it dawns on me that the sheriff is doing this on purpose. He *wants* Colton to attack him. And he wants it done publicly so he can arrest him for it.

I won't let that happen.

Before I can think it through, I gather all the saliva and blood in my mouth and spit it directly into Andy's face. "You are both disgusting," I snarl.

The act is unexpected enough that Colton stills and the entire diner goes silent.

Andy wipes the blood-smeared spittle from his mouth but doesn't say a word. Knott, however, claps his hands in delight. "Congratulations, Miss Adder," he says, "you just assaulted a peace officer! Andy, cuff her."

Andy frowns and reaches for his utility belt.

Shit.

Methodically, he conjures a fake, sinister smile and reads me my rights before placing my hands behind my back. He pats down my shorts and under my bra to make sure I don't have any weapons, and a second later, cold, metal handcuffs bite into my wrists. Before I really understand what's happening, I'm led outside and placed in the back seat of Andy's Bronco.

Knott crosses the street and approaches the window, looking like a villain straight out of a movie. He motions for Andy to roll it down. "We almost had him. Good fucking job. One of these days he'll throw a punch and that will be it for him."

Andy sits up straighter. "Did you see his face when I placed her in cuffs? I think this might be harder for him than if he was the one being arrested. I'll let her go after a few hours. He got the message."

"A few hours?" Knott exclaims. "We can hold her for up to seventy-two without filing charges. Make sure she doesn't get released a second before those seventy-one hours and fifty-nine minutes are up. I'm proud of you, Andy. You're finally showing some promise."

My heart sinks.

Three days?

I'm glad it was me, though. I can only imagine what Knott would have done to Colton if he was the one in custody.

Andy rolls up the window as the sheriff heads toward his patrol car. The engine grumbles to life and only once Knott's driven out of sight does he speak to me, his eyes locked on mine in the rearview mirror. "Are you okay?"

"Yeah, I'm fine. Sorry I spit on you. I thought Colton was going to lose it. I had to do something."

"It's fine. I knew that's what you were doing. I think you saved my nose from being broken, so thanks. Also... I'm sorry I grabbed your butt."

There is a moment of silence and then we both burst out laughing.

"I didn't think that would work so well. Did you see the way Knott looked at me? He has never been more proud in his entire life. I can't believe I'm related to that asshole," Andy says.

I let loose a long breath as the muscles in my body relax. "We did it, then?"

"We did it."

A sense of calm washes over me, and I latch on to it. I'm going to need every ounce of strength to get me through these next three days, but it was worth it to help the Jackals and keep Andy safe. It was worth it to keep Colton out of Knott's greasy hands.

Chapter Thirty-Two

According to the clock down the hall from my cell, I've been twenty-three years old for two whole minutes. I never thought I'd spend a birthday in jail, but here I am.

On a more positive note, I haven't seen a single person since I was processed. I thought the sheriff would have come by to harass me by now, but he hasn't. While a part of me knows his absence is a good thing, I can't help but wonder if his plan is to bore me to death.

If it is, it's working.

I tap my foot and press my face against the bars to look at the clock again, but only a minute has passed since the last time I looked.

Turning my back to the bars, I slide down to the floor, my butt landing on the dirty concrete with an audible *thump* that barely muffles the growling in my stomach. I'm freaking starving.

Desperate for a distraction, I lean the back of my head against the cool metal bars, and start my third count of the dots on the ceiling tiles. I make it to 2,031 before I hear a sound down the hall. To my relief, I recognize Andy's brown locks as he lumbers in my direction.

When he stops at my holding cell, I don't bother standing or turning around. I know it's not his fault, but I'm frustrated and hangry and I need someone to blame besides myself right now. Wordlessly, he takes a seat on the ground.

If he's waiting for me to acknowledge him before speaking, he's going to be waiting a long time.

"You okay, Rylee?" he asks with a scratchy, tired voice.

I glance over my shoulder, giving him the best side-eye I can manage. For some reason it makes him smile. It's so out of place in this dirty hallway and on his obviously exhausted face. He should have gone home hours ago.

"Why are you still here, Andy?"

"I had to wait for a few people to go home before I could turn off the cameras and sneak in."

"Why did you—" I can't even finish my sentence before the cheesy, meaty smell assaults my senses.

Pizza.

Oily, cheesy, pepperoni-topped pizza. I turn to face Andy, using the bars to speed my progress, and see two paper plates in his hands. In an instant, my hands are through the bars.

Andy chuckles and helps me fold one of the plates through the metal gaps. "I had to microwave it, and one of these is for me, but I can get you more if you're still hungry."

I bounce my head in acknowledgment as I take my first incredible bite. It's so warm and melty. I groan in satisfaction and have all three pieces devoured in a matter of minutes. I hold my stomach, leaning my forehead against the bars. "Thank you."

Andy offers me his last piece, but I wave him off. I couldn't eat another bite if I tried. His brows knit together. "I really did try to get you out of here."

"I know."

"Legally we have up to seventy-two hours. Obviously, I'm not pressing charges, and this won't show up anywhere on your record, but Knott doesn't care. He won't let us release you." His frown deepens. "I'll sneak in here as often as I can to check on you, but there's another Jackal here, Deputy Jessica Yates, that you can trust. She's the only one, though."

"Andy, you can't risk yourself or this will all have been for nothing."

"I know. Jack and Danny said the same thing. But I feel awful."

I reach through the bars and pat his hand. "Don't. I'm fine. I promise."

<hr>

Two and a half days later, the sun is bright and blinding as Deputy Yates escorts me outside. I take a moment to savor the crisp, clean air, blinking several times before fully adjusting to the light and my newly found freedom.

Leaning against the hood of his Chevy is Colton, his inked arms wide open, and I can't help but run into them. His hug is soft and delicate, like I'm fragile. I squeeze him tighter, even when he doesn't squeeze back.

After a beat longer than I'd like, his shoulders finally unfurl, and he crushes me against his chest. I breathe in that sunshine-and-spice scent that is so uniquely him, and he kisses the top of my head. When he leans down to find my lips, I dodge the kiss. "I haven't showered or brushed my teeth in three days. I smell."

Colton grabs my chin and forces me to look him in the eye. "I couldn't give a single fuck what you smell like, only that you're okay and that you're still mine after this mess." He kisses me on the lips, and I melt into his touch.

"I'm okay, I promise." I try to give him a smile, but I'm so freaking tired I only manage to scrunch my face up. Once we're safely in his car, Colton slides me across the bench seat and tucks me into his side. He rubs my arm and glances down at me every mile or so like he needs to reassure himself that I'm really here. "Colton, I'm fine. I promise. Knott never showed up, and Andy and Jessica kept me company when they could. I'm good."

Colton's fingers flex on my arm. "Fucking Andy. You might be fine, but some of us were struggling. Holly's losing her fucking mind. I thought she was going to kill Jack when she found out."

"Holly knows I was arrested?"

"The whole town knows. I'm taking you to her right now, if that's alright? She needs to see for herself that you're okay." He moves his eyes from the road back to me. "It was torture not being able to do anything while you wasted away in jail. I won't force you, but I think you should go see her, if you can stomach it."

"I wasn't *wasting* away." Really, I was just thinking. I had a lot of time to think. I scan Colton's face. His eyes are red and there's deep-purple bags under them. It looks like he hasn't slept in days. I knew he'd be worried about me, but not this worried. I rest my head on his shoulder and let loose a long, stinky sigh. "I'll go see Holly."

Not thirty minutes later, we pull into the familiar gravel drive of Holly's bungalow. It's a little after two o'clock, and although I expected Holly to be asleep, she's pacing back and forth in the window. Colton cuts the engine and grips the steering wheel. "I should have mentioned this earlier, but Jack wants to see you, too. Do you want me to come inside with you, or should I wait out here?" His hands flex on the wheel and he won't look in my direction.

"I might be in there a while. I need to shower after I speak with Holly, and—"

"I'll wait. I don't mind." He turns toward me and runs the knuckle of his index finger down my jawline. Despite his reassuring touch, there is something else lurking beneath the surface of his actions, but I'm too tired to analyze it now.

I lean into his hand. "It won't be that long, but come in if you hear things breaking, okay?"

He cracks a tiny smile and reaches over to open my door. "I'm sure you can handle it on your own, Tiger. Just don't get arrested again."

When I step outside the car, Holly is waiting for me on the porch in an oversized T-shirt and leggings with her hair in a messy topknot. She looks like she's missed as much sleep as Colton. A tiny sliver of guilt worms its way through my stomach. I never considered how she might be affected by my arrest.

She reaches for me but quickly pulls her hand back. "Are you okay?" she asks.

I nod. "I'm fine, but I really don't have the energy to keep going in circles with you. Colton's the one who asked me to stop by."

"I'm ready to talk," she says, holding the door open.

Holly lets me shower, and when I'm done, she's sitting on the couch with a plate of food on the coffee table for me. Her plate is already finished, and I absently wonder when she started eating complete meals without getting sick. She pats the cushion next to her, and I reluctantly take a seat.

"Before I start, I need to apologize. I should have been open with you from the beginning and I wasn't. I'm sorry." She bites her lip. "I think part of me thought I was protecting you, keeping you from the same mistakes I made, but now that you intend to join the Jackals, well, you'll find out sooner or later and it's best you hear it from me."

The hairs on the back of my neck rise.

Holly readjusts herself on the couch. "There's no easy way to say this, so I'm just going to lay it all out. Dad is the head of an organization called the Vipers. That's why you might have heard hissing from some of the Jackals. It's why Dad has kept his distance from you. It's the real reason why Mom made him leave. She didn't want us raised around that kind of danger."

Once again, I can't even begin to wrap my head around what she's saying. "Mom made him leave? He didn't abandon us?" I know that I'm concentrating on the wrong part of the revelation and the question makes me feel like I'm five years old again, but I have to know.

"He would never abandon us," Holly says fiercely. "There was an incident when I was thirteen... I was taken by a group of men Dad was feuding with. Even though Dad got me back unharmed, it was the last straw for Mom. She kicked him out, and Dad agreed that it would be safer for me if he left. After that, he went back to Boston and Mom went into hiding so he wouldn't find out she was pregnant with you. When he did find out about you, he stayed away to protect us both. He didn't want any of his enemies using us against him."

My breath catches in my throat. That's not the story my mother told me at all. "Mom lied?"

"Mom lied, and I lied, too. I'm sorry. We've been keeping an eye on you, though. Trying to keep you safe."

My mouth is a desert. I have to swallow three times before I can form words. "We? You and Dad? Or you and the Vipers?" The tattoo coiled around her thigh flashes in my mind. "Wait, are you a Viper?"

"Yes."

"Are the Vipers like the Jackals?"

She shakes her head. "Not really. We're more...illicit."

She's still being cryptic, and I shove down the sudden urge to walk out of the house, forcing myself to stay seated and keep my voice calm. "What does that mean? It's not like what the Jackals do is legal..."

"Dad runs a series of illegal gambling halls that cater to other organized crime groups and wealthy businessmen. He makes a lot of money and is involved in a few other not-so-legal ventures: prostitution, money laundering, corporate espionage, fighting rings... You name it, he probably has a finger dipped in it."

I don't know if I'm too exhausted from jail to think or what, but it doesn't seem plausible that there's been a whole secret world existing right under my nose. How could she keep this from me? How is it possible that my father is an even *worse* person than I originally thought. "So, you're saying Dad is in the Mafia?" Just saying it out loud feels ridiculous.

Her lips purse. "It's not too far from it. But no, and we try to avoid doing business with them as much as possible."

"Why haven't the Jackals put a stop to you?" I ask, half revolted by her answer. It sounds like while the Jackals are in it for justice, the Vipers are in it for themselves.

She flinches. "We're not all bad, and Dad isn't evil. He does what he does with a conscience. He usually only takes from other bad people. He protects those who work for him and gives them a safe place. The Vipers never hurt anyone who didn't already have it coming."

"Why—"

Holly holds up a hand. "There's a lot more. If you could let me finish before you start asking questions, I promise I will do my best to answer them. I need to tell you how I ended up here in Eden."

"Fine," I say with unmasked annoyance.

"When I was still a Navy nurse, I was on an aid mission in South America—the same mission I met Jeremy on, actually." She smiles faintly to herself before shaking her head and continuing. "We came to this little village out in the middle of nowhere. Most of the town had no access to running water and no electricity. I'd never seen anything like it. The only buildings there that weren't falling apart were a mine and a factory. I'll give you one guess as to who owned both."

Ice prickles on the surface of my skin, pulsing through my body in nauseating waves. "Charles Eastmann."

"Charles Eastmann," she confirms. "Or, technically, one of his subsidiaries, East Mining Company. You should have seen the working conditions for the villagers, Ry. It was abysmal. The most populated portion of the town was the cemetery. I can't even think about it without feeling sick to my stomach. Unsafe working conditions, almost weekly workplace accidents...their average life expectancy was somewhere around thirty."

Rage swirls in her irises. "I tried to report it," she says with tears clinging to her lower lids and a firm set to her jaw, "but my superiors insisted it was outside of our jurisdiction and not our concern. I was told we were there to *provide aid for a week and move on.*' I resigned my commission a few months later and joined up with some activists stateside. Without money, we couldn't affect real change, though, and that's when I turned to Dad and met the Vipers."

A shadow of a smile flashes across her lips. "Turns out, Charles Eastmann was already on Dad's radar, and he wanted to get back at him as much as I did. Dad agreed to help me bring him down, but as soon as we started digging into Eastmann's operations in South America, there was a chemical leak in the factory in the village. No survivors. A week later, the mine mysteriously collapsed, effectively covering up all violations committed by East Mining Company."

Holly heaves a humorless laugh. "Sound familiar? It's the same stunt he pulled in Eden years prior." She lets that declaration sink in before continuing. "Eastmann Incorporated is impervious to hackers, and it quickly became clear that we weren't going to get information the usual way. Dad and I needed a man on the inside—or, in this case, a woman. I officially joined the Vipers and was hired at Eastmann Incorporated headquarters as part of the janitorial night crew. My job was to break into the server room and download the information we needed to expose Charles Eastmann. Unfortunately, I got caught during the download and barely got out. Dad and I released what little information I got to the public, and Eastmann Incorporated's stocks plummeted. The information was only about one of his newer departments, but it took him years to recover the financial loss. He's been after me ever since. I needed to disappear, to find a safe place to lie low for a while. Jack owed Dad a favor, and I ended up in Eden.

"You can imagine how surprised I was to find Jeremy here and learn that the Jackals were trying to bring down the same man as me. I was only meant to be here for a few weeks, but things between Jeremy and I took off. We got married, and I stayed here as a liaison of sorts between the Jackals and the Vipers. I guess the rest is history." She reaches for my hand. "I couldn't bring you here because I was on the run. It wasn't any safer with Dad. We both wanted to keep you out of all this shit to protect you. Then you started dating Logan, and we thought Charles Eastmann would use you as leverage to find me."

"You think Logan was using me?" My voice is squeaky, my pulse so rapid I might pass out.

Black spots form at the corners of my vision as she says, "It seems a little too coincidental, doesn't it? But he never made a move. And then when Jeremy—"

"Jesus fucking Christ, Holly. You think Logan has something to do with Jeremy's death?" My voice is rough as her insinuation rocks me to my core.

She shakes her head. "We still don't know who killed Jeremy, but when he went missing, he was trying to finish what I started. He'd been working undercover in the tech department at Eastmann Incorporated. He called home saying he found something...then we didn't hear from him for four weeks. Andy found him on the bridge not long after."

I sway slightly. I need oxygen. What do I even try to process first? The betrayal from my mom. The shock about my dad being some sort of crime lord. The fact that my ex might somehow be involved in the murder of my brother-in-law. I stand without thinking and start to pace.

Holly watches me. "I know it's a lot to take in, but if you're joining the Jackals, you needed to know. I assume that's why you got arrested? Because you were doing something for them? For Jack?"

If she's part of the Vipers, can I talk about this with her? I don't know what the rules are here at all. I glance out the window, suddenly wishing I'd asked Colton to come inside with me.

"You don't have to say anything. I know how it is." She tries to hide her hurt under a smile, but it only makes her look constipated. "You were right about needing to get out of Eden. I'm going back to Boston, to the Vipers. My last shift at the hospital was yesterday. I know a lot has changed, but Colt told me you got into Northeastern. I was hoping we could still go together?"

"I don't know," I say automatically.

Holly recoils from my words as if they were a slap to the face.

"I still haven't heard back from all the schools I applied to," I say a little more softly.

"I understand. There's one more thing I wanted to talk about. Rylee, I'm—"

A knock at the door interrupts her train of thought, and Colton cracks open the screen, not waiting for a response. Needing refuge, I throw myself into his arms before he's fully inside.

"You've been in here for a while, I was just checking on you. I can step back outside if you guys are still talking?"

I shake my head against his chest. "We're done, I can't handle any more revelations today." I turn back toward my sister, but don't let go of Colton. "Thank you for being honest with me. I needed that. I'm not mad, but that was a lot to take in. And although I still have questions about Mom and Dad and the Vipers, I don't think I'm ready for the answers just yet."

Holly sags back into her chair. "Are we okay?"

I close my eyes and rub the middle of my forehead, hoping for some sort of clarity on my feelings. "I want us to be okay. But everything I ever thought was true is a lie. I don't know yet."

Holly's face pales. "I understand. I'm leaving the day after tomorrow. Can you stop by before then? There is one more thing I wanted to talk to you about before I leave. Any time before eight works for me."

I glance up at Colton, who's looking down at me and rubbing small circles on my back. The tiny gesture lets me know he's with me and reminds me I can make whatever choice I want. "I'll think about it."

There is a long pause after my noncommittal answer.

Finally, Colton clears his throat. "We should head over to Jack's. Did you need to grab anything before we go?"

Most of my clothes are already over at his place. Anything still left at Holly's is shoved into a duffle under the couch. "Nope, I'm good."

I turn back toward my sister. While part of me resents her for her secrets, I wonder if I've also let her down. She looks sad right now, but so much healthier than when I first arrived in May. I don't know if she'll ever recover fully from the loss of Jeremy, but she's clearly faring just fine without me. Despite her obvious disappointment with the way our conversation ended, her posture is strong and confident, like in deciding to go back to the Vipers, she's refound her purpose in life.

I, too, feel like I have purpose and direction now. All those hours alone in jail really clarified things for me—one thing in particular.

I look up at Colton and despite the earth-shattering revelations from Holly, I feel confident in the path I've chosen.

Chapter Thirty-Three

The sun is just starting to dip below the hills as Colton and I park at the end of Jack's driveway. When he cuts the engine, sweet summer air drifts in through the open windows, slowly replacing the familiar and subtle smell of fuel that accompanies the old muscle car.

Colton rolls up his window, and I start to gather my things, but he stops me with a calloused, inked hand on my bare thigh. "This meeting is between you, Jack, and Danny. I won't be going in with you. But before you go, I wanted to give you something." He leans over and takes out a small brown paper parcel from the glove compartment. "Happy belated birthday," he says, placing the box in my hand. "I wish we could have celebrated together."

"Colton, you didn't have to—"

"Just open it," he says, fussing with his collar. I scan his face, trying to name the odd tension that's been hovering over us since he picked me up from jail, but I can't.

A bead of perspiration hangs on his forehead, waiting to

fall. He's nervous, but if it's about the present or something else, I can't tell.

I set to opening the carefully wrapped box, gently peeling back the layers of black tissue paper until the contents are revealed. My breath hitches as I clasp a perfectly preserved marigold encased in clear resin. As if frozen in time, the elegant bloom is the brightest yellow-orange flower I've ever seen.

I stare down at the beautiful creation, speechless.

After a moment, I hold it up by the leather necklace-length string looped through the top to get a better look. When the resin catches the last rays of the fleeting day, it glows and almost sparkles, like my very own little piece of the sun. It's the best gift I've ever received.

An unnamed emotion bubbles in my chest. Only, it's not unnamed anymore. I spent most of my time in jail mulling over exactly how I feel and the conclusion I came to is as natural as breathing.

I love this man. I love Colton Archer.

It feels too soon and part of me wonders if telling him might ruin it, but the way he's looking at me now, like I might be as precious as this beautiful flower creation, tells me I'm not the only one feeling this way.

He wipes his hands on his jeans. "I tried to make you earrings, but it's harder than it looks, so I made you this pendant instead. You can use it as a necklace, keychain, whatever you want." He gives an awkward laugh I've never heard from him before. "I like the way your face lights up when you see these, and I wanted to give you a piece of Eden, a piece of me to take with you to Boston. This one is from the stream near my parents' old house."

"It's perfect, thank you." I place it around the rearview mirror. "I don't want to forget it at Jack's."

Colton grabs my hand and runs his fingers lightly over the

marigold tattoo on my wrist. The sensation burns and chills all at once, sending shivers up my neck, muddling my brain. He follows the trail of goose bumps up my arm, wrapping a hand around the base of my skull and placing our foreheads together until we're resting against one another.

"I know you spit on Andy to protect me and keep me from attacking the sheriff." I open my mouth to argue, but he places the rough pad of his finger against my lips. "You acted like a Jackal and if you'd done it for anyone else, I would have been so proud of you. But *never* put yourself in danger for me again. Not ever. Knott could have done anything he wanted to you in that jail cell." His grip tightens almost painfully on the back of my neck. "I wanted to tear that place apart brick by brick to get you out. We both need to be smarter when it comes to one another. We can't let our feelings get in the way. Never put yourself in danger for me. Do you understand what I'm saying?"

I nod, and our foreheads rub together with the movement. I disagree, but I understand. There is no point in arguing right now.

He inhales, breathing me in before exhaling forcefully. "Go. Get inside before I decide to drive us both away from here."

I jerk my head away from his, and I'm met with an icy stare I haven't seen since I first arrived in Eden. It's like he's looking past me, and I hate it. People have been looking past me my entire life, and seeing Colton do it again reignites a fire in me.

"Actually, no." My back stiffens at the strength in my words. "Andy and I were tasked with convincing Knott of Andy's bullshit loyalties. We did that. You getting arrested was not part of the deal. You are vital to the Jackals. I see it in the way they look at you when you walk in a room. I see it in the way Jack consults you before making a decision. If I had to do the whole thing over again, I'd do it the same way, especially if it meant keeping you out of Knott's claws. Do you know why? Because you're worth protecting, too. So don't tell me who I can and can't protect, Colton Archer. My life and my safety aren't any more important than yours or anyone else's."

Colton brings our foreheads back together and laughs. "You are the best thing that ever happened to me, you know that?"

I want to tell him he's the best thing that happened to me, too.

I want to tell him I love him.

But I choke down the words.

He kisses my forehead and then my lips. My chest heaves against him as the kiss becomes more desperate. His lips feel like they're trying to tell me something, but the message is lost in a tangle of moans and tongue. When the kiss begins to slow, and I can finally pull myself away, we're both breathless. Colton's cold mask is also back.

"I'll see you later?" I ask.

"Go inside, Rylee," he says, stone-faced, hands clenched tightly in his lap.

As I walk away, I swear I hear something that sounds suspiciously like a fist slamming into glass. The splintering noise cracks through the quiet night air, making my limbs go cold.

Jack insists on feeding me before discussing whatever it is he summoned me here for. It's such a dad move, and I can't help but love him more for it.

Only once I've finished my last bite and Danny has cleared the table does Jack begin.

"I wanted to talk to you about what happened at the diner the other day," he says with forced casualness.

My mouth goes dry, and it's suddenly hard to swallow.

"Andy tells me Sheriff Knott bought the act. You did good, *mija*. You did very good. But I need to know why you spit on Andy and got yourself arrested." His lips thin and his eyes narrow in assessment. All of a sudden, I'm back in grade school and have been called to the principal's office.

Here goes nothing.

"Danny stopped Colton's first punch, but Knott kept egging him on. It was clear he was going to keep baiting Colton until he got a reaction. I think Knott wanted him to attack in public. I had to do something or Colton was going to get himself arrested. So, I acted."

Jack's head moves methodically in a north-south motion. "You see, *mija*, we have a bit of a unique situation with your relationship with Colt. Our members and their significant others are usually Jackal–Dove combos."

Danny leans forward. "You probably already put this together, but a Dove is what we call someone who is affiliated with the club and under our protection, but not a member. Alex and Holly are Doves," he clarifies.

Jack runs his tongue over his teeth and scoots back in his chair, his ringed fingers clicking on the armrests. "The club has never had a serious Jackal–Jackal relationship before. There is some concern among the members that if you were to become a Jackal, you might have conflicting loyalties. There's talk that we need a new rule—no inner-member relationships. If you were placed in a similar situation and club interest *and* Colt's safety were on the line, which would you choose?"

My leg bounces. "I don't understand. Isn't all member safety a club issue? Especially Colton's?" I'm going on partial information here, but hopefully I sound like I know what I'm talking about.

Jack lets out a heavy sigh, and I can't tell if he's annoyed with me or the situation. "Most of the time, yes. But the bottom line is that we need to know: if you could only choose one, would you choose Colton or the club?"

My teeth are clenched so tight that it strains my back molars. This isn't a hypothetical question. It's an ultimatum, and I can't believe I didn't see it coming. "To clarify, I can choose to stay with Colton or I can choose to give him up and join the Jackals?"

Danny grimaces and struggles to meet my gaze. "Yes, and you have to decide now."

For the past few weeks, every time I thought of the future, I saw Colton in it. I saw us in Boston, coming home to Eden on the weekends and holidays until I was finished with school. I saw us working together to make a difference. Now, with one question, I don't know what I see. To me, Colton *is* the Jackals. They are one and the same. I've never had to separate them in my mind before.

I don't know what being a Jackal would be like without him. Could I still do this and work with Colton if he wasn't mine? Ashlynn's beautiful face pops into my mind. Would I leave town like she did? Would I run back to Charlotte the second I had to watch Colton date someone else?

No. I wouldn't. I know I wouldn't. I couldn't run from the Jackals because that would be like letting Charles Eastmann get away with murder. If it means helping other families like the Graces, then I'm in it for the long run. No matter what happens with Colton in the future, I'm going to see this through.

For little Anna, for Danny's mom, for Jeremy.

For myself.

Besides, I also honestly don't know if Colton would ever look at me the same way if I picked him over the Jackals. The club is his whole life. It would always hang in the air between us.

The weight on my chest is so crushing I can barely move. This is a ridiculous choice to have to make, but I know for a fact that if I pick wrong here, I'll lose them both.

With that realization, I already know my decision.

My resolve cracks a little as I look at Jack, who's trying to keep his face neutral. "You are family," he says. "You've always been family, even before we met you. You still have a seat at this table, no matter what you choose, *mija*."

My hands ball into fists and my toes curl in my shoes as my belly fills with dread.

"If I can only have one, I choose the Jackals."

The choking sensation that follows my declaration is immediate. I want to claw the words back down my throat and take them back.

Danny lets out a sigh, and I watch as a slow, proud smile spreads across Jack's face. Their reactions don't touch me. I can't feel anything except the massive ball stuck in my throat.

"It's settled, then. The vote for your membership will be next month, but your first Jackal meeting is tomorrow. We have new information on Jeremy's murder and the pack needs to get a feel for you being part of the team. Now, can someone go find Colt? I have dinner waiting for him on the counter." Jack gets up and starts whistling while he washes the dishes.

A new wave of anguish crashes over me. "What just happened?" I ask Danny after finally sucking down a gulp of oxygen.

He shakes his head. Standing, he grabs my arm and leads me outside. The first thing we both notice is the cracked driver's side window of the Chevy.

"Colt did that?" Danny asks.

The memory of our last kiss and the crack I heard walking away turns my stomach sour. "I think so." I should have gone to him immediately. How can I face him now, after not choosing him?

"I'll be right back." Danny leaves and when he returns, he's carrying a small first aid kit. The scent of lilies from Jack's walkway wafts with him as he comes to stand beside me. "Colt was supposed to wait outside. Obviously, he had other plans. You'll probably find him at his parents' old house. It's five miles down that way. Big clearing, you can't miss it." He points east and places car keys on top of the first aid kit, handing me both. "Take my truck." He makes a *shooing* motion with his fingers.

Clearly, he expects me to go tell Colton that things are over between us and that I chose the Jackals over him. I guess it's best to get it over with, but that doesn't make it any easier. I feel like an absolute piece of shit, and the only thing I want to do is go bury myself in bed, which I guess is back on Holly's couch.

My eyes burn as I shuffle my lead feet toward the truck. Turning the ignition and driving away from the house feels like sealing my own fate.

I guess I don't deserve Colton if I can't place him first anyway.

A little over five miles down, the tree-lined road opens into a massive clearing. The path is littered with potholes and cracks in the pavement, and it's a relief to step out of the truck and put my feet back on solid ground, even if my legs aren't working properly. It takes a minute for my eyes to adjust to the total darkness, but when they do, I see Colton silhouetted on a small hill overlooking a valley. The ground barely makes a sound as I approach his back.

"She picked me, didn't she?" His head drops, and I realize that he must think I'm Danny. "I can't blame her. Had the tables been turned, I would have picked her, too. That's how fucking deep I am in this shit, man." He snorts. "I'm still going with her when she leaves. What are you and Jack going to do, kick me out? Burn the Jackal mark off my neck and back? Good fucking luck trying to find someone else to do what I do." He pauses. "And another thing—"

Colton whirls around, and his eyes shoot open as he takes me in. He steps toward me, but I step back. "Rylee?" Pain and confusion taint his voice.

A single tear falls down my cheek. "I didn't pick you." My stomach is in such knots right now that I might throw up. I am the worst, most stupid person in the entire world not to pick him, especially considering he just admitted he would have picked me over his brothers if he'd been in my position. Tears sting and pull at my eyes. I'm seconds away from falling apart.

Colton's mouth falls open. "You what?"

It only takes the sound of his shocked voice to know I've made a huge mistake. I cough-hiccup, barely able to get the words out. "I-I picked the Jackals."

Colton runs at me, scooping me up and twirling me around and kisses every inch of my face.

"You." *Kiss.*

"Perfect." *Kiss.*

"Beautiful." *Kiss.*

"Insane." *Kiss.*

"Woman." *Kiss.*

When he puts me down, he places a hand on each side of my cheeks and spreads his legs wide on the dirt so that our faces are nearly even.

My head is spinning and my heart is breaking at his confusing reaction. I have to bite my lip to control the quiver. "I didn't choose you. How can you say that?"

"Don't you get it? One of the reasons I love you is *because* you picked the club. This was your test, Tiger. Your loyalty test. If you picked the club, then you're in. That's it."

My brain hurts trying to understand what he's saying. "But Jack said I could only have one: you or the club. How can we be together if I— Wait... You love me?"

Colton lets loose a barking laugh and then begins to pepper my face in kisses again. "It was just a test. We can be together. Your choice shows that you are willing to put aside your own happiness for the good of others. You're a true Jackal. You're fucking perfect, and I don't deserve you. And of course, I love you. I'm *in* love with you. Have been for a while, I think." He wipes away my tears with his thumbs.

"I love you, too," I breathe out.

He kisses me, and somewhere in between the tears and soul-searing passion of his lips, I get the overwhelming sensation that this is where I belong.

In his arms.

In this place.

In Eden.

Chapter Thirty-Four

The following morning, I wake up with Colton's mouth wrapped around my nipple and his hand dancing across my lower abdomen. I gasp when his skilled tongue slides across my breast, nibbling playfully. As soon as my eyes flutter open, his hand dips between my legs, finding me already wet and ready for him.

An hour later, he lifts his head from where it rests on my upper thigh, a satisfied smile on his lips as he kisses my stomach and makes his way back up to my mouth, which is still quivering from my last body-shaking orgasm. "We have the meeting soon. You get dressed, and I'll go make us some breakfast."

I make a nonsensical sound and burrow myself back into the pillows, still reveling in the afterglow of pure ecstasy.

A cold shower wakes me up enough to dress, and I make my way into the kitchen where I find Colton serving up three plates of eggs and sausage. Danny is sitting at the counter with a cup of steaming coffee in hand. He has bags under his eyes and barely looks at me when I take the seat next to him.

"Tired?" I ask conversationally.

He takes another sip of coffee. "You guys know you're loud, right? Even when you're trying to be quiet. You're so fucking loud." He shifts uncomfortably in his seat. "I never thought I'd mind. But, Rylee, you're like my sister. It's just not right."

"You'll have the place to yourself soon," Colton says, not looking up from the silverware he's gathering.

Danny's eyebrows shoot up in surprise. "Are you guys getting a place?"

Colton freezes at the counter, and his eyes lift to meet mine. He said he'd be in Boston with me, but we never discussed the details of exactly what that meant. My heart drums against my rib cage, waiting for his answer.

"We haven't talked about it. But I'd like to, if you want to," he says, looking at me with a hopeful expression.

I nod enthusiastically, trying not to float off my seat. With a coy smile, Colton slides a plate in front of me and Danny. "Then, yeah. We're getting our own place." A small blush creeps over his face as he fights and fails to contain his grin.

"When do you have to officially decide on a school?" Danny asks me through bites of sausage.

"I'm waiting to hear back from one more. Either way, it will be Boston." I don't want to admit that I'm more nervous that I might actually get into MIT than I am that I'll be rejected.

What if I'm not smart enough without Minho's constant tutelage?

"Minho's got a stack of grants and shit for you to apply to when you decide which program you're choosing. The Jackals will help pay off the rest, so don't let cost sway where you end up," Danny says around a mouthful of food.

Egg literally falls from my mouth back onto my plate. "Wait, really?"

"Of course. It's an investment in the future of the club."

"I'm sure that money could be used somewhere else, on someone who needs it more," I counter.

"Trust me, you're worth it," Danny says, finishing off his plate. "Every dollar we put into you will go back into the community a hundredfold. You'll understand better after the vote. But trust me, you'll more than earn the cost of that degree back for the club."

A warm sensation spreads up my neck and into my cheeks. Colton comes around the counter and opens his mouth like a baby bird. I shove a sausage into it a little too forcefully, and he pretends to choke before bending down to kiss my neck.

"You guys make me sick, you know that?" Danny says without sounding the least bit annoyed.

When Colton takes a seat and starts in on his own breakfast, I decide to change the subject. "So, how does the initiation thing work? You guys make it sound like I'm already in, but you and Jack said something about a vote?"

Danny gets up to pour himself another coffee, refilling Colton's mug before he answers. "Initiations usually start before the new member is ever aware the club exists. We find a person we think might serve the cause and for a while, we watch."

"You watch?"

Danny shrugs. "We try to get a feel if the person is a good fit for our little family. If they're deemed trustworthy enough, then it's put to the council in what we call a consideration vote. That's where the Originals and a representative from each of our charters vote on whether the person should be considered for membership."

In my mind, I see Jack holding court at The Pack the night Colton and I first slept together. Those people at the table must have all been representatives from the other Jackal organizations.

"If the vote is yes, then we start dropping hints and slowly show the prospect what we do. The prospect then has to declare their interest in joining the club on their own, like you did to Jack at the memorial and again at his house the night we had dinner."

Colton pipes in, "Every initiation is different. Some people have to prove themselves over the course of years, like your buddy Andy, before they even get a consideration vote. For others, it's a much shorter process." I don't miss the sarcastic, almost bitter, quality to his voice as he spits out Andy's name. "But everyone has at least two tests, one for usefulness and one for loyalty. That being said, your initiation was all fucked up and out of order from the very beginning. First, we had to decide if you were an Eastmann spy. After we voted that you weren't, Jack had us vote on your consideration for membership that same night."

One of Colton's dimples makes an appearance, like he just remembered what else happened that night. "Shortly after, Minho confessed that he had already been using your study sessions to see if you had the computer skills to replace Jeremy's position in the club."

Danny interjects, "Jeremy and Minho were our hackers. Minho's been struggling to keep up without him."

"Anyway," Colton continues, "Minho reported that with a little training you could more than fill the role. So, your usefulness test was technically complete before your consideration vote."

"Wait," I interrupt, "then what was the diner thing, with Andy and Knott?"

"That wasn't a test," Colton says through gnashed teeth. "A club member needed help and Jack insisted you were the best person for the job. The president always has a little more leeway with the rules than the rest of us. I think Jack was trying to show the club that you're not a Viper, and you did that with flying colors. Vipers don't take one for the team the way you did."

"Anyway, that bullshit at Jack's last night was your loyalty test. And that's that. A notice has been put out to all members for your initiation vote next month. Anyone can come from any of the charters. All the Original Jackals have to vote, and a representative from each charter also has to cast a vote. It's usually the VP or another ranking member."

"At the initiation, you will be asked questions by any member that has one, and at the end, we all vote. If we vote yes, you get the Jackal mark. If there is a single no, then the person who voted no has to explain why and we vote again. If there is a no again, you won't be initiated."

All this time I was already being tested.

I'm not sure if I should be angry or impressed. "Is there anything else?"

"Well, every prospect has to have a sponsor, someone in the club willing to take them on, someone who can be held accountable if they fuck up," Colton says nonchalantly.

"Who's my sponsor?"

Colton and Danny exchange a significant look, and in unison they murmur, "Jack."

The tone of their voices has a wary quality to it. "Is he a bad sponsor or something?"

"We wouldn't know. Besides the other charter heads, he's never sponsored anyone," Colton says.

"I'm the first?"

Danny answers this time. "Jack said he saw something in you the first day he met you. I guess you didn't back away when he almost ran you over with his truck? And then you stepped between him and Holly or something?"

I remember both those instances like they were yesterday

and yet it feels like another life. I remember the jealousy at seeing the way he protected and cared for Holly the day of Jeremy's funeral. I remember the quiet way she took comfort in him as I sat on the sidelines. How different my life is now. Back then, I was on the outside looking in. Now, Holly has removed herself from the warmth and love of the Jackal family, and I've somehow slithered my way in.

Later that same day, when I see Jack at The Pack, I can't help but wrap my arms around him. I doubt the embrace is appropriate for the setting, but he hugs me back, and I revel in his strength and how grateful I am to have met him. He's the closest thing I've ever had to a father figure. To know he was the one to sponsor me means more than I'll ever be able to tell him with words. He gave me this family.

Jack places a hand on each of my shoulders and holds me at arm's length to scan my face. "Everything okay?" he asks. I can feel the metal of his rings and each callous of his worn hands on the bare skin of my shoulders.

"I'm just happy. Thank you for bringing me in," I say, trying to keep my emotions in check.

"That's what I do." He takes a look around the room, skimming over the faces of the men and women gathered for the meeting. His last look falls on Colton and Minho, who are chatting animatedly with a few rough-looking bikers. Then he brings his gaze back to me. "It's selfish, really. I find all the good ones and bring them into the fold. You are one of the good ones, *mija*. You'll be a great fit here. You can't sit in the circle just yet, though, not until the vote next month, but I'm glad you came. Do you mind helping Alex?"

I don't know what circle he's referring to, but I agree and head over to the bar.

"There she is." Alex hands me a towel, and I start in on all the clean, wet glasses. His normal grin is noticeably absent.

"Minho tells me that once you're voted in, he has to start training you before you leave for school. Looks like I'll be looking for another bartender after all." He sounds disappointed, but there is another emotion I can't identify—maybe jealousy?

"I still want to fill in when I can," I say, trying to smooth over a hurt I don't quite understand. "I know it was just a few shifts, but I've really enjoyed working with you."

His smile returns. "If you have the time, I'd love that."

A large group of people walk through the doors, and Alex and I scramble to get them drinks. While we pour, the room erupts into a chorus of screeching chairs and heavy footsteps. After doling out the last order of drinks, I look up to find the room transformed. All the tables have been moved and stacked to the side while sixty or so chairs have been brought out and placed in a circle. As people take their seats, I lean over to Alex and whisper, "Why a circle?"

"All Jackals have an equal seat at the table. Every voice counts."

I become very still as I take in the room. Jack, Colton, Danny, and Minho all sit apart from each other. Jack's seat or position in the circle is no different from anyone else's. It's like they're the knights of the round table. I love it.

Jack calls the meeting to order. "First off, I want to thank you all for lying low this summer. I know it's been difficult and at times it might have felt like we were doing nothing to avenge Jeremy's murder, but I think we've been quiet for long enough. It's time to move forward. Parker, you have the floor. Please bring everyone up to speed."

A lanky guy in a plaid shirt and dark-wash jeans stands. I've never seen him before, but the rest of the Jackals seem to know him well enough. He clears his throat before speaking. "It's looking more and more like an Eastmann henchman is the one who took out Jeremy. We all know that Jeremy missed his first check-in four weeks before we found his body. We can assume the reason for his radio silence was that he was caught stealing information from Eastmann Incorporated and that he followed protocol and went into hiding. Initially, we didn't know where he was during that missing time gap, but after a thorough search of all our safe houses, we finally found something.

"We put together that Jeremy stopped at a series of safe houses between Eastmann Incorporated headquarters and Eden. Per protocol, it looks like he stayed in each one for a few days to make sure no one was following him. At the last safe house, the cabin just outside of town, we found the rest of Jeremy's things. We also found this." He holds up a silver rectangular object with an odd-looking triangular USB port at the end. As the metal glints in the bar lighting, an odd sense of déjà vu creeps up my neck.

"The problem is," Parker continues, we don't know how to get the data off of it. Minho's been trying, but any attempt to open the device will result in an erasure of the data inside. We think it can only be read by a very specific type of computer, which are only given to the most trusted employees at Eastmann Incorporated."

A gear in my brain clicks.

That is the exact same shape as the USB ports on Logan's work computer. If that device was taken from Eastmann Incorporated, I bet Logan's computer would be able to read it.

I shift on my feet, trying to work up the courage to say something, but before I can, Parker takes a seat and Jack stands, walking into the center of the circle. The mood of the room darkens. "I called this meeting because in a few minutes I am going to ask for another volunteer to go back inside Eastmann

Incorporated. We need one of their computers in order to retrieve the data that Jeremy sacrificed his life for."

A murmur ripples through the crowd. My gaze shifts immediately to Colton, who's looking at me with a hard expression. I ball my fists.

He's going to volunteer.

I tremble at the thought and shoot my hand into the air, smacking into a beer bottle and sending it clattering across the countertop. Every face in the room turns in my direction and my cheeks heat with embarrassment.

Jack shakes his head. "Sorry, Rylee, while we appreciate the offer, you can't volunteer until you've been initiated."

I forcefully swallow the lump forming in my throat. "I wasn't volunteering, but I know where you can get a computer to read that device."

With a slight look of surprise on his face, Jack motions for me to continue.

"Logan kept a work computer in his loft. He only used it for traveling or late-night meetings. It had strange triangular USB ports on the side that looked exactly like the storage device Parker held up. You don't need to send anyone undercover; we can just take the computer from his loft."

The faces staring at me shift from confusion to mistrust. Even Colton's expression narrows.

Great. I think I just reminded them all that I used to sleep with the enemy's son.

"I still have the key. It's in the glove box of my car. I can get the computer for you, too, if you want," I offer, as if this might somehow absolve me of my past sins.

Another rumble of comments swells through the crowd.

Danny spreads out his legs. "We can't send you on a mission of this magnitude until you're initiated. I'll get the computer from the Eastmann spawn's place. I trust Rylee's information."

God, I want to hug him. The answering chorus of comments sounds much more amenable this time around. Somehow, Danny's trust in me is enough to sway the momentum of the crowd. Well, most of the crowd. Moments later, a big guy in a leather cut pipes up, "If there is any chance this could go south, why risk the VP?"

Colton drops his chin to his chest and won't meet my stare. Jack takes a step toward the big guy and places a hand on his shoulder in a calming manner. "Garrett has a point. This is a stealth mission. We need someone who can make it look like a break-in and someone to examine the device."

Minho exchanges a brief look with Alex and then with Colton. They nod once at each other and stand. "We'll go," they say in unison.

Jack's lips thin into a tight line. "This one might be too personal for you, Colt. I could use you here. Let someone else—"

"No. I trust Rylee, and this will keep the rest of the club out of danger. I'm going, end of discussion." Colton's arms fold across his chest as he scans the room, daring anyone to contradict him.

"Wait," Garrett says, shaking his head. "Now we're sending half of the remaining Originals on a mission based on information provided by the baby Viper princess? The same one who used to fuck Logan Eastmann?"

Although his words sting, they also bolster me. "Baby Viper princess? How many times have you been in the same room as my dad?"

"I don't know, ten, maybe twenty times. I go to the fights he hosts. Why?" Garrett scoffs back.

"I've been in the same room as him a total of four times.

And one of those times was at Jeremy's funeral. So, it sounds like you know the man better than I do, which makes you more of a Viper princess than me. And as far as Logan is concerned, I didn't fucking know. I barely saw the guy. But if putting up with that idiot for a few months ends up getting the Jackals the information they need to bring Charles Eastmann down for what he did to this town *and* avenges Jeremy's death in the process then I'd gladly do it again."

My shoulders rise and fall with the effort to regain my composure. Across the room, Colton's head bobs, the glint in his gaze dipping down to my heaving chest. The corner of his lips quirk up into a roguish smile, letting me know he's more than okay with what I just said.

"Well, shit," Garrett says. "I guess I'm the new Viper princess, then. Does that mean I get to go home with Colt tonight?" The tension lifts and the crowd laughs. Then, to my surprise, he gives me a wink, which I think is meant to be an apology.

"Does anyone else have any concerns they'd like to bring up with the proposed plan?" Jack asks, taking his seat. No one says a word. "Good, then it's settled. Rylee, please give the key to Colt and go over any information that might prove useful to them. Danny, I want you to run point on this one from Eden. Colt, Minho, you leave tonight."

There are a few other items of club business discussed. They talk a lot about some sort of fighting ring, but most of what they say goes over my head. All I can think about is the distressing feeling that I don't know what I'm sending Colton into. I never saw security at Logan's place, but now I can only assume there must have at least been cameras. The sickening realization that Logan may have watched me when he wasn't home is enough to make my stomach roll, and I almost lose my sausage and eggs from this morning.

Alex, seeing my distress, pours me a ginger ale with a shot of bourbon. The combination settles my stomach and takes the edge off just enough to get me through the rest of the discussions.

When the meeting ends, Colton is the first one up. He bounds across the room and scoops me up in his arms, spinning me in a circle before taking us back toward the offices.

"You did so fucking good out there, Tiger. They needed to see you hold your own before your initiation vote next month. You were incredible." He kisses me, and for a moment I am lost in the sensation of his lips against mine. "Now tell me about the layout of Logan's place."

I spend the next three hours going over everything I can think of with Danny, Minho, and Colton. I tell them when Logan leaves for work, when he goes home, and what clubs he likes to go to. I even draw a pretty decent map of the inside of the loft. By the time we're done, my brain is fried.

Colton takes me to get the key from my car, which has been sitting at Holly's for over two weeks. I breathe a little easier when I see she's not home. Although I'm no longer mad at her, I need a minute alone with Colton and if she was here, that would be impossible.

Everything is happening too fast. The thought of Colton leaving in a few hours, possibly heading into danger, makes my insides twist and knot. Especially since it was me who suggested the plan in the first place. It should be me going, and it's on the tip of my tongue to remind Colton how easy it would be for me to sneak in and out of Logan's apartment, but I think in doing so I would undermine the faith he placed in me at the meeting. I have to trust him to do this.

"You're sure this is a good idea?" I say, bending over to retrieve the Faraday bag from my glove box.

Colton whistles at the view of my ass I'm giving him. "It's a great idea. If it works, it will keep a Jackal out of Eastmann Incorporated. All thanks to you."

When I'm standing beside him again, he kisses my temple and reaches into the Faraday bag. He places its contents—my old cell phone along with the burner phone, the Cartier bracelet, and Logan's key—on the hood of my car. The delicate, rose gold bracelet looks out of place against Colton's tattooed hands.

The jewelry never belonged on me, but those hands sure do.

I flick the bracelet across my hood. "Do you think you could bring that stupid thing back to him? Just leave it in a drawer or something?"

"Nah, let's sell it. We can use the money to furnish our new apartment when we get to Boston. We can buy a big, comfy sofa and a massive king-size bed." His smile is absolutely devilish. The look has blood rushing to my cheeks and the muscles in my abdomen seizing. Right now, I'd like nothing more than to lick that grin right off his chiseled face.

Sensing the change in my mood, Colton wraps his arms around me, pulling me flush with his body. I gasp as he moves his mouth to my neck and presses his rigid cock into my stomach.

I guess his thoughts were right in line with mine.

As his tongue trails across my collarbone, I lean back to give him better access. This only makes our bodies slam into my car and sends my old phone crashing to the ground, the screen splintering into a million pieces the second it hits the gravel, effectively breaking the heat of the moment.

Chest still heaving, Colton picks up my now-useless cell. "You know, we really do need to get you a phone. This antiphone shit Holly has going on is a little too much, even for me."

His statement catches me off guard. "I rarely see you on a phone. Do you even have one?"

"Obviously I have a phone. It's a little difficult to function without one anymore. I'm just usually with the people I want to talk to, and we don't bring them into The Pack or our other places of work. Minho runs Ghost Rider on our phones, so even if we did, we'd be fine. I know Holly is rightfully a little paranoid after her run-in with Eastmann, but not having a phone nowadays is crazy." I must look confused because Colton clarifies, "They tracked her phone while she was on the run. It's part of why your dad sent her here to us. You didn't know that?"

"No, I didn't..."

"We're all cautious, but Holly goes overboard. Did you know she had Minho wipe nearly every trace of her from the internet? Or that she uses a fake name at work and on her nursing license? Sarah James, or something like that."

A jolt of electricity fires through my body. Sarah James was our mother's name.

Oblivious to my reaction, Colton continues, "She got new identification papers when she moved here and retook her nursing exams and everything. Even for me, your sister is a little over the top. Frankly, I'm surprised you turned out so normal."

He runs his hands down my sides until I've forgotten what we were talking about and am giggling like a maniac.

In a more serious tone, he says, "Maybe you should talk to her again before she heads out? I know she unloaded a lot on you the other day, but since we'll all be in Boston, it might be good to clear the air."

We're both quiet as he lets that sink in for a second. "We're raiding Logan's place the second he leaves for work. Half an hour inside to get the computer and stage the break-in, which means I should be back no later than one o'clock tomorrow afternoon. You'll have plenty of time to talk between now and then."

I nod evasively.

Colton glances at the sun steadily creeping westward. With each inch it sinks into the sky, that gnawing feeling in my gut grows.

"I should get going. We're meeting up at Jack's to go over the final plan. Do you want me to drop you off at home, or do you want to stay here and wait for Holly?"

"I think I'll stay here and wait for her before heading over. You don't mind if I stay at your place while you're gone?"

"Not at all. In fact, I'd prefer it. At least this way you won't be alone. And I hope this doesn't make me sound like a chauvinist pig, but I kind of like the idea of you waiting and ready for me when I get home." He places two hands on my ass and squeezes.

I lean up to kiss him, trying to show him the words that I cannot form. But, after a few slow kisses, I get lost in a new sinking sensation.

I hate that he's leaving.

He pulls away, somehow sensing my unease. "This is literally the least dangerous thing I've ever done for the Jackals."

"That doesn't make me feel any better."

Colton pats me on the ass, and with one final peck on the cheek, he hops in his Chevy. The engine roars to life, and he smiles at me from the open window. "I'll be fine. And Tiger?" He pauses. "I love you."

He speeds off down the dirt road before I can respond, and a creeping sensation claws up my spine as I wonder if I'll ever get the chance to say it back.

Chapter Thirty-Five

At 7:00 p.m. the next day, Colton and Minho still aren't back.

To say I was panicking would be an understatement.

Overnight, my guilt from staying behind grew with each passing minute. By morning, the tips of my fingers were raw from repeatedly tapping them against the kitchen counter.

It only got worse when Danny left to go meet Jack at the diner and I opted to stay behind. Without anyone to distract me, I spent the rest of the day worrying that my idea to steal Logan's computer might get someone hurt...*or worse.*

My only solace has been in knowing that every tick of the clock meant Colton was another minute closer to being home.

Until it wasn't.

Now each minute that passes is another agonizing lifetime for me to worry that something went wrong.

Looking down at my feet, I half expect to see a path worn into Danny's wood floor from my pacing. This is torture. If only I had a phone, I could call someone. Well, I guess I do have a phone, but it's sitting shattered on the counter back at Holly's.

I'd brought it, along with all the other contents of the Faraday bag, inside while I waited for her to come home last night and accidentally left it there when she didn't show. Even if it wasn't broken, what good would it be without Colton's phone number?

I could go to Jack's or go find Alex at the bar, but I don't want anyone thinking I'm not cut out to be a Jackal, or that I'll fall apart every time Colton leaves on a mission. Besides, I bet they're busy. The last thing they need is me in their hair. Which leaves Holly. Even with her aversion to technology, she has to have a number for Colton.

Unable to shake the nagging thought that something is wrong, I'm in my car and speeding toward her bungalow before I can talk myself out of it. All I need to do is send him a quick text from the burner phone to put all my worries to rest. Even if I'm wrong, talking to Holly will be a distraction from waiting for Colton.

When I pull in, I'm surprised to find an unfamiliar black Mercedes parked behind Holly's car. Interesting. I guess someone from Boston came to help her pack? God, I hope it isn't our father... That prickling in my gut intensifies, and I roll my shoulders as I step onto the porch, trying to shrug it off, but my hand quakes as I place it on the doorknob.

Jesus, am I really this nervous to talk to Holly?

You can do this, Rylee. You just have to be nice to your sister and ask for Colton's number.

I take a deep, steadying breath, which is ripped from my lungs the second I open the door.

In the kitchen, a tall, bleach-blond frame hovers over Holly's bound and gagged body on the floor. A tear slips down her temple as she blinks pointedly at me, her eyes wide with terror.

"Run!" she seems to say. *"Get out of here!"*

I do neither. Frozen in place, I gawk as the man turns, his glare piercing though my haze.

"Logan?"

Although he's got the same stupid hipster haircut and his usual tailored gray suit, his face is so contorted with anger that I hardly recognize him.

"Rylee, so glad you could make it," he sneers, my name sounding like poison on his thin lips. A lock of yellow-white hair falls into his eyes when he glances down at my sister. "Holly, look who finally decided to show up. And to think, you told me she left town." Logan makes a tutting noise as he crouches down by my sister. "Another lie. What's Rylee going to tell me next? That you're not actually pregnant?"

He grinds something black into her temple, and she winces. It takes me a moment to realize he's pressing the barrel of a horrifyingly large handgun into her head. Utter terror almost overshadows his revelation.

My sister is pregnant?

I blink, as if that might somehow change the scene in front of me. "L-Logan, what are you doing? Let her go," I croak, my throat so dry my voice is barely a whisper.

For a second, I'm the old Rylee back in Charlotte. The one who didn't ask questions or speak up for herself when her boyfriend did something she didn't agree with. The one who stood by and let him walk all over her for a warm place to sleep at night.

I thought I was stronger than this, so why can't I move?

Logan tuts again. "You couldn't have made it easy and just let me come with you. No, instead you made me do it the hard way." He grabs Holly and roughly rips her up from the ground before slamming her into one of the chairs at the kitchen table. The wood creaks with the violence, and the motion makes

Holly's tank top go askew. For the first time, I notice the subtle swell of her belly. My heart squeezes.

She really is pregnant.

She starts crying in earnest now, and all the blood drains from my face. I need to get her out of here, but my limbs are iced over with fear.

"Logan, why are you here? Let Holly go. I'll do anything you want. Please—"

Logan's laughter slices through any hope I had that my plea would work. "Why am I here? Well, I guess that's one thing that went right. I thought for sure that the P.I. would have tipped you off after he caught me snooping in his office."

I never read the email from the private investigator...

"You still don't get it, do you? Do you really think I came all this way for you? Did you think you were special? That I actually wanted to be with *you*?" Logan grabs Holly by her hair and yanks back, exposing her throat. "I came here for this stupid bitch." He shakes her head cruelly and lowers his mouth to her ear. "Did you tell Rylee about how you broke into our database? How you released that information to the public? Did you tell your baby sister that the only reason I fucked her was to get to you?"

Holly's scream is muffled through her tears and spit-stained gag.

"Did you know I had just taken over the department you stole from? You made me look like an idiot. Now you're going to pay." Logan turns back toward me. "The only reason I even asked you out was to find this thieving cunt. Do you know how much effort it took to persuade the owner of your apartment complex to sell the building to me just so I could evict you? Do you know how annoying it was to have to convince you to move in with me, to let you into my home, to let you touch my stuff, only to find out you don't even talk to your sister? And then, when you finally did talk to her, you broke up with me and left in the middle of the night like a fucking rat." He spits on the ground. "What a fucking waste of time you turned out to be."

"Do you know what wasn't a waste of time, though, Rylee?" He runs the barrel of the gun down Holly's cheek. "What wasn't a waste of time was the tracker I planted in that bracelet." My eyes dart to the Cartier bracelet sparkling on the counter where I left it yesterday. "The second you took it out of whatever signal-blocking device you had it in, I knew exactly where to find you and your bitch of a sister."

A tracking device?

My mind runs through all the times Logan guilted me into wearing that stupid bracelet. He was tracking me. He wanted to know if I was meeting up with Holly. A surge of revulsion turns my stomach. Logan spent *six* months with me just to get to my sister. She wasn't paranoid, she was being safe, and I brought the enemy right to her doorstep.

And she's pregnant.

Fuck.

I can't let him do this. I can't let him hurt her. I'm stronger than this.

Tilting my chin up, I look into Logan's eyes. "It will hurt Holly more if you take me instead. Punish me, tell your dad I'm her. I don't care what you do, just let her go."

"Oh, I was counting on that. It's why I'm taking both of you. Besides, there was only one thing you were good for and that was a quick fuck. As soon as we get out of this shithole of a town, we can have some fun and your sister can watch. Maybe then she'll have a little taste of what she did to me. Maybe then she'll know what it feels like to be humiliated. I'm going to take everything from her. No one steals from the Eastmanns."

He sounds like a movie villain. It would almost be laugh-able if it wasn't happening to me. But I believe him when he says he's going to take everything from her. He's going to kill me. He's going to kill Holly and her baby.

He was playing me from the very beginning, which means...

"Did you kill Jeremy?"

His face contorts in annoyed confusion. "Who the fuck is Jeremy? God, you always did ask the stupidest questions."

My face heats and my fingers flex at my sides. "Jeremy, Holly's husband, did you or your father kill him?"

At my words, Holly thrashes violently in her seat. Snot pours from her nose, mingling with her tears, and in one swift motion, Logan brings down the butt of his gun on the back of her head. Holly slumps in her seat, and I rush forward to help her, only to be backhanded with the same gun. The impact is brutal and blinding, and I go sprawling to the floor, my head connecting with the wall. My vision swirls and the collision leaves me dazed. Before I can right myself, Logan is there, binding my wrist in front of me with what sounds like duct tape. He says something as he roughly shoves my wrists together. I try to focus on his words, but they seem to swim and muddle in my head.

"—so no, I didn't kill Jeremy and neither did Dad. But I wish we had. God, that would have been even better than killing you." He yanks me into a standing position and forces his hand up my shirt, groping me painfully. The shock of it is enough to bring me to my senses.

When my eyes are able to focus, I see that he's frowning as he removes his hand from my shirt. "Just making sure you don't have a weapon on you, but I forgot how small your tits are."

Hot shame spreads up my neck and across my face—not at his words, but at this whole situation. My chin drops to my chest. This is all my fault. Holly and I are both going to die because I wasn't smart enough to see what a monster Logan was.

All the energy drains from my body and without fighting, I let Logan lift me up and lead me outside. I have a fleeting thought that maybe if I don't fight, Holly will wake up and be able to make a run for it. The hope that idea elicits is quickly washed away when Logan digs the barrel of his gun into my back and pushes me toward the driveway.

The spineless part of me realizes it would be easier if he just killed me now. At least that way I won't have to endure the violation of my body or have to watch Holly be tortured.

That might be the most cowardly thought I've ever had.

I'm so repulsed by my own defeatist attitude that I hardly register Logan shoving me into the back seat of the Mercedes or the door slamming closed against my arm. I shift uncomfortably before the locks click into place and he retreats back inside.

Unwilling to abandon Holly, I don't bother trying to open the door or run. When Logan returns, Holly is slumped over his shoulder. After knocking her head on the doorframe, he heaves her into the seat next to me and slams the door. In another second, he's blaring rap music and reversing out of the driveway.

While my hands are bound in my lap, Holly's are taped behind her back. The odd position of her hands leaves her unbalanced in the seat, and she falls against my shoulder with the first turn in the road. I use my arm to try to nudge her awake, but she remains motionless.

A few minutes later, the combination of my pestering and the loud music finally does the trick. Holly's eyes flutter open and widen as she takes in her surroundings. She tries to spit out her gag, but whatever is shoved in her mouth is too big. With her eyes, she pleads for me to help, but all I can do is stare.

This is my fault. I got us here and now we're both going to die.

Holly doesn't let up. She pulls back her lips and bares her teeth in my direction.

"What do you want me to do?" I whisper. She bares her teeth again. "You want me to bite him?" She shakes her head, frustration evident in her flared, snot-covered nostrils. She directs her eyes pointedly downward and tries to push out her gag.

"You want me to bite out your gag?" I whisper.

She nods, and I glance forward to make sure we haven't been noticed. Logan is in the seat directly in front of me, rapping loudly to whatever horrible song he's listening to. I can't see him very well, which hopefully means he can't see me either. I shift left, letting Holly slide into my lap. She turns her head toward me and I try to fish out the gag. Our teeth clank with each attempt to grab what I now realize is a dish towel. Each time our teeth connect, I freeze, nervous that Logan will hear the sound and stop the car. He never does, and somewhere near my seventeenth attempt, I finally snag the towel. It takes another minute to pull the whole thing out and when I do, Holly instantly starts coughing.

"Shut the fuck up, Rylee," Logan yells over the music. "We've got a long drive ahead of us, and it's not going to go by any quicker with you being fucking annoying."

Holly mouths a "thank you" in my direction, and I lean down to place my forehead against hers. She tries to whisper something, but her mouth is too dry for me to make out the words. She swallows a few times, and I place my ear against her lips.

"Choke him. Crash the car," her hoarse voice whispers. "If he gets us out of Eden, we're dead."

In my heart, I know she's right. We don't stand a chance if Logan gets us to Charlotte or wherever he's taking us to.

"What about the baby?" I ask. She nods, and I realize we're

all dead anyway if I don't do this. Slowly, I inch her back into a seated position. I wait until we're through the lights of Main Street and darkness shades the back seat before covertly buckling her seat belt and then my own.

"I love you," she whispers against my ear.

"I love you, too," I mouth back, though it's too dark for her to see. The missed words make me think of Colton. I never got to say I love you back when he left yesterday.

I might never get to say it again.

The realization makes my heart hurt. I wish I could see him one last time.

We pass the back of the Welcome to Eden sign, and I send up a silent prayer to whatever god might be listening.

Let me be strong. Let me save my sister.

I wait until we're across the bridge and approaching the curve in the road before flinging my bound wrists around Logan's neck. Shoving my feet against the seat for leverage, I pull back as hard as I can. Logan's gasp is cut short as I cut off his air supply. Over and over again, he slams his fists into my arms and attempts to claw open my hold on him.

The car swerves violently, and for one terrifying moment, everything slows and I'm weightless. The car flips and glass shatters. When we finally grind to a metal-squealing stop, everything is still. Only the stupid music keeps playing. Afraid that Logan is somehow still alive, I pull back on my hands and hold them there for another minute. The duct tape cuts painfully into my skin, warm wetness streaming across the spot where my thumb connects to my wrist.

Still, I don't stop pulling.

Logan doesn't move.

"Rylee?" Holly's voice echoes in the distance as my pulse pounds against my temples.

"Rylee," she says more forcefully. This time her voice snaps the world back into place. The rap music is still playing and there is a grinding, dripping sound from the engine. Somehow the car is upright.

"Rylee!" Holly says again. I turn my head in her direction. "You can let him go now. He's dead." With her wrists still bound behind her, she places her cheek gently against my arm. "We need to find a way to cut off this tape. You can let go now."

It takes more effort than I thought it would to remove my hands from Logan's neck. When I do, my forearms are speckled with blood. I don't know if it's mine or his. After a moment of fumbling around on the dark floor, I find the dish towel I took from Holly's mouth and wrap it around a large piece of glass. I unbuckle Holly from her seat belt, but when I go to cut the tape from her wrists, my hands are shaking too badly.

"It's okay," she soothes. "Take your time. It might be easier if you find the end piece and just unwrap it."

With messy, quaking fingers, I use the glass to cut into the tape and then slowly unwind it from her wrist. When I'm done, Holly takes the makeshift blade and cuts me free before removing the binding at her legs.

How I ever thought she might be able to run is beyond me. I stifle a giggle.

I might be in shock—it's hard to tell with the adrenaline pumping through my veins.

Careful to avoid the glass, Holly extricates us from the car. We've ended up off the road, smashed up against a tree. When I try to look at Logan in the front seat, Holly blocks my view and guides me away, helping me take a seat in the dirt.

"I'm going to make sure he's dead. You sit here and don't move," she says.

I hear the *ding-ding-ding* of an open car door and then the rap music cuts out. Holly is back a moment later, pressing on my neck and spine. "Does your neck hurt? Or your back?" I shake my head, and she walks me through a series of commands and questions.

"Can you squeeze my fingers?" I do.

"Can you wiggle your toes?" I can.

"And there is no pain anywhere when you do that?" Numbly, I shake my head.

"Well, I don't know how, but you saved our asses and we don't seem to be too damaged."

I look up at her from the blade of grass I've been staring at. "We're okay? The baby's okay?"

"We're all okay. You saved us." Her smile is warm and bright, but her eyes are hollow and shadowed. "We need to head back. Do you think you can walk?"

I make some sort of noise that she takes as a yes, and she hauls me to my feet with one grunting pull.

"You're really pregnant?" I ask once I'm standing.

"I am." She cradles her belly with a soft smile.

"It's Jeremy's?"

"There's been no one else. According to the last scan, it happened the last time he and I were together."

"How long have you known?" I sound like a freaking robot, but I know these are the things I'm supposed to ask. It's what someone who hadn't just killed their ex-boyfriend would ask.

"I've suspected for a while, but I wasn't sure until a few weeks ago. Turns out, morning sickness is a real bitch." She laughs. It's a sound I haven't heard from her in weeks. Surrounded by the silent forest with the car wreck and Logan's body behind us, I don't know if I hate her for it or love her all the more.

"How are you so calm right now?"

"I thought I was dead. Then you walked in, and I realized that even if I was going to die, at least you came to see me one last time. At least there was one person left on the planet who loved me after how bad I fucked everything up with you and with the Jackals." She reaches for my hands and rubs gentle fingers over my bruised wrists. "You saved us, Rylee, you saved me and my baby. You are so strong. The Jackals are lucky to have you. I know all I've been doing is apologizing lately, but I think part of me was jealous that they picked you. When they voted on whether I could join, the answer was no. I couldn't even be considered because I was a Viper. That was always a barrier between Jeremy and me. I think I was jealous that you and Colt would never have to deal with that."

The last of my anger toward her dissipates and some of the fog in my mind clears. "They still love you. I can't wait to see Jack's reaction when you tell him he's going to be a grandfather."

Holly's footsteps falter along with her smile. "I don't know how to tell him. Now more than ever, we can't stay in Eden. It's going to kill him to have the baby raised by Vipers."

I'm unsure if the *we* she is referring to is her and I or her and the baby. Either way, I don't feel the trepidation I thought I would feel from her declaration. Colton and I want to go to Boston anyway. If that's where she's headed with the baby, we can all make it work together.

Holly takes my hand in hers. "Thank you again for saving us."

I squeeze her hand. "I love you, Holls."

We walk hand in hand across the bridge that leads back into Eden. Once we cross, Holly suggests that we wash off in the river in case anyone in town drives by and offers us a ride. It's not a bad idea, considering we're both covered in blood splatter and Holly's face is caked with dried snot and runny mascara. She also has new cut on her forehead that looks like it will leave a permanent scar.

We clumsily make our way down a small embankment to

where the river rushes over a set of large boulders. Crouching, I bring the cool water to my face and cup it over my neck. Against the warm summer air, the water is shockingly cold. Once the blood and grime of the evening are gone, each pass of the cool water is almost like a baptism, like the river is somehow washing away all the fear and pain pumping through my veins and leaving me a new person.

A person capable of protecting the people I love.

A person who can go up against Logan *and* Charles Eastmann and make it out alive.

Unfortunately, the absence of adrenaline reminds me why I went to Holly's in the first place. Colton's still not back, and if Logan was here, his computer is probably back in the Mercedes. As soon as Holly is safe, I make a plan to go back and check the car. Maybe there will even be something in there about Jeremy, but then I remember what Logan said.

Holly is already halfway up the embankment when I call out to her. "Holly, I need to tell you something." She waits for me to catch up and places an arm over my shoulder. For some reason, the gesture makes what I'm about to tell her even harder to say, but I say it anyway.

"Logan said that he and his father didn't kill Jeremy. I don't know how trustworthy he was, but I think if he had been the one to do it, he would have been rubbing our faces in it."

Her lips thin. "If the Eastmanns didn't kill Jeremy, then who did?"

A car door slams toward the top of the ridge. Overhead, an oily voice yells, "Get up!" The *thunk* of a fist connecting with flesh echoes in the darkness, accompanied by a pained groan. "I said get up! I'm going to make you kneel exactly where I killed that boy of yours."

Chapter Thirty-Six

Holly and I exchange a look before silently scrambling up the embankment where Sheriff Knott is dragging a handcuffed Jack into the middle of the road. Every muscle in my body stops working at the sight. I don't even blink.

"Kneel," Knott says, kicking the back of Jack's knees. "This is the exact spot I killed your oldest boy. Can you feel his blood soaking into your knees through the pavement?"

My stomach tightens, but Jack hardly responds. His head just sways, and he keeps doing a weird thing with his eyes like he can't focus.

Knott kicks him viciously in the shoulder, and Jack drops to the ground, his cheek slapping against the pavement. He moans but doesn't do anything to right himself. White-hot rage surges through my body. Why isn't he fighting back? Is this what I looked like when I gave up with Logan?

I want to scream at him to get the hell up and fight.

Knott snorts. "You might be a little too drugged to fully understand what I'm about to do. That's okay, we can wait a little." Sheriff Knott moves to the hood of his police cruiser and starts cleaning his nails with a knife.

I turn to my sister. "Logan had to have had a phone in his car. You have to go back and call someone. Call Danny, call the Jackals. We need to get someone here."

"We should both go," she says with heaving breaths.

I shake my head. I won't leave Jack, and I need to get Holly and the baby away from this situation. I lean in close. "No. It has to be you. I promise not to do anything stupid, but I can't leave him. The quicker you go, the sooner you can call for help. Can you make it back across the bridge without being seen?"

She bites her lip and glances over her shoulder. "This late in the summer, the river isn't deep. I'll go that way." The resolve is clear in her voice, like all these years later, the military training still comes out whenever Holly needs it.

"Go."

She gives me a fierce hug, and this time I make sure she hears me when I tell her I love her. She slides down the hill and there is a small splash when she enters the water. Thankfully, the roar of the river covers most of the sound. Sheriff Knott doesn't so much as glance in our direction. After a minute or two, Holly crawls out of the water on the opposite bank of the river. She wrings out her clothes and takes off at a run.

She made it.

My shoulders relax a fraction of an inch.

From the road, I hear another noise that sounds more like a gurgle. I expect to see Jack moving, but to my horror, the sheriff starts pulling another set of legs from the back seat of his car. Danny's head bounces hard off the pavement as his motionless body is dragged from the cruiser. Knott struggles to haul the deadweight across the road and unceremoniously drops his body next to Jack's. His breathing is labored and way too slow— I can barely see the rise and fall of his chest.

He doesn't move or make a sound.

"Your boy doesn't seem to be able to handle his sedatives too well, or maybe it was the morphine? Either way, you seem to be tolerating them much better. Do you have a drug history I should know about, Jack?" Knott taunts.

"Drugs?" Jack slurs.

Sheriff Knott rolls his eyes. "Yes, Jack, drugs. Maggie laced your meals at the diner for me with enough sedatives to take down a horse. I'm surprised you didn't taste it. Once I was able to coerce both of you into the cruiser, I injected the morphine." The sheriff shrugs. "I may have gone overboard with Danny's dose. He's not doing too well, is he?" He pauses as if thinking, then gasps and grabs his chest. "You know what? I just remembered that there is a reversal agent in my belt. I don't think I'll use it, though. You need to experience what it's like to be helpless to save your children. I want you to watch your son die. I want you to know I took both your boys from you, the way you took mine."

"Jeremy?" Jack asks, as if hearing this for the first time.

"Jesus, Jack, you really are high. Yes, Jeremy. I already told you, you're lying in the exact spot I took his life. I caught him up near that cabin of yours after a neighbor reported a trespasser. You can imagine how surprised I was to find your boy all alone away from the rest of your stupid club." Knott scuffs the pavement with his boot. "Like I said earlier, that's his blood staining the road. Soon it will be Danny's. And then yours."

Jack grunts in what I think is meant to be a scream.

Knott laughs before sobering. "Why did you have to call him, Jack? It was both of their days off. You were supposed to be down in that godforsaken mine, not him. Not them. If you hadn't called Dale to cover for you, Abel wouldn't have driven him and gotten roped into working another shift. You're the reason my boys are dead. You and your fucking hopeless crusade. How many more people have to die, Jack? How many before you're satisfied? Actually, I can answer that. Only two. You and Danny."

This time Jack really does scream, he thrashes against his restraints similar to the way Holly fought against Logan's earlier. Jack's head rears back, and for a brief moment our eyes lock.

I lean forward, ready to make a run for him. "No!" he screams, his voice penetrating straight into my soul and locking my muscles in place. He shakes his head ever so subtly, and I fall back onto my heels.

"Yes, Jack. There is no one here to help you and nothing you can do to stop me," the sheriff says, oblivious to our exchange.

No one here? Think again, buddy.

I won't sit by and let this happen the way I let Logan take Holly and me. I'm done hiding. I'm done letting evil win.

This time, I'm going to stop it.

I assess my surroundings. I need to be smart about this. Jack, Danny, and the sheriff are about twenty feet from me in the middle of the road. From my position, tucked up next to the bridge behind the shrubs, I don't think I'm very noticeable, but Jack saw me, so I need to be careful. I move back an inch and try to stay hidden under the cover of the bridge while I search for something that can help me.

Knott has a pistol holstered at his right hip and the knife he used to clean his nails is now tucked haphazardly into his utility belt. I'm not sure I'd be very useful with either of those weapons, and the awkward way his uniform sits on his chest means he's likely wearing a bulletproof vest anyway. When he turns his back to me, I avert my attention to the men on the ground. Both Jack and Danny have their hands cuffed in front of them and seem too drugged to help me fight off Knott. I find nothing else that might be useful.

I'm so screwed.

My only hope is that Holly brings help soon. I glance to the road.

"You're pretty awake now, Jack. Looks like you're ready." Knott grabs some sort of clear tube from his pocket and attaches a needle to the end. "This vial has a high enough dose of morphine to kill Danny in a matter of minutes, if not seconds." He grabs the knife from his belt. "Or I could slit his throat. I'll give you the choice my boys never had. Which will it be, Jack, the knife or the drugs?"

Jack lets out a guttural scream, and the glass syringe winks at me in the moonlight.

That's it.

That's my only chance. I might not be able to overpower the sheriff, but if I can knock him off balance and inject him with that syringe, I might stand a chance.

There is no time to second-guess this. With my pulse thudding in my chest, I allow myself one steading breath before I burst through the bushes. Adrenaline ripples through my muscles as I run at the sheriff's back. These twenty feet are the most important run of my entire life. I channel every ounce of my strength into lengthening my stride and drop my shoulder right before I slam into the sheriff's ribs. When we collide, he goes flying, his head hitting the pavement face first with an audible *crack*, a spray of blood exploding from his forehead. It's not enough to keep him down, though, and he's standing before I can crawl to my feet.

"You stupid bitch," he says with a donkey kick to my chest. The pain steals my breath and sends me spiraling flat onto my belly. I grasp at my ribs, trying to ease the hurt and catch a breath that won't come. The sheriff pulls his gun and advances on me.

No. I can't let it end this way...

I shift again, and I'm in the process of mustering the strength to stand when something hard digs into my sternum. I move my hand and feel the glass syringe.

Wrapping my fingers around my only weapon, I loosen the cap on the needle, and ready myself for a fight.

There is a sudden commotion from my right, and I whip my head around just in time to see Jack throw his legs out, bringing the sheriff slamming to the ground. "Now, Rylee!"

I whip around, fighting through the pain in my ribs and the dark spots in my vision to launch myself on top of Knott. One second, I'm straddling the sheriff, the next I'm shoving the needle into his throat and injecting the drug with every ounce of strength I have left.

An exuberant smile spreads across my cheeks as the vial empties.

I did it, I saved—

An explosion makes me squeeze my eyes shut and cover my ears with both palms. When I pull my hands away, my ears ring, and I barely make out the sound of a gun clattering to the ground.

Sheriff Knott looks at me triumphantly. "Did you think you won, stupid girl?" he slurs. His head lulls to the side as he struggles to keep his eyes open. I run my hands over my body, frantically searching for blood, for a bullet hole, but find nothing.

Relief floods my veins. He missed. He didn't hit me.

When I catch my breath, I bring my fingers to Knott's neck. His pulse is slow now. So slow that I only count two pumps of his dying heart before realizing he's no longer a threat. Something snags my shorts when I try to stand, and I reach down and grab the sheriff's keys, pocketing them just in time to hear one last sputtering breath escape his lips. Then silence. Not even a cricket chirps.

My chest swells with pride.

I did it.

"Rylee?" a soft voice calls me from behind.

I turn, still smiling, to see Jack with his cuffed hands clutching a heavily bleeding wound in his stomach. My face drains of blood and my lips turn cold. I run to his side, scraping my knees as I slide across the gravel on the road. I place my hands over the wound and press down. Jack winces, but I don't let up.

"Is he dead?" he asks.

"I think so." My voice is squeaky, and my hands shake with the effort of trying to stop the bleeding.

There is too much blood.

The viscous liquid is hot and slippery beneath my fingers, and I struggle to keep my hands in place. Blood pools under my knees. I shift my hands and press harder, but it just keeps pouring out.

What do I do? How do I stop this? My panic is making it hard to think.

Jack only smiles up at me. "Good, you did so good. But I need you to do one more thing, *mija*. I need you to go get the morphine antidote from Knott's belt and give it to Danny. It's called naloxone. It will be in a side pouch. Hold it up to Danny's nostril and plug the other one so he has to inhale it."

"But I need to hold pressure," I plead, tears clouding my vision and streaming down my nose. "Holly went to get help. Someone will be here soon."

Jack smiles like a patient father. "Danny doesn't have that time. Look at his breathing."

I turn and look over my shoulder. Danny's breaths are even more shallow now.

"Rylee, you can do this, but Danny needs you to do it now. *I* need you to do it now. Go."

"Okay," I whimper.

I back away from Jack and search the sheriff's belt. Already his face is pale and his lips have taken on a bluish tint. He doesn't stir as I remove the antidote and administer it to Danny the way Jack told me to. Seconds after he inhales the naloxone, Danny shoots up into a sitting position and begins spewing his guts out. I turn him to the side so he can continue to barf and then I go back to Jack.

When I return, Jack's breaths are labored and his eyes are closed. I shake him awake, and his gaze darts to where Danny is sitting up and wiping his mouth. "You did so good, *mija*. I'm so proud of you." Behind me, Danny begins to vomit again. Jack only smiles at the sound. "Next to my boys, bringing you in is the thing I'm most proud of. You and Holly are the daughters I never had. You are a Jackal, through and through. I am so proud of you."

Tears of love begin to fill my eyes, and I do my best to hold them back as Jack struggles to stay awake. I place my hands back on his belly. He doesn't wince this time. "Jack, I need to tell you something." If these are his last moments, I want them to be good ones. "You're going to be a grandfather."

His face lights up so bright it's almost as if the sun is rising on this horrible night. "You and Colt are pregnant?" he asks, his voice barely audible.

I shake my head and a tear falls onto his cheek. "No, Holly is. It's Jeremy's. Turns out, there's a reason she's been acting so crazy all these months." I make a choked half-laughing, half-crying sound.

Jack laughs, too, but it quickly turns into a horrible wet,

hacking cough. His lips quiver and his mouth contorts as tears fill his eyes. "Jeremy's?" The pride in his voice makes my own chest hitch with emotion. I nod to confirm. "You take care of that baby, Rylee. And you take care of my boys. They are going to need you after this."

"I promise."

"Tell—" Jack gasps for breath. "Tell my boys I love them."

Something brushes my shoulder, and I turn to see Danny at my side. He's dazed and wobbly, but he places a hand over my own and Jack's. Jack smiles at us both, but it's almost as if he's looking past us.

"I love you," Jack says to Danny with sudden strength and clarity in his voice.

Jack's blood slows beneath my fingers, and a few seconds later he takes a shuddering breath as his heart beats for the last time.

Danny collapses next to me, and I let go of Jack. My chest is being crushed by the weight of a massive boulder, but I drag myself to Danny's side anyway only to be swatted away. "I just need a second," he says, silent tears streaming down the side of his face.

He covers his eyes and screams.

The blood-curdling, anguished cry reverberates across the river and into the night sky, slashing across my already damaged soul like a blade.

When the echo of his scream dies down, I take the sheriff's keys from my pocket and free Danny. He doesn't fight me, and when his hands are released, he uses his forearm to cover his face.

I scoot myself back over to Jack. Reverently, I remove the cuffs from his wrists and place his hands over the bloodied wound on his stomach. Already his fingers are cool to the touch.

Gently, I move toward his head and place it in my lap. He's heavier than I thought he would be, but once I have him situated, I smooth his hair to the side. "I'll wait with you," I whisper to the only father I've ever known.

In the distance, a siren wails.

"I'll take care of them, Jack. I promise."

<hr>

Minutes, maybe hours later, I'm vaguely aware of a Bronco pulling up and screeching to a stop.

"Rylee?" Andy calls out.

Hands land gently on my shoulders, but I shrug them off. Andy reaches down to Jack's neck. He shakes his head once and then tries to move him.

"Don't touch him," I snap, like a feral animal.

Andy raises his hands and takes a step back.

"Danny needs help," I say a little more softly.

"No, I fucking don't," Danny calls out.

I let out a humorless laugh, which comes out as more of a snort from choking on my own tears. "Knott drugged him with some sort of sedative and morphine. I gave him one dose of the antidote. He might need another one. I don't know."

"Okay, I got it. Colt's on his way." Andy gives my shoulder a squeeze, then touches Knott's neck before moving to kneel beside Danny.

I don't know how much time goes by, but eventually the roar of an old engine approaches, followed shortly by two car doors slamming. The smell of iron is replaced by the smell of sunshine and cloves as Colton lifts Jack off my lap.

He makes me stand and gives me a quick once-over to check for wounds, ensuring that the blood I'm covered in isn't mine. Although I don't flinch, every time he moves me, the pain in my ribs nearly brings me to my knees.

He starts to wipe my crimson-stained hands on his jeans, but it is futile. It's not just my hands that are stained. I will carry what happened tonight for the rest of my life. Whether you can see it or not, the blood will always be there.

After a few more unsuccessful wipes, he takes off his sweatshirt and tugs it over my head, dressing me like I'm a child. He rubs my arms, and I think he's saying something, but I don't hear it.

"Why were you late?" I ask, still in a daze. I can't feel my legs. I can't even focus enough to look him in the eye.

"Fuck," Colton says, running his hands through his hair so roughly that some of the blond strands come away with his fingers. "The computer wasn't at Logan's. We tore the place apart looking for it. I had no way to call you, and Jack and Danny weren't picking up." His eyes dart to the ground behind me where Jack lays.

"The computer is in Logan's car." My lips barely move as I say it.

"I know," he says, rubbing my arms again.

"I killed Logan." My lip quivers.

Colton places his hands on either side of my face and brushes his lips against my forehead. He pulls my body flush with his, cocooning my head in his arms. "I know. Minho and I found Holly and what's left of Logan's car on the way in. We got his computer from the trunk. Holly is here, too. She's safe. She told us what happened."

Violent shivers start to wrack my body. Despite Colton's sweatshirt and the warm night, I'm suddenly cold.

"Jack," I croak. "I tried, but Knott was going to kill Danny—"

"I know." Colton's voice is tight and stretched, like he's

fighting back tears. The small crack in his composure causes a ball to form in my throat.

This is all my fault.

I have to tell him the rest of it. I have to get it all out or I'll combust. "Knott killed Jeremy. He did it to punish Jack. He did it out of some sick idea that it would avenge his sons that died in the mine collapse." My heart is beating so fast my vision starts to turn black around the edges. "He was going to kill Danny in front of Jack. I wasn't fast enough." My stomach heaves as I bend over, but nothing comes out.

Colton clenches his jaw and turns his head skyward. He paces a few times, running his hands violently across his face before placing them on his knees. After a few too-quick breaths, he cups the back of my neck and forces eye contact.

"None of this is your fault. You saved Danny. You saved your sister. You should have never been put in this position in the first place. I should have been here to protect you. None of this is your fault. None of it, do you hear me?"

My lower lip shakes, and I give him the tiniest nod. He shouldn't be comforting me right now. I should be comforting him.

My gaze drifts to Jack's inert form. Danny and Andy are off to his side, talking in hushed tones. One of Jack's hands has fallen off his abdomen and onto the ground. I kneel beside him, placing his hand back over the other. Colton crouches beside me, one arm around my waist, the other draped over Jack as he bows his head.

Andy clears his throat. "I hate to be that guy, but we need to do something about this and quickly, before someone drives by."

Colton nods and pulls me to my feet. He stares at me for a drawn-out moment that feels like an eternity. His lips thin and his eyes turn black as they run over the contours of my face. I see the exact moment his expression changes, hardens somehow. He steps away from me. "You need to go."

Every muscle in my body goes slack. All I can do is blink. "What?"

Colton takes another step away. "Take my car and drive until you can't drive anymore. You need to leave Eden."

Behind us, Andy drags Knott's body onto a tarp and Minho, who I hadn't even noticed was here, grabs one of Knott's limp feet to help.

"I'll come for you when it's safe, but you have to go. Now." His voice is cold and unfamiliar.

I reach for him, but he ducks out of my grasp. "I don't want to leave you. I promised Jack I'd look after you." My voice is barely audible. My eyes drift to Jack's body, where Danny is now crouched over his head, whispering words I can't hear.

"Go," Colton says forcefully.

"I—"

"Goddammit, Rylee, you need to fucking go! I have to take care of this. I have to take care of Logan's body and make sure you don't go to fucking prison. I can't let any of this fall on you. I have to dispose of Knott, and I need to bury my father. You need to go now. It's not safe in Eden anymore. I can't keep you safe right now. Can't you see that?" His eyes plead with me, but it's his words that cleave my heart in two.

I'm breaking. Shattering into a million pieces right here on this road.

Holly walks out of the darkness and takes my arm. "Rylee, please. We have to get out of here," she implores, a hand on her belly.

Colton's already kneeling next to Danny with one hand on his shoulder. He doesn't turn to look at me as Holly pulls me down the road toward the Chevy.

I know that she and Colton are right. Eden isn't safe, and I will just be in the way, but that doesn't make the ache in my chest any better. "You'll come find me?" I call out to Colton. I have to see his face one more time.

He looks up with icy blue-green eyes, the Jackal on his neck strained with how tight he's clenching his jaw. "When it's safe, I promise I'll come find you."

Epilogue

I don't know how long I stare at my trembling, blood-soaked hands, but when I come to, Holly is gently scrubbing my face with a wet towel.

Her forehead is still bleeding, and as she leans over to clean my arms, a few droplets land on my cheek. I don't bother wiping them away. Instead, I let them slide down my neck and inside Colton's sweatshirt.

Logan's blood. Knott's blood. Jack's blood.

I am soaked in the blood of others. What difference does it make if Holly's is added to the mix?

"I think you're going into shock." Holly's voice is muffled, like she's far away. "I'm going to drive to a hospital and get us checked out. Just sit tight, okay?"

I try to nod, but I'm not sure if the idea transfers into action. I'm numb, and I can't seem to move my hands. Maybe a part of me is afraid to try because if I do, then all this has been real.

Holly says something about taking back roads and the next thing I know, I'm sitting in a noisy emergency department while she puts on a green hospital gown. I'm vaguely aware of someone looking at my ribs, an X-ray machine being hauled into the room, and Holly speaking to a nurse while she's hooked up to various wires and machines, but I can't make sense of what they're saying.

My body is here in this stark, white room, but my head is still in Eden on that road.

I bet they've moved Logan's and Knott's bodies by now.

I wonder where Jack is.

I wonder if he's already cold.

The memory of his bright smile and fatherly presence assaults my mind like a crushing physical blow. He was the father I should have had. The father none of us deserved. Why didn't I ever tell him how much he meant to me, to the town, to Colton?

I can't imagine the Jackals without him. I can't imagine an Eden where he doesn't exist.

A static *whoosh* fills the room, followed by the thundering sound of galloping horses.

I blink the room into focus through the fog. There is an ultrasound tech and a doctor standing over Holly's jellied, barely protruding belly.

"That must have been one heck of a car accident for you to smash your head like that. I'm glad you came in. Everything looks good," the doctor says. "Baby's heartbeat is strong, and all your tests came back normal. You're both doing great. Just make sure to follow up with your ob-gyn next week and return for any new or worsening symptoms, okay?" She smiles warmly at Holly, and the ultrasound tech gathers up their gear to leave.

"Was that the baby's heartbeat?" I ask after they leave the room. "Is it supposed to be that fast?" New worry eats at my stomach.

Holly nods and wipes away the silver tears forming in her

eyes. "He's perfect. Look." She hands me a string of grainy black-and-white ultrasound pictures.

My eyebrows lift as I take the shiny paper from her. "He? It's a boy?"

"It's a boy." A sob escapes her lips, and in an instant I'm across the exam room and hugging her. The pain in my ribs makes the embrace feel like torture, but I pull her closer anyway.

"I'm going to name him Jeremy," she says through sobs. "Jeremy Jack, we can call him JJ."

My breath lodges in my throat.

Holly places my hand over her belly, and a tiny flame flickers to life inside me. This baby has no idea how incredible his namesakes were. Jack would have stopped at nothing to make sure this baby was safe and taken care of. If he and Jeremy can't be here, I have to step up.

"That's perfect, Holls. I'm going to be the best aunt you can imagine. I'll be there every step of the way. We're going to take such good care of him, okay? You're not alone. It's the three of us together from now on. I promise."

It's everything I should have said when she confirmed she was pregnant. At least I'm saying it now, and at least they're both okay. I'm going to do everything in my power to keep them safe.

Holly nods. "We can't go back to Eden. Charles Eastmann will be looking for Logan, and we can't put JJ in danger."

My blood turns molten at the mention of Charles Eastmann, but quickly cools with the thought of never going back to Eden. I know she's right. I know the baby has to be our priority, but I love Eden, and Colton is there. It's the only real home I've ever had.

I quickly clear those thoughts from my head. One problem at a time. "Where do we go, then? Where will we be safe?"

"We still go to Boston. We have to get to Dad." She takes a deep breath and places her hand over mine. "We have to go into the Vipers' Den."

End of book one

The adventure continues in *Summer Sparrow*, Book Two of the Jackals and Vipers Duet.

Acknowledgments

Thank you for reading *September Doves*!

To my husband–none of this would have been possible if you hadn't convinced me to take this project out of manuscript-jail. Thank you for your constant love and support, and for letting me read the first draft to you on our eighteen-hour road trip. You are the best partner a person could ask for and I am madly in love with you.

To my critique partners and author friends–I would be entirely lost without you. Thank you for your wisdom, advice, and for generously sharing your knowledge with me. I am so lucky to have you guys in my life.

To my editor–you are a goddess. Thank you for your patience and for making this book shine. I can't wait to continue learning from you.

I'd also like to give a shout out to my mother-in-law for being my first reader and my biggest hype-person!

To you, the reader—thank you for taking a chance on September Doves. I am forever grateful!

About the Author

Emmerson Hoyt lives in Austin, Texas with her husband and a small horde of animals. When she's not writing, she's playing video games or finding an excuse to get another floral tattoo.

Check out her website for the latest news!
www.emmersonhoyt.com

Also by Emmerson Hoyt

<u>Jackals and Vipers Duet</u>

September Doves

Summer Sparrow

<u>Deadwood Duet</u>

The Endless Fall